MISTRESS OF MAGIC

THE REALM OF MAGIC, BOOK 2

Susanne L. Lambdin

Author's Note: This book is a work of fiction. Names, characters, places, and incidents are the product of the authors' imagination. Locales and public names are sometimes used for atmospheric purposes. Any resemblance to actual people, living or dead, or to businesses, companies, events, institutions, or locales is completely coincidental.

Mistress of Magic / Susanne L. Lambdin
ISBN-13: 978-1726348409
ISBN-10: 1726348407

Book Cover by A. R. Crebs

For Valerie.

Map of Caladonia

For a larger version, go to:
https://susannelambdin.wixsite.com/realm-of-magic

Prologue

Snow swirled in a white flurry, the first winter storm of the season, brought down from the Stavehorn Mountains by a fierce northern wind. Ice cracked under the hooves of a frightened large elk as it crashed through the pine trees, its ears tucked back to listen to the howls of pursuing wolves. A pack of four small gray wolves trailed on the heels of a larger red wolf with strange green eyes, keen for the early morning hunt. The scent of blood was thick in the frigid air. Scruffy and half-starved, the pack trailed behind the alpha, unaware she was *Wolfen*, a cousin to werewolves. The pack followed the red wolf because they were hungry and sensed she would catch their prey.

Taliesin, the Raven Mistress, in her *Wolfen* form, possessed a sharp killer instinct. She ran through the forest, her eyes on the tracks in the snow, hastened by the elk's shrill snorts. The wolves were young. Able to communicate with the wolves through snarls and body language, she had assumed the role as a temporary alpha. She had found the former pack leader left dead in a trap. The pack was eager to learn and participate in their desperation for meat.

A large black male showed the aggression needed to lead, yet differed to her, running on her right side, a few feet behind out of respect. She knew this part of the forest and flushed the elk toward a ravine, her nips meant to prod, not lame. One bite from her jaws would taint the meat. Saliva from a *Wolfen*, not the bite, spread the disease, and she wanted the pack to feed. If she made a mistake, it would be difficult to convince four hungry wolves not to eat the carcass. The moment the wolves ingested tainted meat, they would turn into the Night Breed, true werewolves, with an insatiable lust for blood, and turn on her.

9

Taliesin's thoughts drifted to the shack she lived in by the Pangian Sea, on the southwestern coastline of Caladonia. At the base of the mountains, she had lived with Ysemay the Beguiling—an old witch—for the last month. The wolf pack was more than welcome to eat the entire elk, for a dinner of fried fish awaited her. The witch relived her glory years from a thousand years earlier and spent her time reading old spell books while Taliesin ran with the wolves. Life was easier in her animal form, for the only concern was to find food and shelter, protect the pack, and nothing more. This type of freedom was not a permanent solution to her problems as a human, and eventually, she had to return to the world. She had a future, unlike the elk that stopped at a rocky ravine to make its last stand, and she focused on the kill.

In a desperate attempt to fight off the wolves, the male elk turned, antlers lowered to give battle. Foam flew from its thin lips. It tossed its head and missed striking Taliesin by an inch. She dipped low to avoid a second strike from its sharp hooves, while the pack slunk closer and nipped at one another in excitement. The elk was close to the ledge and Taliesin held back. The icy ground beneath its hooves broke, and it jumped toward her to avoid toppling into the ravine. The elk let out another piercing snort as it dropped down on its front hooves and shook its mighty antlers. It was a fatal error, and the remaining section of the cliff collapsed beneath the animal. With a shrill cry, it toppled over the side and fell to the sharp rocks below.

Taliesin and the pack scampered down the side of the cliff to where it lay on its back—neck and spine broken. With a final shudder, the elk expired. Giving a nod of her head, Taliesin watched the black male approach the dead elk. The wolf sniffed the exposed belly, the juiciest part, and savagely ripped into the soft flesh. The three females joined him, pulling flesh from bones while leaving steaming hot guts lying in the snow. Taliesin used her claws to pull the pink intestines from the carcass. She sat on her haunches on the hard snow and ate the soft, gooey flesh without reservation. After all, it was food, she was *Wolfen,* and she was hungry.

"*Taliesin.*"

The haunting voice caused Taliesin to stiffen. The wolves growled in response but continued to feed. She lifted her head, blood on her muzzle, and turned. A white-haired woman, small of stature and dressed in a light blue cloak, watched Taliesin from where she stood among the tall pine trees. A shiver ran through Taliesin's body as she stared at a beautiful face framed by a hood trimmed with fox fur. Something about the woman looked familiar. Taliesin felt certain she had seen her before, in a dream or imagined from a story told to her as a child. Every nerve ending tingled as the woman turned and faded into the trees, leaving behind the scent of lilacs and a strong urge for Taliesin to follow. Her wolfish thoughts faded, replaced by human reason as the lines from a poem written by Glabber the Glib, a poet long since buried, entered her mind.

'*With a ghostly, pale hand, the specter beckoned I follow.*
To the gates of heaven or hell, I was to be led.
Leaving my loved ones alone in grief to wallow.
Better to have company, thought I, in the land of the dead.'

Taliesin trotted forward and sniffed at a set of footprints left in the snow, able to smell the strong scent of lilacs. She followed the track that led into a section of the forest where there was no haunted cry of an owl or even wind to stir the trees. Her ears pricked forward as the woman appeared ahead of her, winding through the trees, leaving behind a trail of magic that created the scent of flowers. The woman made her way to an outcrop of rocks, where a heavy mist lay all around. From a cave entrance, she stood watching Taliesin with strange purple eyes. A pale hand lifted and beckoned Taliesin forward before the woman turned away and disappeared within the shadows of the cave.

Feeble sunlight shined upon the cave and revealed what it had once been, an ancient temple with elegant letters from a language long since forgotten carved into the sides of the stones. Taliesin crept forward, nose to the ground. Broken pillars covered with frost lay on the ground. Small footprints led further into the cave. She tensed as she entered and found a red cloak spread across the cave floor like spilled blood and sniffed the material. For a moment, Taliesin thought of Ysemay, for the old witch would have cautioned her not to enter the cave. Taliesin wanted to find out who the woman was and why she had sought her out. She assumed the cloak was for her to wear. With a single thought, Taliesin turned into her human form and donned the scarlet garment. Tall and slender, red hair flowed down her back and blended with the cloak. It dragged behind her as she walked. The cave floor revealed cracked tiles the shade of a summer sky. Faded, beautiful mosaics of the ancient gods of Mt. Helos painted on the walls showed a figure similar to the woman she followed.

"*Taliesin*," called the soft, female voice.

Coming to a flight of stairs carved into the rock, Taliesin ascended into a chamber lit with the golden light of torches. She heard her name again spoken and hastened her steps. It felt as if she had walked into a dream as strange energy made the hairs on the back of her arms stand on end. Her mind scrambled for an explanation among the many stories about the gods of Mt. Helos. Stroud, the All-Father, was the beloved of nobles, beggars, and the Eagle Clan, whose four-headed dog Nidus guarded the mystical door leading to Mt. Helos. His wife Broa, the Goddess of Crops, bore him twin daughters; Navenna, the Goddess of Enlightenment and Fertility, and Mira, the Goddess of the Moon. The Raven Clan prayed to Heggen, the God of the Underworld. His pet raven, Vendel, often seen on battlefields, carried the souls of the most valiant warriors to the Underworld. There was Ragnal, the God of War, and his two supernatural wolves, Cano and Varg, worshiped by warriors as well as the Wolf Clan, who offered blood sacrifices to win his blessing before a battle and burned the dead afterward in his honor.

Taliesin had never questioned their existence. The temple being where it was, and the woman appearing when Taliesin needed guidance the most, was surely no coincidence. She entered a chamber and found a stone altar. There was no ornamentation on the walls or floor, nor was the goddess visible. Torches on the walls sparked to life and offered a golden light. She knew immediately the strange woman was the goddess Navenna.

"Where are you, Navenna?" Taliesin stared at the altar. The torchlight flickered, and she noticed someone had spelled out her name in a layer of dust.

"*I am here,*" the voice said. "*I have come with Ragnal.*"

Taliesin turned to find two figures standing behind her. She pinched her arm to make certain she was not dreaming. On closer inspection, she saw Navenna wore a silver crown and a silver brooch with a heart-shaped ruby clasped at the neck of her cloak. The goddess serenely gazed at Taliesin with no malice in her eyes. Beside her stood Ragnal, a dark man in ebony armor with narrowed, cruel, dark eyes. He held two iron leashes attached to spiked collars worn by giant wolves. Cano, white as bone, and Varg, black as a dragon's talon, glared at her with yellow eyes. Saliva dripped from their jaws as they growled, pulling back their lips to reveal sharp fangs. Cano, legend said, had created the Night Breed with his bite to create true werewolves. His child born of a mortal woman was Varg, half-man and half-beast, who in turn created the *Wolfen.*

"Is this real? Am I dreaming?"

"*There is little difference between dreams and reality,*" Navenna said. "*Be not afraid, Raven Mistress. We have a great purpose in coming here to meet you.*"

"What do you want of me?"

Ragnal bristled. "*War, blood, death. What you mortals call* Varguld, *the Age of the Wolf,*" he replied. His voice was deep and grating. He had a large sword buckled on his side and rings worn on every finger. His long black cape, trimmed with wolf fur, created a dark shadow around his massive frame that matched the darkness in his eyes.

"*Dark times are upon us, it is true,*" Navenna said, giving Ragnal a sharp look. "*It is said a* Sha'tar *will be born to the Eagle Clan to restore magic to the world. Many believe the last heir of the Raven Clan will spring from nothing and find* Ringerike *to defeat all enemies. So too will a great warrior from the Wolf Clan lead their armies to victory, bringing about the rise of the Age of the Wolf. We believe you represent all three, Taliesin, and this is why we are here. It was believed it would be three heroes who would fight on behalf of my sister, Mira, Ragnal, and me, and this is why you now struggle to find yourself...to find your destiny.*"

"*She has tasted flesh,*" Ragnal said. "*This one belongs to me. She will fulfill her destiny, marry Prince Almaric, and restore glory and fame to the Wolf Clan.*"

"*The blood of Korax Sanqualus, the true king of the Lorians and the rightful leader of the Raven Clan, runs through her veins,*" Navenna said. "*This one prays to me, and I would see Taliesin sit on the Ebony Throne of Caladonia and restore peace to the realm. Mira wants the return of magic, for the Eagle Clan prays to her in secret, and their lord and their heir are sorcerers. The Eagle Clan seeks magical weapons and items throughout the realm, for they want to rule everything, and this is why their clan and the Wolf Clan now hunt to find you.*"

"*One way or another,* Varguld *is coming,*" Ragnal said.

Taliesin shook her head. "No, I won't let it come to that," she said. "I will not see either of those clans dominate the Raven Clan. I am mistress of my own fate."

"*Silence,*" Ragnal snarled. He turned to Navenna. "*My patience runs short, Navenna. A week or two more running with the wolves, and her wild side will grow stronger. She is mine.*"

The two wolves growled low. Varg suddenly snapped at Cano. Before the two broke into a fight, Ragnal yanked on the leashes and brought them to heel.

"*The decision is yours, Taliesin,*" the goddess said. "*All three clans claim you for their own purpose, as do we three immortals. If you truly desire to serve me, then return to the dukedom of Garri-*

dan, reclaim Ringerike, and restore the Raven Clan to its former greatness."

"Join the Wolf Pack and serve me, and I will make you the most powerful warrior in the land. Do not, and I will see you die," Ragnal said, curling his upper lip.

"Or chose Mira and become the most powerful sorceress in the realm," Navenna said. *"You cannot serve all three of us, Raven Mistress. You must pick who you will serve and what will come to be."*

"Blessed and cursed," Taliesin said. She was frightened. Her problems had grown larger in a matter of minutes. She had prayed to Navenna since childhood, and serving her seemed the right thing to do, yet she hesitated to pick. "The House of Sanqualus was wiped out centuries ago. The Raven Clan is no more. I want only to be left in peace."

Ragnal snarled, furious, and let the wolves run the distance of their leashes to snap and snarl at Taliesin. She felt fur grow on her ears and her teeth turn into fangs.

"It is obvious she is mine, sweetheart," he said with a rumble.

Navenna gave Taliesin a sad smile. *"Of course, you want to restore your clan,"* she said. *"Even now,* Ringerike *calls to you. Take your true name again. Rosamond Mandrake. Use the sword, claim the Ebony Throne of your ancestors, and rule Caladonia as its rightful queen. Find a way to control your magic and* Wolfen *side. If you do not, then no one can stop the Age of the Wolf."*

"I can give you everything you desire." Ragnal held out a beefy hand and offered her a ring with a black stone. *"Lead the Wolf Clan, as you are meant to, Taliesin. Together, we shall turn the strongest into* Wolfen *and let them loose upon the world. Be my warrior* Wolfen *queen, and you will know the taste of victory and fame. Fight against me, and you will discover I am not a forgiving god."*

Under the leadership of Chief Lykus, the Wolf Clan had destroyed the Raven Clan. At Wolf's Den, in a vision, she had seen their clan turn into *Wolfen* and eat the Raven Master and her friends she had known all her life. In the Salayan Desert, Captain Wolfgar had captured her and bitten her repeatedly.

Yet, she had managed to escape and join her friends in Garridan. The castle had fallen into the hands of the Wolf Clan. Held prisoner, Phelon had seen to it that she drank human blood and turned *Wolfen*. No, she would never join their clan, nor serve the bloodthirsty god.

Taliesin shook her head. "I will not fight for the Wolf Clan," she said.

"*Then consider yourself my enemy,*" Ragnal replied.

"*Since you were a child, you have prayed to me,*" Navenna said. "*Find your way and restore peace to this world, and I shall see you have whatever you desire. Marry Sir Roland Brisbane, or sit on the throne, or both. It is your choice.*"

An image of Sir Roland appeared in Taliesin's mind. When he had been a member of the Raven Clan, he had gone by the nickname Grudge. He was the only man who understood her, and she had allowed herself to believe they had a future together. Now that she knew King Frederick had sent Sir Roland to infiltrate her clan to find out if the rumors about the birth of a *Sha'tar* were true, she believed he had never loved her. All Roland had wanted was to convince her to use *Ringerike* to help the king defeat his rebellious sons. She searched her feelings. In another time, another place, she would have gladly married Grudge. Her feelings for Roland were conflicted, yet Navenna made her feel it was possible to reunite with him. It seemed selfish to think about her own happiness when thousands might die in a civil war she might be able to prevent. She took a deep breath, her eyes on Navenna, and exhaled.

"I have made my decision," Taliesin said. "I will find a way to restore peace and magic, unite the clans, and sit on the throne." She offered a thin, nervous smile, still uncertain what she really wanted. "This is a dream, after all."

"*Foolish. Reckless girl,*" the God of War snarled. He turned his back on Taliesin as a golden doorway opened. The great beasts followed him through, and they vanished.

Left alone with Navenna, Taliesin felt her fears and doubts subside. A ray of hope entered her heart to see love expressed on the face of the goddess. Taliesin knelt and lowered her head, aware she was turning into a wolf as a hand stretched out to touch her head.

"I sense conflict within you. If you decide to control your own destiny, then I cannot help you, and you will need help in the days to come," Navenna said. *"Take my advice, Raven Mistress. Be careful whom you trust and whom you give your heart. Those who call themselves friends are not always true, and your enemies may become your allies. Rely on your instincts. Retrieve* Ringerike *from the sea. Without* Ringerike, *you will fail, and if you fail, then there is no hope for the world. Be wise, Taliesin. Be very, very wise."*

Taliesin closed her eyes and heard the sounds of wolves gnawing on bones, soft growls, and an occasional vicious snarl. She lifted her head, looked down the end of her muzzle at blood thick and fresh, and licked her fangs. Indigestion had made her imagine gods, temples, and three paths that led to her destiny.

Next time, she would not eat the soft parts.

* * * * *

Chapter One

A light layer of snow fell from the sky. Taliesin stood naked on the shoreline and watched waves crash against the rocks. She felt neither the sting of the wind nor the frigid temperature as foamy water receded over her feet. For the last few weeks, she had refrained from brushing her reddish-gold hair that now hung in twenty long braids resembling the tentacles of an octopus. A basket of fish tied to a spear stuck into the sand rolled as the surf gave a push and pull.

The strange encounter with the gods of Mt. Helos had left her confused. Taliesin had spent an hour searching for the ancient temple. With no tracks left in the snow to guide her, either human or wolf, it was impossible to find, so she assumed it was nothing more than a dream. Leaving the company of the wolves, she made her way to the beach to fish and swim in the Pangian Sea. Ysemay preferred fish for breakfast, and Taliesin felt responsible for feeding the old witch as she had the young wolf pack, while other duties she neglected.

She had left her Raven Clan friends Rook, Wren, Hawk, Jaelle, and the wizard Zarnoc behind in Garridan to sort out her priorities. After leading them into the Salayan Desert, on a mission to find her clan's ancestral sword, *Ringerike*, they had ended up in the dungeon at Dunatar Castle. Phelon had killed the duke, taken his castle, and expected Taliesin to join the Wolf Clan. When she resisted, he made certain she tasted human blood before leaving her to kill her friends. As the tide slowly crept through a grate in the floor and flooded the chamber, Taliesin gave in to the urge to turn *Wolfen*. Her supernatural strength allowed her to break her chains and free her friends.

19

Beneath the shadow of the late Duke Richelieu's castle, Taliesin had struggled with her wild side and the urge to bite her friends. Untrained *Wolfen* were dangerous, she knew, so she had tossed *Ringerike* into the sea and fled before she could hurt her friends. Her guilt at abandoning her little clan and not knowing their fate weighed heavily on her mind. Phelon and the Wolf Pack surely no longer had control of the castle. When she left, an army led by Sir Roland and Prince Sertorius lay siege to the castle. Weeks had passed since she had seen them. She wanted to return, and after all, Navenna had told her to return. She needed to find *Ringerike* and her friends, and then she would decide what to do with the rest of her life.

"Taliesin!" The shrill voice carried to her ears on the breeze. "Where the bloody blazes are you, you stupid girl? Where is my breakfast? Where are you, child?"

Ranting continued within the small shack with a shingled roof and faded green shutters on the edge of the cliff. Strings of seashells hung from the corners of the shack and jingled merrily in the breeze. Smoke, white upon a cloudless blue sky, rose from the chimney, and the fire inside kept the witch warm. Taliesin ignored the voice. She was not a pet. As she walked out of the surf, a thick layer of fur appeared on her body, and fangs scraped her bottom lip as they grew. Her pointed ears filled with the music of the chimes, and she forced herself to calm down in order to turn back into a human.

"I'm coming, you dirty old hen," Taliesin grumbled. She yanked the spear out of the sand, picked up the basket, and ascended a rocky path up the side of the cliff. It would have been easy to turn around and walk away—she owed nothing to the witch. Not friendship or loyalty. Not even breakfast.

A layer of magic spells shrouded the shack and kept it from view in case any ships passed along the coast. Marauders and northern barbarians operated in the area, and the witch had not left anything to chance. Ysemay did not want to be found. Nor did she want anyone looking for Taliesin to arrive on her doorstep.

"It's about time you got back here with my fish. Stupid, lazy girl," the witch said. Her loud voice echoed from inside the shack, its tenor so deep and her temper so strong it shook the pots and pans hanging from the rafters. Most witches had familiars like cats, birds, or frogs and snakes to aid with casting spells. Not Ysemay. Her familiar was a nasty, hairy spider that waited on the steps of the hut, watching Taliesin with eight black eyes.

"You're an awful thing. I should squish you."

The spider scuttled toward the door, still watching her.

"Get inside, Benedict. You first."

Taliesin let the spider inside. Eight shaggy legs propelled it forward. She imagined the spider had eaten its share of cats and toads in its lifetime. Since it was not a normal spider, she could not tell how long it had been alive. Its mistress was more than one thousand years old. While the witch had the ability to look young, there was nothing about Ysemay the Beguiling to warrant such a title. She entered the hut behind the spider. It climbed the wall and positioned itself in a corner to observe her.

"I'm hungry," Ysemay said. "And I don't like waiting for my breakfast."

"Be thankful I bothered to catch you anything at all."

The banter between them was normal; no real malice was intended. Neither liked the other, and like all parasitic relationships, one gained more than the other did, though they traded roles without conformity. Taliesin placed the basket of fish beside a rickety table and snapped her fingers. Clothing appeared on Taliesin's slender body. A soft pair of leather britches stuffed into tall boots, a thick wool sweater, and a leather coat trimmed with raven feathers suited her. Unfortunately, the pants were on backward and both sweater and coat turned inside out. Instead of making another attempt and giving Ysemay the satisfaction of seeing her fail, Taliesin undressed and put everything back on.

"Stupid girl," Ysemay said. "You can't even dress yourself. You will never be worth your spit if you don't learn to concentrate before willing an item to respond. There's a balance to everything in the universe. For every action, there is a reaction. One cannot exist without the other, and consequences occur when a magic user becomes sloppy. The guidelines are so easy a child could learn the most basic magic rules.

There are four elements, Earth, Air, Fire, and Water, and each corresponds to both a season—winter, spring, summer, and autumn—and to a direction—north, south, east, and west. First, ground yourself, and then focus, and when you feel you are balanced with all four elements, then cast your spell."

Taliesin flopped onto the bench and rested her elbows on the table, her chin in her hands. Beside her sat a stack of dusty, old books and rolled parchments Ysemay had procured for Taliesin to aid in her studies. The table wobbled beneath her weight. It was poorly made, like the rest of the furniture which were collected from ditches and had been found left behind on the road. The bench also wobbled, with one leg shorter than the rest, which upset its balance. The other three mismatched chairs pushed under the table were starting to splinter. Ysemay expected Taliesin to repair the furniture using magic, not her hands, and so far, she had not been successful. On a shelf were a collection of chipped cups and plates Ysemay demanded to be turned into gold. In fact, most of the items in the shack were broken or defective in one way or another, either found that way or sabotaged by Ysemay in an attempt to force Taliesin into making repairs.

Aim high, fall hard—the witches' motto. Sadly, Taliesin's magical abilities were pathetic at best. Despite her reluctance to fully appreciate Ysemay's assistance or take her studies seriously, she knew this was an opportunity of a lifetime.

All magic was outlawed in Caladonia more than two hundred years ago during the reign of King Magnus Draconus, and the majority of people had never met a magic user. In fact, the likelihood a farmer or a knight would ever come across a witch or a wizard was highly improbable. The Magic Wars was a time of bloodshed and murder, for King Magnus had executed hundreds of actual, practicing magic users. A few had managed to escape, like Ysemay and Taliesin's dear friend, the wizard Zarnoc. They were the only two magic users she'd ever met. King Frederick had no tolerance for magic users, and keeping to Magnus' royal edict, arrested anyone suspected of being a dabbler, gave them no formal trial, and ordered an immediate execution. Ignorance was blind to justice, and people feared magic.

This prejudice was instilled in Taliesin at a young age, yet she'd always known she was different. Even as a child, she had an uncanny knack for finding magical items, from dancing spoons to magical weapons. Such items were either disenchanted or destroyed during the Magic Wars. Many noble families still possessed ancestral swords with dormant magical properties, despite the king's attempt to rid Caladonia of everything magical, a goal he had failed to achieve.

During the tedious hours spent reading old tests and scrolls stuffed with important information on the nature of spells, spell casting, and a wide variety of magical charms, Taliesin tried to remember other magic users learned in this same fashion. If she wanted to learn how to control her magic, she needed to study from a superior magic user.

Wizards were men who practiced magic, including casting spells, alchemy, and potion making, as well as astrology. These men had keen minds, very similar to scientists and physicians, and used the flow of the energies of the earth, stars, and planets in harmony to gain enormous insight and power. There were once magic guilds where pupils who showed promise could join and study under the best minds in the world. She always wondered if the magic guilds remained, hidden away from the world in the Magic Realms or Skarda. Wizards were ranked the highest, followed by sorcerers and sorceresses, and then warlocks and witches; but all were referred to as magic users.

The term *magician* was not associated with the three ranks of magic users. Magicians were ordinary people who traveled with actors, bards, and poets and pretended to use magic. They performed tricks, such as pulling a hen out of a hat, making mice dance, or card tricks. The ever-popular dancing spoon only required a strand of hair tied around it and a dexterous finger. As far as she was concerned, these were parlor tricks and not real magic.

Of course, it was not necessary to be a member of a secret magic guild. There were long-time practitioners like Zarnoc, who was a first-rate magic user. Ysemay had studied under Zarnoc and possessed exceptional powers.

Taliesin was something different. She was a *Sha'tar*, a natural born witch. One in a million were born in every generation, yet not since the Magic Wars had one survived beyond infancy. *Sha'tars* did not need to learn magic from books, for their gift came naturally. It was a matter of self-will, of being able to control thought, and to visualize an event coming into being, and thus into reality.

Among the common folk were seers, able to predict the future through dreams or visions, while gypsies relied on Tareen Cards dealt in a variety of patterns to predict birth and death or great fortune. Alchemists, also called apothecaries, were found in most towns and sold potions and draughts to the populace to cure a variety of ailments and disease. Since the crown did not consider them magic users, they could ply their trade for money or barter without fear of persecution.

Taliesin knew Ysemay was jealous of her natural gifts. She suspected the witch had an ulterior reason for helping her, and a lack of trust existed between them. Taliesin only stayed with the old woman because she lacked confidence in her magical gift, which made it next to impossible to cast a spell. It did not help Ysemay was extremely critical and in a perpetual bad mood.

"Where have you been, young lady? I have been calling you for the last few hours. The only ones who answered are those mongrel wolves that live in the forest."

"Fishing for your breakfast. You said you were hungry."

"So, you went hunting with those scrawny wolves, and then you caught the fish," Ysemay said in an unpleasant, manly voice. "Those wet-nosed beggars hang around the hut looking for scraps. Feeding strays will only bring them harm. They should be able to hunt without you, Taliesin. Young wolves must learn to fend for themselves, or they will die."

Ysemay's long salt-and-pepper hair hung in a shaggy mane. Her crooked teeth had yellowed, and her breath smelled no better than elk guts. Dressed in a moth-eaten gown with a black shawl that had seen better years, the only thing the witch lacked was a wart on the end of her nose. Muttering under her breath, Ysemay took the basket to the fire where she gutted the fish with a thin knife and placed slender pieces in a pan. The old woman smelled of fish and urine. She never took a bath and preferred to make use of a bucket whenever she wanted to relieve herself, instead of venturing outside. Taliesin had at first thought the old witch refused to bathe because she was lazy. After the last few weeks, she realized the witch expected her to make things right. If she couldn't fix the chair, mend the cup, or rid the shack of the fetid odors Ysemay continued to create, Taliesin didn't know how she was expected to make the witch's world a better place to live in.

"I suppose you want to leave me to go back to Dunatar Castle," Ysemay said. She paused in her work to scratch under her chin.

"How would you know? I never said I wanted to leave."

"Private thoughts have a way of escaping out your ears. I pick up every unspoken word you say. I told you before your friends are dead. Forget about them and do what you came here to do, Taliesin. After we eat, you will perfect the art of transfiguration until you are able to turn a seashell into a proper skillet."

"Studying spells is a waste of time. I forget them the moment I walk out the door, and I'm not staying inside this shack with you all day," Taliesin said. She picked up a cup and hurled it across the room. The display of a childish tantrum did not make her feel better. "What good is being a *Sha'tar* if I must use spells to invoke magic? I was born with this gift, Ysemay, yet it didn't protect me from being bitten. A *Sha'tar* should simply be able to *wish* for what they want, and it happens. Magic should come...well...*naturally*. All I'm doing here is wasting time."

Ysemay shook a spoon at her. "Wasting time, are you? You've been wasting a great deal of my time since arriving. If you want to be able to *wish* magic to happen, you must do what I say, Raven Mistress! Every magic user has had to study their craft to perfect their skills," she said. "This isn't my first time teaching a *Sha'tar* how to utilize her gifts. I have taught quite a few in my lifetime, and none has been as difficult as you have, so stop making excuses and apply yourself. All natural-born witches lack discipline, and it's discipline that's required if you ever hope to return to the world of humans."

At the far end of the table lay the instruments every magic user required to practice their trade. There was a crystal ball partially wrapped in a strip of purple velvet. Twenty small jars contained key components for casting spells: sage, lavender, rose petals, garlic cloves, basil leaves, caraway seeds, copper flakes, gold dust, snakeskin, frog eyes, raven feathers, and crystals. Three wands cut from rowan, hawthorn, and oak trees lay on a homespun cloth. A silver chalice, missing one of the many flat amethyst crystals that adorned the sides, needed to be reset with a new stone. The final item was a double-edged knife with a bone handle that Ysemay used for all manner of things, including blood sacrifices. To contain the blood of her victims, usually mice or birds caught in Benedict's webs, she had an iron cauldron placed on the bricks near the fireplace.

"*Fire is fire. Fire is power. Fire is my tool. Fire is my will,*" Taliesin muttered. The flames in the fireplace roared to life and then lowered. "See! I am trying, Ysemay."

"Not hard enough. That pack is a bad influence on you. You can't expect to learn how to use your magic when you prefer to run with wolves and hunt. Rely on your intelligence. Use your mind, not your animal instincts. Tame the beast. Concentrate. If you can't mend a little cup, then I don't see how you're ever going to be able to control *Ringerike*. Korax was just like you. The king lacked discipline and thought he could rule by imposing his will on everyone. I warned him what would happen if he didn't respect magic, but he didn't listen until it was too late."

Taliesin knew there was no sense in arguing with the old witch. Anything she said sounded like an excuse not to study, and perhaps that was precisely what was wrong with her. She had inherited her magical powers from the paternal side of the family, something that was extremely rare. She was twenty-six years old, a bit late for training when most magic users were chosen when they were infants and began to study the moment they could walk.

Master Osprey of the Raven Clan had adopted Taliesin. Her magic, however, was a gift from her real father, John Mandrake, who had secretly been a warlock and one of the finest swordsmiths in the kingdom. When she was a child, Mandrake had died. Zarnoc later told her King Frederick had given the order for her father to be killed. The wizard had given her to Master Osprey, who had brought her back to his clan and adopted her. Everyone had believed the line of Korax Sanqualus ended with his death, yet somehow his heirs had each survived discovery, until now. Both the Eagle Clan and Wolf Clan had tried to kill her, while others had tried to recruit her to fight either for or against the king.

"Don't tell me you care what happens between King Frederick and his eldest son, Prince Almaric?" Ysemay asked. "The Royal House of Draconus knows nothing except war. Caladonia was a community of sheepherders and farmers under the reign of King Korax. The Lorians forged *Ringerike* to ensure the Raven King maintained peace. When Korax died, the Draconus kings made certain your clan suffered and reduced them to the status of lowly scavengers. The Raven Clan will never be great again. Let it go and study, child. That's all you need to do."

"My friends are waiting for me. So is *Ringerike*. I have to go back, Ysemay."

The witch wiped her nose on the end of her sleeve and went about cutting and cleaning the fish. When the dirty skillet was full of fish fillets, she set it over the fire.

"You never asked why I agreed to train you," Ysemay said.

Taliesin rolled her eyes. "Fine. Why are you helping me?"

"I train you because you released me from the Raven Sword. A strong woman like you should sympathize with my former plight, and perhaps even desire to taste revenge on my behalf. A woman scorned, that's what I was, and that's why I live here, away from the world. I was trapped in that sword for one thousand years, placed there by a man for his own petty reasons until you came along and freed me. You say you want to restore your clan. I think what you really desire above all else is for women to rise in power, to be equals to men. I wanted the same thing long ago. All these centuries, shut away in that cave and living inside a magical sword, I was unable to do more than watch and wait and make plans. You could make a difference, Taliesin. Not just for your clan, but for all women. You could make us more than servants and wives and slaves and chattels."

Taliesin understood why Ysemay was bitter. She had a right to be. She'd been a prisoner, locked away inside *Ringerike*, and Zarnoc was the one who had done it. What happened between Zarnoc and Ysemay was something she'd always wanted to ask. Ysemay wanted her to share her anger toward men, and to blame all men, not just Zarnoc, for what happened to her. Caladonian women took care of their children, catered to men, and had no real rights of their own. They took pride in who they married and what their husbands owned. The Ghajar were gypsies and moved freely through the eight dukedoms to peddle their wares and to breed and trade horses. They considered women of lesser value than men, though the Shan's daughter, Jaelle, was one of the finest warriors Taliesin had ever met and a member of her clan. Becoming a powerful *Sha'tar* was not going to change the laws or the minds of men. Nor was it going to wipe away the memory of Ysemay's suffering.

"I'm not here to exact revenge, Ysemay, though one day I hope the laws will change, and women will have the same rights as men. Nor am I going to kill Zarnoc for you. He has always been kind to me. You must have done something horrible, or he wouldn't have locked you away inside *Ringerike* for one thousand years."

Ysemay turned the fish over with a wave of a wand that was bone from tip to handle and engraved with ancient runes. She set out two plates and refilled her own cup with wine from the never-emptying bottle.

"Mind your manners, you slouch. You sit hunched over like a *Wolfen*. A man did that to you. He bit you, and cursed you, and yet you feel no need to seek revenge," the old witch grumbled. "As for my relationship with Zarnoc and what happened between us, it's none of your concern. What he did to me was cruel and heartless, and one day he will pay for it."

"I want to know what happened. You are both Lorian," Taliesin said. "I always thought the fairy-folk were a kind, gentle people. Am I wrong to think this?"

A sorrowful sigh escaped the witch's lips as she turned to the fire and flipped the fish fillets over again. Taliesin stared at the woman's back and found it difficult to imagine her as a beautiful sorceress in the court of the Raven King.

"You want to know the truth? *My* truth?" Ysemay peered over her shoulder into Taliesin's eyes as the fish sizzled in the skillet. "Oh, I know what you're thinking. I did not always look this way, child. I was the prettiest and cleverest witch at Black Castle, desired by knights and noblemen alike. Even King Korax Sanqualus noticed me, and while his queen looked the other way, he was known to take many lovers. Zarnoc had every right to be jealous, for I was his mistress before I bedded the king. After all, King Korax was powerful, brave, and handsome. Korax had a way with women. No woman could resist his charms, and no man dared stand in his way. We were all helpless when it came to giving Korax what he wanted."

"Zarnoc was Korax's advisor and best friend. You came between them."

"That I did."

"You know you don't have to live like this, Ysemay. You don't have to be a recluse. Why don't you use your magic to look young and beautiful? Why not move to a city and live in a house? You might even find another pet! A witch should have a cat as a familiar, not an ugly spider."

Benedict quivered in the corner. While they spoke, it had been busy and created a web. What the spider lacked in personality, its web collected bugs that seemed attracted by Ysemay's uncleanliness. Everything had its use, Taliesin thought. She still wanted to squish the thing underfoot when the witch wasn't looking.

"Haven't you been listening to a word I say? I don't want to attract a man. I'm done with romance. Besides, it's a waste of magic," Ysemay said with a snort. "Nor do I want to live in a city surrounded by people making a great deal of noise, and you would do well to be nice to Benedict. Spiders have been known to lay eggs in people's mouths when they are fast asleep."

Taliesin glanced in alarm at the spider. "You wouldn't dare!"

With a snicker, the witch removed the pan from the fire and set it on the table. The fish was burned black. She used a fork to stack the charred pieces on a large platter set between them. The fire died down, and lit candles appeared around the room, while a cold wind howled behind the shutters. Ysemay sat down at the end of the table, eyed Taliesin, and filled her plate with crispy morsels. Taliesin imagined Zarnoc finding Ysemay in bed with Korax, a terrible quarrel ensuing, and the words spoken that only made things worse which resulted in her imprisonment and the king's death.

"Your unspoken words flutter about the room like butterflies," Ysemay said, stuffing her mouth with a fork full of fish. She smacked and chomped like a cow busy with its cud, and small flakes dropped onto the table. "Perhaps you did not know Lykus and Arundel were knights and lived at Black Castle during all this. Lykus later became the leader of the Wolf Clan, and Arundel now leads the Eagle Clan. How they both came to power are interesting stories, best reserved for another time. They were only knights then, and served King Korax, while Zarnoc was the court wizard. I never liked Lykus or Arundel."

"That's one thing we have in common," Taliesin said. "Go on."

"Both knew I was seeing the king in private. Lykus kept his mouth shut. Arundel, a lover of intrigue even as a young man, had to stir the pot and tell Zarnoc."

Taliesin was not surprised to hear Lord Arundel of the Eagle Clan had been the one pulling strings. She imagined Arundel, tall and pale, whispering to Zarnoc and telling him about the lovers while Lykus merely listened and watched.

"One night while I was visiting the king, Zarnoc appeared and found us together," Ysemay said. "He was furious. Korax tried to talk his way out, as he always did. It usually worked, only not this time. They had a terrible quarrel that roused the entire castle. I begged Zarnoc to forgive me. Pleaded and begged him to understand that to refuse the king was an insult. I was just another conquest to Korax, you see. It made no difference, for Zarnoc could not forgive us for such a betrayal. Zarnoc vowed to take his revenge. Before he left Black Castle, on the eve of battle, he placed my soul inside *Ringerike* and then buried my body in an unmarked grave."

An image of Zarnoc digging a hole in the ground and dumping the woman's body formed in Taliesin's mind. She hated to think of Zarnoc as a murderer. She also hated to think Zarnoc had left his king on his own to fight against Prince Tarquin and a great army from the north. Arundel and Lykus had clearly not been of much use during the battle, for Korax had been killed. An unsettling image of King Korax wielding *Ringerike* against Prince Tarquin and the sword failing him when he needed it most, struck her as Ysemay's fault.

"What happened then?" Taliesin asked.

"Korax rode out to meet them, with his knights and his army."

Taliesin shivered. "And you were inside of *Ringerike* during the battle," she said. "Did you cause *Ringerike* to lower its guard? Is that how Prince Tarquin Draconus managed to kill the Raven King? Did you betray Korax to try to make amends to Zarnoc?"

"Something like that," the witch said. "*Ringerike* has a mind of its own. We were in a constant quarrel during the battle, the sword and me. When all was said and done, Tarquin Draconus was simply more skilled with a blade. Tarquin always used *Calaburn* in battle, a magical sword made to fight against *Ringerike*. He left *Calaburn* behind at Ascalon Castle with his eldest son and chose to fight with *Graysteel*. It proved the right thing to do. *Graysteel* made me want to kill Korax, and I convinced *Ringerike* to lower its guard. A foolish thing to do, but I couldn't help it, I really couldn't."

"*Graysteel* is the sword that killed the Raven King," Taliesin said. "No bards ever wrote about *Graysteel*. It's always been thought *Calaburn* did the killing."

Ysemay glared at her. "I give you facts, and you interrupt," she snapped. "You seem to care more about magical swords than me. If you must know, *Graysteel* is the Sword of the Lorian Kings. Someone gave it to Prince Tarquin to use. I have always suspected Queen Dehavilyn, the Fairy Queen, persuaded Tarquin to use it. She had her own reasons to hate Korax, for he was the younger brother of King Boran, and the brothers never liked each other."

"I didn't know about that either. It makes sense Korax wanted his own kingdom, so he left Duvalen and took Caladonia," Taliesin said, wondering why the royal fairies had turned on Korax. The Lorians seemed to be a cruel people, and it almost made her wish she did not share the blood of Korax and Boran. "Why would Dehavilyn turn on her brother-in-law? Tell me that part of the story, please."

"The Vorenius family ruled Duvalen. The brothers had a fierce rivalry that revolved around Dehavilyn. She's the one who kept a wedge between them, ever whispering in Boran's ear and churning up trouble," Ysemay said. "When *Graysteel* cuts, it freezes whatever it touches. I made *Ringerike* lower its guard for one second, and in that second Prince Tarquin thrust his sword into the heart of King Korax. The Raven King turned to ice and dropped dead, and Caladonia fell into the hands of the Draconus family. Black Castle was destroyed, and Tantalon Castle was built on top of its ruins by the son of Prince Tarquin. Your clan was reduced to grave robbing and scavenging for a living."

Taliesin nodded. "I've spent most of my living searching for magical weapons on battlefields," she said. "You never get rid of that smell. If I had my way, I'd rebuild the Raven Clan, and we'd make a living finding and selling magical weapons."

"Magic is outlawed, and you'd only end up burned at the stake," Ysemay said, flashing her eyes. "Tarquin Draconus is called the King of One Day. He put the crown on his head, proclaimed himself king, and rode out to accept surrender terms from Sir Arundel and Sir Lykus. Korax's knights had set a trap. In the ensuing skirmish, *Ringerike* refused to fight for King Tarquin, and Sir Arundel slew him. I had no part in that, my dear, though I rejoiced in Tarquin's death."

"Arundel killed Tarquin?" Taliesin was shocked and disgusted to think the slimy Eagle Clan lord had ended the life of the Draconus prince. "Then Arundel was the one who caused the fall of the Raven Clan. He was the one who set things in motion, and now the Eagle Clan and Wolf Clan are in power."

"Yes, yes," Ysemay replied. "After Tarquin was killed, Arundel and Lykus flew into the mountains. Titus, Tarquin's eldest son, allowed the rest of the Raven Clan to leave Black Castle and return to Duvalen. King Titus buried his father at Ascalon Castle. He buried *Ringerike* inside the Cave of the Snake God with Korax's body, never knowing of my own plight. Nor was anyone else aware of what happened to me. For centuries, I waited to be rescued, and then you found *Ringerike,* set me free, and now I am here."

"I didn't mean to free you, but I'm glad I did," Taliesin said. "You never should have been placed inside *Ringerike* by Zarnoc. Never! Yet, I wonder why Zarnoc didn't come back for you and *Ringerike*. He had to know you had a hand in Korax and Tarquin's death. Isn't that what he wanted?"

"I cannot say what Zarnoc wanted," she said, "only that he never came for us. *Ringerike*, of course, blamed me for what happened to Korax. It was a miserable existence, stuck inside that sword, to be sure. *Ringerike* should have defeated *Graysteel*. Had I not been inside the sword, filling it with hate and anger, I am sure things would have ended differently. Dehavilyn gave her husband's sword to Tarquin, but Zarnoc crippled *Ringerike* by placing me inside. Zarnoc killed Korax, not me." She let out a little sob. "I know I should feel sorry for what happened to Korax. I feel sorrier for myself. Forgotten, unloved, and unwanted."

Taliesin was used to Ysemay thinking only of herself. There was so much more to the story. She took a sip of wine, eager to hear more. "What happened to *Graysteel* and *Calaburn*? Where are they now?" she asked.

"Of course, you'd ask about the magical swords and not about my broken heart," Ysemay said with a scowl. "*Graysteel* was returned to Duvalen. *Calaburn* remains in the ruins of Ascalon, buried with Prince Tarquin, just as *Ringerike* was buried with King Korax. I wouldn't think about trying to find either sword, girl. Leave it be."

Taliesin remained silent as the witch snapped her fingers. Benedict lowered on a web and scuttled across the table to reach her lap. Ysemay stroked the creature with a loving hand, while it stared at Taliesin with eight, beady, black eyes.

"Zarnoc! Zarnoc! He ruined my life," Ysemay lamented. "He will ruin your life as well, girl. That old wizard is not your friend. Like all men, he only thinks of himself. He cares nothing about you or about me. He is just like Korax."

"You mean Lorian."

"I mean faithless, you stupid girl!"

The witch fell silent and fed the rest of the fish to the spider. In her frustration, she left nothing for Taliesin to eat. Ysemay refilled her cup yet again with wine from the never-emptying bottle. She guzzled wine to forget her trouble and stroked her spider. Taliesin drank and ate nothing. After hearing such a sad tale, she didn't want anything from Ysemay's table. Nor did she intend to stay in the little shack by the sea with a woman broken and ruined by a past she had helped create along with her spider.

"How long must I stay here?" Taliesin asked, thinking of *Ringerike*.

"That's up to you now, isn't it? Learn something. Keep something between those two holes in the sides of your head. I am not the one keeping you here. Your inability to pick up the most rudimentary of spells and put them to use, along with your willful wolf pride, keep you here. Practice your magic and control your temper. Do that, and you might be able to leave this place and restore the honor of your clan."

A lone howl outside the hut made Taliesin smile as she helped herself to a handful of nuts. The wolf pack had followed her home. She knew if she looked out the door, the four young wolves would be watching from the safety of the trees, waiting for her to join them for another long run in the forest. The wolves lived in a small, cozy cave she had found for them not far from the shack. The elk would keep them fed for a week. Not having named them, she hadn't developed a fierce devotion to the pack and refrained from answering their calls.

Taliesin focused on a broken cup surrounded by odd-shaped bowls filled with shells, wild berries, and nuts. Three skulls, found by the witch on one of her excursions into the forest where she collected herbs and miscellaneous items for her magic spells, lay in a neat row from large to small. A collection of junk that had washed onto the shore lay in a heap on the side of the room beneath a window with panes smudged with dirt. All manner of jars, old lanterns, a few torn battle banners, and the dried-out bodies of squirrels, rabbits, and several varieties of fish hung from the beams overhead.

Since the dead animals couldn't be eaten, Taliesin assumed bits of their bodies were tossed into the myriad of potions Ysemay brewed over the fireside and then emptied outside the hut. The patch of land used for her dumping was blackened and gave off a peculiarly unpleasant feeling that Taliesin avoided.

"Mend the cup," Ysemay ordered.

Taliesin gazed at the cup. There were a number of simple spells, almost childish when recited, that she might use to fix the crack. Long ago, someone else had figured out the spells through trial and error, figuring out what worked or not, and had written them down. She didn't want to recite stupid, old spells. Using her willpower should work just the same, she thought. Ysemay muttered the spells aloud and waved her hands or wand about like a jester. Performing witchcraft reminded her of an actor on the stage, and all the drama seemed like hocus pocus nonsense.

Her effort ended in failure, for the crack grew larger and the cup instantly broke in half. A scolding cluck from Ysemay brought a soft growl from Taliesin as she picked up both halves, pressed them together, closed her eyes, wished it were in one piece, and opened her eyes. Not only was the cup mended, but it also looked brand new.

"I fixed it!" Taliesin exclaimed, setting the cup aside. "All it took was imagination. I think I'll try cleaning the shack and making things look brand new. You could use a makeover, too."

"You fixed it on the second try, and I'd rather you not play about with magic to make repairs. If it isn't broken, don't fix it." Ysemay snorted and wiped her arm under her nose. The spider climbed onto her shoulder and hid beneath her mangy hair. "You'll have to do better than that if you're going to defeat a king." She glanced at the empty plate. "Oh, did you want any fish?"

"I prefer it raw, Ysemay. You know that. Besides, I already ate...."

"...something nasty in the woods," the witch said.

Taliesin hated the fact Ysemay knew what she was thinking. The tragic story about Ysemay and the Raven King only made her want to go after *Ringerike* and set things right. *Ringerike* lay at the bottom of the Pangian Sea where she'd left it, and it *called* to her. She didn't see herself leading an army to reclaim a throne. She just wanted to see her friends, including Zarnoc, and hear his side of the tragic story.

"I have tried for weeks to train you to be a proper witch, yet you resist. You prefer to be a warrior more than a *Sha'tar*. If you could combine the two talents, you would be more powerful than anyone in Caladonia," Ysemay said. "Of course, you should retrieve *Ringerike*. The Raven Sword has intelligence and is a unique sword, my dear. I hold no grudge against *Ringerike* for my imprisonment."

At the mention of the witch holding a grudge, Taliesin thought about Sir Roland and his former nickname with the Raven Clan. The knight wouldn't be at Dunatar Castle waiting for her, wanting to apologize and make amends for the past. He had most likely returned to Padama, the royal city, to defend his beloved king. It was foolish to hope otherwise, and her sigh brought a scowl to Ysemay's wrinkled face.

"Pining for a lost love is a waste of time," the witch said. "Before you leave me, perhaps you should see what's happened at Dunatar Castle during your absence. You may change your mind about going there."

"What do you mean?" Taliesin asked. "Do you have a magic looking-glass?"

"Something like that," Ysemay said. "If I do this for you, how will you repay me? My services are not for free, child."

Taliesin smiled and spread her hands across the table. "Freedom isn't enough for you," she said. "What do you want then?"

The old woman laughed. "What I want, you are not able to provide," she replied. "Not yet. I am patient. I can wait a bit longer. You want to see Zarnoc and talk to him. Let me arrange it for you. Perhaps he will convince you to stay here."

Ysemay walked to the middle of the room, placed her hands together, closed her eyes, and began to hum. A sparkle of light appeared, and the outline of a door, painted green with tiny flowers etched along the border with a large gold handle, took shape. The door grew solid and seemed familiar. Taliesin had seen it somewhere and recalled something similar at Dunatar Castle in a hallway that led directly into the grand hall. Behind the door, she heard music and laughter.

"If I walk through this door, I'll rejoin my friends?" Taliesin asked.

"In part," the witch said. "You will be a spectral, able to see all, yet touch none. Zarnoc is there. He alone will be able to interact with you. The moment you enter, you will have only a few minutes before you must return. Now go and see if you find answers to your unspoken questions."

Taliesin approached the door. She reached for the handle and, quivering with anticipation, opened it. A bright light filled the shack. As she stepped through the door, she heard Ysemay laughing, but it was too late to change her mind.

* * * * *

Chapter Two

The grand hall of Dunatar Castle was resplendent, dressed with garlands of white lilies and long candelabra that held white candles, the tiny flames dancing in time to music played by a quartet. Guests sat at five long tables covered with white cloths, set with gold plates and floral arrangements. Every nobleman and his lady in the dukedom, as well as the turbaned leaders of the nomad Djaran tribes, enjoyed a sumptuous banquet. Taliesin's friends sat among the nomads. There was Rook with his dreadlocks, the pirate Hawk, his sister Wren—carrying Rook's child—and the exotic auburn-haired Jaelle of the Ghajar gypsies. Zarnoc, in bright yellow robes, poured wine into a silver chalice for Prince Sertorius, dressed in gold and seated beside a young woman wearing a silver wedding dress with the veil pulled back to reveal a plain face.

"May I be the first to congratulate you on your marriage, Prince Sertorius," Zarnoc said. "And to you, Lady Lenora. May your days be merry, and your nights filled with love. May you have many pretty children with strong teeth and straight legs, and may you never want for money, a home, food, or friends. There. I think that should cover it."

"Thank you, Zarnoc," the bride said as she smiled at her husband.

"Eat, drink, and be merry," Prince Sertorius called out and lifted his goblet high. The seated knights banged their fists on the tables and raised their glasses with the rest of the guests. "Let us all toast the god Stroud for making this wedding feast possible. For the man who does not pray to the gods and offer his thanks each day is a man who appreciates neither the beauty of a sunset nor the softness of a woman's inner thigh."

Sir Morgrave, Sir Barstow, Sir Duroc, and Sir Gallus, all in dark black tunics embroidered with a red skull, raised their goblets higher. They were Knights of Chaos, created by Prince Sertorius who they had served since he was a boy and full of imagination. Sertorius had wanted his own order of knights, and his father, being indulgent, had allowed him to form the order. Each knight loved his prince and served him well. Taliesin didn't like a one of them.

The old wizard looked at Taliesin and smiled. No one else noticed her arrival since she wasn't really there. More ghost than flesh. An invisible witness to a tragic affair.

"Your hair is a mess," Zarnoc said. "And you're late."

"Zarnoc, is that really you? Am I really in Dunatar Castle?"

"Of course, it's me, and yes, you're at the castle," he replied.

Zarnoc set the decanter of wine onto the table and walked over to Taliesin while the prince and his bride engaged in light banter. The wizard looked neither surprised nor concerned and was clearly able to see her, as though she stood in solid form and not a mere play of light. Zarnoc did not attempt to touch her. He appeared to speak to thin air and garnered a few concerned glances from the guests.

"I have tried for weeks to send word through the wolf pack," he said. "I'm annoyed you didn't bother to try to talk to them. Why in the world did Ysemay send you here at this late hour? She has certainly gone out of her way to make things difficult. There is nothing you can do as a spectral, my dear. Unfortunately, the spell she's woven around you prevents me from bringing your body here. You might as well be a ghost."

"I wasn't ready to return. I'm still not. Is *Ringerike* safe?"

"Under the sea and covered by sand. Sertorius knows it is nearby. He questioned your friends, and they told him what happened. I am his prisoner, you see. All of your friends are prisoners. The prince keeps us here and waits for your return, and for you to bring him *Ringerike*."

"Sertorius didn't wait for me," Taliesin said. "He has married."

Zarnoc pointed toward the groom. "After you left, the prince arrived with Sir Roland and an army. Together, they defeated Master Phelon and the Wolf Pack," he said. "Don't think too harshly of the boy. When weeks passed, and you still hadn't turned up, Sertorius decided to wed the duke's daughter. I think it was his plan all along. I rather thought you hoped Sir Roland waited instead."

Taliesin gave a shake of her head. "I don't know what I think," she said. "Maybe part of me thought Roland might stick around a bit longer."

"My, my, you are a fickle girl. Roland has returned to Fregia with the Knights of the White Stag, no doubt, suffering from a broken heart. As for Sertorius, did you really think he loved you?" Zarnoc asked. "Perhaps it is for the best both men are out of your reach, my dear. You're *Wolfen* now." He pointed at her friends. "I've had to keep a close eye on Hawk, you know. I was told you saved him after he nearly drowned. Mouth to mouth resuscitation was not a good idea. One drop of your saliva and he might have turned *Wolfen* as well. Had you even thought of that?" He paused. "Your ears are turning fluffy."

"Because I am angry," Taliesin said. "If you knew where I have been all this time, why didn't you just come for me? I am not Ysemay's prisoner."

Zarnoc looked at her sadly. "As I said, Ysemay prevented me from contacting you. She only sent you here to show you why you shouldn't return," he said. "However, the roast beef is delicious, and the wine is the best in the realm. As you can see, power has gone to the prince's head. Marrying into the House of de Boran has made Sertorius Draconus far more powerful than his brothers. Garridan is the wealthiest of the eight dukedoms, and he now has his own personal stronghold and a large army at his disposal. Since the twelve Djaran tribes have sworn their loyalty to Sertorius, no one can cross the Salayan Desert and attack his fortress. All he needs is

Ringerike to lead the greatest army ever assembled and take control of Caladonia. It is a sound plan, Taliesin. I think he looks happy. Don't you?"

The youngest prince of the Royal House of Draconus held the hand of his young bride. Lady Lenora knew exactly how to behave. She laughed when appropriate or offered a maidenly blush when called for. Taliesin felt jealousy stir when Sertorius kissed his bride. A sense of betrayal filled her with such anger she felt her ears turn pointed and her fangs grow.

"This is his wedding night, Taliesin," Zarnoc said. "You can't prevent what is going to happen. Nor can I, even if I wanted to, and I do not. Even if you had arrived earlier, Sertorius could hardly marry a wolf girl."

"Now I know what Sertorius is made of," Taliesin said, "And to think I believed Sertorius was in love with me. He's no more trustworthy than Sir Roland. Neither man ever loved me. All they want is *Ringerike*."

"Oh, one of them loves you more than you realize," Zarnoc said with a sigh. "Roland didn't have the stomach to remain and participate in this wedding. You missed him by three days. The knight did mention you on a number of occasions."

Taliesin stared at him. "So, the great Sir Roland Brisbane of the Order of the Knights of the White Stag has left the scene of the crime," she muttered. "Roland took the Raven Clan Service Oath, but it never meant anything to him. The oath is sacred, a promise to serve the clan until death, and not to be taken lightly. I liked him so much better when he pretended to be Grudge. I'm glad he's gone."

"Such a fickle girl," Zarnoc repeated.

"How can you say that? I never said I loved Sertorius, but I did love Grudge. He was my equal, and I miss him!" Taliesin gritted her teeth. "I wish I'd never met Roland!"

The wizard frowned. "You really must stop saying 'wish' all the time. You are a *Sha'tar*. When you make a 'wish,' it could cause something to happen. So, stop saying that word until you know how to wish properly. I can see now why

Ysemay sent you to me. Tsk tsk. You haven't learned a thing during your absence."

"I'm doing my best," she snapped. "And I have a right to be angry! Both Roland and Sertorius led me on. I don't care if Sertorius married another, but I do care Roland pretended he was Grudge, only to find out he's a King's Man!"

"Clear the cobwebs of romance out of your ears and listen," the wizard replied. "I intend to make good our escape this night on your winged horse. Thalagar is well taken care of, I assure you. The prince has seen to your horse's comfort, and that's more than I can say for the rest of us. *Ringerike* will remain hidden until you come for it. By then, we will be far north of here. I intend to take your friends to the Lorian kingdom of Duvalen. If you choose to come here, then find and release Master Phelon from his cell. I fear he's the only one who will be able to teach you to come to terms with your *Wolfen* side. Only be careful, for Phelon will try to get you to fight for Almaric, and that is something you must not do."

Taliesin tried to touch Zarnoc. Her hand passed through him. "Should I come to Duvalen to find you?" she asked.

Duvalen was only a legend, she thought. No one went there because no one knew where to find it. If she retrieved *Ringerike* and her magic Deceiver's Map, she would be able to locate anybody, anywhere. The map was in a pouch fastened to her sword harness, which had two straps worn around her middle, and fastened over her shoulder with the scabbard worn across the back. By now, the leather belt had probably softened in the salt water, or fish had nibbled on it, rendering it useless.

"Yes, come to Duvalen, my dear. That's a very good idea," Zarnoc said. "For now, you must return to Ysemay. Do not stay longer than one night." He didn't explain further. "Off you go. People are beginning to stare. Come to me when you are ready, and not before. And tell Ysemay..." he paused, and scratched at his whiskered chin, "...best tell her nothing, for I have nothing nice to say to her." He wiggled his fingers. "See you soon, my dear."

The wizard snapped his fingers and vanished, along with the shadows and voices of the castle. Taliesin found herself seated at the table. Ysemay was cracking chestnuts between her fingers and tossing the husks into the flames of the fire.

"Did you enjoy yourself?" Ysemay asked. "See what you needed to see?"

"Yes," Taliesin said. "And I'm leaving at first light."

* * *

At dawn, Taliesin left Ysemay snoring in her bed and slid out the door of the shack.

She took the familiar path to the beach. Her anger grew as she imagined Sertorius waking in bed with his new bride, and she felt her body respond. Morphing into a large red wolf, she headed away from the cliff and the forest and traveled due south along the coastline. Her anger grew as she sped across the sand. Her large pads left deep impressions as she thought back to the events that had led to all her problems.

A few months ago, the Raven Clan had arrived at a field where a battle was fought between the Fregian duke, Hrothgar Volgan, and Prince Sertorius. Though the Raven Clan was to scavenge, and her particular job was to pick up swords of great value from the dead, she'd come across Sertorius' banner, a scroll that was actually a coveted Deceiver's Map, and the golden sword called *Doomsayer* that allowed her to speak to the dead. She had taken all three back to Raven's Nest, the clan's home. Soon after, Captain Wolfgar and the Wolf Pack arrived and demanded she turn over the items to them. Sir Roland, then masquerading as Captain Grudge of the Black Wing guards, had sent the Wolf Pack running off with their tails tucked between their legs. The next day, Secretary Glabbrio, from the Eagle Clan, had arrived to claim *Doomsayer* and offer his lord's protection to the Raven Clan. Master Osprey had packed up his clan to go to Eagle's Cliff and had sent Taliesin with her friends to hide. The clan had been caught on the road by the returning Wolf Pack, taken to Wolf's Den, and either killed or turned into monsters. Had she not taken the items home, she wondered if Osprey and the rest of her clan would still be alive.

Guilt kept Taliesin on the move. Pausing only to seek fresh water to drink or to regain her strength by catching fish, she returned to Dunatar Castle the same way she'd left. She had five hundred miles to cover before she reached the coastal city of Dunatar. Fifty miles took one hour, if she pushed herself, and it was dark by the time she saw the large white castle lit by torchlight that sat on a hillside and overlooked the sea. The seven towers of Dunatar Castle were as impressive as the sprawling city beneath the hill, protected by a great circular wall that opened only to the sea. The harbor was filled with fishing boats and ten warships that displayed the lion flag of Prince Sertorius.

Hidden by darkness, she ran to the exact location on the beach where she had tossed the sword and harness into the water. All she had to do was dive under the water, find her possessions, and then swim through a tunnel to the dungeon in order to free Master Phelon. The tide was in, which meant the dungeon would be submerged, as would Phelon. *Wolfen* could not drown since it took silver and fire to kill their kind. Phelon would be alive and wide-awake beneath the water. She doubted Phelon, as selfish and nasty as he was, would agree to help her, but Zarnoc had told her to free the heir of the Wolf Clan, and that's what she was going to do.

"First things first," she said.

Diving beneath the water, Taliesin changed into something part human and part wolf, using her instincts to lead her to where *Ringerike* lay in the soft sand. Fish swam out of the way as she descended 30 feet. She swam along, scratching at the sand with her claws until she felt her mind connect with the sword. Her canine feet touched the bottom, and she hunched over to retrieve the scabbard that held *Ringerike* on the sea floor. The pouch remained attached to the slippery belt. The sword was happy she had returned for it and communicated with images, not words.

As she kicked to the surface, Taliesin saw King Frederick of Caladonia talking to his third-born son, Prince Dinadan, discussing battle plans. The scene changed to the scarred face of a tall man with long blond hair, wearing an ermine robe over his gold armor, and she knew it was Prince Almaric, the renegade, whose own army gathered in the eastern dukedom of Scrydon. The image again changed, and she gazed at a table where Lord Arundel and his Eagle counselors had gathered studying a map similar to her own Deceiver's Map. Then she saw Lord Arundel's son, Master Xander, riding beside Sir Roland of the Knights of the White Stag, heading with a Fregian army toward the royal city of Padama. Her heart lurched to see Roland's rugged face. His skin was tanned from hours in the sun, and he had wrinkles at the corners of his brown eyes. He had no laugh lines despite being fifteen years her senior, for he seldom laughed. With dark curls peeking out beneath a silver helmet, she remembered he had once worn a thick beard that scratched her face whenever they kissed. She wondered what Sir Roland would think if he could see her now, for fur covered her entire face.

When her head broke the surface, the images faded from her thoughts. Her efforts focused on dog paddling, while she fastened the sword belt over her shoulder, for *Ringerike* was a broadsword, and as long as she was tall. The leather had softened in the seawater, otherwise, it remained in surprisingly good condition. Taking a deep breath, Taliesin again submerged to search for the tunnel built beneath the lower section of the castle that led into the dungeon. She had no trouble locating the grate lying in the sand where she'd left it. With a hard kick, she swam through the tunnel to reach a staircase covered in slime. As Taliesin ascended the steps, she wished for the water to recede, and felt it rush past her, flowing out the tunnel despite the force of the tide. It required concentration to keep the water at bay. By the time she reached her former prison cell, it had returned to knee-level. She needed to act fast to release Phelon before it flowed back into the dungeon, with its slime and wretched odor of brine, fish, and rotting corpses.

Two torches at the top of steps provided feeble light. Taliesin sensed Phelon inside the cell. The other prisoners on this floor had drowned at some point. She smelled the foul stench of death, an odor all too familiar to her nose, and through it caught the strong odor of wet wolf. As she approached a heavy iron door, a fish flopped about on the stairs, attempting to make its way back to the water. Of no concern to her, she ignored the fish and broke the lock with her fist. She pushed the rusty door open with her shoulder, its loud creak a nuisance, and entered the damp cell.

"I knew you would come back," a voice said in the corner of the chamber.

In the dim starlight from a window high above, she spotted Phelon chained to the wall in the exact place he had once chained her. Seeing the Wolf Clan heir dangling on the wall recalled her transformation into a *Wolfen*. Phelon had caused her to drink blood when she refused to kill another prisoner and then waited for the tide to enter the chamber, knowing that when her friends were about to drown, she would have to transform into a *Wolfen* to save them.

As she gazed at Phelon, she was surprised she did not feel hatred for him. A passing cloud cast the cell into inky black darkness. Taliesin narrowed her eyes, still able to see Phelon without difficulty, and took pity on the man. His skin was red, raw, and bleeding beneath the silver cuffs hooked to the wall. He was too weak to pull free and hung against it like a broken puppet. His captors had not been feeding him. His clothes were nothing more than rags, revealing an emaciated body.

"How are you enjoying your stay at Dunatar Castle?" Taliesin asked. "Are they treating you well?" She laughed despite his deplorable condition.

"Your attempt at humor fails to amuse," Phelon snarled. He shook his head, sending droplets of seawater flying from his flaming red hair. "Get me out of here before a guard comes down here to check on me."

"No one is coming, Phelon. The tide is in, and you're supposed to be underwater. Pity you didn't defeat Sertorius when you had a chance. If you don't like being a prisoner, win the battle. Are there any more *Wolfen* down here?"

Taliesin stared at the silver chains, considering how to free Phelon without burning her skin. He pulled at the chains, snarling in pain and anger.

"There is no one else alive," the son of the Master of the Wolf Clan said. "Sertorius does not know the meaning of mercy. Since I was the one responsible for turning most of the people here to the *Moon Side*, he wanted to punish me. *Moon Side* is how people in polite society refer to *Wolfen*. After Sertorius and his soldiers spent the day hacking and slicing our kind with silver blades, he burned the bodies. I have smelled scorched flesh for weeks."

"Let's get you out of here."

Taliesin reached up and slid her hand around *Ringerike's* hilt, aware the sword wanted nothing more than to kill the creature chained to the wall. She pulled the weapon half out of the scabbard and illuminated the room in bright blue. Several skeletons lay on the floor. Phelon had killed two Eagle Clan envoys weeks before, which accounted for two of the skeletons. She had no idea who the third belonged to, though she suspected it was a *Wolfen*, for a silver dagger remained inside the ribcage. When she glanced back at Phelon, she noticed his eyes had started to glow amber.

"You feel it, don't you? The mutual attraction of our kind is hard to ignore," Phelon said in a silky-smooth voice.

"I feel something, it's true."

Phelon looked triumphant. "I knew it was only a matter of time before you turned fully *Wolfen*!" He gave a shake to his silver manacles, making the chains hit the wall. "By Ragnal's Beard! You're one of us now! Set me free, Taliesin. Let's be gone from this dreadful place. I hear soldiers on the stairs. Don't you?"

Taliesin heard the voices of men down the corridor. She lost her concentration, and the water flowed fast into the cell. "First, tell me if Zarnoc escaped last night," she said as she pulled *Ringerike* free. The guards would surely notice the bright blue light it cast. She raised the blade high. "You would have heard if my friends left the castle, surely. I suspect Sertorius raised the alarm when he found them gone."

"Zarnoc and your Raven friends escaped," Phelon hissed. "I have no doubt the wizard told you to free me because he wants me to teach you how to control your wildness. He knows I am the only one who understands the alterations you are experiencing. Isn't that why you came here, to ask for my help?"

"*Ringerike* wants to kill you," she said. "You cannot be trusted."

Phelon's eyes flickered upward, burning gold in color. The tips of his ears had sprouted fur, and she noticed his teeth were slowly turning into fangs.

"Free me, and I will train you. No tricks. I give you my word of honor."

"Very well," she said.

Taliesin hit the manacles on his wrists and ankles with *Ringerike*, sending up sparks and breaking the silver cuffs into pieces. Phelon let out a sigh and staggered away from the wall, exhausted, holding Taliesin in his yellow-eyed gaze. The water seeping through an iron grate in the wall and in through the open cell door had reached their waists. Taliesin sheathed her sword on her back, grabbed Phelon under his arms, and together they waded to the entrance of the cell. She dragged him up the steps and out of the water. Torchlight grew stronger, along with the footsteps and voices of the prince and his guards.

"Why do we delay?" Phelon asked. "Show me the way out, sister."

"Come with me," she said.

Taliesin considered using the drainage pipe but felt compelled to see Sertorius one last time. She wanted to see the look on his face when he saw she'd retrieved *Ringerike* and freed Phelon. She left Phelon leaning against the wall and drew *Ringerike* from its scabbard as two guards appeared in the corridor. The sword refrained from glowing as she struck them both unconscious with the flat of her blade. She gave a low whistle. Phelon appeared at her side and quickly stripped one of the guards. He put on the clothing, minus the armor, as a detachment of soldiers appeared on the stairs and headed toward them.

"Do something," Phelon begged.

Taliesin grabbed Phelon's hand, closed her eyes, and wished for them to turn invisible. She hoped it worked and pulled him aside as armored men rushed past them. She tugged on Phelon's hand and led him up the stairs, down a corridor, and into the grand hall. The feast was over and the hall nearly deserted. Servants had yet to remove the leftovers from the tables. Several nobles sat with their heads in their plates, apparently passed out from too much drink, while two knights with great stamina continued to drink as they played a card game. Neither man paid Taliesin and Phelon any attention as they approached the table. She sheathed her blade in order to reach with her hands. Phelon grabbed handfuls of wild boar left over from the feast and stuffed it into his mouth. She was no less messy, so ravenous she could have eaten everything in sight and paused between bites to wash it down with wine.

In the process of chewing a large piece of meat, Taliesin heard the slightest intake of breath. She spun around and spotted Prince Sertorius in a doorway, sword in hand. Handsome, tall, and lean, he wore an expensive tunic and looked refreshed after a night spent with his bride. His expression was hostile as he pointed the sword at her.

"So, you came back," Sertorius said.

"Heggen's Beard," Taliesin muttered, caught by surprise. She wiped hands on the tablecloth. "We're supposed to be invisible. Why can you see us?"

The prince laughed. "I wear a charm that reveals magic," he said. The sword remained pointed at her. "I wonder why you felt the need to release Phelon. I was not aware the Raven Mistress had joined the Wolf Clan. In fact, I thought you hated them as much as I do."

"Call the guards, and I'll kill you," Phelon snarled with his mouth full of meat.

Taliesin lifted one corner of her mouth. "Finish eating, Phelon, while I talk to Sertorius." She approached the prince. Her sword quivered, warning her to take caution. "Congratulations on your marriage, Your Grace."

"The marriage is purely for political reasons. There is no reason to be jealous, my dear. Surely you know I love only you?"

Sertorius held his sword aside and stepped closer. His dark blue eyes glimmered with emotion as he leaned toward her for a kiss. Her wolf instincts prevented her from kissing him, and she stepped back with a shake of her head. Their eyes locked together, and for a few seconds, they swam in the memory of their former relationship.

"I didn't come here for an admission of love. I came for my sword and for him." Taliesin pointed toward Phelon. "I'm taking Lykus' son with me, and there's nothing you can do about it. Call your men, and you'll find out just how deadly I can be. I have *Ringerike*, and it's not for you. Nor am I."

"Phelon received the same treatment he showed you," Sertorius said. He was too angry to continue to try to charm her. "You have no idea what type of man he is. Nor do you seem to care how I feel. What was I to think? You were gone, and so was *Ringerike*. I decided to marry Lenora and take this castle and its lands as my own. Had I thought you truly loved me, I would have waited. Was I wrong to think otherwise? Do you love me, Rosamond the Fair?"

Her heart was beating so fast she was afraid she'd turn *Wolfen*. Taliesin felt sick to her stomach when she heard Phelon wolfing down his food and was greatly confused as Sertorius gave her a longing look.

"*Ringerike* belongs to the Raven Clan, and I am the Raven Mistress. You couldn't wield the Raven Sword even if I gave it to you, and that I have no intention of doing. I never did, Sertorius. Nor did I ever intend to marry you."

"Take a look around you," Sertorius said, casting a hand into the air. "I didn't travel a thousand miles to this dukedom merely on the hope my childhood sweetheart stood ready and waiting to marry me. I am the youngest of five princes. I may never rule Caladonia. You are aware of how important *Ringerike* is to me. Give me the sword, and I'll annul my marriage. I will marry you, and we can rule Caladonia side by side. What do you say?"

Taliesin felt like telling him her blood was bluer than his own. She knew revealing the secret she was both Lorian *and* Korax's true heir would only compel him to take what he wanted by force. She heard footsteps and saw guards gathering in the hall behind the prince. Sertorius lifted his hand and held them back.

"Perhaps I loved you once," she said. "Even if you had waited, I still wouldn't be inclined to help you claim the Ebony Throne. Your love is no more than a handful of sand in a windstorm."

"Rosamond, let's not fight," Sertorius said, using her real name in a deliberate tone that was soft and gentle. "You know I cannot let you take Master Phelon. He is my leverage against the Wolf Clan, who is my enemy as it is yours." He took a step toward her. "It does not have to be like this, my love. Let me kiss you. Allow me to hold you. Let us be as we once were."

She held her hand up, holding him back.

"Do not touch me," Taliesin said. "I am bitten, Your Grace."

His eyes shot wide open. "You are *Wolfen*?"

"Phelon turned me," she said. "I could no more be your wife than your mistress. A drop of blood or a bead of sweat is all it takes to turn *Wolfen*. Despite how I may feel about you, I do not desire for you to be cursed as I am."

Taliesin scrutinized the man she'd loved since childhood. In Sertorius' eyes appeared revulsion for the *Wolfen* prisoner. For the first time, she actually felt compassion for Phelon and the Wolf Pack, since it seemed they were hated and feared by everyone. She caught the scent of a strong, musky scent on Sertorius' face and wrinkled her nose.

"I smell your bride."

"The consummation of the marriage was necessary. It does not mean I love Lenora, but I did love you." Sertorius did not attempt to touch her again, and his soft voice turned bitter to match the reflection in his dark blue eyes. "Let us not pretend I alone have been unfaithful to our childhood vows. You were Sir Roland's lover long before I stepped back into the picture. That night you came to my tent, when the moon hung low over the desert, I wondered why you would not let me touch you. It is Roland Brisbane you love, not me."

"Don't try to justify your actions by accusing me of being unfaithful," Taliesin said, not caring to share her feelings about Roland. "I understand why you married the duke's daughter, Sertorius. Your reason and tactics are sound. Like any good general, you took the offensive and came away with a great prize. Mark my word. You will never sit on the Ebony Throne. Nor will you see me again after tonight."

"Pity," the prince said as he signaled his men forward.

Taliesin lifted her finger to ward them off. The guards hung back, uncertain if they were to arrest her or to engage her in battle. They seemed afraid to do either and remained ten paces back.

"Your magic has grown stronger since we last saw one another," Sertorius said. "Zarnoc told me he spoke to you last night. I was grateful to hear you were alive and angry you did not return to me sooner. No, you wanted to study magic. You must know I do not trust magic or magic users. I locked up the wizard for this very reason. Perhaps I should do the same with you, especially now that you're cursed."

"I am not staying long enough to be your prisoner," Taliesin said. "In fact, I mean to return magic to this kingdom. Farewell, Your Grace."

"Stop her!" Sertorius shouted.

Taliesin turned and ran to Phelon as the guards rushed into the grand hall. She grabbed Phelon's hand, and they turned invisible. Sertorius attempted to point them out as they ran to the door. The guards gave pursuit. With a wave of her hand, Taliesin slammed the door shut, willed it to remain closed, and never looked back.

* * * * *

Chapter Three

"Very impressive," Phelon said. "It won't take Sertorius long to summon the guards. I trust you have an escape plan."

"We'll leave through the front gate," Taliesin said as they ran across the courtyard. She memorized the smell of the seaside city as she inhaled deeply through her nostrils. The odor was so strong and the stars bright. In all the excitement, she feared she was going to change into a wolf.

Phelon sensed her discomfort. "Sertorius' men dumped my dead warriors' belongings into a pile behind the barracks," he said. "We can get harnesses to store our gear while we travel on four paws. Every harness is outfitted to carry weapons, clothes, supplies, and water. It will not take us long to cross the desert unless you prefer to head north to the Stavehorn Mountains. I assume you have some destination in mind?"

Taliesin gazed at the moonless sky. "We go through the mountains," she replied, not mentioning she intended to find Duvalen, home of the Lorians.

Angry shouts and frantic footsteps announced the arrival of Sertorius' guards as they flowed into the courtyard from several doorways. Phelon led her behind the barracks, and she stood guard while her companion located two harnesses still loaded with supplies.

Taking no time to converse, Phelon stripped out of his clothes and revealed a well-muscled, hairless body. He was more attractive with his clothes off, Taliesin noticed as he stuffed the garments into a large pouch with drawstrings fastened to the top of the harness. Next was his damp boots and two flasks of water. He tossed two extra flasks in her direction and pointed at the harness he meant for her to use.

"Don't be shy," he said with a snicker.

Taliesin removed her clothes and boots as he'd done and stuffed everything into the drawstring backpack. She wrapped her sword belt around one of the side poles until it was so tight, she doubted she'd ever get it off again without having to cut through the leather. She used rope to tie the sword and scabbard to the side of the pack. The jewels in *Ringerike's* hilt glittered in the faint torchlight. She tore a piece of material from a bloody tunic and used it to hide the hilt.

"Always put on the harness before you alter your shape," Phelon said as he slid the large harness across his shoulders and tightened the straps. It fit his body with three straps, one in front, and two at the sides. Several different-sized sheaths held blades carried lengthwise down his sides. The harness covered his entire back and lay across his backside. He caught her staring and smiled as fur sprouted down the length of his body. "The harness is designed to fit our human and wolf shapes. Go ahead and tighten the straps now," he continued. "It will be a snug fit when you first turn *Wolfen*. The straps adjust to fit your body mass, though you need human hands to tighten them."

Taliesin had not considered it possible to have human hands and a wolf body, but she put on the harness and pulled the straps tight. Phelon gave a satisfied nod, and they headed toward the main gate.

"Some of our kind are so skilled at changing, they never experience mid-transformation, what you call monsters, only that's when we are at our strongest," Phelon said. "If you simply think like a wolf, you can go from human to wolf with no in-between. To be *Wolfen*, just focus on your inner rage and let it transform you."

Her ears tingled as she heard a large number of guards and soldiers headed in their direction. Within the grand hall, men used a battering ram to break through the door. Taliesin felt her head throb each time the ram slammed into the wood, and with a sudden groan, broke off contact. The door collapsed, and the shouts of excited men filled the courtyard.

"'Think like a wolf,'" Taliesin repeated. She was far too angry with Sertorius to morph into a wolf and felt her height grow as her legs bent backward—a painful experience, to be sure. Her breasts flattened as her muscles thickened, and fur sprouted on her body.

Phelon had transformed into a fine-looking wolf, she thought, impressed by his large size, red fur, and black-tipped ears. His lips twisted strangely, and she realized he smiled. She attempted to calm down on the run and felt her body tremble as a tingle spread through her. Thinking only that she was a wolf, she shuddered and dropped onto all fours, and a thick red coat of hair covered her body. She noticed she was much larger and stronger than the male at her side.

With a soft bark, Phelon led the way to the main gate as the sun appeared on the horizon. The portcullis was lowered, the bars too close together to pass through, and they took to the stairs that led out onto the battlements. A guard called out a warning too late for the archers to fire. Taliesin and Phelon jumped over the wall, landing fifty feet below, uninjured, and entered the fortress city of Dunatar. Keeping to the sides of the buildings and in the shadows, they dashed through alleys, down the steps of a brothel, and into a dank opening that led into the sewer that ran beneath the streets. They rushed along the narrow side of the sewer, beside a meandering stream of sludge, until the passage widened and joined a flowing stream that flushed the sewer into the sea. The tunnel opened to the beach, the air filled with the sounds of insects, and an occasional loon on long legs strode across the tide pools. They raced across the beach beneath the gleaming white walls of the city and left it far behind.

For twelve days and nights, they traveled on a northeastern trail along the Stavehorn Mountains, a natural border between Caladonia and a savage wilderness in perpetual winter. Garridan, the largest dukedom, known for its seaside towns, and the Salayan Desert, which they wanted to avoid, swept to the south of the mountains. The next dukedom was Fregia, home of both the Order of the Knights of the White Stag and of Sir

Roland. They ran across snowcapped peaks where the winter breeze blew colder. Somewhere along the way, the four scrawny wolves she'd met at Ysemay's shack caught up with them, as well as two more wolves that had joined the pack. Older and bearing old injuries, the two wolves, shunned by their former packs, ran behind the large black alpha wolf. Taliesin's little pack had accepted them, and soon she realized the older pair had taught the youngsters to hunt. The pack followed at a safe distance, hunting on their own, while Taliesin and Phelon killed their prey in private. They never shared what they ate with the pack, and covered their urine and feces, to make certain the pack were not infected.

One evening, dark clouds filled the sky and a sudden drop in temperature concerned Taliesin for the safety of the pack. They had left the upper trails and entered Fregian territory, for the simple reason she was not ready to find out what lay on the other side of the mountains. Crystalline shapes of frost appeared on the leaves of trees and bushes, and on the wolves' thick fur. Tiny white clouds appeared each time the pack panted. Phelon, ahead a good distance, seemed willing to keep traveling by night. His fast pace made it difficult for the pack to keep up.

Taliesin took pity on the wolves and halted. Using her keen night vision, she scanned the surroundings until she found a windfall. She ran to the opening, peered beneath the canopy of dead trees, and sniffed. There was no smell of humans or other animals. She let out a sharp bark and backed away from the entrance.

"What is it?" Phelon asked after he joined her.

"We're camping for the night. The pack is tired."

"There is no need to keep them with us, Taliesin. We do not build packs with wild animals," he said. "Let's kill them and be done with it."

"Don't you dare," she said, glaring at Phelon. "We're making camp, and that's the end of it. I happen to enjoy their company more than yours."

"Fair enough," he said with a growl. "I suppose there is safety in numbers."

Taliesin moved away from the windfall. The black male rushed by her and entered the den. One after another, the wolves entered the shelter and assumed a huddled mass for warmth. She let out a sigh that sounded more human than wolf as she crawled in beside the wolves. Phelon joined them as light snow began to fall. She felt the heat rising from his body, generating so much warmth the ground and air around them felt balmy. The six wolves yawned with contentment and nestled closer. The harnesses prevented Taliesin and Phelon from curling up as the wolves had done. She was surprised when Phelon morphed into a human and slid off his harness. He removed hers as well and set it aside before he crawled to the opening and waved her over.

"Come and see this," he said.

A soft growl rose in the back of the black wolf's throat. Taliesin growled back, and the male settled down. Joining Phelon at the entrance, she caught her breath when he pointed out a meteor that streaked across the sky.

"Did you see it, Taliesin? Make a wish! You're supposed to, you know?"

Taliesin thought about Zarnoc and her friends, and silently wished they would find Duvalen. She turned back into a wolf before she backed into the den. Phelon sat beside her, still human, and petted her as he would a dog.

"I admit, I have started to enjoy running wild," Phelon said. "Life as a wolf is uncomplicated. As long as we avoid humans, we are virtually free from all worries. I feel like I am on holiday. I'm actually happy, and I am seldom happy."

Phelon reached into his pack and drew out a cloak he wrapped around his nude body. His behavior struck her as odd, for he could have turned into a wolf. Nor did he need clothes to remain warm. A shy smile cast in her direction made it clear he had done so out of embarrassment.

"Sometimes I can read your thoughts," he continued. "It's normal in the Wolf Pack to share each other's thoughts and feelings, and it makes warfare much easier. There is no need to shout commands, for it is instinctive. You communicate with your wolves in the same way. The alpha male has bonded with you. If you were a real wolf, I believe he would choose you as his mate."

She let out a loud yawn. "That means I'm tired."

Phelon smiled. "I know you don't like me, and I can't blame you. I did try to kill you and your friends. You can't blame me for wanting to taste Prince Sertorius' blood. He is not your friend, yet he insists on calling you Rosamond. That's reason enough to bite him, for I know you prefer to go by your clan name."

"I don't want to talk about the prince," Taliesin said, ending with a threatening growl. Her voice in wolf form sounded deeper than normal, and the wolves had to find it strange she was able to speak, for several growled at her. "I want to sleep, Phelon. Must we talk?"

"Must you remain in wolf form? Fregians are known for killing wolves for their pelts. It will be safer to travel as humans, and I again caution you against bringing your pets along with us. You should try to convince them to stay here. This forest is as good as another."

Closing her eyes, she sent the wolves comforting thoughts, assuring them she meant no harm and wanted only to protect them. A thought was projected from the leader, the black male, and it wasn't conveyed so much in words as it was in an image of him getting up the courage to nuzzle her to show his appreciation. The black wolf trusted her. If he trusted her, so did his pack, and she let him know their safety was important to her by sending him an image of herself in human form hugging his furry body and then as a wolf nuzzling him back. The wolf understood and sent her an image of trappers slaughtering his parents and siblings.

Before she was aware of what she was doing, Taliesin felt her body changing into her human form, lying face down. Phelon covered her with his own cloak. He fished around in his pack and pulled out a long white ruffled shirt he put on and pulled down to hide his privates and thighs. She noticed he was aroused. She was somewhat flattered and felt a blush on her cheeks as she sat up, pulled the cloak around her shoulders, and closed it in front.

"You were communicating with the wolves, weren't you?" he asked.

"Yes," she admitted. "I don't know how it's possible, it just is."

"I cannot communicate with them as you do. It must be because you are a *Sha'tar*. I imagine you can talk to any animal you want to. Try to convince them not to make this journey with us. It's for their own good, Taliesin."

Phelon continued to rummage about in their backpacks, producing a blanket to sit on, a bottle of wine, a loaf of bread that looked as hard as a rock, and a piece of yellow cheese that had turned green on the edges from mold. He cut off the mold with a knife while she re-established the link with the black wolf, warned him about hunters, and cautioned him to remain in the forest.

"I am your friend," she said. The black wolf pressed against her and rubbed his head against her body. "You are a beautiful animal, so very beautiful. I'd like to call you 'Korax,' after the king of my own clan, for no other wolf is as brave, beautiful, or trusting. You must not come with us." She felt a tongue, wet and warm, flick across her hand. Letting out a sigh, she leaned over the wolf and hugged him. He allowed the close contact and pushed back against her.

"Now that it's settled, come have some wine and cheese."

"In a minute," she said. "I'm making friends. You never know when I'll meet them again. I made it clear not all humans are friendly. This is a once in a lifetime occurrence, so let me enjoy it."

"Whatever you want," Phelon replied.

Taliesin hugged the black wolf and kissed him repeatedly on top of his head. The pack stirred behind them. She turned to see the wolves had lowered their heads to the ground, whimpering, and inched closer to her, tails beating the hard ground.

"Do you want a fire?" Phelon asked as he crawled out of the den.

"Don't bother on my account. I'm perfectly content."

"Then I won't make one. We have one skin of wine I have been saving, and I wouldn't mind getting drunk tonight. Come join me."

"I said I won't be long."

Six wolves soon surrounded Taliesin, sniffing her, licking her, and making quite the fuss about what felt like a family reunion. As the alpha wolf watched her, his expression one of tolerance, she greeted each wolf, pulled them close, put her head over theirs, and rubbed her cheek against their faces. She felt no reason to fear the wild animals and sensed no fear in return. One of the new wolves was female. Her coat was white. The she-wolf had a gray eye and a blue eye and a jagged scar across her shoulder that at one time had been deep. The female was older than the rest, and by the looks of her tits, had produced several litters.

Taliesin liked the white wolf almost as much as Korax and felt an impulse to name her new friends. The white wolf was 'Minerva,' for her deceased adoptive mother. The four other wolves were similar in color and markings. The other new wolf to the pack was male. Since he avoided letting her pet him, she called him, 'Hedge.' The three females she already knew. They were smaller than Minerva was, and she named one 'Boots' due to her black feet. She named another 'Molly,' because the red fur under her shin matched the hair of a barmaid who had given her a free bottle of wine years back when she'd slipped her a pretty necklace for good service. Lastly, she named the brown wolf with green eyes 'Emerald.' This female was lean and had particularly soft fur. She found this wolf the most beautiful and conveyed in thought to Korax this female would make him a fine mate. After she'd introduced herself to all the wolves, she gave the leader a final pat on the head with the reassuring thought he should rest while she guarded the pack. She slid out of the den and joined Phelon.

"The wine is tolerable." Phelon handed her the flask. "You spent too much time getting friendly with the wolves. You must set them free, Taliesin. They are wild creatures, wilder than us, and could turn on us upon any provocation. Our kind does not befriend real wolves, though on occasion, when extremely hungry, we might eat a few."

"One more day with them won't hurt." Taliesin took a drink, handed the wineskin to Phelon, and tore off a large chunk of cheese. "I don't know why they trust us more as humans than in our wolf forms. I think it's because we're so much larger. Korax understands they may not eat after us, or they'll fall ill."

"Still holding onto your Raven Clan legacy and bestowing nicknames? Soon you will not care about your past and will come to enjoy your new life as a *Wolfen*. After we meet with Almaric and give him *Ringerike*, we will visit my father at Wolf's Den and make you a real member of the Wolf Pack. The ceremony is quite special and is always conducted on the full of the moon. A few of your old friends from the Raven Clan are there as well. You can rejoin Minerva and the twins, Falcon and Talon. I'm sure there are others eager to see you again."

"It's not possible, Phelon," she said. "I'm going to Duvalen to join Zarnoc and Hawk. I love running with these wolves. Being a member of the Wolf Pack is not the same, and you know it. There's no reason for me to meet Almaric since I refuse to part with *Ringerike*. I thought you might come with me."

Phelon took a swig from the bottle. "I have never known wolves to run with *Wolfen*," he replied. "The only story even close is about a small boy raised by wolves in the forest. I don't mind if they stay with us a few more days. When we reach Almaric's camp, you must send them away."

"Did you hear what I said? I'm not coming with you. I am going over the mountains to find Duvalen and my friends."

His eyes glittered bright yellow. "Why would we want to go to Duvalen? I don't think it even exists. If it did, I still wouldn't go there. Legend says the fairies of Duvalen are cruel. Their world is a dangerous place for anyone who is not Lorian or one of the ancient breeds. No, Taliesin. I would not go there for any reason. Nor should you. Come with me and meet Almaric."

"I'm sorry. My answer is no."

"Then, if you truly want me to come with you, make it worth my while," Phelon replied in a husky voice. "Lay with me tonight."

Taliesin felt a blush warm her cheeks. She put a hand to her hair and felt a tangle that reminded her of a bird's nest. Phelon reached out and pulled her arm down, his brown eyes filled with tenderness. When he kissed the back of her hand, as a nobleman would do with a lady, she felt her blush spread down to her neck. The impulse to kiss him made her laugh, and as she pushed him back, she took another drink.

"After tonight, we will part company," Phelon said at last. "Unlike Sertorius, I won't try to stop you from leaving. My path is to the east. I will join my father and Prince Almaric in Scrydon and go to war."

"I'm not interested in war," she said. "Nor will I pick sides."

Phelon scratched behind his ear. "You are female, and therefore by nature treacherous," he said, though he laughed. "The last woman I trusted was my mother. I am told at my birth she took a disliking to my red hair and briefly considered eating me. My nursemaid took me from my mother, presented me to my father, returned while my mother was sleeping, and slit her throat with a silver knife. While I have my nursemaid to thank for saving my life, she still killed my mother. I was only five years old when I pushed my nurse off a cliff and thereby won my father's approval."

"That's horrible," Taliesin said.

"It's the way of our clan."

Taliesin took the wineskin from Phelon and finished it. She placed it between her legs, crossed one over the other, and picked at the cheese. It was tasteless and stuck in her teeth. Her mind was full of thoughts of conspiracies and betrayal. She wanted more wine, enough to get drunk and sick on, and in the blink of an eye, the flask was full again. Phelon gasped when she handed it to him.

"If you can refill this, why not simply wish for a basted turkey and feed your pack and us?" Phelon asked. He drank the magical wine and seemed tipsier for it.

"Jealous?"

"A little. Any other wizard would have recited a spell or used a charm to make wine and cheese. You can merely think it and make it happen. That is the mark of a true *Sha'tar*," Phelon said. "Why don't you create a shelter for us for the night? I wouldn't mind sleeping in a tent."

Taliesin thought of a tent with a large bed covered with pillows and blankets. She ended up creating a tiny tent with one thick blanket to share. Phelon stretched out on the blanket, and the edges magically curled over his body. A lantern, with a small flame that danced about, hung at the top of the shelter. Taliesin held the flask up, toasted Phelon, and squeezed wine into her mouth.

"Not quite what I imagined. It's good enough for one night."

"Don't underestimate your abilities, Taliesin. A *Sha'tar* is born one in a million," Phelon said. "Long ago, their notoriety led to jealousy among the people of their villages, and even among magic users, and many were killed out of fear, while others never learned to use their gifts and lived ordinary lives. No one ever planned for a great resurrection of magic. You know, I'm almost tempted to come with you to see if it's possible or not."

"Then let's find out where we can find Duvalen," she replied.

Taliesin wished *Ringerike* and the sword belt were in the tent. She laughed when they appeared on her lap. Phelon's eyes grew wide as she reached for the small pouch attached to her sword belt, pulled it toward her, and unfastened the cords that tied it closed. *Ringerike*, resting across her lap, inched partially out of the scabbard and started to glow bright blue on her lap. In the eerie light, she reached inside the pouch to remove a small, folded piece of parchment. She unfolded the map, spread it across her lap and the sword, and thought of the place in Lorian where Zarnoc was born. One thousand miles to the north a twinkling star appeared, marked in glowing letters with the name 'Duvalen.' Other images appeared, highlighting magical weapons along the way.

"There are six magical weapons between here and Duvalen," Taliesin said, excited. "I have no problem picking up a few weapons if you're coming with me. If not, I'll return with Zarnoc and my friends to retrieve them."

"The map is blank," Phelon grumbled.

"This is a Deceiver's Map. Only magic users can read it. The map also can show you whoever you want to find, and the names of all secret places."

"Are we being followed?"

"Let me see."

Taliesin stared hard at the map. A dot appeared to represent her and the pack. "We're in Fregia, as we know," she said. "This is the Tangers Forest, and there's a Fregian town two days from here if we continue east. It's the village of Ruthenia, Sir Roland's birthplace, and I don't want to go there. No one is following us. There are a couple of lone hunters in the forest. I also see several *Wolfen* patrols about two hundred miles to the south, moving from west to east. They must be going to join Prince Almaric."

"I can't see a thing. Show me," Phelon said.

Taliesin willed the map to appear to Phelon and pointed out where Prince Almaric had gathered a large mercenary army in Scrydon, not far from Wolf's Den. The *Wolfen* were crawling all over the map in that area. They were at the Black Tower, home of Duke Fergus Vortigern, the Lord who controlled Scrydon, and Almaric's strongest ally.

MISTRESS OF MAGIC | 67

"The House of Vortigern owned the magical sword *Trembler*, which causes terror among its enemy when drawn in battle. I found it long ago," she said. "All I have to do with any dormant magic sword is touch the blade to return its powers. I did the same with *Doomsayer*, which was taken by your father. I suppose Almaric has it now."

Phelon nodded. "I'm sure the eldest prince does," he said. "What about your clan? There are only five of you. I know you care about your friends, Taliesin. You seem to care about everyone, including me. I must warn you not to trust me. When I said I would help you and not force you to go with me, I meant it. Just know that if we encounter any *Wolfen*, I will have to take you prisoner."

"And if any Fregians show up, I'll turn you over to them, so we're even."

Taliesin thought about Zarnoc and saw his name written at the top of a mountain where a tiny blue crystal appeared, indicating the fairy fortress of Duvalen. She again thought about magical weapons, and the name *Calaburn* appeared no more than twenty miles to the northeast in the ruins of a once-great castle build by Prince Tarquin Draconus.

"*Calaburn* is nearby, in the ruins of Ascalon," she said. "It possesses the powers of turning into flame in the hands of its rightful master. The blade cannot be broken, can cut through rock, and will never dull. It also causes depression and night terrors. It's made of gold, not silver, so it won't harm you."

"You would give *Calaburn* to me? We are not friends."

"To tempt you into coming with me," Taliesin said. "There is a cave beneath the ruins of the castle where the sword is kept. It would like to be found."

"How do you know all this?" Phelon asked.

"Sertorius called me Rosamond because I'm Rosamond Mandrake. My father was John Mandrake. Only a few of his swords were enchanted. I owned one called *Wolf Kill*er, only I lost it back at the Caves of the Snake God. One day I'll go back and get it."

Ringerike gave a little jerk on her lap, indicating it was jealous at her longing for *Wolf Killer*, and made her immediately regret having said too much. She sensed the sword's annoyance with her for confiding in Phelon. It didn't think he was her friend and warned her Phelon would turn on her in the blink of an eye.

"Your father was Mandrake? I had no idea," Phelon said, delighted to receive such tasty information. "No wonder you are able to find valuable weapons on any battlefield. If I were not the son of Lykus, I would join the Raven Clan, help you collect every magical weapon in the realm, and sell them to the highest bidder."

"Some magical items are evil, Phelon. I know the names of most of them and who made them, though not all. There were far too many evil sorcerers and evil weapons being used, and that's why the House of Draconus outlawed magic. There are other magical items, like horns and wands and even harps. Perhaps I'll find them all. I won't decide until I go to Duvalen. For now, let's concentrate on finding *Calaburn*."

Phelon bowed his head. "I am honored you would even think of me," he said. "Of course, I'll come with you and help find this sword, and then we'll part company."

"Then we'll part company," she repeated.

He set the bottle aside and lay down on the blanket. She put the map inside her pouch, slid *Ringerike* all the way into its scabbard, placed the sword between them, and lay down beside Phelon. The blanket curled over both of them, coming together at the center like a neat, little cocoon. Taliesin smiled when Phelon curled up against her. As soon as she heard him snore, she allowed herself to doze off.

In the morning, she found the wolves had left the den and were gone.

* * * * *

Chapter Four

Shadows appeared on the side of the mountain as Taliesin and Phelon, in *Wolfen* form, scaled a jagged escarpment to reach Ascalon Castle. The ruins, built into the side of a mountain, were accessible after a freehand climb using a narrow path cut into the stone that led through crumbling gates. Their harnesses, too cumbersome to wear on their big bodies as they made their ascent, dangled below them on ropes and slowed their movements. Taliesin reached the stairs first and reached out with a clawed hand to grasp Phelon's arm, leaving gouges as she pulled him up beside her.

"For a moment, I thought you were going to leave me behind," Phelon said, morphing into his human form. A thick beard covered his face, and his hair had grown much longer. "You're a much better climber than I am."

"I wasn't about to let you fall," she replied. "Sorry I hurt you."

Phelon shrugged. "No complaints. Better to be alive than dead," he said.

The cuts on his arm healed quickly, leaving splotches of blood on his arm. He untied the rope around his lean waist and tossed the harness to the ground. Taliesin followed his example. She opened the large pouch fastened to the harness, removed her clothes, and dressed. It was the first time she had worn clothes in weeks, and they hung on her lean, muscular body. Belting *Ringerike* onto her back, she left the rest of her gear at the base of a tall pillar that stood alone, grabbed a flask of water, and stood at the entrance gates as she drank every drop.

"There's no snow up here. How is that possible?" Phelon asked. He joined her, his own flask in hand. His red hair stood out in contrast to the dark-blue uniform he wore. He swallowed a mouthful of water and saved the rest.

"The air feels a little warmer, too."

"We need to take a look around before we look for the sword. Something made the snow melt." He hooked the flask to his belt. He drew his sword. "This place could be inhabited by all manner of dark creatures. You go first."

Grinning, Taliesin left *Ringerike* in its scabbard and entered a large courtyard with huge flagstones that retained a hint of their former colorful appearance. Cracked and worn, the flagstones spread across a wide expanse of flat ground, surrounded by mounds of rubble that had once been a castle. Two broken towers overgrown with dead vines remained. Nothing else was left of Ascalon, which Taliesin recalled from the poems of Glabber the Glib had been a formidable fortress during the era of King Korax Sanqualus. Ascalon had belonged to Prince Tarquin Draconus. As Lorian troops withdrew from Caladonia, defeated and bitter, they destroyed everything in their wake before vanishing into the Stavehorn Mountains and from the records of history. Glabber the Glib's poem about 'Mighty Ascalon' was one of his first, written before he'd become famous. Taliesin tried to remember what he'd said about the place and recited a stanza.

"'Six spiral towers glittered like emeralds in the winter sun,
A sacred place loved by many, ruled by a Draconus son,
Let all remember there was no finer castle than Ascalon.'"

"You like Glabber the Glib's poetry? I think the poem ends with, 'no finer place was Castle Ascalon, an emerald jewel lay to ruin in a winter sun.'" Phelon's eyes twinkled. "I'm surprised you'd like an Eagle Clan poet, considering how much you hate Lord Arundel and Master Xander. The Wolf Clan eats poets." He laughed coarsely. "They taste like chicken."

"Glabber is my favorite poet and playwright," Taliesin said. "I had his entire collection of works at Raven's Nest. Glabber can't help he was born into the Eagle Clan. and don't remind me the Wolf Clan ate his son, Secretary Glabbrio, along with the entire Raven Clan. Cannibalism is nothing to laugh about, and if the day comes that I ever put human flesh to my mouth, I will fall upon my own sword."

Ringerike let out a mournful note. She placed her hand around the hilt.

"When we are *Wolfen*, we are not human," Phelon said as if this made all the difference in the world.

"You'd still remember who you ate for dinner. Don't make excuses."

After a thorough search of the area revealed no sign of any living creatures, Taliesin stopped at a section where the foliage was blackened, as if a great fire had scoured the area and left the dirt uninhabitable for plant life. She found the head of Prince Tarquin's statue under a dead bush, his face still recognizable and undeniably handsome, though the rest of the statue had turned to dust. Not far from the head, she spotted a marble staircase that had avoided the erosion of time. With Phelon's assistance, they broke through dead vines that partially covered the entrance and gazed into darkness. The stairs descended into the lower levels of the castle. Large scratch marks covered the walls, and sections of the stairs were gone.

"Let's get an exact fix on *Calaburn*," Taliesin whispered. She used a block of stone as a table and spread out the map. A quick scan showed her *Calaburn* was, in fact, on the lower level. A tiny image of a skull and crossbones gave warning there was danger beneath their feet.

"There are a lot of bones and carcasses nearby," he said. "It looks like some animal has been using this place as its lair. I smell something, but I can't quite put my finger on it. It's not a familiar odor. Do you see anything on the map?"

"It keeps changing on me. One minute I can see the castle as it used to be, and then it turns into rubble. *Calaburn* is here. Whatever left those bones behind must be on the lower level, only the map won't reveal what it is." Taliesin folded the map and slipped it into the pouch. "Let's see if *Ringerike* can tell us anything."

"The Raven Sword talks to you, too?"

She nodded. "I can also talk to birds."

Taliesin reached up with her right hand to grasp *Ringerike's* hilt. The sword trembled as she closed her eyes and concentrated. Images of Ascalon appeared in her mind, and she gazed at a beautiful castle of green stone and flagstones painted with murals. Gentle folk inhabited Ascalon, seated on benches reading poetry and performing plays in the shadow of six slender towers. A path from the north led to the castle. Knights and ladies on liveried horses rode into the beautiful castle. They were greeted by Prince Tarquin, a tall, handsome man, and a regal lady with long blonde hair who wore a crown of flowers.

"The Lorians didn't destroy this castle like Glabber claimed in his poems and stories. *Ringerike* says there is a gold dragon that lives here, sitting on a mound of treasure. The fairy folk hired the dragon to destroy this place, and in payment allowed it to remain and guard the royal treasure."

Phelon gave a shudder. "I didn't know dragons still existed," he said, his voice lowered. "I thought they were all killed during King Magnus's reign two hundred years ago. Why didn't you mention this before? We've been talking, and it probably heard us. Apparently, you do not fear anything, even dragons."

Taliesin opened one eye, frowned, and shut it again, as the last battle fought within the walls of Ascalon appeared in her mind. Knights in silver stood at the wall and used giant crossbows; a wizard in the main tower used magic to deflect the dragon's fire; and the second son of Prince Tarquin, a boy of ten, and a Fregian duke, both whose names were unknown by the sword, commanded the troops. Finally, a giant gold dragon landed in the courtyard and killed all in a rain of fire. She didn't know why the map hadn't warned her with a large description that read 'beware of the dragon,' and made a mental note to always double-check with *Ringerike* before she believed anything on the Deceiver's Map.

"The Lorians sent a dragon here to kill Tarquin's family. First, Queen Dehavilyn gave *Graysteel* to Tarquin use in battle against Korax. At the Battle of Tripleton, where the three streams cross, Prince Tarquin and King Korax fought. Korax died that day, and Tarquin died on the following afternoon. The Raven Clan took *Graysteel* back to Duvalen, but Dehavilyn wasn't done yet. She sent the dragon to kill Tarquin's family and the royal court. Titus, the eldest son of Tarquin, went with his father to Caladonia. He was later crowned king and built the Draconus dynasty and Tantalon Castle on the ruins of Black Castle."

"I didn't ask for a history lesson," Phelon said. "How do we kill a dragon?"

"Well, I fought an eight-headed hydra and an army of the undead at the Cave of the Snake God," Taliesin said. "A gold dragon can't be any worse than a hydra. A few whacks with *Ringerike* should do the trick."

Phelon looked at her as if she'd turned green and sprouted feathers. "Have you ever seen a dragon?" he asked. She shook her head. "Gold dragons are said to have been the most ferocious in battle. Have you seen *any* dragons at all? No! Because if you had, you'd most likely be dead. If a dragon has survived this long without discovery, especially one that guards *Calaburn*, then you can be sure that's exactly what will happen when we meet it face to face."

She had never heard Phelon sound so frightened. "Do you want to leave?"

"Run? From danger? You really do not know me at all."

Phelon stabbed his sword into the ground, stripped out of his clothes, and morphed into a *Wolfen*. His red fur gleamed in the sun, and he towered over Taliesin in his half-turned state; his thin black lips peeled back to expose long fangs that oozed saliva. With a snarl, he walked on his hind legs to the staircase, sniffed the foulness coming from the dark, and dropped down onto his front legs. Taliesin heard something stir within and imagined the dragon sleeping on a hoard of treasure, wishing it would fall asleep by the time they reached the bottom of the stairs. A glance at Phelon in his hideous half-turned form made her glad no one held up a mirror when she was in a similar form; it was hideous.

Phelon hung back as she preceded him down the stairs with *Ringerike* held high and a bright blue light cutting through the dark. Centuries of trash littered the stairs, from rusted and melted weapons, human skeletons, to half-eaten carcasses of animals left to rot. The sword was steady in her hand as she descended into the thick gloom that reeked of ammonia and sulfur. At the foot of the stairs, she gazed at an immense chamber carved out of the side of the mountain. Her arm rose of its own accord, lifted by the sword, and *Ringerike* pointed across the great hall to the remains of a throne made of green quartz and covered with cobwebs. Phelon joined her, and together they walked across the chamber and stopped in front of the throne.

"The map indicates the sword is beneath the throne," Taliesin whispered. She gestured for Phelon to move the throne aside and kept guard.

Phelon mustered all of his strength and gave a hard shove that sent the throne flying across the room. The crash on the far side was so loud and thunderous, Taliesin was quite certain if the dragon wasn't awake in its lair, it certainly was now. Aware he'd blundered, Phelon morphed back into a human, naked and trembling with fear. She gave him an angry look, and he immediately turned back into the beast.

"Sorry," Phelon growled. His voice echoed in the chamber.

Taliesin glared at him again and gazed around the space. Where the throne had been was another staircase that led down into darkness. Taliesin kept her thoughts on the dragon, willing it to sleep and demanding anything living within the dark chamber be still, calm, and extremely tired. She led the way downwards, guided by the bright light of *Ringerike*, which allowed her to see 20 feet in all directions. The stairs, carved out of the living rock and in fair condition, wound down in a circular fashion and took them deeper into the mountain. The odor within the cave was foul. A stench of decay and death assailed her nostrils, worse than a battlefield strewn with the bodies of ten thousand men and horses rotting in the sun. If this was the perfume of a dragon, she thought, it was no wonder King Magnus had ordered their extermination. It was a putrid odor. She had half a mind to kill the damn thing for crapping where it slept.

"Sleep, sleep," she said. "Sleep foul beast."

Taliesin staggered forward as Phelon's unconscious body slammed into her legs from behind and knocked her off her feet. Too late, she realized she had not specified which foul beast she meant, and they tumbled down the stairs. She lost her grip on *Ringerike* and watched as the blue blade spun away and fell onto a pile of gold coins before they crashed at the bottom of the stairs. Phelon made no move to rise, and she kicked him several times in the ribs out of pure malice. The sword lay no more than ten feet from her, glowing bright, and sent a warning to proceed with more caution. As soon as she retrieved *Ringerike*, the light dowsed. Something moved, something very large, in the darkness.

"Heggen's Beard," Taliesin muttered.

Her voice echoed as *Ringerike* glowed bright blue, revealing giant stalactites and stalagmites that looked like colossal fangs, purple mushroom-shaped things that littered the floor. Green mold covered everything. On closer inspection, she realized the green mold was dragon dung. It was apparent her host had not ventured far from its lair in the last two hundred years.

"If there be a dragon here, please know I mean you no harm."

"There *be* a dragon," a loud, booming voice replied.

The Raven Sword trembled in her hand as the ground beneath her feet began to move. Loud breaths emitted hot air that hit Taliesin in the face. She jumped back, trying to move out of the way, as a large form, illuminated by the sword, rose from the cave floor. Treasure cascaded from it, gathering at her feet as a long neck extended, and an enormous head appeared. Gold scales covered the dragon, and emerald-green eyes peered intently at the sword's bright blue light. The dragon had survived, she thought, because it was the smartest and strongest of its kind. Despite its enormity, she found the creature beautiful and felt no fear, until a tongue lashed across its spear-sized fangs that made her feel like a tasty snack.

"Well, you do smell delicious. Be glad I have already eaten," the dragon said. "I should warn you that I can read your thoughts. Telepathy is a trait of gold dragons, for we are magic users, my dear."

"That's comforting, and also disturbing. You are a great deal larger than I imagined, though, in truth, I've never seen a dragon before." Taliesin bowed her head. "Forgive me for trespassing, great one. I am the Raven Mistress, and this is *Ringerike*. I am not here to harm you."

"Harm *me*?" The dragon laughed.

Taliesin trembled as the dragon lifted its head and belched a great ball of fire that sped across the cavern and vanished with a puff of white smoke. The dragon lowered its head, steam rising from its flared nostrils, and its eyes widened as she held the sword up before her.

"Your true name is Rosamond, daughter of John Mandrake, a gifted swordsmith, and your mother...," he paused, "you don't know who your mother was, do you? Interesting. *Very* interesting."

"Do you know who my mother was? Will you tell me?"

"There is a time and place for everything, and that time has not yet come," the dragon rumbled. His eyes widened as he noticed the sword. "*Ringerike*? I know this sword. John Mandrake was descendant from the Royal House of Sanqualus, which is the only reason the Raven Sword is so ready to defend you, my dear. This sword belonged to King Korax, forged a thousand years ago by the Lorians." The dragon lowered its head until its nostrils were close enough to puff hot air upon Taliesin. "Tell me, Raven Mistress, who forged this sword for the King of the Raven Clan? Give me the name of the Lorian swordsmith, and I will spare your life."

The weapon let out a soft hum. An image of a woman, fair of face, yet strong of hand, appeared in Taliesin's mind. She watched the fairy maiden, sweat on her brow, pound a sword, forged in a fire made by the same black dragon and laid upon an anvil.

"Her name was Ardea. A fairy sorceress," Taliesin said, silently thanking the sword for its help. She breathed easier when the dragon nodded its immense head. She was glad he had not asked the name of the fire-breathing black dragon since her sword did not know the name of this particular dragon.

"Ardea was a lover of King Korax," he said in a lecherous voice. "Ardea is still alive, for as you know, fairies live as long as dragons, and we live a very, *very* long time. I am incredibly fond of Ardea and occasionally visit her in Duvalen, a place you are most anxious to visit. You have fairy blood, yet you are much more than that, Mistress Taliesin of the Raven Clan."

"What dragon helped Ardea make *Ringerike*?"

"Ha! Something you don't know," he said, narrowing his eyes. "Vargus the Dreadful provided the fire that made Ringerike invincible. It was Vargus who killed Prince Tarquin's family, and it was Bonaparte who killed Vargus."

"Who is Bonaparte? A knight?"

The dragon sucked in his breath and exhaled through his nostrils, displaying fancy little balls of red fire that puffed out of its nose one after another like leaping sheep. The dragon sat with one front leg bent at the knee, resting on a rocky ledge to support its great weight, and the other front leg held upwards with sharp claws spread out as if he were a gentleman of leisure throwing his hand out in absolute disdain.

"Ascalon is now my home," the dragon said. "All you see belongs to Bonaparte. I am Bonaparte, and I will allow you to address me as such, Raven Mistress. Over the centuries, I have accumulated great wealth."

The treasure filled the chamber, wealth and riches only kings ever acquired, and servants merely dreamed about.

There was enough gold to paint the entire three miles of wall that surrounded the town of Dunatar. The gold dragon had accumulated a vast amount of treasure in its lifetime. Its long tail, with a large triangular tip, curled around the base of the mound of gold. The enormous green eyes, as luminous as pools of water in the moonlight, regarded her thoughtfully and held her gaze, displaying so much intelligence and emotion, she asked herself if dragons had souls.

"Of course, we do," the dragon said in its deep, resonant voice.

"I don't like people reading my mind, Bonaparte."

"Then guard your thoughts, Raven Mistress, for I also know you travel with Master Phelon, the heir of the Wolf Clan. Do you really think Phelon is worthy of *Calaburn*? He is *Wolfen*!" A flash of fiery smoke snorted out of his nostrils.

Taliesin held his gaze. "Phelon is my friend. And I am *Wolfen*."

"Yes, I know, my dear. It is strange you are not scared of me," the dragon said. He flashed his enormous white teeth. "Through the ages, I have destroyed thousands of villages and millions of humans. I have roasted to death countless knights who dared come here. Many have come looking for *Calaburn*. None ever left this place. I have also eaten a few *Wolfen* for dinner. Tell me. Do bards still sing about dragons?"

She lowered her sword, for, despite its length, the Raven Sword was a toothpick in comparison to the size of Bonaparte's teeth. All the dragon had to do was bend down his head, open his massive jaws, and swallow her whole.

"Bards still sing about dragons. There was Shavea and her brother Klakegon, Malagorigaz, and Tagallagon the Black, to mention a few. There was also Huva'khan and Ūerdraine, a blue and a gold dragon that often-pestered Black Castle during the Raven King's reign. The bards say black dragons were distempered, red chaotic, blue cunning, while and silver want only to fly, and the green yearn to nest."

"What about gold dragons?"

"Gold dragons are obsessed with treasure."

"Bonaparte does like gold," he said.

"And I have a knack for finding magical weapons." Taliesin's voice was unwavering, though she knew the dragon was sizing her up for dinner. "I am sure you have many magical items here—surely you could part with one little sword? I'm not sure about protocol when addressing a dragon. Do you require I guess your name to avoid being eaten, Your Greatness? I mean your true name, for I know dragons have nicknames, and Bonaparte is a nickname."

The dragon gave her a wink. "You are quite clever, Raven Mistress," he said in a rumbling voice. "No one knows my true name, not even your sword. I know *Ringerike* helps you see the past and present, but it cannot predict the future. Nor does it know my secrets. Perhaps I should take a closer look at you...before I decide to *eat you*."

Taliesin caught her breath as bright-burning torches appeared on the cave walls, bathing the room in a golden sheen, and watched, amazed, as the giant dragon turned into a tall, powerfully-built man in gold armor. Black hair fell to his trim waist, and he held her with his bright green eyes, almost human except for a slit of gold in the center.

Ringerike, annoyed she found the dragon-man handsome, thumped her leg as she stepped forward to meet Bonaparte. He wore a jeweled ring on every black-nailed finger and a gold crown with a large emerald on his brow. His strange eyes sparkled, and he offered a courtly bow, one arm extended high and the other across his middle as he dipped low.

"Bonaparte welcomes you to his home," he said. "Because Bonaparte killed Vargus, he is allowed to stay here and guard his treasure unmolested by ghosts. This castle is both enchanted and haunted, my dear. You are very brave to come here, and Bonaparte admires bravery, especially brave female warriors."

The dragon-man stopped three feet from her, placed his hands on his lean hips, and started to move in what reminded her of a serpent, twisting and turning as if he danced to music. He placed his hands on his thighs and slid them all the way up to his armored chest, giving her a provocative look that made her flesh crawl.

"Do you like what you see, Raven Mistress? Do you like Bonaparte?"

"Yes, I do," she admitted.

Taliesin admired his square, clean-shaven jaw and his perfect nose—straight, long, and with flared nostrils, just the way she liked a nose to be. His large green eyes slanted at the far corners, and he had high cheekbones. Her gaze settled on his wide, full lips, and she licked hers at the same time he licked his own.

"Are you going to eat me?" Taliesin asked. "I'm a bit tough."

"Oh, I think not. Bonaparte has other plans for you. Bonaparte likes you."

The dragon-man's arms wrapped around her waist and pulled her against his body. His hard scales which she had mistaken for gold armor, softened, and reminded her of the flesh of a snake. Her sword arm sagged, and the tip of *Ringerike* scraped against the floor and sent blue sparks into the air as Bonaparte kissed her. She sensed trust from the sword, trust of the dragon, and approval to share a kiss, for *Ringerike* felt charmed by the dragon as well.

The kiss grew passionate and Taliesin, in her excitement, accidentally bit the dragon-man's tongue. His blood was thick and tasted sweet as honey.

The moment she tasted his blood, images of dragons appeared in her mind. Dragons once roamed the planet, as plentiful as the birds in the air, and many yet lingered hidden in their caves, forests, and beneath the sea. Bonaparte had lived a long time and during his life had loved many dragon and humans. She was the first *Wolfen* he had ever kissed, and he wanted more from her. Careful not to upset him, she slowly pushed him away, only willing to provide a kiss.

"Fortunate is the man who wins your heart," he said. "Never before has anyone kissed me with such tenderness. There is confusion within your mind. You do know whether you will find happiness on the road, true love, or security building a home among the trees. Raven's Nest is destroyed, yet you would rebuild another and rule as the Raven Mistress."

"Did your blood cure me?" Taliesin asked.

Bonaparte took hold of her hand and kissed it. He led her to a chest filled with gold coins, closed it, and they sat together, gazing into each other's eyes.

"Unfortunately, no, my dear. Nor am I cursed," he said. "You are now connected to Bonaparte and always will be. Bonaparte has decided he loves you, for your heart is pure, so he will tell you his secret. The real names of dragons are magic words, and to those who know them, it allows you to summon that dragon. I have never told my true name to anyone. I am *Tristakus*. Should you ever need me, say it aloud, and I will come to you. Be warned, girl. Tell no other, or you will betray my trust. You do not want me as an enemy."

"I will keep your secret," Taliesin said. She licked her dry lips, feeling incredibly thirsty, and noticed they felt chafed. Her stomach growled with hunger. "It was daylight when I arrived, and now it is dark. How long have we been here? The kiss surely didn't last all night."

"To properly kiss a dragon, as you did, takes a *very* long time. Your friend left hours ago. He watched for a while and finally left. I would gladly kiss you again, Taliesin. Bonaparte is also hungry. Bonaparte must go out and hunt, and you must take what you came here for. Bonaparte will give you *Calaburn* in exchange for your sweet kiss and the knowledge that now you love him. It is a fair trade, however, if I had wanted more from you, know that you would have given me anything."

"A magical kiss is quite enough," she whispered.

"Yes," he said. "Bonaparte is quite satisfied."

Taliesin wondered why the dragon-man kept referring to himself in the third person whenever he used the name Bonaparte yet used the first person when he spoke as the dragon-man *Tristakus*. He did not explain and tried to pull away, his manner dismissive. She held onto his arm. She wanted to ask him about Duvalen since he had been there before and could tell her how to get there, what to avoid, and whether or not the fairies were dangerous.

"Zarnoc is indeed waiting for you, my dear," Bonaparte said. "I cannot say if your friends Hawk, Wren, Jaelle, and Rook are in Duvalen, for I cannot see their faces. I do see a winged horse named Thalagar who has been sent by Zarnoc to find you. I could tell you much more about Duvalen, for I have many stories to tell. All you need to know is be careful in the land of the fairy-folk, for there are many strange creatures in the northern forests, and they eat little girls like you."

"Will I see you again?" Taliesin wondered if her reluctance to see Bonaparte was due to his enchanted kiss. She did feel love for the dragon, and when he was gone, she would miss him.

"Of that, I have no doubt, my dear. When you need me, call my name, and I will come. You should only do this if you are in great danger. Otherwise, I will be angry, for I am not to be trifled with," the dragon said. "Do send my regards to Zarnoc the Great. Oh, I know the wizard quite well. Now go before I change my mind and keep you here as a pet, Taliesin. Take *Calaburn* with my blessing and go find your friends."

"If I go, you will be alone," she said.

Bonaparte slid his fingers through her hair, and the tangles and snags loosened, combed out with his touch. Her tresses turned silky, long, and flaming red. He drew a handful of her hair into his fist and pressed it to his nose.

"I wish you could stay longer. Not even I dare risk angering the gods," he replied. "They have plans for you, Taliesin. You did not dream you met them. You really did have a rare encounter with the gods in that forest. I have read your thoughts, and I know Ragnal, Navenna, and Mira compete with one another in the hope you will do their personal bidding. Ragnal wants the Wolf Clan to rule the world. He would see the Age of the Wolf come to fruition, and this cannot be allowed to happen. You must control your *Wolfen* side, and dragon blood will help in this regard. Navenna, the goddess you pray to, desires you to become the Queen of the Raven Clan, though I would not be so quick to trust her if I were you. As for her sister, Mira, she wants magic restored to the land. Oh, yes. I know this and many things about you. Bonaparte knows everything."

"Ragnal brought two enormous wolves with him," Taliesin said, "one gray and one black, held on chains. They are the reason there are werewolves and *Wolfen*."

He cupped her chin in his hand. "Be careful of Varg and Cano. One day, you will have to kill them, and perhaps Ragnal," he said. "The gods are capricious by nature and allowed my kind to be hunted and killed to near extinction. There are a few of us left. Just a few. We have no love for the immortals and refuse to take part in their games. It is for you to decide what path to take, Taliesin. Choose wisely, or you will forever be a slave to them."

"I will be careful, my dragon lord," she whispered.

Bonaparte stood and moved away from her, sinking into the treasure, until he reached a cleared area. In a glimmer of light and magic, he turned into a large gold dragon. His immense body filled the chamber and left only a small, open area between her and the staircase. He indicated with a nod for her to look in that direction. Taliesin stood and spotted a gold sword sticking out of a pile of coins. She crossed the chamber to the blade. Her fingers closed around the hilt, and she pulled it free. *Calaburn* was a longsword, a versatile weapon capable of cutting or thrusting, and was far lighter than her broadsword. She sensed it was intelligent and its darkness came from a frustration that it had not fulfilled its own destiny; something they shared.

"Don't worry, *Ringerike*. No other sword can replace you in my heart," Taliesin said. *Ringerike* gave a contented hum. She lifted the Draconus in the air. "Be reborn!"

Magic flowed from her hand into the longsword. *Calaburn* burst into bright, intense flames, and she heard the dragon's deep, rumbling laughter as he departed through a tunnel at the back of the cavern. The sweep of his tail allowed fresh air to enter the chamber. She looked at the mounds of treasure until she spotted a scabbard made of black dragon scales. The flames died as Taliesin slid the blade into the scabbard and belted it around her waist so it hung on her right side. As she walked toward the stairs, she passed many intriguing, magical items that had long turned dormant. From the moment she had entered the cave, each had started to absorb her unending supply of magic. With their powers now restored, they wanted to go with her.

Zarnoc had once told her magic came with a price. His jewel of knowledge returned as a little voice in the back of her mind, reminding her the balance between good and evil was a precarious perch, and only a few mortals could maintain perfect balance for long. Yet one could not exist without the other. *Calaburn* was touched by darkness. She understood it was necessary in the scheme of things, for *Ringerike* represented law and order. Even the gods served good and evil, or light and dark, and so it was with magic. *Ringerike* touched her thoughts and offered reassurance and love. In comparison, *Calaburn* resonated with a fierce jealousy. Oddly enough, both swords agreed she should take nothing else from the dragon's hoard.

"I'm sorry I can't take all of you with me," Taliesin said.

No sooner had she apologized, she noticed a silver ring with a large sapphire that glittered on the bottom step and begged her to pick it up. She bent down and slid it onto her right index finger. An image of Prince Tarquin entered her mind. He was handsome and dark-haired, with one blue eye and the other covered by an eyepatch; the ring had belonged to him.

"This ring was forged in the heat of Huva'khan's breath. The one dragon most feared by the Lorians," a male voice said in her mind. It was the voice of Prince Tarquin Draconus, she knew at once. *"Keep it. It is my gift to you, Raven Mistress."*

In the blink of a raven's eye, Taliesin felt a strange tingling sensation, rather like the crawling of an army of ants across her skin, all over her body, from head to toe. As she pulled at the ring and found it refused to budge, a suit of armor made entirely of the scales of a red dragon appeared on her. *Ringerike* and *Calaburn's* scabbards remained on the outside, along with the belts, for the dragon-scales appeared beneath them, accommodating her gear. The breastplate molded to her shape, yet it felt sturdy, and though her long legs were encased in armor, it was easier for her to move about than if in ordinary chain mail and a steel breastplate. She lifted her hand to her head as she felt scales grow out of the back of her armor and extend over her head to form a helmet. She slid her fingers along the long nose guard in the shape of a dragon's tail. There were cheek pieces and a neck guard, and the helmet was crested with the figure of a dragon, wings spread wide and flat to the sides of the helmet. She dropped her hand and flexed her muscles in the armor, finding it weightless and flexible. She lifted her scale-encased feet, testing her new footwear for strength and comfort.

"Surely Bonaparte won't mind. There can be no harm in keeping the prince's ring," Taliesin said. "I do need armor. And this is the finest I've ever seen."

Ringerike provided an image of Prince Tarquin wearing the red dragon scales in another battle when he was younger, and she saw how it repelled fire. It again warned her not to take anything else. She felt another's thoughts in her mind. *Calaburn.* Before the new sword could add its opinion, *Ringerike* interceded and ordered *Calaburn* to remain silent, making its dominance clear. There was an order of precedence in the magic world, and although *Ringerike* tolerated *Calaburn*, it expected obedience and cooperation. It was not to interfere unless asked. She kept the sword and ring, and as she ascended the staircase, she found a large gold scale from the flank of a dragon. It was Bonaparte's scale, she thought, someone had turned into a shield, for there were straps fastened to the backside.

"Every warrior needs a shield," Taliesin said. "This is the last thing I am taking, I swear, *Ringerike*. Bonaparte will not miss it, and after all, he did not say I couldn't take what I wanted. After all, it was a special kiss we shared."

She picked up the shield, placed the straps over her left arm, and continued up the stairs three at a time until she arrived at the courtyard. A faint reddish glow appeared on the eastern horizon where Bonaparte could be seen flying through the clouds. It had snowed during the night. She saw no tracks made by Phelon and felt guilty he'd left on questionable terms. There was nothing to be done about it, for he had left her, and she intended to go north without him.

As she took a sniff of the cold morning air, Taliesin wondered if dragon blood had improved her sense of smell. *Wolfen* were able to smell a thousand different things at once. With Bonaparte's blood enhancing her olfactory system, she smelled the musky scent of a horse before she spotted the black stallion flying over the mountains. She watched as Thalagar flew toward the ruins of Ascalon. Her vision had also improved. Every hair on Thalagar's body was visible, even at a great distance, brushed back by the wind as he swept toward her and landed.

"Hello, old friend," Taliesin called out.

The black Andorran stallion folded his large raven wings against his sides. His thick, glossy mane and tail were neatly braided. He wore neither a saddle nor a bridle. Thalagar stomped the ground with his front hooves as she approached and let out a friendly whinny.

"I have missed you, too."

Taliesin placed one hand on the side of Thalagar's face and pressed her forehead against his, as they always did. In an instant, the shield vanished from her left arm and reappeared as gold scale mail on the horse's body, and the leather straps had turned into a bridle. Every inch of the horse was now protected by armor as if specifically handcrafted with Thalagar in mind. He appeared more like a dragon and less like a horse, though his giant wings remained as before, black, glossy raven feathers that fit his large size.

"It's time to see Zarnoc," Taliesin said, feeling more optimistic than she had in months. "You know the way, old friend, so take us to Duvalen." She gazed at the morning sky, searching for the dragon without any luck. "Farewell, Bonaparte. Farewell, Ascalon. I may never pass this way again."

As she turned to mount the horse, she spotted a ghostly form, holding the hand of a transparent fair lady, coming up the staircase. She knew at once it was Prince Tarquin and the beautiful woman was his wife. He looked troubled, and Taliesin felt a throb on her index finger. *Ringerike* had warned her not to take more than *Calaburn*. Try as she might, she could not remove the ring from her finger. Nor was she certain how to remove the armor from her horse. Thalagar gave a snort and stomped his front hoof as the royal specters drifted closer, warning them to keep back.

"I mean no disrespect, Your Grace," Taliesin said, as she met Tarquin's gaze. She imagined he had been a formidable opponent in battle. His expression softened, and he smiled, knowingly. "Bonaparte said this castle was haunted. I didn't think I would actually meet you, Your Grace. I thank you for the gift of the ring and the sword. May I also have your blessing, so we may part as friends and not enemies?"

"*Granted,*" Prince Tarquin said in a smooth voice. "*Out of respect to your mother, Calista, I offer my blessing. Go in peace, Raven Mistress, for I shall always be a part of you from this day forth.*"

"Wait! My mother? Who was Calista?"

The two ghosts turned, glided across the courtyard, and faded into the dawn in a twinkle of lights, leaving her with a mystery to solve. She had been told her mother died in childbirth. Her father, John Mandrake, had never talked about her mother, and she longed to know more about Calista. Zarnoc would have the answers, she thought, and as soon as she arrived at the fairy city, she intended to ask.

Taliesin climbed into the armored saddle, slid her boots into the stirrups, lifted the reins, and lightly tapped her heels to Thalagar's flanks. Leaping, the stallion beat the air with his wings and lifted upwards. He circled the ruins three times and then flew over the Stavehorn Mountains, headed toward the mythical city of Duvalen.

* * * * *

Chapter Five

Thalagar dropped out of the clouds and flew over the northern mountain range of the kingdom of Skarda—a land of ice, snow, and great forests that hid their villages and lodge houses from view. Taliesin spotted men beneath her in winter clothing mounted on small, wooly horses. There were no visible villages, and this surprised her. Perhaps the northern people lived in caves or hid their villages within the densest parts of the forest to avoid detection. She had no idea since she had never been so far north, nor had she ever seen so much snow, yet her dragon armor kept her warm and snug, just as it did the flying horse.

Frost appeared on Thalagar's wings, for the air was bitterly cold, and it threatened their safety, yet all she did was *wish* his feathers to be free of ice, and the wings appeared dry and clean. They flew low above the treetops of an ancient giant forest and across a frozen lake. The stallion snorted and turned his head, alerting Taliesin that he had seen something in the snow. She looked down and spotted a human figure pursued by a large polar bear. Alarmed for the safety of the stranger, she pulled back on the reins and nudged her heels against the horse, indicating she wanted to land.

"We must help him," Taliesin shouted. "Land, Thalagar. For Navenna's sake, land before it's too late!"

Taliesin found herself fighting with Thalagar as the horse refused to come out of the sky. The polar bear spotted them and let out a roar. Its prey kept running. Another yank on the reins, and the horse relented, flying down to land ahead of the figure in a bright blue cloak and wool cap. Taliesin drew *Ringerike* in her right hand, and the sword released a bright blue light as it quivered in her hand, eager for action, as the young man ran up to her. The bear charged at full speed. The man cowered as Thalagar wheeled and charged the polar bear. Taliesin leaned forward, sword pointed at the chest of the animal, which rose upon its hind legs and tore at the air with large clawed paws. It opened its mouth, exposing sharp yellow teeth, and gave a thunderous roar.

"Don't kill him," the man shouted. "He's my friend!"

Taliesin heard the ridiculous cry for mercy as the bear's front paw swung toward her horse. Fearing for Thalagar, she swung *Ringerike* downward with the intent of slicing off the bear's paw. The sword cut through cold air and snowflakes. A tiny growl brought Thalagar to a sudden halt. Taliesin gazed over the side and gawked at a small bear cub. Somehow, the massive beast changed size, appearing less menacing. The horse whinnied in response. She dismounted, reached under the Thalagar, and caught hold of the bear by the nape of its neck. As she lifted the wiggling cub into the air, the young man arrived. He sunk into the snow to his knees and lifted his arms for the baby bear. Taliesin handed him the animal and lowered her sword, taking a closer look at the strange pair.

"My name is Tamblyn, a bard by trade, and this is Ursus. He is my guardian," the young man said. He appraised her dragon armor with curiosity. "Who are you? You're not Skardan. Your armor...."

"It's a dragon scale," Taliesin said.

"I've seen it before. It belonged to Prince Tarquin Draconus."

"If that is the case, then you must be quite old," she said, taking note of his fine apparel, stitched with gold thread. She assumed the bard had to be a Lorian, and his bear under an enchantment for it to be able to grow or shrink at will.

"In human years I am old, but not for a Lorian," he said.

"Then you are fairy folk. I was right." She smiled. "I am Taliesin, the Raven Mistress, and this is *Ringerike*. I am not a thief, Tamblyn. The prince gave me his ring and his sword, with his blessing, of course. My horse is Thalagar. He wears the prince's shield-armor. I have just come from Ascalon and now travel to meet my friends in Duvalen."

Taliesin studied the young man with a stern eye. He appeared to be around 20 years of age. With no facial hair to keep his face warm, he looked bone-cold and exhausted. His nose appeared a bright, cherry red. His fur cap was covered with frost, and strands of blond hair clung damply to the sides of his head. What stood out the most was his eyes, colored a strange, light blue. A lute with broken strings hung over his shoulder. She wanted to know more about the young man and the cub that whimpered and nuzzled his neck.

"I am headed the same way," Tamblyn said as he eyed her sword. "While I am grateful you stopped to help us, I should warn you that we are being followed." He balanced the bear on his left hip and pointed in the direction they had come. "The creatures that follow us are great in number. We must leave here at once. It's not safe, for the hunting pack grows closer every second."

Taliesin held out her hand. "I suggest you climb onto my horse, Tamblyn," she said in a steady voice. "Give me the cub. I won't hurt him."

"Ursus will only let me hold him," he said.

"It's either that or we face whatever hunts you. If you want to stay and fight, then your polar bear needs to be full-grown." Taliesin wondered what manner of creatures pursued the man and bear. No information was offered, nor was it needed, for at that moment she heard the piercing cries of wolves.

"Ursus, you will help our new friend." Tamblyn lifted the bear cub into the air. "No complaints either. This lady-warrior needs your help. I'm afraid I am not any good with a sword, and my lute has broken strings, so I can't put them to sleep with a song."

Taliesin lifted her sword, prepared to fight the wolves, while Tamblyn set the cub on the ground. It grew in size and let out an angry roar as movement spread through the trees. A feeling of sheer evil spilled out of the darkness of the ancient forest, stretched around them, and enveloped them in an oppressive grip. Taliesin perked up her ears and heard growls and snarls coming out of the forest. The young man panicked and sank into the snow, whimpering as the bear stood before him and snarled with rage. Taliesin grabbed Tamblyn around the middle with one arm and lifted him onto Thalagar's back.

"You must truly be brave," Tamblyn said, "for these aren't ordinary wolves. They are *Wolfen*, and they do not take prisoners."

Twenty large, dark forms rushed out of the trees with a loud howl as the horse flew upwards with the bard. It was the Wolf Pack, traveling as giant wolves. Taliesin suspected Phelon had sent the hunting party after her. They certainly hadn't parted on good terms, and he'd betrayed her confidence the moment he had the opportunity to send his men after her. She tried to contact the wolves and warn them she was one of them. They ignored her and charged across the snow, howling louder than before. The bear stood on his hind legs, waved his claws in the air, and prepared to fight at her side.

Holding *Ringerike* to the side, she pulled *Calaburn* from its scabbard. She doubted the young man knew how to fight, for Tamblyn clung to Thalagar with fear in his eyes. Fortunately, her warhorse was trained for combat. Thalagar flew into the air, circling low enough to strike with its hooves. Armed with both swords, she held her ground as the Wolf Pack attacked from all sides. The polar bear dropped down and charged the lead wolf, ripping it apart and splattering blood upon the snow.

Taliesin held tightly to both hilts and let the swords do their work. She twisted and turned in the snow, slashing and hacking with each sword. *Calaburn* reacted to its first kill and burst into flames, while *Ringerike* glowed bright blue and hummed as it cut down a large gray wolf. Her skill and speed far outmatched the *Wolfen* warriors. The two swords worked as a team and propelled her arms, slashing and striking of their own accord and creating a circular field of red in the snow. Any *Wolfen* touched by *Ringerike* was cut through to the bone, leaving them unable to regenerate and bleeding out in the snow. Those stabbed, or even merely touched by *Calaburn* were immediately set on fire; each sword had its own value.

The polar bear was ferocious, and the wolves tried to keep away from the beast and targeted Taliesin instead. Thalagar fought from above, striking the heads of the *Wolfen* with his hooves and flying out the way whenever the wolves tried to snap at him.

"Be careful!" Tamblyn shouted. "One bite and you will be cursed!"

Taliesin ignored the bard and focused solely on the wolves, not what her horse was doing, and continued to hack away at the furry forms moving around her. Surrounded, her thoughts centered on killing everything that moved. Taliesin knew from the way the Wolf Pack attacked without fear or caution that the blood lust was upon them. Until she'd tasted Bonaparte's blood, it was something she had felt and thought unable to control. Now that she had dragon blood in her veins, Taliesin fought with a cool head and remained in human form, methodically killing her opponents.

Soon, with the help of Ursus and Thalagar, twenty Wolfmen lay dead. Piles of ash blew away on the breeze and dismembered body parts lay without twitching or morphing back into their human forms. To be safe, she used *Calaburn* to touch the remains, which burned on contact. When nothing was left, she stuck the blade in the snow. The fire died out, and she slid the sword into its scabbard. She kept *Ringerike* in her hand as its blue light and humming faded away.

"I see someone in the snow," Tamblyn shouted, as the horse landed. He slid out of the saddle and ran to the polar bear drenched in red blood and stroked its gruesome nose to calm him. The bear growled. "Ursus saw a foot twitch! One is still alive!"

Taliesin walked to where a naked man lay on his back. His long blond hair and thick beard were matted with blood from a deep gash across his forehead, where he'd been kicked in the head by Thalagar's flailing hooves. She sheathed *Ringerike* on her back and knelt beside the still form, placing her hand upon his brow.

"The Wolfman is alive," Taliesin said.

"Kill him before he revives!"

"No need to shout. I know this man. This is Captain Wolfgar. He's been tracking me since I left Dunatar Castle, no thanks to Master Phelon. His wound is serious, for it does not heal, as it should. We need to get him to Duvalen, or he will die. Give me something to bind his head with, Tamblyn. And give me your cloak, too."

The bard removed a yellow silk scarf from his pocket and handed it to her. Taliesin tied the scarf around Wolfgar's head as Tamblyn placed his cloak around the injured man. She noted the bard wore an elegant gray tunic made of velvet covered with diamond studs. A rich bard, she thought. While Tamblyn watched, unsure what to do to help, Taliesin picked Wolfgar off the ground. The young man gasped as she showed off her incredible strength and placed Wolfgar over Thalagar's saddle. Somewhere in the forest would be the Wolfmen's harnesses, weapons and gear, and clothes. She didn't want to go in search of the captain's belongings, so she tucked the cape around him.

"I can't believe you are helping the same man who tried to kill us," Tamblyn said. "He is a werewolf, after all. My parents say they should all be rounded up and destroyed. They're not allowed inside Duvalen or in the Magic Realms. I'm sure troops will be sent out to scour the area for more of their kind. I can't even recall when I saw a *Wolfen* — it's most strange."

Taliesin turned toward the bard. Tamblyn clearly didn't know what he was talking about, she thought. He put his hands on his hips, clearly in a mood to argue, despite the fact they stood on blood-covered snow, and snowflakes were falling. She wanted to set the matter on werewolves straight.

"The Wolf Pack are *Wolfen*," she said. "The Night Breed are the real werewolves. Ragnal, the God of War, has two supernatural pet wolves, and Cano, the older, created the Night Breed. Men bitten by werewolves turn at the full moon and have no memory of their nefarious acts. It's Cano's son, Varg, whose mother was human, who created the *Wolfen*. The *Wolfen* have three different forms — man, wolf, and beast. They are not controlled by the moon like werewolves, and they remember their human natures when in animal form."

"Both breeds will fight side-by-side one day. The Age of the Wolf will bring about the end of the world as we know it, for *Wolfen* and Night Breed will join and attempt to turn all humans and fairy folk. I'm aware of the difference, Raven Mistress," he said, clearly insulted. "Both species eat people, however, so if you're going to chastise me like my mother always does, then have your facts straight."

"I can't argue with you there, but I'm still bringing Wolfgar with us."

Tamblyn gave a shake of his head. The polar bear let out a low growl.

"You can't bring that *thing* with us," Tamblyn countered. "I am Lorian and know our laws, not you. I tell you the king and queen will most certainly kill him. It would be better to leave him here to his own fate, Taliesin. You do him no favor bringing him along."

"I can't leave him behind," she said. "I too am *Wolfen*. Don't be afraid. In Ascalon, I met Bonaparte, and the dragon allowed me to taste his blood. It seems to help me control my anger, and if I'm not angry, I don't turn. I can control it, so can Wolfgar, if he wants to, and he doesn't seem to be any shape to cause any trouble."

"Don't say I didn't warn you. Come on; let's go home."

Tamblyn reached for the polar bear. Ursus sniffed the air, his eyes suspicious, as he lowered his shoulder so Tamblyn could climb onto his back. With a snort, Ursus turned and ran at top speed across the snow. Taliesin leaped onto her horse. She kept a hand on Wolfgar's back to keep him from sliding off as Thalagar bounded into the air and flew over the trees, headed toward Duvalen.

* * *

The journey to the fairy city of Duvalen was much shorter than Taliesin expected. Within the hour, her horse flew into a valley shrouded in a fine white mist that parted to reveal a beautiful castle that twinkled like crystals in the morning sun. The polar bear vanished in the trees beneath them as they flew toward the city and castle. Forest, green and thick, surrounded Duvalen. The castle, its spiral towers painted white with blue shingles, was built in the center of the city. There were twelve towers in all with a mighty keep with stained glass windows.

The polar bear reappeared at the drawbridge and galloped through the gate. Thalagar flew over the wall and landed in a courtyard filled with spring flowers and green lawns, as Ursus charged up to them. Tamblyn jumped off his bear, which again shrank to a cub, waved at Taliesin, and turned to wait as Lorians streamed toward them from the castle and all parts of the city. The fairies didn't look threatening or cruel, which she'd imagined they would after hearing stories about them from Ysemay and Bonaparte, and all had pointed ears. She'd never actually seen Zarnoc's ears since his hair was long and usually unruly, yet assumed they had to be the same. Dressed in elegant tunics and gowns of bright colors, with sparkling jewels and long cloaks, the fairies struck her as beautiful, though she wondered if it was skin deep. Seeing Ursus drenched in blood caused alarm among the fairies until they caught sight of Taliesin on an armored, winged horse and gathered around them.

"Prince Tamblyn has returned," a man shouted.

Tamblyn glanced over his shoulder and looked at Taliesin, embarrassed.

"You might have mentioned you are a prince," Taliesin said as she slid off Thalagar's back. She joined Tamblyn, holding the reins of her horse loosely in her hand, should he need to fly at any sign of treachery. No one approached the flying horse, for the fairies seemed more interested in her and the Wolfman lying across the saddle.

"I told you I was a bard. I'm also a prince," Tamblyn replied. "Sometimes I visit villages and play my music. My parents don't approve. They don't approve of anything I say or do. Stay here and let me do the talking. All you need do is play along."

"Music to my ears," she said. "I'll play, Prince Tamblyn, as long as you keep my secret." She wasn't quick to trust people. It was strange that she felt she could trust the fairy prince.

Tamblyn laughed. "Of wolves and ravens and eagles, there are secrets upon secrets," he sang out, "and I, a poet with a lute, will sing their songs, and a legend will be born."

Unsure of what Tamblyn implied, Taliesin watched as the prince picked up Ursus and approached a man with long silver hair, eyes dark as coal, wearing a lavender cloak and a crystal crown set with rubies. It was King Boran, she thought, disappointed he did not wear *Graysteel* at his side, for she'd wanted a closer look at the sword that had killed his brother, the Raven King. Tamblyn bowed to his father and spoke to him as Queen Dehavilyn stepped forward. Taliesin scrutinized the infamous queen, thinking how her interference in the past had caused the deaths of so many innocent people, and she reminded herself to be cautious. The queen was a beautiful woman with black hair coiled in braids at the sides of her head. She was taller than everyone else and dominated the crowd. On her head was a crystal crown set with a large blue stone, and a blood-red cape covered her slender form.

"Put Ursus down, son, and give your mother a kiss. You have been missed," she said in a commanding voice that held no affection.

Tamblyn set Ursus on the ground. The bear scampered to Thalagar to play beneath the horse's long legs, tumbling, rolling, and showing no fear of the winged horse. Taliesin dropped the reins, bent down to pull the cub away from her horse, and watched as the prince kissed his mother. She turned back to Ursus, patted the cub on the head, and set him aside. Ursus yawned before he grew in size. The polar bear towered over Taliesin and her horse and bowed before the king and queen. The crowd applauded, and Tamblyn motioned for Taliesin to join him.

"I told you not to leave the city, Tamblyn," his mother said. "Something happened. Something terrible. Ursus is covered in blood, and you look shaken."

"We were attacked by the Wolf Pack. This warrior saved my life. She is my friend."

A pale finger pointed at Taliesin. "Who are you?" the queen demanded. "And why have you brought a *Wolfen* into my fair city? Our laws prohibit the *Wolfen* and the Night Breed from entering the walls. The dog will have to be put down, for it is the law."

Taliesin reached up to place her hand on the hilt of *Ringerike*. Tamblyn quickly stepped in front of her and placed his hand upon her shoulder. She lowered her hand, aware *Ringerike* did not trust the queen, and *Calaburn* felt equally hostile in the presence of the Lorian royalty. The dragon scales glowed bright red beneath the prince's hand, and people in the crowd started to whisper, both curious and frightened.

"Allow me to introduce my new friend," Tamblyn said, as he turned to face his parents. "This is Taliesin, the Raven Mistress, the one Zarnoc told us about. Captain Wolfgar is her prisoner. She came upon us on our return home as the pack was hunting us. Taliesin risked her life to fight the wolves and Ursus fought beside her. We are both very fortunate, mother."

The queen stared at Taliesin and finally motioned for her to approach. A haughty look appeared on the queen's brow that Taliesin didn't like as she bowed low. The crowd quivered with excitement as if they expected trouble. Taliesin felt *Ringerike* thump her back. She put on a smile, tapped the ring, and the armor vanished. The sapphire ring sparkled in the sunlight and caught the queen's eye, and Taliesin could see the queen desired it. Taliesin placed her hand behind her back and felt the queen's disapproval, but Taliesin wasn't about to part with it.

"I brought your son home in one piece, Your Highness." Taliesin caught Tamblyn's worried look. He had told her to play along, and she had spoken out of turn. It was too late to take it back, though, and she continued. "Where are Zarnoc and my clan members? I thought they would be here to greet me. Zarnoc invited me to Duvalen."

"She's been invited. Did you hear that?" Tamblyn asked. "If an outsider is invited, father, then we must treat her as a guest."

His father glared at Taliesin. "I am King Boran Vorenius, and this is my wife, Queen Dehavilyn. Zarnoc has been sent for, Raven Mistress." He glanced at his son. "You know I do not like you traveling outside the city without a royal escort, Tamblyn. Ursus, thank you for protecting Tamblyn, yet again. I seriously doubt this red-haired girl helped that much. She is a woman, not a warrior, though her armor and swords are impressive. Since you claim she saved you, not because Zarnoc invited her, we will allow the Raven Mistress to stay here, for the night at least."

"My husband and I both welcome you to our home," the queen said, though she did not sound like she meant it. "You have brought powerful magic with you, Taliesin of the Raven Clan. The ring you wear belonged to Prince Tarquin. I recognize his armor. So too do I recognize *Ringerike* and *Calaburn*. Odd, for one was made to destroy the other, though they never met in battle."

"They fought well together, Your Highness," Taliesin said. She didn't like the way the fairies snickered and whispered together in an altogether unpleasant, gossipy way. Pristine in their tidy, immaculate garb, she assumed they felt she was a threat in her dragon armor, armed with two powerful swords. Thalagar snorted behind her and pawed at the ground. No mention had been made of Hawk, Wren, Rook, or Jaelle, which greatly alarmed her. She was resolved, however, not to show the slightest trace of fear.

"The Wolfman is to be placed in our dungeon," Dehavilyn ordered. "Guards! Take him away!"

"I mean no disrespect, Queen Dehavilyn," Taliesin said. "As the Raven Mistress, I have every right to keep my prisoner. Wolfgar belongs to me. I will put a chain on him if I must. As you can see, he needs the skills of a healer. I would not have him caged."

"You speak to us with familiarity," the queen replied coldly. "Zarnoc claims you are the rightful heir of King Korax Sanqualus. If there is Lorian blood in your veins, it is minimal, at best."

Taliesin's green eyes narrowed. "I have enough Lorian blood to claim the right to own *Ringerike*," she said in a firm voice. "And I have a right to keep my prisoner, Your Grace."

"Distantly related," Boran said, with a yawn. "I admit you do resemble Korax. My younger brother chose the last name Sanqualus and the raven to be his symbol. Those who left Duvalen with him to enter into Caladonia became the Raven Clan. Korax, despite my wishes, proclaimed himself the Raven King and King of all Caladonia. The last I knew of *Ringerike*, it was buried with him in the Cave of the Snake God. Did you see my brother in the cave? Tell us, how did he look?"

"He was undead, Your Grace," Taliesin said. "I fought against Korax and the hydra to lay claim to *Ringerike*. The sword was won in battle, and the Raven King has been laid to rest." She didn't mention Captain Wolfgar had killed the zombie fairy king, knowing such news would end in his own death. As long as no one knew, she didn't see the harm in keeping it a secret.

"There is an odd smell about you," the queen said. "You have seen Bonaparte. It's a wonder he didn't eat you. Dragons cannot be trusted."

The king glanced at his wife. "This woman has dragon blood in her veins, my dear," he said. "She has indeed visited Bonaparte at Ascalon and seen Prince Tarquin. Notice how the swords remain docile. She clearly possesses great magic, as Zarnoc claims."

Tamblyn frowned. "Shall we go inside and find Zarnoc?" he asked. "I'm sure he's smoking his pipe and spinning a dream weaver, unaware he's been summoned. I want to be the first to tell him about the battle."

"Stay here," the king said. "He has been sent for. As for your friends, Raven Mistress, Zarnoc came alone. Your clan is destroyed. There are no Ravens here."

"Find the jester," Queen Dehavilyn ordered, motioning to a young man with silver hair. "Zarnoc has a new position in court."

Taliesin wondered how a great wizard had come to play the role of a jester in the royal fairy court and where her Raven friends had gone. If a prison cell was what Wolfgar could expect, she wondered if the same fate had befallen her little clan and if the same was in store for her.

The page ran toward the castle, shouting Zarnoc's name, and sent a flock of doves flying from a slender white birch. Maidens and lords scattered, and guards hurried forward, rattling spears against shields, to form a defensive line behind the king and queen.

"So, you are my cousin," Tamblyn said, grinning wide.

"Distantly related, as your father said," Taliesin replied. "The bear fought bravely, Your Graces. He is a worthy companion for your son. I am impressed."

The prince walked to stand beside the large polar bear. Of all those present, only the bear and his master looked upon Taliesin with appreciation and gratitude. The bear's soft brown eyes were moist, and she heard him say, *"thank you"* in her mind. Ursus' mood changed in an instant. He growled as the page, shouting he'd found the wizard, ran back to the king.

"Zarnoc is coming, Your Grace," the page said, breathing hard from his effort. "I found him in the kitchen."

"As soon as Zarnoc arrives, we will find out just who this woman is," King Boran said in a snide tone. "Let's not take any chances. Guards, come forth! The law has been broken!"

More guards, in silver armor etched with elegant engravings and carrying slender spears, stepped out of the crowd. They surrounded Taliesin, Wolfgar, and Thalagar. A groan from Wolfgar caused the guards to quiver as he slumped from the saddle. Taliesin caught the man as he fell from the horse and lowered him to the grass. Clearly, the kick from Thalagar, reinforced by the dragon armor, had caused more damage than she realized. Tamblyn, concern in his eyes, joined her and placed his hand on the captain's brow. There was a startled cry from the crowd when Tamblyn pulled the cloak tighter around Wolfgar's large frame.

"This man needs medicine," Tamblyn said. "Send for the royal physician."

"In due course," his mother said. "First we must decide if he will live or die."

Blood streamed down Wolfgar's face and neck. The scarf wrapped around his head was stained. One bare shoulder, muscular and dirty, was exposed. Taliesin wished Wolfgar wore clothes and smiled when leather pants, a bulky sweater, and boots instantly appeared on his large frame. A number of women in the crowd looked disappointed, for he was an exceptionally handsome man.

"She is a *Sha'tar*," someone in the crowd murmured. Others whispered it as well until the queen motioned the fairies to be silent.

"Send for a healer," Dehavilyn said. "We cannot deny a Lorian and her prisoner assistance, no matter how many generations removed. If the Raven Mistress proves to be of royal blood, every courtesy will be extended. Tamblyn, come away from that beast."

"Not until a stretcher arrives, mother. I take full responsibility for Taliesin and her prisoner. There is no reason to fear this man, but he will die if we do not help him."

"Then we will help him," Dehavilyn said.

* * * * *

Chapter Six

"Make way! Make way!"

Zarnoc, wearing a short yellow tunic and laced sandals, ran through the crowd to greet Taliesin. He was shorter than the rest of the Lorians, and his long white hair and beard looked wild, giving him the appearance of a hermit. He pushed past the guards, a hand pressed to his ribs, visibly out of breath.

"I came as soon as I heard you arrived," the wizard said. "King Boran. Queen Dehavilyn. This is my dear friend, Rosamond Mandrake, the daughter of John Mandrake, also known as Taliesin, the Raven Mistress. Tell your guards to stand at ease and let's get this man into bed. It makes no difference if he sprouts fur and a tail. I won't have it said Lorians aren't understanding of the limitations of lesser species."

"Very well, Zarnoc. Guards! Take this Wolfman inside and have the royal physician look after him. Son, you may go with them," Boran Vorenius said.

The guards brought forward a stretcher. Taliesin and Tamblyn eased Wolfgar onto it. Four slender men lifted the captain and carried him toward the castle. Tamblyn ordered Ursus to take Thalagar to his stable and went with Wolfgar. The horse's armor vanished, leaving behind a small triangular scale on his forehead. The polar bear walked beside the horse, his large bottom moving side to side, with the stump of a tail twitching as they disappeared from view.

"Zarnoc!" Taliesin waved at her friend.

"Welcome, welcome," Zarnoc said. He threw his arms around Taliesin. "Did I not tell you Duvalen is a beautiful place? Of course, you shall have Korax's old room, and we can talk all about your adventures."

103

The Lorians seemed to relax as servants brought out trays filled with wine glasses, minstrels under the trees started to play, and dancers held hands and frolicked in circles as a carefree attitude turned away the former grimness in the air. Fairies sat upon the lawn, drank wine, and ate sweets. The royal couple motioned for Zarnoc to follow, entered a colorful pavilion, and sat on two portable thrones. Their friends flopped down onto large pillows and chattered among themselves. No one paid any attention to Taliesin or Zarnoc. A servant handed them each a glass of wine and went about refilling glasses. Platters of food were placed on pillows before the guests. The odor of roast beef reached Taliesin's nose, and her stomach growled.

"Please, be seated. My court jester seems quite taken with you, Raven Mistress," Queen Dehavilyn said. "Alas, we must decide what to do with Taliesin and her prisoner. A law has been broken—a Wolfman has been brought into our city."

Taliesin remained standing beside Zarnoc. He lit a slender pipe made of ivory and puffed smoke out the corner of his mouth as he grinned at her.

"I suppose I should call you niece, no matter how many times removed," King Boran said as he sipped his wine. Jeweled rings sparkled on every finger, and his manner was refined, in sharp contrast to his temper. "If you were not family, I do not think I would allow you to remain, Raven Mistress." He snapped his fingers. "Zarnoc, give her something to eat. She must be famished. And change your garments at once, for you are not appropriately attired."

Zarnoc's clothing changed into the comical costume of a jester, complete with belled hat and shoes. He looked quite miffed when his pipe turned into a colorful stick ended with a miniature doll head that looked very much like the wizard.

Taliesin was offered a turkey leg on a gold plate. She shook her head and placed the glass of wine on the tray. Until she knew her fate, as well as Wolfgar's, she had no interest in dining with the Lorians.

"You have my younger brother's red hair and possess a rebellious nature as he did," King Boran said. "I realize you saved my son's life. Nevertheless, you must be judged to see if you are worthy or not to bear the title of princess and *Sha'tar*. Isn't that right, Dehavilyn? She must be judged."

"Yes, she must be. It's the law."

"Frankly, I'd prefer a hot bath and a soft bed, *Uncle* Boran," Taliesin said. "The title of 'princess' does not interest me. As I am family, no matter *how* many times removed, I expect to be treated as such."

The king smiled coldly. "You are outspoken, too, like my brother."

"We do not allow magic to be used in our city," Dehavilyn said. "Humans are unable to use magic properly, and in their hands it is dangerous. Long ago, we fought against a Caladonian king who sought to destroy all magic. We returned to the mountains and promised him no magic would ever find its way back into his realm. By taking you in, we have no other choice and must keep you here, *niece*. Permanently."

Boran took his queen's hand. "Korax had a temper. All redheads have tempers, my love. Proceed with caution. She is well-armed." He caught Taliesin's gaze. "Let's be honest with one another. What do you want, Taliesin? Do you want only to be a *Sha'tar* or do you seek a crown of your own like my brother?"

"To restore my clan's former greatness," she replied.

"I see. You would have the Raven Clan be what it was under my brother's reign. A noble pursuit," King Boran said. "Everyone who comes brings us a present. Since you offer nothing, you will give my wife Tarquin's sapphire ring. I'll take one of your swords, but you should decide which one to give me."

"Don't you dare, Taliesin," Zarnoc piped in. "My nephew has no manners, even if he is king. The gift of your company is quite enough for both of them."

"Nephew?" Taliesin dropped her jaw. "You never told me you were from the House of Vorenius."

Zarnoc sighed. "I saw no reason to tell you when we first met, Taliesin, for I had to be sure you were a Sanqualus, though technically, you are a Vorenius," he said. "Now you know why I was so keen to rescue you from King Frederick and place you at Raven's Nest. We are related, my dear."

"Be silent, jester," the queen commanded. "We have rules, and they must be followed, Zarnoc. Take Taliesin to see the Augur. If the Augur says she is, in fact, Korax's heir and a *Sha'tar* blessed by the gods, then we will reconsider what is to be done with her. If the Augur pronounces her to be a fraud, then Taliesin and the werewolf will be executed in the morning."

"Yes, quiet," the king said. "Those are the rules. My brother broke the rules when he left Duvalen to find a kingdom of his own. My brother strayed from the path. Korax mingled with humans. Worse, he insulted us by marrying a Hellirin. As far as I am concerned, your bloodline is tainted, girl. You are nothing more than an outcast. We do not approve."

"A Hellirin? What is a Hellirin?" Taliesin asked, glancing at Zarnoc.

"Be silent, girl," the queen shouted.

Taliesin bristled from head to toe. She held her tongue though she sorely wanted to tell the royal fairies precisely what she thought of them. The crowd murmured their disapproval of Korax, and from what Taliesin could gather among the whisperings, he'd left home against his parents' wishes. Zarnoc had gone with Korax. It was obvious the Lorians didn't think much of Zarnoc, even though he was a royal, and this angered her even more. She was surprised when she didn't grow fur or fangs. She remained in control, a big step in the right direction.

"Korax was a great king," Taliesin said. "His people loved him, human and fairy alike. The Raven Clan discriminated against none. Everyone was welcome at Black Castle. People still sing ballads about the Raven King and *Ringerike*. There are poems and plays every Raven knows by heart."

"Your clan is dead," Dehavilyn purred. "Destroyed by the Wolf Clan."

"I'll make the Raven Clan strong again, Your Grace. Have no doubt about that."

"Do not disagree with my queen," King Boran snarled, the anger in his voice making it clear he was on the verge of a dramatic demonstration of royal emotions. His cheeks turned red, his gray eyes turned beady, and he breathed through his nostrils, making an odd little noise that greatly annoyed his wife. "She is rude," he said. "Just like Korax. All redheads are rude."

"I said nothing except what is true. King Korax was loved by the Raven Clan, past and present members included," Taliesin said. "After I see the Augur, I hope you will tell me about your brother, Your Grace. I only know what is said in legends, and I'd like to know what Korax was really like. Though I do know the ladies were fond of him...very fond indeed."

The royal pair gazed at one another, saying a thousand things without words. When they turned back to Taliesin, it was clear they'd silently agreed upon something that didn't bode well for her. Phelon had warned her that the Lorians were not friendly people, and the dragon had told her to be careful. She'd chosen to overlook gossip in the hope family blood meant something to the Lorians. Korax and Zarnoc had obviously not left on good terms with his older brother. The king looked bored. His queen wore a malignant smile on her face that turned Taliesin's stomach.

"Come with me," the wizard said.

Rising to their feet, Taliesin and Zarnoc bowed and left the king and queen in the shade drinking wine with their friends. They took a winding path through a garden, along a shell-covered path, past a skinny, lone tower that shot straight into the sky like a giant tree. Giant sunflowers, daisies, lilies, and rose bushes were beautifully groomed. Butterflies and dragonflies flew to each flower to drink nectar. Taliesin and Zarnoc stopped at a large fountain with a spouting dragon. She glanced at the golden fish swimming in the water and counted thousands of coins beneath them. Fairies made wishes just as humans did, she thought.

"Shouldn't we go see Hawk and the others?" Taliesin asked. "I have no intention of seeing this Augur and letting her pass judgment, and I have no desire to give those snobs any of my possessions. Let's just find our friends and leave. You can tell me your story as we travel."

"That's what I wanted to tell you — they're not here. I changed my mind at the last second and sent them to join Shan Octavio. Jaelle knew where to find her father. Even now, Hawk, Rook, Wren, and Jaelle are seated with the Shan having a proper meal. I said I'd wait for you and join them later. This happened a few days ago. I thought you'd be here sooner. Phelon must have tried to convince you to go with him, which I suspected he would do. Why ever did you go after *Calaburn*?"

Taliesin sat at the fountain and stuck her hand in the water. The goldfish changed in size, grew large teeth, and attacked. She jerked her hand away and stood.

"Everything here is dangerous. The queen is dangerous. Her husband is clearly a pawn, and she has all the power. She's turned you into a joke, Zarnoc. I don't see how this is possible when you are Boran's uncle."

"It's a long story, and we must be careful what we say. Every flower reports to the queen, and butterflies spy for the king. It's a beautiful, yet dangerous place we've come to, Taliesin, and I admit, I'll be glad to leave," Zarnoc said. He looked slightly guilty. "Not all Lorians are perfectly horrible. There are a few, like me, who enjoy the company of humans and delight in the enjoyment of mortal things, like hearing warm laughter, eating good food, smoking stout weed, and, most of all, enjoying the company of dear friends."

"Let them hear us," Taliesin said.

"Dehavilyn and Boran made a bad impression. So have I. I know you expected to find me held in higher esteem. Never fear. I won't be a jester for long. It's their way of keeping me in line. Boran knows I could turn them both into fish with big teeth." Zarnoc snorted and waved his doll stick at the fish. "Just who do you think is in that fountain? Those aren't regular goldfishes, Taliesin. They are cousins who didn't get along with the king and queen. Don't stick your fingers in places they have no business being. Now come along. We must see the Augur. It's the law."

Taliesin didn't care if it was the law or not. She was not happy at being judged by the fairies, and if the Augur was anything like Ysemay, it was not going to be a pleasant meeting.

The sun was riding at its zenith, and the grounds seemed warm and comforting despite the snow that fell on the opposite side of the castle walls. Taliesin walked beside Zarnoc, wondering where they'd find the Augur, and noticed a pair of fawns at play. Rabbits hopped back and forth, squirrels tossed nuts at them, and flowering bushes along the cobblestone path let out shrieks as they caught a whiff of Taliesin.

"Why are you the court jester? What happened?" she asked.

"I turned the queen's hair blue the last time I was here," Zarnoc said. "It was an accident—she drank from the wrong glass. The potion was meant for my nephew, Boran the Bore. I meant to turn him entirely blue for the rude way he greeted me after I had been away for a while. Dehavilyn is the one who runs Duvalen. She only married Boran because he was king. She preferred Korax. Since she wanted to be queen, she remained to marry Boran." He winced and gave her a sideways glance. "When you think hard, like you're doing now, I can hear every word inside your head. Boran is the one who sent *Graysteel* to Prince Tarquin. He wanted Korax to die, and he wanted it done with his sword. I admit it was a spiteful thing to do. However, Dehavilyn was the one who paid your new friend Bonaparte to retrieve the sword and kill Tarquin's family. This was also spiteful. I'd forgotten how horrible they are, so I do apologize. I haven't been here in nine hundred and ninety-nine years."

"Nine hundred and...," she paused. "Just how old are you?"

"Two thousand years old, give or take a few," Zarnoc said, laughing. "When my older brother, Xerxes, was king, this was a lovely place, and people got on very well together. Sadly, as soon as Boran took the crown, things changed for the worse."

"Who are the Hellirin?" The moment the name was out of her mouth, Taliesin felt like she'd said a dirty word and didn't expect to get an answer.

"I'd really rather not talk about them right now," Zarnoc said. "No doubt, they will have heard you are here and will pay a call." He stuck a finger in his ear, scratched about, and his jester's garments turned into a long robe the color of a rob-in's egg. He grew a foot in height, and his beard twisted into a neat little braid tied off with a silver chain. "How do I look? I only ask because I'm nervous about seeing the Augur. This is her tower ahead of us. Actually, it's more of an observatory. The Augur reads tea leaves and speaks to the gods. The king and queen rely on her completely. She's a beastly woman."

"Worse than Ysemay?" Taliesin couldn't imagine a woman more unpleasant than the old witch, though the fairy queen might tie her for first place.

"Oh, by far, my dear."

Zarnoc caught Taliesin by the hand and pulled her up short in front of a tall, slender tower with stained glass windows and an observatory on the top level. The stones of the tower were covered with vines, and the brightly colored windows could be seen like patches in a green quilt work. A female figure with flowing white hair stared down from a balcony built outside the highest window. Taliesin thought about a poem by Glabber the Glib called 'The Lady of Shandrelle,' in which a young girl was kept imprisoned throughout her life by an evil uncle.

"The Augur is powerful," Taliesin said. "I can feel it. Her magic is strong."

"Try not to lose your temper," he cautioned. "It will be hard not to. I've been married to Azniya for one thousand and twenty years. I only lived with her for three months before the 'incident of the blue hair,' and decided to leave with Korax. After all, he was my favorite nephew. My wife doesn't know about Ysemay or the others, so don't mention you know me. I haven't said 'hello' to Azniya since I returned, so she'll probably be in a bit of a snit."

"Your wife? Excuse me?"

The wizard cleared his throat and shrank three inches.

"I was drunk," he said with a shrug. "Pass her test, and then see me afterward. I'll be right here waiting for you, my dear. I imagine you'd like to have a hot bath and wear something soft and clean." He produced his long ivory pipe from thin air, already lit, and started to puff away. "Well, go on, my dear. She doesn't bite...too hard."

When Zarnoc laughed, Taliesin looked at him in alarm, for at that moment, a male peacock strutted onto the path. The beautiful bird took one look at them and let out a horrendous scream. They both jumped back.

"That's her pet, Kadmos. He bites," Zarnoc warned. "Watch your fingers on the way up the stairs. He'll take you to the Augur. Be nice, Kadmos, or I'll cook you for dinner, you ugly thing."

Taliesin walked to the peacock. Kadmos had a beautiful turquoise body and long, decorated tail feathers, and beady black eyes. She followed the proud bird through the open door of the tower and entered a room filled with enough shelves of bottled herbs, spices, strange creatures, and potions to make any sorcerer green with envy. A table set with flowers, four matching chairs, and a tidy kitchen made the lower chamber feel crowded and yet cozy. On the stone walls, a skilled artist had painted dozens of beautiful birds, including ravens. Taliesin had a feeling it was Zarnoc's artwork, for when they'd met, she'd found his drawings of birds and knew he had talent.

On the next floor was a bedroom with a large bed circled by heavy drapes of gold and orange, and a dresser pushed into a corner that lay open to reveal some colorful robes. A large white owl sat perched on a stand in the far corner of the room. The peacock took one look at the owl, lifted its head, and rudely walked by, heading directly up the stairs to the next level. Taliesin caught herself staring at the owl, unable to look away from his wise, old eyes. The owl let out a loud "who" and regarded her intently.

"You are splendid," Taliesin said. "I do so love owls. Do you have a name?"

"Who," the owl said.

"You, sir. I like you. I'll come back and talk to you later."

The owl opened his eyes wider and flapped his wings. A single white feather fell from his tail onto the floor. He glanced at her with his large yellow eyes, and then back down to the feather. Taliesin realized the owl wanted her to pick the feather up, and she obliged, tucking it into the pouch on *Ring-erike*'s sword belt. She stroked the owl's head, for he looked soft and silky. As she touched him, she felt a mellowing feeling come over her and sighed.

"Owls are my favorite birds," Taliesin whispered.

The peacock poked its head around the corner and let out an awful noise. She dropped her hand and nodded at the owl, whose name she knew without being told was 'Umbria,' and it was his job to watch for omens and signs of both good and bad. It also meant she had passed her first test. The owl found her worthy. The peacock was not as easily convinced and remained on guard as it climbed the stairs. It paused to see if she was following and then moved on.

"You have very nice tail feathers, Kadmos," Taliesin said. She reached out to touch his tail. The peacock moved *fast* and nearly bit her hand. She jerked back and tried not to laugh. "I really wasn't going to pull your tail. I am a Raven, you know, and we birds all come from the same nest, in a manner of speaking."

The peacock made its horrible noise and stopped outside a door on the top landing. Engravings of birds were etched into a door painted orange. There were two slender windows on either side of the tower, and hawks, owls, an eagle, and a raven, along with a number of smaller birds, occupied some perches on an overhead rafter. They all sang out in greeting to Taliesin. With shudders and shakes of their wings, a dozen feathers floated down and landed upon her head and at her feet. She reached up as the peacock paced before the door, waiting for it to open, and pulled a raven feather from her hair. She kissed the feather for good luck, and placed it inside the pouch, along with the owl feather. The Deceiver's Map remained inside and had taken on the form of a silk scarf. It was clever the way it could take any form she wanted, and she didn't want it to be a map, not at that moment. If the queen found out about the map, Taliesin feared she might want it as well.

"If you are ready to go in," the peacock said, in a human voice, "I suggest you knock. The owl, by the way, does have a name. Her name is Umbria."

"I already know that," Taliesin said. "If you were nice, you would have introduced me to Umbria."

"And you might show more manners. You've excited every bird here with your presence. My mistress will be angry Umbria gave you a feather, let alone that you have chosen a raven feather and not mine. I am not surprised, for you are the Raven Mistress."

Taliesin wanted to give the peacock a hard kick in the side. "I'll come back and pluck one from you," she said in a stern tone. "This shouldn't take very long. You can hide until then, you old coot."

"Arrogant fool," the peacock snapped. "Now go in. She's waiting for you."

Taliesin knocked three times on the door, which vanished beneath her fist on the third rap, and found she stood in a small room with glass walls and a glass, peaked roof. Birds flew overhead and sat upon a hundred perches above her. The entire room reeked of bird droppings. At the far side of the room, in a bright ray of sunlight, stood Azniya, a medium-built woman wearing a long white robe, carrying a peacock feather. Her eyes were cerulean, and black eyebrows shaped like feathers stood out in sharp contrast to her pale skin. Azniya was neither attractive nor unpleasant to look upon, and like all Lorians, her ears were pointed, her chin was small, and she radiated strong magic. She pointed the peacock feather at Taliesin, who immediately dropped to her knees.

Both swords were humming, distressed and wanting to help. Azniya waved her wand and wrapped Taliesin in a transparent magical cocoon. She tried to break free and found herself unable to do so. The Augur was indeed powerful.

"So, you think you are the next *Sha'tar*, do you, little bird?" the Augur said in a silky voice. When she walked, she strutted like a heron. "You might have spent time in the company of Zarnoc. I see he has failed to teach you how to use your magic. Zarnoc was once the royal sorcerer in Duvalen, but that was a very long time ago. When we first met, I knew he would one day fall from grace, although I never expected him to run off with Korax. Now there was a wild, young man with delusions of grandeur. We'll see if you have Korax's blood in your veins, or only that of a very old, crusty dragon that happens to prey upon young girls like you."

"Bonaparte is my friend," Taliesin said.

Angry, Taliesin concentrated on the invisible cocoon and this time wished she were free. She freed herself in a twinkle of fairy lights and stood. The Augur looked in stunned amazement as Taliesin stepped forward. Not breaking stride, she walked to the fairy, removed the raven and owl feathers from her pouch, and touched the woman on the face with each feather.

"I'm not quite as defenseless as you think. I hope it burns."

The Augur let out a scream that shook the rafters, as loud as a lion's and as ferocious as any dragon. She grew in stature and loomed over Taliesin, waved her hands about her, and caused a great gust of wind to blow the warrior off her feet. The feathers fell from Taliesin's hand as she skidded backward twenty feet and slammed into a large birdcage painted bright blue. The eagle inside let out a cry, caught hold of the bars with its great talons, and snapped the air, trying to reach her face as it beat its great wings. Taliesin crawled to her feet, moved away from the cage, and looked at the Augur, who had shrunk to her former size and looked far calmer and more composed.

Taliesin kept some distance between them, watching the fairy. She was ready to wish her into oblivion or to draw *Ringerike*, although *Calaburn* begged to let it kill the old witch. She grew more anxious as the Augur walked toward her in the curious heron gait.

"You do have magic," the Augur said, "or you would not still be alive."

"If you want a magical showdown, I'll do my best. Zarnoc sends his regards, by the way. I can't say I'm impressed with the king and queen or with you. It's no wonder he left you after the wedding night, considering you aren't very nice."

"What a sharp tongue you have and such beady little eyes." The Augur drifted toward her, white robe flowing, and halted in front of Taliesin. Her cerulean eyes narrowed as she regarded the tall female warrior. "I sense great power in you. I also sense danger. You are not sure which side you fight for in the civil war that ravages Caladonia. Your clan has been slaughtered by the Wolf Clan, and you and your friends are on the run; that much is known to me already. There is no doubt you are John Mandrake's daughter. Your name is Rosamond. I cannot tell who your mother is, for someone has placed a spell on you so I cannot probe deeper."

Taliesin thought of Prince Tarquin's comment about her mother. It was possible Zarnoc had put a spell on her. It seemed more likely Bonaparte had done so. To keep the Augur from further reading her mind, she recited the alphabet backward. The Augur stared hard at her and suddenly laughed.

"Zarnoc was present at your birth. Did you know this?"

"I believe he mentioned it," Taliesin said. "My magic comes from my father, not my mother. Who she was is no concern of yours, Augur. You are to judge whether I have Lorian blood or not. Well? Am I Korax's heir or a fraud?"

"Just like Korax, you expect everyone to do your bidding. Let's see if you do come from his bloodline, Raven Mistress."

Azniya reached out her hand and placed it on Taliesin's right arm. The fairy's touch was cold, and the sensation startled Taliesin. *Wolfen* were normally immune to cold and heat. With dragon blood in her veins, much to her surprise, she felt a slight chill. Taliesin felt the Augur's mind contact hers and picked up mental images—scenes of violence and of debauchery in Duvalen that left Taliesin feeling sick to her stomach. Korax had been Azniya's lover before Zarnoc wed her. He had also been intimate with Dehavilyn, which Boran discovered and swore to exact his revenge. When Korax left, he took five thousand Lorians, along with Zarnoc, and built Black Castle in what was now the dukedom of Maldavia.

"No more," Taliesin said. She pushed the woman's hand off her arm and immediately ended the mental link. "I don't need a history lesson from you."

The Augur reached for her again, this time trying to grab her arm. Taliesin moved out of the way with a sidestep and reached for *Ringerike's* hilt, while *Calaburn* burned hot on her hip, desperately wanting to kill the witch. It was starting to grow dark outside, and shadows reflected in the glass walls moved of their own accord, sweeping about as if ghostly specters. Hearing Azniya laugh, Taliesin knew the shadowy creatures had been summoned to harm her.

"So, this is what you want? To see me fight? I will not hesitate to use my magic if they try to attack. In fact, the Raven Sword insists on an introduction."

Taliesin drew *Ringerike* and pointed the broadsword at the Augur. The sword hummed softly and radiated a strong blue light. A tap on her leg made her aware *Calaburn* was about to ignite. She reached with her right hand and jerked it out of the scabbard. The sword burst into flames and tried to lunge at one of the ghostly things that had stopped to stare at her.

The Augur laughed. "Finish her off," she shouted. "Kill the Raven Mistress!"

Dozens of floating specters darted off the walls and flew high into the air, shrieking all the louder as they turned and nosedived toward Taliesin. She reacted with speed and slashed a wide arc with *Ringerike* while thrusting *Calaburn* toward the wall. The broadsword cut through the ghosts, and they evaporated on contact, an impressive feat nearly overshadowed by *Calaburn* as it pierced a ghost and lit it on fire. More phantoms attacked Taliesin, who danced in a circle as she swung her giant sword and thrust with the smaller. Together, the swords destroyed every phantasm, until none was left. Only then did Taliesin, confidence restored and the determination to leave pressing on her mind, address the Augur.

"Well, I'm not dead! Did I pass your test?" Taliesin demanded to know.

The Augur nodded. "Oh, I am impressed," she said. "*Ringerike* responds to you just as it did for Korax. Even *Calaburn* obeys you. As I suspected, your magic is strongest when you are in combat. Again, just like Korax. I think the Queen will be very interested to see you in action, so let's not disappoint your *aunt*."

Taliesin wondered what the old Augur meant and was afraid she was about to find out.

* * * * *

Chapter Seven

Taliesin felt a strange, tingling sensation and the scene changed in an instant. She stood in a brick-lined pit, fifty feet deep and fifty feet wide. Hundreds of fairies sat in bleachers at the top of the pit, drinking wine, laughing, and placing bets. There were four large wooden doors built into the walls of the pit with small barred windows. Behind each door, she heard snarls and angry shouts. Whatever lay hidden behind the closed doors, the fairies obviously meant her to fight. If she was to be their entertainment, Taliesin intended to be protected. The flames produced by *Calaburn* died down as she kissed the sapphire ring worn on her right hand. Red scale armor appeared on her body, including a winged helmet on her head, and a blue orb surrounded her. Both swords were willing to do whatever it took to protect her, and she held her weapons in front of her, poised for battle.

"Amazing," Azniya said where she sat on the front row. "She wears Huva'khan's scales! It is the armor of Prince Tarquin Draconus! I'd recognize it anywhere."

The King and Queen of Duvalen sat beside Azniya. A railing ran before the front row of chairs, keeping the crowd back as they dropped flower petals into the pit. Sand covered the ground beneath Taliesin's feet. The moment the petals touched the sand, they shriveled and turned black. Whatever custom this was seemed to excite the fairies. Taliesin frowned when the crowd grew most thrilled. Several zealous maidens in front stood and tossed bird feathers into the pit. Most were eagle feathers, an insult Taliesin did not miss. One lone peacock feather fluttered to the ground, and the crowd silenced.

A door in the side of the pit opened. Zarnoc was pushed out by two guards with long spears, and tumbled into the arena, lost his balance, and fell flat on his face. The crowd roared with laughter. Taliesin walked to Zarnoc and stood at his side as he rose to his feet. He wore a jester's costume, with a belled yellow hat and red pointed shoes. It was hardly fitting to see royalty treated in such a disgraceful manner. Taliesin shook her swords at the crowd, furious, and watched as Zarnoc dusted off his tunic made from scraps of multi-color material and green tights. A single, white owl feather was pinned to his chartreuse lapel. Taliesin recognized the feather belonged to Umbria, which seemed quite odd. Someone had taken the time to see he wore it, and she wondered if Azniya had given it to him.

"Am I expected to fight you?" Taliesin asked.

"Doubtful," Zarnoc replied.

Something in the dark hallway, beyond the door Zarnoc had walked through, let out a heinous snarl. The royal couple waved their hands, and the crowd started to chant, "kill them, kill them."

The hairs on the back of Taliesin's neck stood on end. The growls echoed from the tunnel as the shape of a furious blond *Wolfen* charged forward. The beast reached the end of the silver chains attached to cuffs worn on his ankles and wrists, which were held by two green ogres of considerable size and ugliness. The ogres' heads were enormous, and long fangs hung over their thick bottom lips. Both carried spears and held the chains with one hand. The *Wolfen* released a piercing howl that sent a shiver down Taliesin's spine. Zarnoc lifted his hands, prepared to use magic.

"Here is our star of the evening," King Boran shouted. "You will fight Captain Wolfgar. His strength has been enhanced so he won't be so easy to kill."

Tamblyn appeared next to his father, a furious look on his face. His parents ignored him, and he gazed at Taliesin, unable to offer assistance or put an end to the madness.

"Why are they doing this?" Taliesin asked the wizard.

"You broke the law by bringing Wolfgar here, and I'm the one who invited you to Duvalen," Zarnoc replied. "Together, we should be able to handle him."

Wolfgar turned and rushed the guards. A momentary struggle ensued, and pieces of green ogre sprayed into the pit as the crowd laughed and applauded. Zarnoc darted behind Taliesin, bells tinkling, and covered his ears with his hands as the howls grew to a thunderous level. More guards with spears appeared in the tunnel to force Wolfgar to leave his meal. With a snarl, the blond beast rose onto his hind legs and backed into the pit. The sounds of fairy laughter angered him further, and he turned. The door clanged shut behind him. Taliesin spotted an ogre guard grin wide through a barred window.

"Your family is horrible, Zarnoc. They are the reason Korax and Tarquin are dead," Taliesin said. "Now it's our turn. You should never have asked me to come to this awful place."

"Yes, well, it's a little late for regrets. Perhaps I can turn him into a mouse."

Wolfgar, eyes glowing bright amber, lifted his head and howled. Whatever magic they used on Wolfgar had enlarged his muscles, and she watched, horrified, as he grew twelve inches taller. With a snarl, Wolfgar took a step forward on his hind legs, snapped his jaws, and slashed at the air with clawed hands. Taliesin pointed both swords at the beast. Wolfgar lowered his massive head and snarled.

"What are you waiting for?" Taliesin asked. "Turn him into a mouse, Zarnoc. I have armor, but you only have pointed shoes and a belled hat. Use your magic!"

"No magic is allowed, Uncle Zarnoc!" King Boran shouted. "You are to fight to the death, Raven Mistress. You and your *Wolfen* captain. Attempt to use magic, and my archers will not hesitate to shoot you, my uncle, and the captain! Now, fight!"

"No magic?" Taliesin stared at the royal couple. "Are you serious?"

The queen pointed at Taliesin. The gesture caused every guard in the upper gallery to point their arrows at the contestants. A surge of magical energy rippled through the pit like a fine breeze. In an instant, *Ringerike* and *Calaburn* were jerked out of Taliesin's hands and floated high above her. Her armor, along with her helmet, vanished, and she felt Zarnoc pull on her arm.

"Oh dear. This isn't good," Zarnoc moaned. He took off his belled cap and hurled it at the advancing monster. "He's coming, Taliesin! Do something!"

Fists raised, Taliesin prepared to fight the *Wolfen*. One woman was nothing more than an insect in Wolfgar's path. After he ripped her apart, Taliesin knew the captain would kill Zarnoc and attempt to crawl the walls of the pit to eat the fairies.

"Use your magic," Zarnoc shouted. "You're a *Sha'tar*!"

Taliesin glanced at the wizard. He emphatically pointed at Wolfgar. She turned back, mesmerized by the sheer size of his fangs, and with a gulp, she *wished* Wolfgar would turn human. Nothing happened. *Ringerike*, overhead, emitted a piteous sound overhead as its blue light dimmed, and *Calaburn* lost its flames. She tried again, wanting Wolfgar to fall asleep, failing to manifest even a yawn. Zarnoc let out a gasp as magic sputtered from her fingertips like sparking fireworks and fizzled out.

"You need to be confident if you are to defeat him," the wizard said as he turned and ran.

Wolfgar snarled and charged forward in all his hellish rage, snarling savagely as he leaped toward her. Using quick footwork, Taliesin sidestepped Wolfgar and watched in horror as he headed straight for Zarnoc. The wizard raced around the side of the arena, pursued by the *Wolfen* that ran after him on its hind legs. At a swipe from Wolfgar, Zarnoc lost his footing and rolled into the middle of the pit. Wolfgar held the remains of the multi-colored coat in a clawed hand, took one sniff, and ripped it to shreds. He tossed the coat aside and glared at Taliesin as Zarnoc crawled away on his hands and knees.

"It's me, Wolfgar," Taliesin said, in a calm voice. "I mean you no harm. You must fight the blood lust. Control your temper...as I do."

There was no penetrating the fog in Wolfgar's brain. It had been relatively easy to dispatch the Wolf Pack in the forest when she had been armed with *Ringerike* and *Calaburn*. Now the swords floated overhead, quivering and humming with frustration, too high for her to reach. She had no choice but to grapple with the giant beast. Her instincts took over as she morphed into a giant red wolf. Her clothes ripped, and fell to the ground, while the sword belt and scabbard shoulder straps dug into her muscles. Wolfgar's eyes widened into yellow saucers. His jaws opened, exposing two rows of sharp fangs the size of daggers, and he lifted his clawed hands, equally as lethal.

Cheers from the fairies and the snarls from Wolfgar sounded loud in her ears. Taliesin thought about Bonaparte and the dragon blood in her veins, mingled with the *Wolfen* curse, and felt a sudden jolt of strength. Her confidence boosted, she lunged at Wolfgar. He knocked her away with one arm. Taliesin landed on her side, jumped up, and gave a shake to her thick red coat. The fairies on the front row gazed over the rail, shouting and waving their fists. Wolfgar froze as he sniffed the air and stared at Taliesin with recognition, for a moment, his amber eyes turned blue.

"It's me. It's Taliesin. You just need to calm down."

Before she could anticipate Wolfgar's next move, he dropped to all fours and rushed her, froth slathering his jaws. She leaped into the air and slammed into a wall of sheer muscle. His arms wrapped around her, his fangs sank into her shoulder, cutting deep, and blood flowed freely from the wound. Crying out in pain, Taliesin broke free from Wolfgar's deadly embrace and morphed into a *Wolfen*. Standing a foot shorter, she traded blows with him, snapping and biting, and managed to knock his feet out from under him. The other *Wolfen* crashed to the ground.

"That's the spirit," Zarnoc shouted on the far side of the pit.

Wolfgar climbed to his feet, shaking from head to toe, and rushed her. Taliesin turned her head as the great jaws snapped at her muzzle and summoned every ounce of strength as she punched Wolfgar in the stomach. He fell to the ground, and she jumped on him. He struggled to throw her off as she clung to his body, digging her claws into his rib cage, refusing to be tossed.

"*Ringerike,*" Taliesin called out. "Help me!"

The sword, now glowing bright blue twenty feet above, trembled violently and tried without success to return to her hand. *Calaburn* jerked about as if held in the hand of a fool in combat, likewise unable to break the fairies' spell and come to her. Frustrated and angry, the longsword burst into flames and directed bolts of fire toward the fairies. The Lorians warded off the flame bolts and sent them spiraling back into the pit, where they hit the ground on either side of Taliesin and Wolfgar and left behind craters.

"I am part Lorian," Taliesin shouted. "You cannot keep *Ringerike* from me!"

Taliesin lifted her furry head and roared. She was startled her voice carried impact, for some fairies staggered back from the rail, a few fell to their knees, while others slammed into the ceiling and fell into the crowd. Emboldened, Taliesin jumped off Wolfgar, landed on her feet, and morphed into a human, naked and proud. She lifted her right hand into the air as *Ringerike* broke through the invisible barrier and streaked toward her. She caught the hilt in her hand and pointed the blade at Wolfgar. Her clothes reassembled and appeared on her body, as she concentrated, willing *Ringerike* to subdue her opponent. The blue light shot from the sword and surrounded Wolfgar, holding him in an orb of light. His fur vanished as he morphed into his human form. He stared at Taliesin, unsure what was going on, lifted his hand toward her, and collapsed.

"It seems we have two *Wolfen* in our city," Dehavilyn said. "Whatever shall we do with them, my love?"

"Kill them," King Boran shouted. "Kill them all!"

The Lorian king, in a fit of rage, threw his goblet of wine at Taliesin. *Ringerike* moved of its own accord and knocked the goblet aside, which whirled back toward the startled king and struck him in the head with a good, solid *thwack*. With a grunt of pain, the king slumped against the railing and fell onto his back.

"Look to the King!" a guard shouted.

A commotion ensued at the railing as guards converged around the indisposed king. At a wave of the queen's hand, the door to the pit opened and twenty guards, each wearing a long blue cloak, marched in and pointed slender, silver spears at Taliesin. She paid no attention to them, instead staring in horror at the large, red welts that covered Wolfgar's body like latticework. He'd been whipped with a silver chain until the skin lay open to the bone. The wounds were slow to heal, and she knew Wolfgar must be in immense pain.

Zarnoc slunk up behind her and shook his finger at the guards. "Don't think for a moment I don't know each of your names," he said. "I never forget an insult. This is no way to treat Boran's uncle and Korax's heir. I've a good mind to turn you all into slugs!"

"We need to see to Wolfgar," Taliesin said.

While Zarnoc continued his chastisement of the royal guards, Taliesin bent down on a knee and placed her hand on Wolfgar's feverish forehead. Blood covered his face and mouth from when he'd bitten her. She knew, without looking, the wound in her shoulder had already healed. The dragon blood ingested by Wolfgar, however, battled against his *Wolfen* strain. She suddenly realized, the older the *Wolfen*, the more poisonous dragon blood was to their system. It was not the same for her because she had fairy blood, and even a small amount had allowed her to become stronger. A sickly pallor hung on Wolfgar's face, and his pale blue eyes appeared overcast.

"Kill me, Raven Mistress," Wolfgar groaned. "Please...."

"Not today, Captain Wolfgar. I'm going to save your life."

She nodded at Zarnoc and watched as he joined them. The wizard held his hand over Wolfgar's face and turned a latch on a turquoise ring on his finger, allowing a white powder to sprinkle upon the man's lips. Wolfgar licked the powder off, and his eyelids grew heavy, sagged, and closed.

"Is he...?" Taliesin caught her breath.

"The dragon fever is upon him. He is sleeping," Zarnoc said. "Fear not, child. I will not let them harm your captain. You have my word of honor."

Taliesin stood tall and slid *Ringerike* into the red leather scabbard on her back. She glanced upwards. *Calaburn* remained above, trying desperately to reach her, and an image of Prince Tarquin, seated on his throne with two large hounds at his feet, appeared in her mind. He clapped his hands twice. *Calaburn* appeared in his hand, and the image faded. She likewise clapped her hands twice, and the sword fell into her hand. At the sound of bowstrings being pulled back, Taliesin spotted forty bowmen aiming at her. She sheathed her sword and attempted to appeal to the crowd.

"People of Duvalen, listen to me!" Taliesin stared at the pale faces lining the railing. "From what I've seen of your city, it is fair and lovely and represents all that is magic and beauty. Tell me! What good is magic if you use it for evil? You live behind high walls, shut off from the world, and pretend life is a party. I know you are afraid. Afraid of humans and *Wolfen*, and most of all, you fear change. I am *Wolfen*, yes, but I am also one of you."

"You are both monsters," the Queen said. "We do not tolerate your kind in our realm. Kill the captain, or you will both die! Do it now, Raven Mistress!"

Taliesin stubbornly shook her head and remained beside Wolfgar.

"Is he worth dying for?" the wizard asked.

"Yes, he is, Zarnoc," Taliesin said. "Wolfgar is loyal to the Wolf Clan, as I am loyal to the Raven Clan. I can find no fault for what he has done. He was following orders. I wish I had warriors in my clan as strong and loyal as Wolfgar. I wish I *had* a clan."

"If wishes were fishes, the sea would be overcrowded. And I have warned you for the last time not to make wishes." Zarnoc stood in front of Taliesin with his arms held wide, offering his body to block the arrows. "Will no one speak on our behalf? No one?"

Taliesin, determined to die with Wolfgar, gathered the captain into her arms. In his drugged induced sleep, Wolfgar buried his face against her chest. His breath was warm on her skin, while his temperature was boiling. He whimpered, the sound reminding her of a puppy, and she held him tighter, *wishing* someone would put an end to the madness.

"I will speak for you!"

Tamblyn jumped onto the stones that ran along the edge of the pit, the railing at his back, and held out his arms. His mother wore an angry look on her face. The king, groggy from the blow, relied on two guards to support him. He stared at his son in shock as the prince addressed the crowd.

"My cousin saved my life, yet you reward Taliesin by making her fight against the wolf captain. Taliesin spared his life twice today. She believes his life has value. I agree with her. Mother, call off your guards and release the prisoners. Please."

"Be still, boy. This does not concern you."

"But it does," the prince said. "I am to be King one day. I do not want to be known as a king who turns his back on a friend in need. Let me prove it to you."

Tamblyn jumped over the railing and landed in the pit. He landed with grace, so light on his feet that he left no imprint behind. He ran to Zarnoc and spread his arms wide, offering his slender body as a shield. The door burst inwards with a crash, and ogres fell to the ground, crushed beneath Ursus' paws as he lumbered into the pit. The polar bear lifted his massive frame, stood on his hind legs, thrashed at the air with his front paws, and shook the very rafters with his roar.

"I am Tamblyn Vorenius, Prince of Duvalen, and I order you to lay down your bows. Do you hear me? You shame the Royal House of Vorenius. You, mother, and you, father, bring shame to us all. There will be no more fighting in the pit. Not now. Not ever!"

The arena grew silent.

The queen floated into the air and drifted into the pit, landing not far from the small group. Diamonds sparkled on her gown and cloak. Against the backdrop of blood-covered sand and brick walls, Dehavilyn seemed to be in her element. Dark, fierce, and cruel. She lifted her right hand, gracefully swept it sideways, and the guards lowered their bows. She walked to take her son by the hand and kissed the back of it.

"Darling, I will respect your request, for it is made out of true friendship," Dehavilyn said. "Uncle Zarnoc, you are forgiven. Forthwith, you are restored to your former status as a royal wizard." Her violet eyes gleamed when Zarnoc bowed low. "As for you, Raven Mistress, there can be no doubt you are the rightful heir of King Korax, for *Ringerike* was made to serve no other. Clearly, you are a *Sha'tar* and able to control magic with your mind. You will be allowed to tend to the Wolf Pack captain, provided you keep him in your room and do not allow him to walk about freely."

With a clap of her hands, guards carried a stretcher out of a tunnel. Wolfgar was placed on the stretcher and removed from the pit. Tamblyn kissed his mother's cheek, and with a motion at Taliesin, he and the bear followed the stretcher. Taliesin bowed to the queen, ran after her cousin, and fell into step beside him.

"Thank you, Tamblyn. You have repaid your debt to me."

"Cousin, I surprised even myself," the prince said. "I am not known for my bravery. I dare say you have inspired me this day. Please, accept my apology on behalf of my parents and our people. You are most welcome here."

Tamblyn caught up with the guards and remained at Wolfgar's side as they walked down a tunnel illuminated by bright green and blue moss shaped into wall sconces. Iron cell doors with small, barred windows lined the tunnel. In the darkness, Taliesin heard voices crying out in pain and suffering at the hands of the Lorians. The wizard caught up with her, hands crossed behind his back, and walked with purpose at her side.

"I suppose I should apologize for bringing you here," Zarnoc said. "I have made my displeasure known to my nephew and his wife. In the past, I tolerated their cruelness, yet I see this only encouraged them to behave even worse. Boran's father never would have treated a guest in this manner, especially not for someone of the bloodline of Korax. I had thought after Korax died that their prior dispute over Dehavilyn would end. I know I regret what happened to Korax. Can you forgive me?"

"This is not your fault, Zarnoc. The more I see of your home, the more I dislike it," Taliesin said. "Watching people fight to the death for entertainment is barbaric. It's something I would expect to find in Skarda."

"We will not stay long in Duvalen. Boran and Dehavilyn were shamed by their son, but it won't last. We're walking on eggshells, and we must both proceed with caution, or we're likely to join this poor lot." He sniffed. "I miss my little Ginger. She's not been eating well, I can tell, for I have indigestion. Cats are very sensitive to violence, you know. I hope Shan Octavio is taking care of her."

"We'll join the gypsies soon enough, and you can be reunited with your cat."

Zarnoc smiled. "Oh, I like that idea," he said. "In the morning, I should think, would be the perfect time to make our departure."

A door opened, and the group entered a corridor in the palace, ascended several flights of stairs, and arrived on the ground floor. Stained glass windows let in colorful rays of morning sunlight, framed by purple and pink drapes. Long silver candlesticks and slender candles with sparkling blue flames replaced the mold for lighting. The ceiling was high overhead, and colorful banners more than sixty feet long hung from the rafters. Paintings on the walls depicted scenes of fairy armies fighting enormous dragons, hordes of goblins, and figures with a deadly pallor and strange pale eyes that Taliesin had a feeling were the Hellirin, though she did not ask. A painting of one particular gold dragon with green eyes looked familiar, and Taliesin smiled as she thought about her new friend Bonaparte. They passed the throne room. Its enormous roof was painted gold and silver, and royal banners hung from the rafters. Two large thrones were cut from diamonds and draped with wolf pelts, and they left Taliesin worried about her little wolf pack. A single servant dusted the thrones with a cloth. They continued down a corridor and arrived at a wide staircase, making the ascent to the next level, where a large number of Lorians had gathered to watch. Taliesin glared at the royal court as she stomped up the stairs.

"Try smiling," Zarnoc said. "Smiles work wonders on frightened fairies." He beamed at an elegantly dressed young couple who walked down the stairs whispering about Taliesin. The man and woman smiled back at him. "See, it's not so hard to be friendly."

"I don't want to be their friends. Where are we being taken?"

"To your bedroom. You need food and rest, my dear."

"There's dark magic all around us. I can feel it," Taliesin whispered. "It's been getting stronger since we reached the second floor. What am I sensing?"

"Well, it's not the royal sorcerer Balboa—he's a real stinker if you ask me. What you are feeling is the ancient magic that comes from the Royal Armory. There are weapons in the palace that sense your presence," Zarnoc replied. "Not only weapons, but horns, harps, and mirrors, to name a few. They feed off your magic and grow stronger."

"Magical weapons?" Taliesin was excited. "So, this is where illegal contraband has been shipped from Caladonia. I wondered about that. I suppose an enchanted hairbrush might come in handy." She finally smiled.

"Even the Lorians do a little grave robbing. Queen Dehavilyn has the largest collection of magical items in the world," Zarnoc said. "Many have been shipped here by the dukes of Caladonia or the royal family to be kept here, out of the way. Out of harm's reach." He pointed at a pair of large red doors engraved with strange symbols and read the words aloud. "'We were the first. We are the mightiest. Blessed above all others are the Lorians, the Ancient Ones, the Keepers of Magic and all things Sacred.'"

"I can hear the weapons inside. They are talking to me."

"You're being summoned. Try to keep your thoughts clear. Ignore everything you hear and keep walking, for behind those doors lies trouble, my dear."

Taliesin sensed *Ringerike* and *Calaburn* communicating in their odd little way to the magical weapons in the Royal Armory. The Lorians had many other weapons behind the doors, and if asked, they would gladly align with her. Even *Calaburn* had lost its dark glow, reinforced by *Ringerike*'s goodness, and it too sought to be worth her praise. She could hear each weapon and magical item silently calling her name from behind the doors, begging her to enter and stroke each of them. In a way, the items behind the doors were prisoners, just as the people and creatures in the cells beneath the palace. If she knew how to use her full powers, she imagined she might be able to free everyone and everything in the palace that needed to be rescued.

They turned a corner and headed down a hall adorned with large paintings of fairy kings and queens of old, including a young Prince Korax standing beside his older brother, a slain deer at their feet. Another painting, larger than the rest, showed every god of Mt. Helos, including Ragnal's two supernatural wolves, Cano and Varg. Their yellow eyes seemed to follow Taliesin as she passed, and she imagined the beasts jumping out of the painting to block her path.

"That painting looks *real*," she said.

"Shush," Zarnoc cautioned. "It is, in a way. If ever there was a direct link to Mt. Helos, it is in that particular painting.

No one knows who painted it. I only know it was here when I was born, and it never ages, nor dulls. I swear, one evening when I was a boy, the goddess mother, Broa, visited me in my sleep and kissed my forehead. I do not pray to the gods. If I did, I would pray to Broa, the goddess of the sun and crops and...and baked loaves of delicious bread."

Taliesin didn't laugh. The painting was behind her, and she feared glancing back, sensing the two giant wolves' heads had emerged, for she heard their deep growls. Walking faster, she hurried down the gallery and through a hall with red carpet. Guards stood at a golden door that was opened so Wolfgar could be carried inside. Tamblyn, along with the polar bear, waited for them at the door.

"If you need anything, cousin," the prince said, "I'm just two doors down on the left. I am very tired and must rest. I'll see you in the morning." He bowed, walked down the hall with Ursus, and entered his bedroom.

Taliesin let out a weary sigh and entered through the golden door into a lavishly decorated room. The carpet was thick and gold, tapestries of jousting knights hung on the walls, and a painting of Prince Korax on a horse hung behind a four-poster bed. Zarnoc hovered over Wolfgar, who had been laid on a coverlet of red velvet. The guards left the room and closed the door. Taliesin walked across the room, admiring a large table cluttered with a collection of daggers and jewelry boxes. Armor suits stood in each corner, and shields lined the walls.

"So, this was Korax's room," she said. "It's hard to imagine he has been gone for one thousand years, for everything looks new. He was very handsome. It's no wonder the ladies found him irresistible." She noticed Zarnoc wince. "Sorry. I didn't mean to upset you. It's just that I have heard so much gossip about Korax. I suppose you think I am as fickle as he was, but I assure you, I'm nothing like him, other than we share the same red hair and green eyes."

"Sometimes it feels like his death happened yesterday," Zarnoc said. "Had I only stayed with him that night and convinced him not to fight Tarquin, he would still be alive, and Caladonia would not be in the middle of a civil war. I'm not sure what you have been told, but Korax was not bloodthirsty like his brother. He was a good king. I regret I let a woman come between us, especially *that* woman. Does she still keep a pet spider as her familiar? A disgusting preference I never understood."

"Benedict is her familiar's name," Taliesin said. "Ysemay told me what happened, Zarnoc. She has suffered a great deal. People do and say things when they're upset that they regret later. I know neither of you can do anything to change the past. It's best not to think about it."

Large glass doors opened onto a terrace with a chaise lounge and potted plants. Taliesin went out the door, letting Zarnoc tend to Wolfgar, and paused at the railing, where she had a view of the entire city of Duvalen. The mountains, capped with snow, sheltered the fairy city, ringed by a thick forest blanketed in white. The city lights twinkled like stars in the skies. Duvalen was lovelier than any place she'd seen. She wondered if her parents, John and Calista, had ever been to Duvalen, though it seemed unlikely. With a glance over her shoulder into the room, she wondered if it was the right time to ask Zarnoc about her mother. She went inside and found Wolfgar sleeping soundly, the covers pulled over his body and a damp cloth placed over his furrowed brow. His face was clean, and his head wound had healed without leaving a scar. His long blond hair was brushed out and shined like spun gold. The fever appeared abated, for his face was no longer flushed, and his chest rose and fell with each breath.

"Ah, that bath you wanted is ready," Zarnoc called out. "I also prepared you something to eat. It's leftovers from the royal banquet. I'm sure it's delicious, only you must refrain from stuffing your belly."

Taliesin sniffed the strong odor of perfume mixed with the subtler scent of food and turned. The wizard had prepared a hot bath in a large gold tub. A feast for a small army was spread on a nearby round table. There were trays of roasted beef, ham, and chicken, along with a basket filled with bread and a jar of butter.

"Phelon must have sent the Wolf Pack after me," she said. "I don't think Wolfgar came here to kill Tamblyn. The prince was simply in the wrong place at the wrong time."

"So, everyone keeps saying," Zarnoc replied. "I suspect Phelon contacted the Wolf Pack and ordered them to take you to Prince Almaric. He'll be blamed for failing to do so himself. Perhaps I was wrong to have you save that whelp. It seemed the civilized thing to do at the time. He is the heir of the Wolf Clan. Phelon has been waiting more than five hundred years to be chief. I suppose he can wait a while longer, for Lykus has longevity unlike any other *Wolfen*."

"How did Wolfgar get here so fast?"

"*Wolfen* are telepathic, the pack mentality you know, which means they communicate even though they are miles apart. You can do this as well, my dear. Phelon most assuredly told Wolfgar where to find you. Be glad you didn't give Phelon *Calaburn*. He'd only give it to Prince Almaric, and he already has far too many magical weapons. I know you have cause to hate King Frederick, but I dare say he is not half as rotten as any of his five sons."

"I haven't met all of the princes, or if I did, I don't remember."

"Never you mind," he said. "A hot bath is what you need to fix you right up, and then to bed, you go. I promise to watch over you while you sleep."

Taliesin watched Zarnoc sprinkle a dash of sparkling powder in the hot water that turned into bubbles. She removed her sword belt and sword harness, placed *Ringerike* on a chest at the foot of the bed, and hung *Calaburn* from a knob that stuck out of one of the bedposts. She kissed her sapphire dragon ring for good luck.

"Zarnoc, I think I should tell you that I met Ragnal and Navenna near Ysemay's shack," she said. "They are playing a game, and I'm their pawn."

"Do you want to tell me what they said, or shall I read your mind?"

"I want you to tell me about my mother. Tarquin said her name was Calista, and if he mentioned it, I wonder if that means she was a Draconus. Ysemay said you were there at my birth. Why have you never mentioned my mother before?"

The wizard was caught by surprise. "You mean the ghost of Prince Tarquin told you about Calista? I suppose Bonaparte did his share of talking, too," he said. "You can never trust a dragon."

"I have a right to know, Zarnoc. Now turn away."

Taliesin clapped her hands. Her clothes fell off her body, and she jumped into the tub, sank into the warm bubbles to her chin, and sighed. Zarnoc carried over a pitcher of warm water and poured it over her head. She picked up a sponge and washed, as Zarnoc sat in a chair, lit his pipe, and produced two smoke rings from his nostrils.

"Sertorius did love you," Zarnoc said with a sigh. "I know people often marry their first cousins, though I thought you might object if you knew the truth. This is why I did not object when he married Lenora. The only reason I didn't tell you who your mother was and sent you all those years ago to live with the Raven Clan, was to protect you from King Frederick. There can be no doubt that he knows you are the daughter of John Mandrake and the king's younger sister."

"My mother was the sister of King Frederick?" Taliesin splashed water over the sides of the tub as she sat forward. "So, I am a Draconus!"

"Yes, my dear. You have bluer blood in your veins than any monarch I know," he said. "Your parents married in secret. Sadly, Calista could not hide the fact she was pregnant, nor ask Frederick to sanction her marriage to a commoner. At the time, no one knew John Mandrake was the ancestor of King Korax, which had Frederick known, might have made him more agreeable to the match. I imagine if Sertorius had known who you are, he still would have wanted to marry you."

Taliesin considered throwing a sponge at Zarnoc. She sat back in a huff and stared at the clouds of a blue sky painted above on the ceiling. "I didn't want to marry Sertorius," she said. "I never loved Sertorius like I loved Roland. I still love Roland, Zarnoc."

"I know."

"Tell me how my parents met. Tell me everything."

Zarnoc nodded. "It's time, I suppose," he said, in a melancholy voice. "Twenty-seven years ago, a young swordsmith made his way to the royal city of Padama. He arrived to make swords and bought a small blacksmith shop in the center of town. One day a royal procession came past with King Frederick and his sister, Princess Calista, who paused to admire John Mandrake's work. The king and your father struck up an immediate friendship. John also fell in love with your mother, love at first sight. They met in secret whenever they could and married a short while later. Most love stories of such a nature end in tragedy. When Frederick learned about their marriage, Calista was already five months pregnant, and he sent her to a convent. Poor John was forced to remain working his forge to make swords for the king. I soon heard Calista was pregnant, so I went in search of her. I was at her side when she gave birth to you, a red-haired child touched by magic, and with her dying breath, she begged me to look after you."

Taliesin wiped away a tear. "So, you brought me to my father...."

"To raise and love, as was proper," Zarnoc said. "The king assumed for many years you were a foundling. When the day came he learned the truth, an assassin was sent to kill your father and you. Master Osprey arrived in time, whisked you away to Raven's Nest, changed your name, protected you, and loved you as his own child. I again interceded the moment I knew Frederick had suspected you were his sister and Mandrake's child. The king ordered Sir Roland to find you and return with you to Tantalon Castle. I had no idea you would fall for Grudge, yet you did, and I believe he fell in love with you. However, knowing the Wolf Clan and Eagle Clan also knew about you and your ability to find magical weapons, I took matters into my own hands. I suggested Hawk find *Ringerike*, and the rest fell into place. You found the Raven Sword, and now you are here...in a tub."

"Do you think Roland still loves me?"

"It seems any man you kiss falls in love with you," Zarnoc quipped. "Fickle just like Korax, going from flower to flower, sucking nectar. If you love Roland Brisbane, you certainly have a funny way of showing it. He did not turn you over to the king. He did not betray you, as you think he did. Roland is a King's Man, but he is honorable just the same."

"I'm glad you like him, Zarnoc. One day we'll be reunited."

Taliesin lifted her face, and anticipation caused her to quiver as the pitcher floated into the air and poured water directly over her head. The water continued to pour until the soap rinsed out of her long red hair. The pitcher returned to the floor, and she finally sank back in the tub with a sigh. Zarnoc refilled his wine glass and poured one for her. He brought it over, handed it to her, and returned to his chair. His clothes turned from the jester's costume into a long purple robe with yellow stars and moons.

He puffed on his pipe and continued his tale, "Calista was beautiful when she was your age, with long black hair, blue eyes, and a sweet, kind disposition. She was ten years younger than Frederick, who loved her with a possessive jealousy, and John Mandrake offered her a temporary safe haven. They both knew it couldn't last, that they'd eventually be found out, but they were in love and reckless. I think if they had left Padama and joined the Raven Clan, or perhaps come here, they might have lived longer. She and John would have been happy here, that is what you were thinking, earlier, when you were gazing at the city. You wondered if they'd ever been to Duvalen."

She nodded. "They would have been happy here, I think. Did my father know you are a Lorian and a wizard? You said you were his friend."

138 | SUSANNE L. LAMBDIN

"As a customer only. I paid top coin, and he liked me very much," Zarnoc said. "I never told him he was the Raven King's heir or that I was a distant relative. He knew I was a wizard, and he knew he had magic—he was a fine warlock, really. Your father was a friend of Osprey, as well. Osprey always stopped at the blacksmith shop when he came to town to trade. We spent many a fine evening together, the three of us, talking about Calista and you. Osprey and your mother knew John was a warlock. They knew me only as a wizard, not as a Lorian royal."

"Am I like them?" she asked.

"You take after your father in appearance and share his hot temper. John looked like Korax, but he did not act like him. He was a good man. I remember Calista Draconus as being gentle and kind. Make no mistake. Prince Tarquin's ring and sword wanted to be with you because of who your mother was, and it's the same with *Ringerike*. Magical items want to be with the family members of their true owners. Oh, I know you took Bonaparte's scale and put it on your horse. I'm sure the dragon does as well, though I suspect he does not mind, after all, you shared a magical kiss."

"Stop prodding about in my mind," she said. "Some things are meant to be private, Zarnoc. It was only a kiss." A kiss that had lasted hours, she thought.

"You tasted his blood. It will help you control your wild nature."

She imagined Ascalon castle, restored to its former beauty as a fortress on a mountain, guarded by a gold dragon.

"Prince Tarquin must have been a kind and forgiving man, despite what people say about him. I know what Queen Dehavilyn did, Zarnoc. I also know Bonaparte killed Vargus the Dreadful after the queen sent the black dragon to kill Tarquin's family. She is a horrible woman, and I don't think much of her husband."

"Hmm? Yes, I suppose Bonaparte is an exceptional dragon," he replied, making no comment on his own family. "Tarquin's domain spread across the Stavehorn Mountains and into much of Skarda. The only reason he and Korax went to war was due to Dehavilyn's meddling. She first persuaded Tarquin to take control of Caladonia with her dark magic, making him lust after the southern lands, and then convinced Korax to build a large army to wage war. The day Tarquin's message arrived, a challenge to fight one another for ownership of Caladonia, winner takes all, Korax had already decided to march on Draconus lands. You know what happened."

Taliesin reached for her glass of wine. "I am a Draconus and a Sanqualus," she said taking a sip. "If Frederick had known the truth of it, he might see that I can restore peace to Caladonia. It's what Navenna wants, that and for me to restore the greatness of the Raven Clan. Ragnal wants only war, while Mira wants magic to thrive again."

"I imagine they want more than that, my dear," he said. "In a way, you are Korax and Tarquin's child. I do believe you are a symbol of peace. You could put an end to the war and take the Ebony Throne for yourself. Roland would make a fine king. Of course, it's up to you to decide if there will be peace or war. *Ringerike* is powerful, Taliesin. So are you. Together, you can do anything you want. You can bring about the Age of the Wolf, return magic, or bring about peace. Tantalon Castle is built on the ruins of Black Castle, and blood has been spilled on both sides of your family."

"I have much to think on," she said. She wasn't angry Zarnoc continued to read her thoughts. 'In one ear and out the other,' Ysemay had often told her. What she needed to learn was how to prevent people from reading her mind, and earplugs were not going to help. "If I decide to restore magic to the realm and take the throne, I can't do it alone, Zarnoc. I wouldn't even know where to start."

"That sounds like a proposition, and I do like propositions coming from a naked lady in a bathtub. Of course, I will help you. You are family, and I think I owe it to Korax, perhaps even to Tarquin, to help you do so."

Rising from the tub, Taliesin found towels neatly stacked on the floor. She wrapped one around her and took another to dry her hair. Zarnoc waved his hand, and a white robe flew toward Taliesin. She slipped it on, found slippers on the ground close to her toes, and slid them on. Zarnoc quietly smoked his pipe as she sat next to him, bringing her wine glass. She set it on the table, reached for bread, and ate without decorum, tearing off big chunks and swallowing them with wine.

"You passed Ysemay's test and the Augur's test. Now you have passed the Queen's test. Three powerful women," Zarnoc said. "I know how you feel about women being treated less than equals of men. However, these three *are* powerful, Taliesin."

"Not as powerful as you," she said. "I know you could have used your magic in the pit. It was your test to see what I learned from Ysemay. No matter what you think, Zarnoc, you are also stronger than I am. I got lucky."

"I didn't get to be the oldest wizard alive because I believe in luck, my dear. Your compliment is noted," he said. "Enough secrets have been kept from you. Ysemay looks like an old woman for the same reason I appear as an old man. It's a way to keep people at a disadvantage because if they think you are old, they usually tend to underestimate your abilities. Frankly, I think it's about time to reveal myself to you."

The wizard put aside his pipe and smiled at her. The facade of an old, gray-haired man altered to that of a man about thirty years of age. His hair was black and long, his beard neatly trimmed, and his purple eyes gazed at her from beneath finely arched brows. Nary a wrinkle marred his face. Zarnoc was not handsome, not really, yet she found him incredibly kind at times, and unquestionably intelligent. With a nod, he resumed smoking his pipe.

"I'm a little older than I told you, Taliesin. I have fought in many wars. The last war was against King Magnus Draconus. Fairies, elves, dwarves, and the last dragons forged an alliance and fought together against the Caladonian army. The battle took place at Pelekus Castle and, as fate would have it, we were defeated. The survivors retreated into the northern mountains, never to return, while I remained at Pelekus where you later met me. Since then, the Magic Realms have remained cloaked in magic to hide from humans. Only the Skardans have ventured into this area, for their leader, Talas Kull has no fear of magic, nor any tolerance for magic users."

Taliesin said nothing as she helped herself to a slice of roast beef and refilled her glass.

"Drink sparingly of the wine, for it's fairy wine," he said. "It's quite intoxicating to humans. Eat only enough to sustain you. Do not allow gluttony to possess you, or you will be bound to this place for all time. Everything here is tainted with magic. Too much will consume even you, so be wary."

"Why eat or drink at all then? I can create my own food out of thin air."

"Magical food has no protein," he said. "You know this, my dear. Simply do as I say, and we'll get out of this mess sooner than you can say 'Eagle Clan.'"

"I wouldn't say that on my death bed," Taliesin retorted.

She chewed a few bites of meat, enjoying the savory taste. She wanted to ask Zarnoc what she was eating, decided she didn't want to know, and reached for a juicy red apple. Zarnoc slapped her hand and pushed the bowl of fruit to the opposite side of the table.

"What was that for? Apples are my favorite." Taliesin immediately thought of Thalagar, for he liked apples, too.

"It's a blood apple. Fairy fruit. Don't eat it," he cautioned, with a wink. "Don't ever eat fruit while in this place. You don't have that much Lorian blood in you, Taliesin. Blood apples make humans a little crazy, and the more you eat, the crazier you become. Nor should a horse eat a blood apple. Don't worry about Thalagar. I have a few friends here, and they are watching him."

"I am not ready for this, Zarnoc. I am starting to wish I never found *Ringerike* and stayed at home."

Zarnoc let out a cry of alarm. "Oh, don't make wishes! Take it back! Take it back right now, or who knows what will befall us all." He counted to ten, enough time for her to take the wish back and immediately explained. "*Any* wish you make, thought or said out loud, manifests in one form or another. I told you this before, my dear. Until you are a full-fledged *Sha'tar*, do not make wishes. In fact, don't ever make them."

"I'll stop," she said. "I do it far too often, I know."

"Get some sleep. I'll be comfortable in this chair, and if not, I'll conjure myself a bed by the fire. This palace always feels a little nippy to me. If you need me, call out, and I'll be there in a moment. Come morning, we'll sort things out."

Feeling her eyelids starting to sag, and a yawn building, Taliesin walked to the bed, pausing to stroke *Ringerike* and give *Calaburn* a pat before she crawled into bed with Wolfgar. She lay on top of the bed and used a coverlet to cover her body. She heard Zarnoc snoring as she placed her head on a pillow and closed her eyes.

She was asleep within seconds.

* * * * *

Chapter Eight

Taliesin, in a world where shadow met light and twisted into nightmares, cried out in her sleep as forty Wolfmen surrounded Master Osprey and his wife, Minerva. Twin blond-haired boys stood beside them, holding their hands. Falcon and Talon, aged ten, were the darlings of the Raven clan and highly mischievous. This night, their little faces were filled with terror. The events that unfolded beneath her eyelids had already happened, and there was Chief Lykus, a tall, bearded man with grim features. He wore black chainmail, and his body was human. His face morphed into that of a *Wolfen*. He lifted a clawed hand to strike each lad across the cheek, creating matching wounds, and then turned on the couple.

"So, you refuse to join us, Osprey of the Raven Clan?" Chief Lykus snarled. "Will you not, for your clan? There are women and children here, and tasty young girls, ripe to the bone. We will take your infants and stick them on spikes for the vultures. The boys, those who are willing, and those who show promise...perhaps I can be enticed to spare their lives."

"May Heggen curse you and your clan! May you know the taste of death as his raven, Vendel, feasts on your eyes and innards," Minerva snarled. A guard struck her, and she fell to her knees.

"Hold," Lykus said, raising his hand. His eyes were red, and saliva covered his beard as he lashed out at the Raven Master. "Why do you say nothing? Do you think Arundel cares about you or your clan? Do you see any Eagles coming to the rescue? No, Osprey! None will come for you this night. You belong to us!"

Osprey didn't beg for mercy, nor did he beg for the lives of his clan, for he knew his words would be ignored. The Wolf Chief dropped his hand, and the guard stabbed Minerva in the stomach with his dagger. She collapsed to the ground as the entire Wolf Clan shed their clothes, morphed into wolves, and attacked the Ravens. Taliesin heard the screams and cries of three hundred people slaughtered by tooth and claw. The twins were pulled away from Minerva as Lykus' pack fell upon Osprey. The old man said not a word as he was torn to shreds and devoured by large wolves.

Taliesin groaned in her sleep as her fear grew and dark shadows blocked the carnage that lay at Chief Lykus' feet. She heard a wolf's howl, forlorn and eerie, and felt herself drawn to the pack, its secrets, and its ghastly rituals. She panted as she dreamed.

A full moon rose above a large black castle built inside a rocky hill hidden deep in a dark, ancient forest. Torches lighted Wolf's Den, and within the high walls, the baying of wolves filled the night with terror. Taliesin stood in the middle of a courtyard lined with dead trees as if she were there in person. The Wolf Clan gathered to watch a ceremony. Minerva and the twins, along with a few younger members of Raven Clan, each marked with a gash across their cheek, stood shoulder to shoulder. All were bitten, and all bled. The officers led a girl in her teens forward, and Lykus appeared in human form wrapped in a dirty cloak. He grabbed the girl by her chin and lifted her face to the moonlight, his cheek pressed against hers, and saliva flew from his lips as he spoke.

"Tonight, is the last night of the Raven Clan's existence," Lykus said, in a deep voice. "Those of you who were once Ravens shall now and forevermore be known as *Wolfen*. The men will run with the Wolf Pack, howl at the moon, and dine on human flesh. The females will be our servants. You shall each serve Ragnal, the God of War, to whom we pray and offer sacrifice on each full moon. It is Ragnal's wolf companion, Varg, born a *Wolfen*, who bit Caninus, the first chief of the Wolf Clan. It was Varg's sire, Cano, who bit a young maiden and created the first werewolf, known as the Children of the Night—the Night Breed. They are our enemy. They are soulless beasts that roam the wilds and kill without reason or thought of consequence. It is only the *Wolfen*, those of us known as the Moon Side, who are blessed by Ragnal. We are able to maintain our humanity when the change comes upon us. We alone kill with purpose and control."

Lykus squeezed the girl's chin at the same time he curled his lip upwards, exposing a row of sharp fangs. As he bent his head, the crowd, male and female alike, changed from human to full wolf forms. They waited for Lykus to offer them fresh meat, snarling and growling as the blood lust seized them. Only the officers of the Wolf Pack, dressed in full chainmail and fur cloaks, remained human. With a sly smile, Lykus dipped his head and ripped out the girl's throat with one bite. At his signal, the officers dragged the dead girl to Falcon and forced the frightened boy to lap at her blood. It was Talon's turn next. He licked the blood spurting from her neck, virgin's blood, and then Minerva drank her fill. The body was cast to the Wolf Pack.

"Tonight," Lykus said, "each and every one of the Ravens is born again as a member of the Wolf Clan. You will learn what it means to be one of the Moon Side. We do not age, and we do not sicken, for only silver and fire can harm us. On this last night of summer, each of you will change from human, to *Wolfen*, and to wolf, as Caninus, the first leader of our clan did centuries ago, and together we shall hunt under the stars."

It was Talon, the younger twin, who turned first. The most innocent, lured by the scent of blood, the thickness still hot in his throat, felt the change. With a jerk and a sudden flurry of arm movements, he turned from human, to *Wolfen*, and to a large blond wolf. He lifted his muzzle and howled the joyous sound of a free soul of the night.

Falcon took longer to change into a *Wolfen*. He was unable to become a wolf like his brother. Not able to turn wolf and never able to run on all fours, his temper was too fierce to be less than a monster. There was no beauty in his soul or allure to run beneath the moon. He desired flesh and lingered to feed with a ravenous appetite on corpses.

The rest of the Ravens, including Minerva, her wound healed, fell to all fours, turning from monsters to beautiful giant wolves. In a rush, the new members of the pack approached Lykus, heads bowed and whimpering softly with their tails tucked beneath their legs. With his tongue, Lykus offered reassurance and guidance, and he touched the tips of their black moist noses.

In her sleep, Taliesin felt a hand slide down her hip. She awoke with a start to find dawn filtering through the windows in colorful sunbeams, the faint odor of last night's fire in her nostrils, and Wolfgar staring at her. His pale green eyes were filled with anger. He leaned on an elbow, put his hand at her throat, and squeezed.

"What am I doing here, in your bed, Raven Mistress?" Wolfgar's fingers tightened on her windpipe, and then he released her. "I could have killed you in your sleep. You dreamed. I heard you say the names of Osprey, Minerva, and Lykus. The memories of that night at Wolf's Den still haunt you. Though you were not there, you saw it happen, didn't you?"

"Yes," she said, pushing him back. "I saw. All of it. You are here because I saved your life yesterday. I had the opportunity to kill you twice, and yet I did not, captain. You should ask me why I spared you."

"Don't think I have forgiven you for leaving me at the Cave of Chu'Alagu," Wolfgar said, his voice deep and gruff. He pressed his thumb to her cheek. "After I killed the Raven King, we fled the army of the undead, only to find ourselves pinned between them and an army led by Sir Roland, his knights, and Master Xander's Eagle legionnaires. In the chaos, we managed to escape and found our way here. You should ask how I knew you were here."

Taliesin caught his thumb and removed it from her face. "Wolf calls, that's how," she said, her anger stirred. "Phelon sent you word through every foul beast in the forest, and when it reached your ears, you came looking for me here. The fairies drugged you and whipped you with a silver chain. Had Zarnoc not healed you, we would not be having this conversation."

Wolfgar watched as she built a wall between them with the pillows. He laid back, arms crossed under his head, and sniffed the air. It grew uncomfortably quiet between them. Catching the lust glimmering in his eyes, Taliesin lifted her hand and struck the side of his head. With a growl, he caught her wrist, and with a hard jerk, pulled her over the pillows to lie on his chest. The look of desire in his eyes set Taliesin in motion. They struggled for dominance, each trying to pin the other on the bed until she managed to knee him in the groin, and as he doubled over, she pushed him off the bed.

Wolfgar hit the floor with a *thunk*. She heard a growl and rolled to the side of the bed, expecting to see a wolf. On all fours, the naked man commenced quivering head to toe in an attempt to turn without results. She said nothing as he concentrated harder, willing himself to change. The harder he tried, the redder his cheeks grew. Frustrated, he caught hold of the mattress, pulled himself upwards, sat on his haunches, and stared at her in absolute horror.

"What have you done to me, woman? Is this witchcraft?" Wolfgar shouted. "Why can't I change? I am certainly angry enough to turn, and that look on your face is not helping. This is not a laughing matter!"

"It is, it really is. You're red as a tomato," she said, laughing. His eyes hiked upwards. "There's nothing wrong with you, and it's not magic. It just takes a little more concentration. You bit me during our fight in the pit. I might have failed to mention that, as well as the fact I tasted dragon blood a few days ago. It's changed me, Wolfgar, and it's changed you, too. Dragon blood has tamed our wild side, but we're still *Wolfen*."

"What you've done is unforgivable! I don't want to be tamed!"

Taliesin noticed a tattoo of a snarling wolf on his bare shoulder before he yanked the sheet off the bed and wrapped it around his body, refusing to meet her gaze. Not knowing what to say, she rose from the bed and went to a basin to wash her face and hands. One look around the room revealed Zarnoc was no longer present. She found a wardrobe in the corner, opened it, and selected a long gray sweater, leather pants, and tall brown boots. While Wolfgar sulked, she slipped on *Ringerike's* shoulder harness and belted on the scabbard that held *Calaburn*. When she finally glanced at Wolfgar, she found him sitting up with hands held out in front of his face, trying desperately to make himself turn.

"I no longer feel the rage inside of me," he said. "I am...calm."

"It's nice, isn't it? Having control makes a difference. I'm sure if you were thinking with your head and not your tail, you could change. Perhaps you don't want to."

Wolfgar threw off the sheet, stood, and placed his hands on his hips, glaring at her across the room. He looked magnificent in the morning light. He was muscular, with a flat stomach and surprisingly little body hair. Lacking modesty, he walked to the basin to splash water onto his face and rubbed the stubble on his chin.

"What dragon are you talking about? They are all dead."

"Not all," Taliesin said. "A few days ago, I met a gold dragon named Bonaparte. I guess I bit him." She didn't want to say how. "I tasted his blood not knowing what it would do to me. I found out silver can no longer harm me. I'm stronger, and my senses are sharper. It's the same for you."

"Are we still immortal?"

"Yes, I suppose so," she said. "I'd forgotten about that part of the curse."

Taliesin sat at the table and poured a glass of wine. Breakfast had replaced the night's dinner. She took nothing to eat and only a few sips of wine, despite the fact her stomach was growling. She imagined Wolfgar was hungry, too. He walked to the wardrobe, selected garments, and dressed before coming to sit next to her. He picked up a bottle of wine and started to drink. The bottle was jerked away. Taliesin poured wine into a goblet and handed it to him. She selected a slice of bread that had neither jam nor butter to add to its taste and set it before him.

"We're in Duvalen, and this is fairy food and drink. Eat only bread and drink only a few sips of wine, or you shall be forever imprisoned here."

Wolfgar ate the bread, finished his wine, and sat with his arms crossed over his chest, glowering at her in an accusatory fashion. She wasn't afraid of him. She had been, once, only now there was no reason to fear the captain.

"Get to the point," he grumbled. "Why did you spare my life? You want something from me, and it is clearly not to be found in bed. What then? I'll not tell you Lykus' plans, nor give you a count of Almaric's army so you can report it to Sir Roland. How is Roland by the way? He is clearly not here, or I would not have awoken next to you. Did you abandon him as well?"

There was no reason to tell him about Roland, or about what had caused their breakup. She felt no inclination to divulge the contents of her heart to the captain. What she felt was private, and she wasn't sure what would happen with Roland when she saw him next.

"I want you to join the Raven Clan," she said. "Lykus took the lives of my clan. I mean to take his captain as one of my own."

"Why?" he snarled. "There is no trust between us. I am your enemy."

"Because I am Korax's heir, and I have need of a champion. Because I intend to put down Almaric's rebellion and tame the Wolf Clan. Because I need warriors to fight for me in order to make that happen. I want only the best. Join my clan. Fight for me."

Wolfgar glared at her. "You're mad," he said. "I'm a Wolfman. I am Captain of the Wolf Pack. Why should I want to help you defeat Almaric and put my clan in chains? If you need a champion, find Roland and ask him. I am not interested."

150 | SUSANNE L. LAMBDIN

For a moment, they gazed deeply into one another's eyes. She didn't trust Wolfgar though she felt they had formed a bond. She also didn't trust the bright sun coming in from the window, the quiet in the room, or the food on the table. Everything about Duvalen was deceptive, and she feared her emotions were swayed by the magic that hid within the castle.

"I'm going to confide in you. We must talk softly so we are not overheard. There are spies everywhere in this dreadful place," she said. "Navenna wants me to lead the Raven Clan to its former greatness. Mira wants me to restore magic to the realm. They compete against Ragnal for supremacy of this world. I am inclined to do the goddesses' bidding and put down this wolf rebellion."

"You are serious. I have been the sworn enemy of the Raven Clan for three hundred years, and you want me to be your champion? I must admit I am surprised to hear you say this," he said, refilling his glass. "It's not easy for me to change allegiance overnight. I have orders to take you to Prince Almaric. Unless you give me a better reason, that's precisely what I'm going to do, Taliesin."

"There are four members of the Raven Clan besides me," Taliesin said, holding his gaze. "As the Raven Mistress, I am responsible for restoring my clan. You are a skilled warrior. Fight for me, as a Raven, and I'll give you a magical sword and make you a lord. You no longer need to fetch sticks for Chief Lykus for the rest of your life. Is that reason enough, or do you like your long leash? When Lykus pulls on it, you must obey. Unless you break free from it entirely, you will remain a slave, and nothing more. What I'm offering you is an opportunity to be a man with a will of your own. I thought freedom might appeal to your human side."

"Freedom," he echoed. "I'm an old wolf, Taliesin, and old habits die hard. Why would you trust me? Did we share more than a pillow last night?"

Taliesin shrugged, not feeling it necessary to answer, and moved the trays of food to the end of the table. She removed the Deceiver's Map from the pouch on her belt and smoothed it out on the table. She wanted it to be leather, and so it was. A blueprint of the castle appeared to her eyes only. The lines changed, showing the armory and every weapon that lay within.

"What are you looking at? I see nothing," Wolfgar said.

"A map. There are forty magical items in the royal armory, and there are another six between here and the Maldavian border. I intend to rebuild my clan and give every new member a magical item. I'm going to rebuild Raven's Nest. I only need to figure out where to build it and how to hold it. Let the Draconus House fight amongst itself, I say."

Wolfgar took a sip of wine and set aside the goblet. "You have changed since we last met," he said. "There is a confidence in you that was not there before, and I can see you are determined to bring this plan into fruition. The use of *Ringerike* alone makes you a dangerous enemy. You will be unstoppable with more magical weapons in your arsenal but building a kingdom on a dream and a prayer is risky."

"We're all opportunists," Taliesin countered. "Don't think for a second I trust you, Wolfgar—I don't. I need your help, and I want the best."

"And since Sir Roland is out of the picture, I'm next in line." Wolfgar leaned back in his chair and chuckled softly. "Don't worry. I know you're not offering more than a sword in my hand, Taliesin. Hawk and Rook are good fighters, but two men are not enough to lead a rebellion. I had but your scent and Phelon's promise you were here to go on. I have been on the hunt for you a good, long time, yet it seems you have caught me."

"Take the Service Oath," she said.

"What then, Taliesin? Will you ask the Ghajar to join you then? They are gypsies and have no need of a mistress. They have Shan Octavio, though he might take you as his new mistress."

"By coming here, Wolfgar, we have started a chain of events that cannot be stopped. I intend to see how things play out, and then I'll take what I want."

Taliesin touched the map, and it turned into a silk scarf. She folded it neatly and placed it inside the pouch. A nudge from *Calaburn* brought a smile to her face, and she removed the sword from its scabbard and placed the weapon on the table. Wolfgar watched, confused, as she pushed the sword toward him. The sword didn't resist and seemed willing to be claimed by a darker soul. He gave her a confused look.

"If you take the oath, *Calaburn* is yours. It needs someone with a darker personality to be at its best, and I have *Ringerike*. I don't need a second sword. Take the oath and be my champion, Wolfgar. My clan accepts all who desire to live their own lives as free women and men. Be rid of your leash. Join me, and *Calaburn* is yours."

The blond man stared at her, not saying a word, and placed his hand upon *Calaburn*. The sword thumped the table, and a spurt of flame shot out the tip. She felt *Ringerike* thump her back, as it reassured her the decision was the right one. *Calaburn*, in turn, found Wolfgar acceptable. She still couldn't help thinking about Sertorius. *Calaburn* would have done wonders in Sertorius' hands, terrible wonders, and that was why she was determined no Draconus would have such a dangerous weapon. With Wolfgar, she thought, the sword would find a master who could control it without wanting to claim a kingdom. He was a man who wanted to follow a strong leader, and that was what she offered.

"I would still take orders from you. A new hand would hold my leash."

"It won't be like that because I won't tell you to fetch or whistle when I want you to come," Taliesin said. "The oath is simple: 'We come from nothing, we say nothing. We swear to protect the Raven Clan, brothers and sisters, eggs, nest, and tree. Family first or comes the grave.' Be sure about this, for it is binding."

Wolfgar nodded. He repeated the sacred oath, his face and tone stoic. When he finished, he gave a shudder. "Is that what you need to hear from me, Taliesin?" he asked. "They are just words."

"No, not just words. We're family now, and I will hold you to your oath. Master Osprey always gave new members a new name. Most were criminals or outcasts hiding from their past. I wish I'd known you when you were a boy. 'Wolfgar' fits you, but you're no longer in the Wolf Clan. Oh, well, I'll think of something."

Taliesin extended her hand, and Wolfgar's hand closed around it. A surge of magic flowed from her hand into his, and before her startled eyes, he turned from a thirty-year-old to a boy who looked no more than twelve. She gasped. Wolfgar jerked his hand back, caught his breath, and ran to a full-length mirror on the wall. With a boyish scream, he held his hands to his face, legs quivering, and turned to stare at her.

"What have you done to me? I'm...I'm a child!"

"Zarnoc warned me not to make any more. Maybe you can only make so many before they start to backfire," she said, trying not to panic. "How was I to know this would happen? All I meant was that I wanted to know you when you were a boy. I didn't actually want to turn you into one."

"Change me back at once!"

"Okay. I wish you were a man again," Taliesin said. Nothing happened and Wolfgar's mouth twisted. She rubbed her hands together and held them out before her, summoning every bit of her magic. "I said, 'I wish you were a man again!' I wish you were thirty years old. I wish I hadn't said anything before, because it's not working, you're still a boy, and I think you're actually crying."

The boy dropped to his knees, face in his hands. Wolfgar not only looked like a child, he thought like one too. She'd apparently wished for too much, too quickly, and it was just too horrible to contemplate. Kneeling beside Wolfgar, she pulled him into her arms and listened to his sobs.

"I'm so sorry, Wolfgar. I promise I'll figure out how to turn you back into a man," she said. "If I can't do it, I know Zarnoc can. Please don't cry."

"You think I am?" he said, with a sniff. "I'm not crying, it's just I can't very well be your champion when I'm not even old enough to shave. You're so mean, Taliesin. I thought I liked you. I thought I'd like being a Raven. Now I'm not big enough to carry a sword!"

Taliesin gave him a hard shake. The boy gazed up at her and blinked.

"Do you know who you are? Do you remember Wolfgar?"

"Yes. No. Who is Wolfgar?" He let out a loud groan and hung his head. "Why can't I remember anything? I'm a Raven, that I know, and I think we're in Duvalen visiting your relatives. Is there something else I should know? Why are you staring at me like that? Did I do something wrong? If someone blamed me for stealing anything, then they're lying because I haven't left this room since last night."

Pale green eyes met her own, and Taliesin felt a pang of guilt for having wiped away Wolfgar's memory and turning him into a child. It was a complete and utter disaster, and a clear sign she had not yet learned how to control her magic. The panic on Wolfgar's face continued to intensify until she noticed a vein throbbing in his forehead and feared it might rupture. Taking pity on the confused boy, which she had plenty to offer, she placed her hand on his shoulder. He was a boney lad and had yet to develop muscle.

"Maybe it's better this way," Taliesin said, offering a smile.

"I can't remember my name."

Wolfgar looked at her with a blank look on his face. It appeared he didn't remember being a member of the Wolf Clan, and if that was the case, she doubted he knew he was *Wolfen.* As long as the boy didn't lose control of his temper, and suddenly grow fangs and a tail, she could handle the situation without any trouble, or at least until Zarnoc turned him back into a man. She wiped the tears from his cheeks, pulled him to his feet, grateful that his clothes at least had shrunk to match his size.

"Well, we need to call you something," she said. "My last name is Mandrake. John Mandrake was my father. You are in the Raven Clan, and you're part of my family, so let's call you 'Drake.' A drake is a male duck. Yes, I think it suits you."

"I'm Drake. That sounds right. And you're my mother."

"That's taking it a bit too far," Taliesin said. "I'm the Raven Mistress, and you must do everything I tell you to do and always be good. There's a very nice wizard by the name of Zarnoc who I'll introduce you to. We're in his nephew's castle, and they are fairy-folk. I suppose leaving today is now out of the question."

"I'm hungry. When do we eat?"

Laughing, Taliesin led Drake to the table. She covered each dish, not wanting him to eat too much or he'd be stuck in Duvalen forever. An unhappy expression appeared on his face as he slid his finger along a dribble of gravy left on the table and stuck it in his mouth. Imaging chicken legs and fried potatoes, Taliesin pointed at a dirty plate and willed the food to appear. A tiny yellow chick and a new potato appeared on the plate, and the boy gave her a questioning look.

"They're not cooked," Drake said.

"A fact I'm well aware of," she muttered. A wave of her hand and the chick and potato vanished and left the boy with an empty plate. He sniffed at the covered dishes, and she had to slap his hand to keep him from the meat. "I hear footsteps. Someone is coming. Maybe you should hide."

The boy ducked under the table as the door handle jiggled and opened for Zarnoc. He entered the chamber accompanied by four guards. This morning, Zarnoc appeared as an old man with a long gray beard, dressed in bright red sorcerer's robes. He carried a long staff with a crystal ball attached to the end and acted as if he were on official business. The guards kept their spears at their sides and coldly regarded Taliesin until they noticed the boy under the table.

"Good morning," the wizard said, as he too noticed Drake. "You must be joking? I am gone for one hour, and I come back to find...," he paused, seeing the boy's lip quiver, "...to find you both ready for our outing. How serendipitous, for the king and queen are having brunch on the lawn, and we are to join them. Taliesin, may I have a word in private, please?"

Zarnoc walked out to the veranda. Taliesin grabbed *Calaburn* on her way out and had fastened the belt around her waist by the time she joined him. The wizard looked very displeased.

"I warned you not to make any more wishes," he said. "Look what you've done to Wolfgar—you've turned him into a boy! From the way he cowers, I suspect he has no memory of who he was, or that he's in hostile territory. Taliesin, this is your mess, and unless you figure out how to turn him back, he'll be young and stupid forever. He's still a Wolfman under that adorable mop of blond hair."

"He's fine," Taliesin said. "Look how happy he is."

Both turned to look at the boy. Drake waved from beneath the table.

"I should turn you into a playmate and leave you both here," Zarnoc grumbled. He reached into his robes to withdraw his long pipe, already lit and producing smoke, and placed it between his lips. "Queen Dehavilyn is having a royal picnic on the lawn and requests you both join her. Those four grim toadstools are to be our escort and make certain we arrive. I don't know what she'll have to say about...."

"Drake. My name is Drake," the former Wolfman said. He ran out onto the veranda, took one look at the wizard, and stood at attention.

"Named after a duck?" Zarnoc chuckled. "How fitting, because we'll all be sitting ducks if you don't come along right this minute. Now that you're a boy, we'll have to protect you every step of the way."

"Maybe it's for the best. The queen can't object to a boy, and Drake is now a member of the Raven Clan," Taliesin replied. "Don't look so displeased, Zarnoc. Drake is taking this far better than you are. Try to look on the bright side. I have learned my lesson. From now on, I promise, I won't make any more wishes."

* * * * *

Chapter Nine

Springtime was in full bloom within the walls of Duvalen, while it snowed outside the city walls, the howling wind kept at bay by an invisible magic dome. Throughout the garden, spread across the ground like a rainbow, were a wide range of wildflowers and roses. Honeybees buzzed, and butterflies glided, as they randomly visited a variety of brilliantly-colored flowers. Their busy behavior reminded Taliesin of fickle lovers, and she imagined Prince Korax hand-in-hand with a 'girl of the hour,' his eyes already set on the next conquest. She held onto the boy's hand and kept him from catching tiny elves seated on the backs of dragonflies, angrily shaking their spears as they sped past on a breeze.

The fairies sat upon blankets and pillows inside colorful pavilions with flower garlands hung along the tops, and they ate a lavish feast from the finest gold plates and goblets. All types of animals had joined the Lorians—a unicorn with flowers woven in his mane and tail, a lioness and her cubs, and an ostrich that stole pastries off a plate and swallowed them whole.

Zarnoc led them to a picnic blanket not far from the royal pavilion, whose majestic red and dark purple color drew the finest and richest fairies to join the king and queen. The four guards stood out of the way, their shadows reflected on the lawn, and kept their eyes on Taliesin and her two companions. The sound of a lute and a young man singing caught Taliesin's attention, and she turned to find Tamblyn, wearing a lavender tunic, performing for a seated audience. The polar bear lay on his back and swatted at butterflies that tried to land on his large belly. A young girl in a pink dress and ribbons, who held a small white rabbit, sat on their blanket. Zarnoc smiled as he set out the contents of the picnic basket. The rabbit jumped out of her arms and hopped to Zarnoc, who winked at Taliesin.

"Everyone has a pet here," he said. "Thalagar could join us if you like. He's eating oats and hay in Ursus' barn and said he's quite content."

"You mean that murderous polar bear is a pet?" Drake asked. A boyish pout appeared on his youthful face. Seeing the girl snickering at him, he picked up a chicken leg and hurled it at her head. She let out a scream and ran off crying, leaving the rabbit with Zarnoc.

"The bear's name is Ursus," Zarnoc said, giving the boy a disapproving look. "And he's the pet of Prince Tamblyn. You may not remember coming here, Drake, but had you injured the prince, you would learn firsthand why fairies are feared by humans. We're not all sunshine, moonbeams, and fairy dust."

"Let's just enjoy the picnic," Taliesin said.

The wizard scratched the rabbit behind its ears and grinned at Taliesin. He leaned down to whisper in the rabbit's ear as it snuggled against his leg.

"Now the old goat talks to rabbits," Drake grumbled.

"I talk to whoever will listen," Zarnoc stated, tapping the rabbit on its pink nose. "Try to do as I do, and all will be well. That means smile whenever possible and take little refreshments. The queen and king have yet to arrive, so I don't know what mood they'll be in."

Taliesin looked at the crowd. All the women wore lovely gowns and headdresses. There was not one female warrior in the midst of fairies. The men wore garments that were slightly effeminate, making it difficult to tell some apart from their female companions. The guards wore sparkling armor that looked like it was made from diamonds. The spears they carried appeared so thin she wondered if she could have snapped them into pieces with one hand.

Drake, in his black tunic, looked handsome. His fair skin and pale blond hair gave him a fairy-like quality. The others seemed suspicions of Taliesin as she placed her two swords beside her on the blanket, for they quickly looked away whenever she caught them staring. Only the pets showed no fear, and soon a fawn walked to their blanket and sat next to her.

"All I need is a bird to land on my head to make this complete," Drake said. He glanced up at the sky as if he feared he'd summoned one. He pushed the plate of food aside, stomach growling, and glared at the minstrels, apparently not fond of music.

"It's a pity you can't try the cupcakes," Zarnoc said. "The icing is sublime. I did warn you about fairy food. Curb that rumbling in your stomach, Captain Wolfgar...I mean Drake. You'll have to sustain yourself on the merry company and fine music. I could create a magical cupcake, only it has no protein, and you'll only be twice as hungry when the effect wears off."

"I want meat!" The fawn glanced at Drake in alarm. "I didn't mean you, little one," the boy said. "I meant a chicken or pheasant. Whoever heard of animals being able to understand humans? Anything I say is going to cause offense."

The fawn did not look any more at ease by this announcement and, along with the rabbit, scampered away to another blanket. Taliesin, Zarnoc, and Drake were left alone with a picnic they were not enjoying, and with a feast that could not be eaten.

"I give up on you," Zarnoc said with a heavy sigh. "Be glad you joined the Raven Clan this morning. When I informed the queen you joined, your fight was canceled, and the mountain troll sent home. I admit the troll was quite disappointed. He's fought *Wolfen* before and won." He chuckled at their surprised expressions. "Tamblyn is filling in the time slot instead. The poor boy lacks any musical talent whatsoever and frequently drops notes. His voice only turned last spring, so they say. When he was your age, Drake, he had the voice of a little angel. It's deepened considerably since he sprouted hairs on his chin and chest."

"He still can't sing," Drake said.

Taliesin laughed at his rudeness, for the boy showed the same lack of manners he had as an adult, yet she found him endearing. She much preferred Wolfgar in his current youthful state, and though Zarnoc awaited her to turn him back, the wizard was going to have to wait a long time. Across the heads of the audience, Taliesin spotted Tamblyn, who in turn saw her at the same time. His face lit up, and he looked genuinely pleased to see her. She smiled, thinking she had been in the company of more princes in the last few months than in a lifetime, and the only one of the lot who seemed remotely decent was the fairy.

Tamblyn walked toward her, strumming his lute while he sang in full voice, "*Behold the flame-haired rider, upon her black-winged horse, flying higher than the eagle she lighted on the spot. Attacked on all sides by werewolves, she slew them two by two, never losing her footing, she struck fast and true.*"

"Does he make up the words as he goes along?" Drake asked, cringing. At Zarnoc's nod, he looked horrified. "He's the worst bard I've ever heard. Not that I can remember hearing any before, but if I had, I would have certainly not listened."

"Mind your manners, you pipsqueak," Zarnoc snapped. "I forgot how much I dislike you. I like you even less than I like Phelon, and I don't even consider him likable." He tapped the boy on the nose. "If you're going to convince me you are worthy of the Raven Clan, you'll have to do more than belly ache and torment fawns. I expect great things out of you, Drake...or else."

"Don't threaten him," Taliesin said. "He's just a boy."

"A boy in sheep's clothing. You won't find him so nice when he remembers who he is, Taliesin. Remember, he is supposed to join his men in a few days, bringing you along as a prisoner. I am told more than half of the Knights of the Blue Star have joined Prince Almaric. The monk-knights devote most of their time in prayer and the rest training for combat; they are the fiercest warriors in the realm. Fortunately, Sir Gavin and his grandmaster will accompany the Duke Elric Galatyn to Padama. The duke carries his ancestral magical sword, *Flamberge*, which will do him little good since its powers are dormant. Have you ever been to Bavol? The city of Antilla has a grand bazaar where you can enjoy public baths, and the Crystal Mosque, where the knights live, is exceptionally beautiful. If Almaric has his way, he'll most likely burn the city to the ground in retaliation."

"I have never been there," Taliesin said. She heard her two swords softly humming, their strange, little way of communicating, and an image of *Flamberge* entered her mind. The sword burst into flames, similar to *Calaburn* in battle, only it lacked the same ferocity, and caused horrible nightmares. When magical swords were forged, a magic user always enchanted them. Some dark sorcerers had an odd sense of humor and included terrible side effects to be suffered by the sword's owner for the sheer fun of it.

"Duke Elric and Sir Gavin must battle their way through Scrydon to reach Maldavia, with the Wolf Clan hot on their trail," he said, as he nibbled on a chicken leg. "Renegade knights and mercenaries from Skarda have also joined Prince Almaric's army. Duke Fergus Vortigern of Scrydon is Almaric's strongest and richest ally, and he pays top dollar to anyone who will join them. Do you know the name of Duke Fergus' sword, girl?"

"*Trembler*," Taliesin stated with confidence. She reached over to ruffle Drake's blond hair. "Whenever the longsword is drawn, it makes men tremble in their boots."

Zarnoc tossed the bone into the basket. As soon as he caught Drake attempting to steal a chicken leg, the wizard slapped the boy's hand, who growled in response.

"Perhaps the queen will allow us to remain here longer," he said. "If not, we'll have to take this *boy* with us to the gypsy camp."

"Where are Shan Octavio and the Ghajar camping this winter?" Taliesin asked, feeling sorry when Drake wiped away a tear. He had to be famished. She pressed her hands together, arched the palms outwards, and created a green apple. Tossing it to the boy, she watched as he devoured it, knowing it contained no nutrients, and he'd be hungrier an hour later.

"In the dukedom of Thule, which has a far milder climate than these other northern dukedoms," Zarnoc said. "The Duke of Thule, young Andre Rigelus, is a King's Man. You found his father's sword, *Traeden,* on a battlefield long ago. I believe the Eagle Clan has that sword, which is a good thing, for they fight for King Frederick."

"Arundel and Lykus are evil men, Zarnoc. I would not be surprised if you told me they're the ones who convinced Prince Almaric to go to war against his father in the first place."

Zarnoc looked troubled. "Possibly, though I'm more inclined to believe the gods played a hand in this," he said. "Prince Almaric is far more cruel and cunning than his father, Taliesin. A prince who is willing to kill his own people, when all he had to do was wait for his father to die of natural causes, to inherit the Ebony Throne is not someone we want to rule. The Wolf Pack will not rest until they capture us, and I'm quite certain the Eagle Clan is just as eager to capture you."

Drake put his hands on his lapel and snapped it sharply. "I'm not afraid. I may be small, but I have the heart of a lion," he said. "I won't let anyone hurt Taliesin."

"That's right. Make yourself sound important, little mouse," Zarnoc grumbled, as he rolled his eyes. "It makes me feel so much better knowing we have a child to defend us against the Wolf Clan. Phelon will have him for lunch."

The last thing Taliesin wanted to do was talk about Phelon. Zarnoc might not like him, but he had helped her a great deal. Without his guidance and assistance, all manner of terrible things might have occurred after she left the dukedom of Garridan. No matter what Zarnoc thought of the Wolf Clan heir, Phelon had not taken her to Prince Almaric, nor had he taken her prisoner. He let her go. Phelon had also proven to be an amiable companion when needed.

Drake moved a bit closer to Taliesin and placed his hand over his head. "I swear to you, Taliesin, that as long as I live and breathe, I shall do my best to be a loyal Raven," he said. "I give you my word of honor, for that is all I have to give."

Taliesin looked upon Drake and silently wished he were a man again. It didn't work, as she'd suspected it wouldn't, and she caught Zarnoc glaring at her. More wishes were not going to turn Drake into his former self. Zarnoc had to be the one to turn him back, or he wouldn't last a day outside of the fairy city. The boy was so naive and trusting. As she put her hand on Drake's arm, she smiled as wide as possible, for at that precise moment King Boran led his queen into the garden, followed by a royal procession of fairies. Trumpets blared, and the crowd started to applaud with delight. Both she and Drake inclined their heads as the king and queen sat on flower-strewn thrones beneath the royal pavilion across the field. A number of guards, armed with silver spears too thin and light to be of much use, took position behind their thrones.

"I do not trust these fairy-folk," the boy whispered.

"Nor do I," Taliesin said, "but pretend you do."

"Try keeping your mouths shut," Zarnoc said, by way of a friendly suggestion. "And keep smiling no matter what. Smile until your faces hurt." He let out a chuckle when Drake put on a wolfish smile. "That's a bit better, though not by much."

The afternoon was spent in the sunshine. When dark clouds rolled in, the fairies took down their tents and headed toward the palace. A trumpet blared in the distance, and Taliesin watched in amazement as the fairy-folk ran for an arched doorway. The king and queen were in the lead and floating, instead of using their feet. Taliesin heard the trumpet let out another piercing blast. Zarnoc had her by the arm as soon as she belted on her swords. He tried to pull her after the others and found she resisted until Drake took her by the hand, as curious as she was to see what the ruckus was about.

"It seems we're under attack," the wizard said in excitement. "Oh, it's not the Wolf Pack. The Hellirin have arrived. I suggest we run. Shall we?"

Zarnoc turned to flee only to be knocked over by a dozen screaming children who ran by with a leopard, ostrich, and a giraffe on their heels. The unicorn, ridden by two young girls who were crying hysterically, galloped by, followed by a long line of butterflies and a stream of smaller woodland animals.

"By all the gods, I'll not run!" Taliesin shouted, jerking free from Drake to draw both swords. She glanced toward the palace. "Why aren't the Lorian soldiers coming out to protect their civilians? They are running inside with everyone else." She glanced at Zarnoc. "Let's climb the battlements and see this Hellirin army."

"I don't know why you want to bother," he replied. "The queen and king won't thank you for it. They never thank anyone for their help. Nor will they spare one soldier to fight the Hellirin. When no one rides out to meet them, they will leave. This is merely a show of force, nothing more."

"Hiding is not what I do, Zarnoc. You know that."

With a reluctant Zarnoc in tow, Taliesin and Drake climbed the steps to the battlements. There were no guards at their posts and no one to defend the castle. Across the field, mounted cavalry advanced through the snow, black and purple banners with the emblem of a white dragon snapping in the frigid breeze.

"I suggest you get off your backside and get these people into the palace," Taliesin ordered. "I will go down and hold them off, Zarnoc. Drake, stay with the wizard. You're too young to help."

"Oh, give him a sword and let him try," Zarnoc grumbled.

"Yes, I can fight," the boy said. "You can depend on me!"

"Maybe with a sword in your hand, you'll remember you're one of the greatest warriors in the realm," Taliesin said, hoping she was right.

Without pause, she handed *Calaburn* to Drake. The blond boy caught the blade and whirled it over his head. He neither changed in size nor remembered who he was, although he behaved in a manner suiting a warrior. The sword showed off its powers without being called upon to do so and displayed lines of flame along the edges. Drake lifted *Calaburn* high, and together he and Taliesin jumped off the wall, dropped to the snowdrifts below, and took defensive stances.

"Now for armor," Taliesin said. She rubbed her ring, and red scale mail covered her from head to toe. She pulled off a scale and placed it on the boy's arm. The single scale turned into a full coat of red dragon scale armor that mirrored her own.

"Be careful," Zarnoc shouted from the battlement.

Taliesin stood beside the armored boy. *Ringerike* glowed bright blue, humming angrily. *Calaburn* burned brightly and made crackling sounds, like burning logs in a fireplace, as Drake waved it over his head.

"Is this all it can do?" the boy asked.

"You'll find out," she said, grinning. "It's an exceptional sword." *Ringerike* jerked in her hand. "Of course, not as fine as you, for you are made for a queen."

Drake glanced at her, unsure if she was teasing or meant it. He had no time to inquire as black-armored riders, mounted upon a breed of horse that looked more dead than alive, charged at full tilt. The horses were coal black, emaciated, and had luminescent white eyes with no pupils as if they'd spent the majority of their lives underground. A helmeted warrior, carrying a long red lance with a gruesome three-pointed tip, rode the back of each. The thunderous approach of the cavalry, somewhat muffled by the snow, mixed with the blowing of a trumpet, sent a shiver of dread down Taliesin's spine, and had it not been for Drake's brave stance at her side, she might have headed after Zarnoc.

"What are those creatures they ride upon?" Drake asked. "They look dead."

"No matter what comes across that field, we stand our ground," Taliesin said. "We have powerful magical swords. They do not. I've been up against worse in my lifetime."

"I am not afraid," he said.

The riders charged the two red-scaled warriors, coming fast. When they reached the middle of the field, a barrage of arrows fired from the fairy palace swept up in an arc and spiraled down to hit its targets. Riders fell, and horses collapsed. More kept coming, row after row, heading straight toward Taliesin and her newest Raven Clan brother. A war cry started to rise from her throat as her excitement and fear escalated. She paused as something large appeared at the corner of her eye. Ursus the polar bear, ridden by Zarnoc, walked out a secret door in the wall and joined them. The wizard slid off the bear, which rose onto its hind legs and roared ferociously.

"You brought reinforcements," Taliesin said.

"I can hardly watch and do nothing," Zarnoc said with a wink. "I might as well put my powers to use and see how strong I have become while in your company."

The wizard lifted his staff, and a wall of flames appeared before the riders, cutting them off at the last second. Two foolhardy souls who charged through the flames were met by the polar bear, which tore them to shreds. Four mounted soldiers, weapons raised high, rode around the flame wall on the right and straight toward Taliesin and her companions. Taliesin bolted forward and met them head-on. *Ringerike* was agitated and let out a fierce humming as it sliced through the neck of the nearest horse. The beast fell to the snow, tossing its rider over its body, where it was met by Taliesin's sword. She knocked aside a wicked-looking blade, cleaved through black armor, stabbed into soft flesh, and watched transfixed as it melted like hot wax, hissing when it hit the snow.

Ursus charged a second rider, knocked the beast and dark elf to the ground, and fell upon them with a savage roar, while Drake charged the third rider. Before the boy reached the rider, a volley of arrows from the battlements pierced the Hellirin's body like a pincushion and dropped him from his horse onto the cold, hard ground.

"Not fair," Drake shouted.

Taliesin remained close to the polar bear, with Zarnoc and Drake behind her, as the strange, undead beasts leaped through the flame wall and charged. Ursus knocked riders from their saddles with his front paws and sent them flying through the air to be struck by Taliesin's sword before they hit the ground. The sword moved of its own accord, and she held on tight. *Ringerike* fought with a will of its own, jabbing here, stabbing there, making quick work of the enemy. Zarnoc used magic to lift riders from their horses and slam them into the wall, giving the boy nothing more to do than shout and point at the enemy coming around the flame wall.

"They're retreating," Drake cried out.

Taliesin stood with corpses at her feet, enormous sword dripping with blood, and watched the cavalry wheel and return to the far side of the field to prepare for another charge. Her gaze was drawn to the knee-deep gore that surrounded her. A stench of death seeped from the mangled black-armored bodies poking out of snow. Their blood was a dark green and reminded her of the color of pine trees, but a putrescent yellow sludge oozed from the emaciated horses.

"In the name of the gods, what are those things?" Taliesin lifted her visor as the firewall lowered, giving her a clear view of ten columns of foot soldiers in black.

"Heggen's creations," Zarnoc replied. He leaned on his staff, stuck a foot into the snow, and acted tuckered out. "The Hellirin guard the gates of the underworld. They live in a subterranean city called Nethalburg and seldom come above ground, which accounts for the weird eyes of their *darkling* horses. The Hellirin soldiers look no better, I assure you."

The boy applauded as another volley of arrows, these on fire, whizzed overhead and struck the lines of mounted troops across the field. Ursus paced in the snow.

"Then Heggen sent them to attack Duvalen?" Taliesin asked.

"Not exactly," the wizard said. "The Hellirin are the sworn enemies of the Lorians. They are the undead and loathed by every Lorian. It's their custom to attack every few months. Today they do seem a bit more aggressive."

"And Queen Dehavilyn allows this?" Taliesin asked. She was disgusted by what she viewed to be cowardice. "Is she afraid of the Hellirin? Who is their commander?"

"Duchess Dolabra," Zarnoc said, wincing as if speaking the name aloud caused him considerable pain. Taliesin followed his hand as he pointed across the field. "See the warrior in silver armor, wearing a helmet with a dark-red plume? That's Dolabra of the Hellirin, a queen in her own right."

"A woman commands the army of the undead?" Taliesin immediately felt like an idiot. Zarnoc glanced at her, amused. "It's just that I hadn't expected to encounter another female warrior. Unless the barbarians of Skarda train their women in swordplay, I assumed I was an exception. What is going on? Is this some type of game played by Dehavilyn and Dolabra?"

"In a way," Zarnoc replied. "A few volleys of arrows are nothing more than a slap in the face to the Hellirin. If Dehavilyn offered a true display of force, it could provoke Dolabra, and a siege is the last thing we want."

"Who is the warrior beside Duchess Dolabra?" Drake asked. He'd stuck the end of *Calaburn* into the snow to cool the flames. He pointed at a rider with a horned helmet, a long black cape, and a battle-ax.

"Ah, that would be General Folando, the Duchess' lover and consort," Zarnoc replied. "Despite his ill-mannered look, he does what she says, not the other way around. See the centaur on Dolabra's right? Don't ask me who he is, because I have no idea. Apparently, the centaurs have joined the Hellirin. I never saw that coming. Centaurs are normally good-tempered."

Trees shook, and limbs snapped as if something large made its way through the forest. Taliesin glanced at the walled castle. She no longer saw any reason to remain outside the wall if Dehavilyn wasn't interested in defending her own home.

"This fight isn't ours," she said, "and it's one we cannot win, magical swords or not. Let's go back inside and let the fairies and *darklings* play their little game."

Zarnoc lifted his staff, a sparkle of light shot from the end, and they vanished from the battlefield, safely reappearing behind the castle walls. Taliesin, the boy, the bear, and the wizard stood in the middle of a rose garden as a crowd ran toward them. The Lorians presented Ursus and Zarnoc with garlands of flowers, and the wizard let out a loud sneeze.

"I'm allergic to flowers," Zarnoc said with a sniff.

The piercing notes of battle horns, accompanied by pounding on large kettledrums, thundered outside the wall. With a shriek, the Lorians hid behind the benches and statues in the garden. Taliesin put her hand on Drake's shoulder and trampled roses underfoot as they accompanied the anxious polar bear back to the battlements. The sound of sneezing let her know Zarnoc had arrived, though not one fairy or soldier, other than Tamblyn, accompanied him. The prince stood beside Ursus and cradled his lute as the army advanced on the castle.

"Duchess Dolabra seems serious this time," Tamblyn said, worried. "My parents and Balboa could certainly chase them off if they wanted to. Our magic is superior to the Hellirin's magic, at least above the ground."

"Maybe the bard can kill them with a song," Drake said.

"Am I really that bad?" Tamblyn sounded insulted. "This is Eevhass, and if wanted to, I could put the entire Hellirin to sleep.

"Doubtful," Zarnoc replied. "Do you know how to play the lute, Drake?"

"No, but I can sing!"

"Then perhaps the two of you can give it a go," the wizard said, motioning at his great-nephew to play his lute. "At the very least, if it's as awful as I imagine it will be, the Hellirin may retreat."

* * * * *

Chapter Ten

Drake sang in a sweet soprano about a girl pining for her lover gone to war, while Tamblyn, following the boy's lead, strummed his magical lute. Their music steadied the nervous Lorian soldiers, two hundred strong and bows in hand, who gathered along the battlements and released another volley of flaming arrows. Enemy soldiers failed to raise their shields, and the arrows struck their chests, setting their tunics on fire before they fell to the snow. As the death toll continued and more soldiers in the ranks of the Hellirin dropped, Taliesin realized this recklessness was an act of defiance. Those not totally consumed in flame, after a moment shuddered, and then stood and removed the arrows, only to repeat the act countless times.

The horror of it chilled Taliesin despite the springtime weather within Duvalen, for the soldiers who dropped had once been Lorians, and through dark magic became *darklings* who defied death. Where the enemy stood in a landscape of snow splattered with green blood, the Hellirin army showed no sign of fear and remained in formation. Taliesin remembered another army of the undead; a battle in a desert fought between the guardians of the Snake God's temple and the Knights of the White Stag and the Eagle Clan and wondered if the same dark magic gave life to the soldiers in the snow.

A monstrous voice that shook the ground bellowed from the other side of the wall and silenced Drake, while Tamblyn continued to play, missing several chords as he trembled. An enormous giant with dark-green pimpled skin and wearing only a loincloth pushed through the enemy lines. He faced the wall as he swung a large spiked mace in the air.

"It's a troll!" the archers shouted.

Five more subterranean trolls of immense size, their pungent odor carried on the breeze, lumbered out of the trees and stood before the black-clad troops. Each held a leash attached to a white dragon, smaller than the trolls, with scales running the length of their backs, and long, thick tails that ended with sharpened spikes.

"*Darkling* dragons," a fairy soldier muttered. "No magic affects their evil kind."

"I've seen dragons before," Taliesin said, her anger rising.

Taliesin lifted *Ringerike*, which glowed bright blue, and shouted, "Fire!" Two hundred slender arrows flew into the air, mixing with the whirling snow, and arced across the field to strike the trolls and dragons. The arrowheads pierced the muscular trolls and sank into hard flesh but merely bounced off the scales of the dragons as they thrashed their tails and snarled, pulling at the leashes, eager to attack. The archers prepared another volley and paused as five cloaked figures in pointed hats joined them on the battlements.

"Ah, the queen's magicians have arrived," Zarnoc said, clearly amused. "The Lorian Magic Guild looks impressive. They aren't as powerful as Duchess Dolabra's sorcerers. Perhaps if I offer assistance, we might be able to eliminate the problem headed our way. Balboa means well. The queen limits what the guild can and cannot do, and a light show is not what we need."

Zarnoc pointed out the royal sorcerer, Balboa, wearing yellow from head to toe. A black mustache with curled tips drooped across his upper lip. The guild members were both male and female, and each looked frightened, with wands hanging at their sides. Taliesin again shouted at the archers and ordered them to fire. This time fewer arrows shot into the air. Disgusted, she turned toward Zarnoc.

"Nothing seems to kill the Hellirin. If Balboa is going to do something, he better do it before those trolls and dragons reach the castle," Taliesin said. "What are they waiting for? Is this what both sides do when they meet? Scare tactics only?"

With an annoyed hiss, Zarnoc walked toward the collection of magic users, pushing through the archers who randomly fired arrows at the enemy.

"Balboa has no idea what he's doing," Tamblyn said, still strumming his lute. "Most of the wizards and witches in Duvalen have little or no experience in real combat. After the Magic Wars, the guild suffered great losses. Zarnoc and Balboa are the only ones who returned home. My mother thinks your arrival has awoken a great evil in this land. She says death is attracted to you, Taliesin. Duchess Dolabra has not used trolls and dragons against us in ages."

Taliesin watched the trolls and dragons wade through the snow. When they reached the wall, the trolls used their clubs to batter the invisible magical barrier that surrounded the castle, while the dragons opened their snouts and breathed fire. Alarm spread among the Lorian soldiers, and their fear kept them from firing arrows despite Taliesin's insistence. Drake slid *Calaburn* beneath his belt, grabbed a bow, and shot arrows at the nearest troll. The Lorians refused to participate and watched Zarnoc and the Magic Guild as if convinced the guilds' magic was enough to drive away the monsters.

"The Hellirin aren't playing around. Your mother still isn't doing anything," Taliesin said. "Why doesn't she help Zarnoc and Balboa? I'd go back down, but if no one else is willing to risk their lives, I see no reason I should."

Lowering his bow, Drake nocked another arrow and pointed it at a troll as its ugly head appeared above the wall. He shot the troll in the eye, laughed loudly, and jumped about. His excitement spurred ten older fairies to shoot at the same troll with rapid fire. The troll fell from the wall with a roar and crashed to the ground.

Tamblyn looked at the boy. "Just who are you?"

"I'm Drake. I'm a Raven," he said. "I can shoot trolls all day. It's fun! I do think Taliesin is right, Prince Tamblyn. Your mother should help the guild. I'm sure with her help they could turn these green giants and dragons into snowflakes."

The prince brightened at the compliment. "My mother is very powerful," he said. "It's just that she's been afraid of Dolabra ever since they were children. You see, Dolabra is my father's younger sister, and she can be quite prickly at times."

"Wait! You mean Dolabra is your aunt?" Taliesin was shocked.

"She *was* my aunt. Now that she's undead, I don't like to call her that anymore. It's rather complicated," he said.

"Someone needs to put an end to this, Tamblyn. Duvalen and Nethalburg should be allies, especially now. If these two queens can't sort it out, then maybe it's time for new rulers."

Tamblyn looked horrified. "I'd be king," he said. "I'm not ready for this type of responsibility."

The magical barrier started to break. Chunks of the wall fell on the heads of the trolls, and black smoke from the dragons slipped through the cracks, filling the air with the foul stench of pumice and a cloud of ash. Tamblyn continued to play, quivering each time a club smacked against the force field and another chip fell to the ground. Drake gave Taliesin a worried look.

"Those dead things are going to get inside the castle," the boy said.

Taliesin grabbed a soldier by the arm. "Lorians, you must fight back! You must show these Hellirin you cannot be intimidated! Nock your arrows, men. Light them afire and take down these trolls! Do it while the barrier still holds!"

The whoosh of arrows fired in unison sent the slender missiles spiraling toward the five remaining trolls that clung to the walls. Taliesin continued to shout orders, and the archers obeyed, peppering the trolls with scores of arrows. One after another, the trolls dropped to the ground, while the dragons struggled to break their chains or used their hot breath to melt them. The Lorian archers cheered.

"The first round goes to us," Drake said.

"I wonder if they're after the weapons in the armory." Taliesin glanced at *Ringerike*. The sword trembled in her hand, confirming her suspicions. "Yes, that's exactly what the

Hellirin are after. If they can get their hands on those magical weapons, General Folando and the *darkling* army will be invincible."

An archer caught her eye. "The Hellirin have always wanted to tear down these walls and lay ruin to Duvalen. Since you have been here, Raven Mistress, the magical weapons have been causing a ruckus. Some of the weapons are evil, and they call to her, and she has answered."

"Well, fight back," Taliesin said. "Give them a taste of Lorian courage and honor!"

Three dragons went airborne and breathed hot flames at the archers. Two more slid out of their collars and started to climb the walls. The archers kept firing, wasting arrows, displaying their willingness to continue to fight. Zarnoc had lined up the magic guild and commenced firing ice missiles at the dragons. All five dragons flew into the air, screeching as they dodged the artilleries, flying upwards until they were out of reach. The army across the frozen field regrouped, and a trumpet blew a piercing note. The Hellirin soldiers started to smack their shields with their weapons, and the Lorian archers fell silent, quivering in fear.

"Tamblyn, what magical weapons do your parents keep here?" Taliesin asked, eyeing the golden lute in the prince's arms.

"Everything you can imagine, including a few of your father's swords."

"Mandrake?" Drake turned from the wall. It wasn't a boy Taliesin saw reflected in his eyes. She saw Wolfgar, and his conniving thoughts were plainly visible. "Ah, I am beginning to see more clearly. We Ravens take weapons from battlefields and sell them to the highest bidder."

Taliesin waved the boy silent. She imagined if Hawk had been with them, he would have been the first one to pick the lock on the door and helped himself to a few magical weapons. Now it seemed the Hellirin had the same idea.

"They've come for *Eevhass*," Tamblyn said. He held out the lute. "Duchess Dolabra was there the day I was presented with this lute. When played, and played well, it *can* put the enemy to sleep. I did it before as a joke when Dolabra came here to celebrate my mother's birthday. My aunt has never forgotten or forgiven me, though it happened eight years ago."

While the Hellirin army regrouped, Zarnoc and the magic guild stopped trying to shoot the dragons out of the sky and concentrated on repairing the damage to the force field around Duvalen. No sooner had they made repairs when another loud horn pierced the air with a mournful note that brought the enemy troops charging toward the castle. The archers on the wall lifted their bows, arrows nocked, and turned in unison to stare at Taliesin, waiting for her command to fire.

"Keep playing, Tamblyn," Taliesin said. "Close your eyes and play something beautiful." She glanced at the archer she had spoken with earlier. "Light your arrows and prepare to fire on my order."

As the archers lit their arrows, Tamblyn closed his eyes; beads of perspiration dotted his forehead as he played the lute. His voice shook, and he sang off key. The polar bear let out a piteous groan. Taliesin didn't have the heart to tell Tamblyn to play better. He tried hard, only he didn't seem able to play the right chords and was all thumbs. Drake tapped his foot on the ground and hummed a four-chord country tune Taliesin remembered from childhood. Tamblyn caught on and strummed the chords, following Drake as he hummed the refrain. The cries and shouts of the enemy drowned out his playing. At this rate, Taliesin thought, the prince was never going to be able to make the Hellirin fall asleep.

Taliesin lifted her sword high and swung it downward. "Fire," she shouted, watching the arrows sail through the snowy sky.

The bear lumbered to Taliesin as flame arrows struck the front lines of *darklings*. The enemy immediately responded by sending a return wave of black arrows soaring toward the barrier. Zarnoc and Balboa had done their job, the force field held, and the Hellirin arrows fell to the ground. The enemy advanced, creating a cloud of white from kicked up snow in their wake, and Taliesin spotted the lead trolls running with a battering ram. She ordered the archers to fire on the trolls. Despite direct hits and the number of arrows in their massive bodies, the trolls never lost their strides and slammed the battering ram against the force field with a thunderous smack. A shimmering spark of lights spread upwards and over the top of Duvalen as the entire invisible wall vibrated.

"Will the wall hold?" Taliesin asked.

"Perhaps," Ursus said. "The battle has never reached this point before, and they've been fighting for centuries."

"Why?"

"Duchess Dolabra fell in love with General Folando a long time ago, though it is forbidden for fairies to love *darklings.* King Boran was furious when he learned his sister had run off with Akyres Folando. Together, they killed the former Hellirin king, and she claimed the throne."

"How did Dolabra become a *darkling*? Did she take her own life?"

The bear nodded. "I do not know the exact details, only that Boran never forgave his sister for joining the Hellirin," he said. "During the Magic Wars, the Hellirin fought with the Lorians against King Magnus, and that is the last time they joined forces."

An excited cry from Drake caught Taliesin's attention, and she looked over the wall. The battering ram reeked of dark magic. It had made a dent in the invisible barrier. The next strike hit the wall with a deafening boom, and the archers started to panic as the barrier shattered. The Magic Guild waved their wands. The ram burst into flames and was dropped by the trolls, who trampled their own troops to avoid a fireball thrown by Zarnoc. A surge of men in black appeared with ladders, placed against the walls, and Hellirin soldiers started to climb to the battlements. Taliesin shouted at the Lorian archers, and they concentrated their efforts on the enemy soldiers.

"Hold the line!"

A female voice shouted above the din of battle. Taliesin spotted the Augur with the owl Umbria perched on her shoulder standing beside Zarnoc. A black helmet appeared at the wall. The Augur and Zarnoc lifted their fingers and blasted the soldier off the ladder. He flew across the battlefield and fell into the midst of his own troops. Balboa joined the pair, and together, the three magic users fought to keep the enemy from climbing over the walls. Drake angrily shook *Calaburn* in the air, eager to fight, and the sword burst into flames.

Taliesin felt *Ringerike* quiver in her grasp and turned to Tamblyn. "You're the only one who can stop this madness," she said. "The Raven Sword says you are the best bard in the world. Play, Tamblyn. Do it now."

"Uncle Korax's sword told you that?" Tamblyn asked, blushing at the compliment. "Do you think I am a talented bard, dear cousin?"

"Yes, I do," Taliesin said. She placed her hand on his shoulder. "Play your favorite song. Simply close your eyes and let the lute lull them to sleep."

The prince closed his eyes and strummed the lute. The music altered and turned into a beautiful melody. Three archers fell asleep at their posts on the wall. Drake lowered his sword, a hand held over his mouth, and yawned.

"Tamblyn, it's beautiful," Taliesin said. "Play louder! Let them hear you!"

The strains of the lute floated through holes in the barrier, and the trolls fell to the ground, followed by the dragons, and then the infantry. Enemy soldiers fell from the ladders and hit the ground. The front lines collapsed in the snow, and the Duchess and her general, stationed at the back of their army, turned their mounts toward the trees. Those among the Hellirin who slumbered were left behind as the rest of the army faded into the forest. Taliesin watched the holes in the barrier fill with a translucent shimmer and cut off Tamblyn's music, although he continued to play. The fairies along the battlements started to topple over. Drake dropped to the floor with *Calaburn*. The sword's flame faded, and it hummed softly, as did *Ringerike*, to the strains of the music. The big bear wheezed where it lay beside the sleeping Lorians. Zarnoc, the Augur, Balbo and the rest of the magic guild smiled, unaffected by the music of the lute, and started to applaud.

"It worked, Tamblyn," she said. "The enemy is withdrawing."

Tamblyn's violet eyes sparkled as he stilled his hand, and the lute fell silent. "I never made this many people fall asleep before," he said. "The rest of the Hellirin are retreating. You're the one who gave me the confidence I needed. Thank you."

"What song did you play? I don't recognize it."

"It's called *Cherished One*," Tamblyn said. He smiled at the magic guild as he blushed to his roots. "My grandmother used to play it for me when I was Drake's size to help me sleep at night. This was her lute, you see. All I had to do was think about her, and suddenly I wasn't afraid anymore, and the lute responded."

Taliesin smiled. "My father also used to sing me to sleep," she said. "He would hum as he worked at his forge. I've always loved music. Keep practicing, Tamblyn. I have no doubt you will soon be putting everyone to sleep."

Laughing at her own little joke, Taliesin sheathed *Ringerike* on her back. Filled with the sudden need to check on Thalagar, she left Drake with Tamblyn and stepped around the archers as they started to wake up. At a quick pace, she descended the stairs and found her way into the courtyard. She was uncertain where to find Ursus' barn until the smell of hay and manure carried to her on the breeze. She hurried along a lane strewn with tiny white shells, passed several gardens filled with pink and purple flowers, and arrived at a large building encircled by pillars. It was the most elegant stable she had ever seen.

She entered the barn and found a stable hand about the size and age of Drake grooming Thalagar. The black stallion stood outside his stall, while the other horses munched on hay and regarded her arrival with disinterest. Thalagar, however, whinnied upon seeing his mistress. He stomped the ground with his front hoof and sent the groom stumbling out of the way. The frightened groom glanced at Taliesin, picked up his brushes, and without saying a word, disappeared into the tack room.

"Hello, Thalagar," she said smiling.

Taliesin walked over to Thalagar, and she threw her arms around the stallion's neck. He nuzzled her with his soft, velvet nose, breathing in her scent while flipping his tail. It was quiet in the barn and far away from the soldiers and magic guild. For a moment, Taliesin considered climbing onto her horse and flying away from Duvalen. She didn't know when the fairy queen would allow her to leave, and she dearly wanted to rejoin Hawk, Rook, Wren, and Jaelle. A rustling sound at the entrance and a push from Thalagar's head made Taliesin turn around.

Queen Dehavilyn, dressed in a gold gown and a large white diamond crown set on her brow, stood behind her. Taliesin stepped away from her horse and gave a simple bow of her head.

"My son insists I thank you for your help," Dehavilyn said. "I saw what you and that wolf boy did. Oh, yes. I know you turned the *Wolfen* into a boy, though I can't imagine why. Did you think I'd overlook the fact he's an animal?"

"I didn't think it mattered, considering he helped fight the Hellirin when no one else would," Taliesin said in a stern voice. "Your soldiers are in serious need of training. If the Duchess returns, and I'm sure she will, she'll level this castle. Your son thinks she wants his lute. I think we both know it's not that simple. If Zarnoc, the Augur, and Balboa hadn't joined forces, the enemy would have made it inside, and many people would have died."

The queen bristled from head to toe. "How dare you speak to me as an equal!"

"I am as blue-blooded as you, Aunt Dehavilyn. Your problems with your sister-in-law are none of my business. Nor is fighting your battles. Since you've made it clear you don't want us here, we'll leave in the morning. I'm taking the boy and wizard with me."

Dehavilyn swept past her, avoiding a pile of dung. Taliesin noticed it turned into gold, along with the wheel barrel that held the contents of a cleaned stall. It was one way of getting rid of manure, but it was also a waste of magic. Manure could be used in the gardens, which is what they did at Raven's Nest. Taliesin doubted the Lorians dug in the soil and planted seeds. They probably relied on magic instead of a hard day's work.

"If you want to protect your people, then I'm volunteering to remove all temptation. Dolabra wants what you have in the royal armory," Taliesin said. "Tell me which weapons she and her general want, and I'll take them with me. Once temptation is removed, the Hellirin will surely stop bothering you."

"My sister-in-law has received a request from Prince Almaric to join him, and that's why she came here today," Dehavilyn said in a shrill voice. "Dolabra also knows you are here and wanted to see what you could do with *Ringerike*, which wasn't all that impressive." She smoothed the front of her gown. "It seems someone has told you far too much about us. I do not appreciate gossip about our family or about what we guard here. Nor do I care to thank you. We have managed for centuries without the help of humankind. I will not let you take one single weapon from Duvalen or steal the lute *Eevhass*. That's what you want, isn't it? You want to steal my son's lute! Well, I won't let you do it, Raven Mistress."

Taliesin eyed the queen. "Think what you will of me, but I warn you, Your Majesty, the Magic Realms must not be divided. If you want to keep all you have, then find a way to convince Duchess Dolabra and General Folando to sign a truce. I'm told King Korax had a truce with the Hellirin. It's your only hope of avoiding the war already at your gates. I helped

182 | SUSANNE L. LAMBDIN

you hold off the Wolf Pack with no thanks on your part, so I know you won't say it now. You're welcome all the same."

"Impertinence!"

"Obstinacy and stubbornness," Taliesin countered. "I am Korax's heir, after all. You are wrong about Zarnoc. He is loyal to you and his nephew. You're also wrong about Tamblyn. With a little confidence, he'll be the finest bard in the realm, and perhaps one day he'll make a worthy king. I don't want to take *Eevhass* from him. If Tamblyn wants to come with us, that's his choice. He already ran away from home once, so I suspect he's waiting for me to ask him to join us. Now, if you don't mind, I'd like to return my horse to his paddock and see he is fed well. It will be a long journey for us in the morning."

Taliesin untied the lead rope and opened the gate. The queen stood and glared at her as she led the horse into his stall. Taliesin eyed a nearby barrel of oats. She left the horse in the stall, grabbed an empty bucket, and filled it with oats mixed with maple syrup, making it sticky to the touch. Taliesin returned to the stall. As she walked past the queen, she noticed the woman's strange purple eyes drift to *Ringerike*, causing the sword to thump Taliesin's back in warning.

"You are far more dangerous than I realized," Dehavilyn said. "I do not think it would be wise to let you leave, Raven Mistress. Nor take my son and uncle with you."

"That's up to them," Taliesin said. "I am going to Shan Octavio's camp tomorrow, with or without your permission."

As Taliesin shut the gate and prepared to find her friends, at least fifty fairy guards, lined in four rows, appeared in the stable entrance. It was obvious from the expression on the queen's face that she expected Taliesin to put up a fight. *Ringerike* quivered, itching to taste blood. Tempting as it was, she wanted no quarrel with the Lorians. Prejudice and resentment already guided Dehavilyn's actions, and killing her guards would only make things worse.

"Was it worth it?" Taliesin asked.

"What do you mean?"

Taliesin felt her anger rise. "Turning on Korax and killing Tarquin's family," she said without fear of the consequence. The queen stared at her in shock. "I suppose you had your reasons, but I'm curious. Were you in love with Korax, or did you merely resent the fact he left Duvalen without you? You could have been *his* queen."

"The Augur was right about you," Dehavilyn said, her eyes narrowed to slits. "No one with magical abilities like you have should be allowed to roam free. Not in the Magic Realms and certainly not in the mortal world." She extended an elegant hand toward her small army. "Come willingly, Taliesin, or I shall order my guards to make it impossible for you to leave. You won't get far without your legs and arms. Now, give me the Raven Sword."

"I don't think so. It's mine."

Dehavilyn pointed a long finger at Taliesin. "I want *Ringerike*," she replied. "I am no fool. I know you will kill my guards if provoked. I expect this type of behavior from a *Wolfen* and you, Taliesin, are an animal, not royalty. It sickens me to think you are Korax's heir. You know nothing about what happened between us, and if I hear you ever mention his name again in my presence or suggest that I had anything to do with his death, I will personally take your life."

"I wouldn't try it," Taliesin snarled.

"Oh, guards! Bring the prisoners forward. If she refuses to surrender the Raven Sword, be sure to cut their throats."

The guards dragged Zarnoc and Drake forward and threw them on the ground, close to a large mound of steaming horse dung. Both were bound and gagged. A spear was offered to the queen. She spun it with great skill and pointed it at Drake's back.

"Give me *Ringerike* or I will kill the boy," Dehavilyn said. "I'm growing impatient, Taliesin. You should know I never intended to let you go. I want that sword to add to my collection. I already have the flame sword."

At a snap of her fingers, one of the guards brought *Calaburn* forward. The queen did not want to touch the blade and waved it away. Drake struggled with his captors, trying to break free. Angered at his behavior, a fairy guard stepped forward and struck the boy in the back of the head with the butt of his spear. The boy's eyes closed and every muscle in his body went lax. Zarnoc was struck next by a guard's heel. The wizard made no sound as he received several more hard kicks in the ribs Taliesin feared would cause serious internal damage.

"Fine," she said. "You win, Your Majesty."

Taliesin unbuckled her sword harness and offered *Ringerike* to the queen, despite the sword's angry protests. Its whines were ignored as Dehavilyn reached for the sword. She screamed the moment her fingers closed around the scabbard and jerked her hand away as if burned. The guards pointed their spears at Taliesin, but none attempted to take the sword from her. Drake and Zarnoc, along with *Calaburn*, were carried away. Taliesin had no other choice but to go with them.

"A wise decision, Raven Mistress," Dehavilyn said. She walked alongside Taliesin into the stable yard. "Perhaps I should thank you for surrendering, and for the winged horse. I fancy Thalagar and shall keep him as my own. As for the boy, once I remove your charm, I'll turn him into a wolf and put a leash on him."

"Just what do you expect me to do?" Taliesin asked.

"Sit in the dungeon until I decide what to do with you."

* * * * *

Chapter Eleven

Taliesin sat on a bench in a damp cell and watched rats play at her feet. A small barred window in the door provided light from torches lining the moldy walls outside. Fur sprouted on her ears and whiskers tickled her cheeks. She was too upset without *Ringerike* to control the urge to turn. Nor did the dragon blood ease her anger or the spread of fur across her arms and hands. A great deal of crying and moaning was heard in the two cells across from her. Zarnoc and Drake were prisoners as well, and the threat of their deaths was the only reason she'd let the guards take the sword from her.

She'd waited the past two hours for the temperamental Queen Dehavilyn to appear and pronounce what manner of death was in store for them. Only the queen did not come. No one came. She imagined all sorts of unpleasant outcomes.

"Zarnoc? Is that you crying?" Taliesin asked.

"It's the boy. I'm the one fussing. If you'd only learn how to control your temper, along with your magic, we'd already been on our way to the gypsy camp. I'd love some cooked mutton and dancing by the firelight and to smoke my pipe with my old friend. But no, you wanted to insult the old girl and spend the night in a cold, dank cell."

Drake sniffed. "I'm afraid. The queen said she is going to turn me into a wolf. I don't want to be a wolf. I like being a boy."

"Do you like having a tongue?" Zarnoc asked. "Then stop whimpering and let me think. I've been in this situation before, in this very cell. My initials are carved into this very wall. I don't think they've cleaned since then. The waste bucket certainly hasn't been emptied, and it's definitely not filled with gold."

At the approach of footsteps, Taliesin hurried to the little window and peered into the corridor, expecting a guard bringing something for the prisoners to eat. Much to her surprise Tamblyn appeared, dressed for travel in a long cloak, tall boots, and a backpack on his back. Tamblyn lifted a finger to his lips, held a single skeleton key into the light, and placed it into the lock of her door.

"Sorry I couldn't come sooner," the prince said in a soft voice. "Mother is upstairs talking with Duchess Dolabra and her consort, making some type of alliance. You are to be given to the Hellirin to do with as they wish, and knowing my aunt as I do, I assure you, they mean to kill you. Everyone else is attending the grand feast to celebrate the alliance."

"So, your mother decided to heed my advice, after all."

"Actually, the Augur insisted both sides sit down to talk," he continued. "As soon as I get this bloody door open and free Zarnoc and the boy, we're leaving. Ursus is waiting for us in the stable with Thalagar."

The lock jiggled and then clicked. Tamblyn pushed the door inwards, its creaks echoing through the corridor, and ducked inside before Taliesin could leave. She gave him a curious look, not wanting to remain one more second inside the cell.

"My mother has locked *Ringerike* and *Eevhass* in the royal armory. *Calaburn* is there, too, as well as a number of other weapons we should steal. I'll help you get in and out without being detected, but you must promise to let me join your clan."

"Agreed," she said. "You and Ursus can take the oath later. Now let's move it."

Taliesin followed Tamblyn into the corridor. He unlocked the two doors, releasing Zarnoc and Drake, both who looked a little worse for wear, and then handed her the skeleton key, which presumably also opened the armory and every door in the palace. Tamblyn passed out dark cloaks he carried inside the backpack. Zarnoc looked delighted as he snatched one out of the prince's hand, threw it over his shoulder, and vanished from sight. They each disappeared when the hoods were raised over their heads, though being invisible proved difficult for Taliesin, who kept bumping into bodies, and their footsteps echoed along the corridor.

"I suggest we keep quiet if we are to get to the armory unseen, unheard, and unhindered," Zarnoc said. He clapped his hands once, and the sound of their footsteps faded away.

The corridor led to a narrow staircase that went up four levels, each protected by guards. They reached the upper level, and a heavy wooden door was unlocked and pulled inward. Taliesin slammed into a small body, knew it was Drake, and kept close to him as they entered a large hallway with a high ceiling. This part of the castle she remembered and hurried forward, taking marble stairs to the second story where the Royal Armory was located. The plan seemed far too easy, and the cloaks worked perfectly, keeping them from being seen as they passed guards at their posts.

From the grand hall was heard the sounds of revelry, along with music, laughter, and the strong aroma of food and drink. As Taliesin walked by the open doors, she spotted *darklings* seated beside the fairies, and at the far end of the room, beneath long banners hung from the rafters, sat the fairy king and queen and their guests, Dolabra and Folando. Taliesin hurried past the hall, heart pounding and senses reeling from the amount of magic that oozed from a door at the end of the hallway. The magical energy grew with each step, and by the time she reached the doors to the armory, it was overpowering.

There were twenty guards posted outside the doors, and each looked alert and ready for action. Taliesin felt a ripple of magic, no more than a light breeze, rush by her shoulder, and the guards instantly froze, unseeing and unmoving. Zarnoc pulled his hood off and, now visible, waved Taliesin over. Since she was still cloaked, the key appeared to float in the air next to Zarnoc as she placed it into the lock, and a click from within verified the door was unlocked. Four shoulders pushed against the heavy doors and opened them wide enough for the would-be-thieves to slip inside the armory.

Taliesin threw off her cloak, as did each of her companions, and searched frantically for *Ringerike* in an enormous chamber covered from floor to ceiling with rows of weapons and magical objects; crystal globes, musical instruments, staffs, and things as ordinary as bouncing balls and dolls. A lithe body pushed by her as Tamblyn scurried across the room, going around tables laden with armor and objects, and winding his way through the menagerie until he reached a glass case which held the long-necked gold lute with twenty-five strings.

"*Eevhass,*" Tamblyn said with a loud sigh.

The prince tried to open the case and found it locked. Zarnoc was at his side at once and helped him open the case without breaking the glass, while Taliesin found *Ringerike* in its red scabbard lying on a chest. The prince sighed. He held the lute in his arms, cradling it like a child, while Zarnoc went about filling a sack with miscellaneous items.

Taliesin wrapped the red leather belts around her middle and shoulder to belt on *Ringerike* as Drake found *Calaburn* on a shelf in a new scabbard. He placed it around his narrow waist, fingers nimbly fastening the buckle. Instantly, every magical weapon in the chamber started to move in the racks and stands, each wanting to be touched by the *Sha'tar*. Taliesin obliged and walked around, touching anything and everything. To avoid a mutiny, she asked each to keep quiet and wait their turn, as she decided what to take with them. She handed Drake five silver Mandrake swords she recognized as the blades made for the five Caladonian princes. The boy eagerly placed them in a magical bag that never grew heavy and accommodated everything placed inside. She slung a carved longbow with a blue bowstring, a scimitar with an ivory hilt, and two army swords that appeared to be a package deal, for they shared the same sword belt and scabbard, over her shoulder. Finally, she chose two rapiers with fancy basket hilts that told her their names were *Fang* and *Sting*. Both blades quivered so much in their narrow black sheaths she thought they would burst out and start stabbing at her friends.

"Are you sure we're stealing the best?" Drake asked, with boyish excitement. "I'd so love an ax, Taliesin. Please, find me one. I'm sure I'll grow into it."

"Let's take a look at my Deceiver's Map, and keep your voice down," Taliesin said.

Glad the fairies hadn't realized what it was, she removed the map from the pouch on her belt and asked to see the names of the weapons stored in the chamber. Every weapon of value appeared on the map, the names shining in bright, gold letters. Tamblyn stood at the door and watched Zarnoc collect items. Drake stood next to Taliesin, bouncing on the balls of his feet, eager to hear the names of the weapons.

"There is a double-edged ax with a black handle wrapped in a gold string called *Lore*. We want that," she said. "There is a throwing ax, plain brown handle, looks like its rusted when not in use, called *Trueblood*, so find that, too."

"I saw such an ax over in the corner, and it's rusted," Drake replied.

"Then get it," she said. "And find *Lore*. No other axes are as powerful as those two. Tamblyn, find the *Spear of Rotan*. It has a green spearhead made from emeralds, and Zarnoc, leave those snuff boxes alone and grab every weapon that literally twitches or makes noises. They want to leave, and so they shall. None of you should have trouble recognizing magical weapons, Drake. Just have to pay attention to what you're do-ing. I wonder where *Graysteel* is."

Zarnoc shot her a stern look. "Of course, you'd ask about that sword," he said. "If we're going to take that one, then I'll manage it. Boran will be furious to find it's gone."

"Every weapon is acting weird," the boy said. "I grab a fist-ful of evil, and I'm a goner, for sure."

"Or you turn into a grown man with delusions of gran-deur. Wait. That *was* you. Just fetch that pair of axes, boy, and leave the evil to me." Taliesin met Zarnoc's golden eyes as he walked around a table with a lovely golden bow and handed it to her.

"Jaelle would like this," the wizard said. "I believe we have something for everyone in the clan, even Hawk. Those two rapiers will suit him quite nicely. I am certain Dehavilyn and Dolabra are aware we are here. We must hasten our steps. Take only the best, and we'll *poof* away." Zarnoc scratched his nose, sniffed, and with a wave of his hand, every weapon on the map at their location vanished, and reappeared inside the wizard's tote bag.

Taliesin stared in awe at the empty shelves and pegs on the walls.

"Worry not, my dear," Zarnoc said, "I noticed the claymore *Graysteel*, and it's in the bag. However, do pick up the black chess piece on the table right over there. That's right, the one that looks like a rook. Into your pocket."

She placed the chess piece into her pouch and caught Zarnoc kissing a tall, slender ivory harp on carved golden lips.

"Look what I found," Drake said. A bag, lighter than what filled it, was slung over his shoulder a sword dangling at his side, and he held a leather-bound book. "The pages are filled with sketches of magical weapons, many which Mandrake forged."

"May I?"

Drake handed Taliesin the book. She glanced at the name written inside. She knew at once that the blunt-edged letters belonged to her father's heavy hand. Each illustration was known to her, along with the stories attached to each forged blade.

"Thank you," she said.

"I do remember things, mistress," Drake said. "What it's like to lose a father, to be robbed of your home, and forced to survive on the road. How it feels when your nightmares turn into reality. Take me to the gypsies, please."

"Promise." Taliesin wheeled. "Zarnoc, if you're done kissing the harp, let's leave before we're attacked. Be quick, all of you. We have enough."

"Last item, this harp," the wizard said. His appearance had changed from an old man to a much younger version. His sorcerer's robe was replaced by pants, cuffed boots, and a long coat with signs of visible wear, patches at the elbows, and each button different in design, color, and size. His beard vanished and his hair changed from gray to blond. He held the harp in elegant, long-fingered hands, against his chest. "Made of dragon bone. Strings made from the hairs of a unicorn's tail. Everyone, this is Ismeina the White Witch, imprisoned in the harp by a jealous wife. The harp is not a weapon, but if the witch were released, she'd be of great assistance. And a fine teacher for you, Taliesin. Yes, Ismeina will be coming with us."

"Zarnoc, you have 20 seconds before the cock crows," a female voice said, coming from the harp. The voice was beautiful, and Taliesin imagined the witch must be as well if the wizard wanted to bring her with them. "We must be gone. Foolish. All of you. Quick now. Depart at once."

"I left you behind once. I will not do so again." The wizard placed the harp inside his bag and motioned his friends to the window he'd opened with a wave of his hand. A warm spring breeze carried the scent of lilacs, orchids, and roses. "You will find Ursus and Thalagar waiting below the window. Now hurry. It's time to leave."

Tossing his cloak to Taliesin, Zarnoc leaped out the window with the vigor of a teenager and turned into a large black raven. With three strokes of his wings, he soared into the moonlight and vanished from view. Drake pulled his hood over his face, and he with the bag of weapons disappeared. As he noisily climbed down a thick overgrowth of ivy that hung from the balcony to the ground, Tamblyn grabbed two more bags of items, slung his harp over his shoulder, flipped his hood over his yellow head, and slid out the window. Unlike the boy, his movements were barely noticeable, for he made little noise until he landed on the ground.

Taliesin counted to ten, to give her friends enough time to make headway in their descent and swung a leg over the windowsill as she heard the crow of a cock. The doors to the armory splintered and collapsed under three strokes from a small battering ram. Helmets were visible in the large hole as the guards attempted to enter the armory.

She jumped to the ground and landed lightly on her feet. Drake stood beside Thalagar, cloak tossed over the horse's rump, leaving only the horse's head and withers in view. At her nod, the boy scrambled into the saddle and moved far to the back to allow Taliesin to mount in front of him. His arms folded around her as Tamblyn rode Ursus out of the shadows.

"Run!" Tamblyn said, close to panic.

The bear bolted, moving so fast he appeared like a whirl of snow. Thalagar stroked the air, and his nine-foot-long raven wings lifted his body from the ground. In seconds, they were flying into the night sky and passing over the wall. She glanced over the side of her horse as a secret door in the wall opened, casting a yellow light onto the snow. The polar bear raced into the wonderland of white and headed south where she lost sight of them in the forest. She turned to look at the palace one last time and found it brightly lit. The battlements swarmed with armed guards, both Lorian and Hellirin, and a shower of arrows shot into the air. The arrows fell short as Taliesin pressed her heels to Thalagar's flanks, and they soared upwards, high above the trees where they were soon joined by a black raven.

"Nicely done," Zarnoc said, pleased with himself. "I assume Ursus and Tamblyn will wait for us at the border of Fregia. Ursus will have no problem getting past any Lorian and Hellirin patrols. Nor will Master Phelon and his Wolfmen cause a problem. Once Lorian polar bears are on the move, they can travel as fast as sound, and nothing on earth can stop them."

"We were lucky," Taliesin said. The hood had fallen from her face, and her hair blew wildly in the frigid breeze. She heard Zarnoc scoff, and he winged into the darkness.

"Is everything alright?" Drake asked.

"Of course," she said. "Zarnoc knows what he's doing." The moment the words were out of her mouth, she wondered why she felt the opposite.

* * * * *

Chapter Twelve

Dawn found Taliesin cruising across the sky on the winged black stallion, with the raven flying alongside, and the polar bear keeping pace below. Taliesin and Drake wore armor, as did Thalagar, and together they created a shadow that appeared like a giant dragon upon the snow-covered peaks of the Stavehorn Mountains. As soon as they entered Fregia, she searched for her little wolf pack among the forests and ice-hardened lakes, hoping they'd returned to Ysemay. The countryside was dotted with castles, most in ruins, but one magnificent fortress that belonged to the Order of the Knights of the White Stag caught her eyes. She wondered if Sir Roland Brisbane was in residence, and she felt tempted to pay a visit. Thalagar flew lower, and she searched the battlements for the tall, broad-shouldered knight. She saw no soldiers in any of the towers, nor standing guard at the walls. The castle looked deserted, and she assumed the White Stags had gone to the royal city of Padama to help defend King Frederick.

As they flew south toward Maldavia, the sun made its appearance on the eastern horizon. The wilderness turned to wide stretches of rolling hills flaked with clumps of trees, small wooded areas, and ravines. The air grew warmer, and the white carpet of snow vanished, replaced by dull brown grasslands kissed by frost, sleepy farming villages with cows grazing in their corrals beside rickety barns, and the occasional walled city and castle. When they finally arrived at Maldavia, with its glens, waterfalls, and fertile valleys, she spotted Padama, home of the Draconus kings, and wondered if Zarnoc had deliberately taken this route to the gypsy camp.

The walls wrapped around a large, overcrowded, and bustling city. Padama was a beautiful city, a magical place while she lived there with her father. In the center of the city lay Tantalon Castle, built on the ruins of Black Castle, a magnificent fortress with twenty towers and high walls. Soldiers inside the castle prepared for a major siege. Their armor glinted in the sunlight as they placed barricades behind massive doors and carried baskets of arrows and buckets of oil to the battlement. Though Prince Almaric's army was nowhere in sight, there was evidence in the fields beyond the city's walls of a recent battle. Freshly dug graves marred the landscape, sprinkled with a light layer of frost.

"Are we landing in Padama?" Drake asked, his face pressed to her shoulder.

"No. Just passing through," she said.

Maldavia might be the home of the Royal House of Draconus, but it was also controlled by Duke Peergynt, the king's cousin, who turned against the king to join Prince Almaric and the rebels, making the area a hotbed of battles between the king's men and rebel Maldavian troops. Wolf's Den in Scrydon was where Prince Almaric gathered his mercenary army. She suspected Wolf Clan patrols watched the gypsies. Shan Octavio was not involved in the war, though it didn't mean the war would not find the Ghajar, no matter where they moved their caravans.

She felt a surge of excitement as she recognized Tannenberg Forest, a bed of thick green one hundred miles wide, on the horizon. The familiar smell of the forest set her heart yearning to see Raven's Nest once more, though she knew the Wolf Clan had left nothing after they set it afire. The old ancient oak tree, referred to as *Mother* by the Raven Clan, had provided shelter at its base, within its trunk, and on its uppermost limbs. For more than one thousand years, from sapling to an adult tree, *Mother* had witnesses countless wars and remained the tallest tree in the forest.

She pressed her heels to Thalagar's flanks, signaling him to fly lower, and spotted the black raven fly past *Mother*, headed toward Miller's Wood. The horse obeyed, dipping and drifting down gracefully until they were skimming the treetops. She knew this forest, every tree, hollow, beehive, and cave. She'd lived there most of her life, and though she'd spent the later years wanting to be elsewhere, it felt good to return home. Miller's Wood was located near Vendrik Castle, home of Duke Peergynt, which she had visited several times, and found it unlikely its owner was in residence if Zarnoc chose this location to land. A creek ran through the woods and created a soft gurgling noise that filled her ears as the horse dropped out of the sky and landed in the clearing.

With a shout of delight, Drake jumped off the winged horse. His armor vanished as he ran toward the polar bear as it appeared out of nowhere and collapsed beside a tree. Tamblyn, fatigued and saddle sore, slid off the bear, removed the bags of weapons, and sat on the ground. Ursus let out a whine and turned into a small cub so the prince could cradle him in his arms. The golden lute, nearly the length of his legs stretched out before him, lay beside Tamblyn. Drake plopped beside the princely bard and rested his head on his shoulder. All thoughts of exploration gave way to a necessity to sleep, though Taliesin knew it would not do to camp in the open.

"We're only a mile from Raven's Nest," Taliesin said. "I'd like to see it again. I could go there and be back in an hour. Do you mind?"

"Yes, I do mind. Make the rounds, girl, and make certain it is safe," Zarnoc said, fluttering to the ground. He changed his appearance from a raven to the old man. His long, gray robes looked wrinkled. He used his staff as a cane as he joined the group seated beneath a young oak tree. "We'll rest here tonight."

"Good, because I can't move another inch," Tamblyn groaned.

Taliesin slid out of the saddle and tapped Thalagar's neck. His armor vanished, returning to the tiny gold scale in the center of her forehead, and he walked toward the creek to drink his fill. Every muscle aching, Taliesin kissed her ring to remove her armor and stretched her arms over her head. Every tree in Miller's Wood looked familiar, like old friends greeting her home. Her biggest concern was the two sacks of weapons that lay at the base of the tree. Though each bag appeared empty, their contents hidden, she sensed the strong magic mixed of good and evil, of dark and light, seeping into the air.

"Go on about your business, girl," Zarnoc said.

Taliesin took a stroll around the area to make certain it was safe. When she returned, she found her friends exactly where she had left them. Drake lay with Ursus pulled against his stomach, and both were sound asleep. Zarnoc turned from a bush, straightened his robes, and gave Taliesin a nod as he walked over to the group.

"How many miles did we travel?" Tamblyn asked with a yawn.

"Too many, lad," Zarnoc said. "Earlier, I sent word to Shan Octavio to move his camp into the Gorge of Galamus. He's had enough time to do so. Look at your map, Taliesin. Make certain our friends are where they are supposed to be."

Taliesin walked over to the stream and sat on the grass before she removed the map from the pouch. Her scabbard pressed against the grass, making her have to sit straight unless she wanted to remove the harness, and she didn't until she was certain they were safe. The map turned from a silk scarf into a wooden board at her silent request. Taliesin located the Ghajar caravan at the bottom of the Gorge of Galamus, a clever move, for they were using the caves to hide their horses and wagons. The gorge was only a few hours away. It didn't look like the gypsies were coming to Miller's Wood that evening, for they remained stationary, presumably also making camp.

"Rook, Wren, and Jaelle are with the Shan," Taliesin said. "They're settling in for the night. I don't see Hawk on the map. Should I be worried?"

"You should always be worried when it comes to Hawk," the wizard said. He sat on a log and smoked his pipe. "Look

at the map again, girl. Make certain there are no hostile patrols in their area. I don't want to run into anyone from the
Eagle Clan or Wolf Clan. Nor do I care to encounter any of
Duke Peergynt's men, though he should be in Scrydon, which
is why I picked this place."

Small patrols from both clans appeared on the main roads,
along with Duke Peergynt and his soldiers. Castle Vendrik
was practically left empty, while Peergynt and his men used
the King's Road to reach Padama. Something else she noticed
was a large force from Erindor had joined the Eagle Clan, each
marked with the king's banner, which meant they had sided
with King Frederick. Eagle's Cliff was located in Erindor, and
the legions marched toward Maldavia. If the Eagle and Wolf
patrols ran into each other, they would fight to the death, also
a pleasant situation to find on the map. For now, she thought,
they were safe. She filled Zarnoc in on the details, put the map
away, and scanned the area with sharp eyes. She listened intently to the sounds around her. She heard a distant hoot of an
owl, and the constant swish of Thalagar's long black tail,
smacking the tall grass at the side of the river. He nibbled on
the grass and cast a look toward her.

"Your horse says Miller's Wood is as safe a place as any,"
Zarnoc said. "I know you are wondering why we didn't join
the gypsies tonight, my dear. I need time to rest and gather
my thoughts. As you know, Shan Octavio would insist on
drinking and talking until dawn. Why don't you use the chess
piece in your pouch, Taliesin, and make camp?"

Taliesin reached into her pouch and fished around until
she felt the chess piece, pulled it out, and held it the palm of
her hand. It appeared like any ordinary rook piece, made of
black granite, and it radiated magic. She didn't see how it was
possible to make camp with a game piece.

"What exactly does this do, Zarnoc?" she asked.

"You're holding one of three existing Travel Castles. When
you place it on the ground and clap your hands three times, it
will transform into a full-size tower made of stone. Inside we

will find provisions for your horse and us. The beauty of it is while we can see the tower, no one else can."

Taliesin turned the chess piece over in her hand. It felt cold at first but warmed the longer she held it and grew steadily hotter until she dropped it to the ground with a cry.

"Move, girl! Move!"

Zarnoc threw his entire weight at Taliesin and knocked her twenty feet from where she'd been standing. The horse, no more than ten feet away, jumped the stream, snorting angrily. Tamblyn, Ursus, and Drake awoke with a start as Taliesin sat on her buttocks and stared at a black tower. The narrow windows glowed from a fire lit within, and a large door facing her opened at her mere glance. Within was a round chamber filled with furnishings, including cushioned chairs and thick rugs that looked inviting and cozy. Tamblyn picked up the bear cub while Drake carried both bags of weapons, and they entered the tower.

"I thought you were smarter than that, girl."

Zarnoc walked over and held out his hand to pull Taliesin to her feet. When she was standing next to him, he let out a giggle of delight, lifted his robes as a woman would raise her skirts, and started to skip towards the tower.

"You seem pretty excited about all this," Taliesin called after him. She whistled at Thalagar and waited for the horse to respond. The stallion gave a shake of his head, tossing his glossy black mane, and trotted to her. She patted the horse on the neck and followed him into the tower, closing the door behind them.

"Home, sweet home," the wizard said.

Zarnoc sat on a large cushioned chair, smoking his pipe with his eyelids half-closed. The fireplace was lit with logs blazing. A large platter of biscuits, eggs, and fried bacon was set out on a table. A pitcher of milk occupied the center of the table, and coffee in an iron pot was warming over the fire. Thalagar walked to a stall filled with hay, entered, and immediately started to eat. Tamblyn sat in a chair before the fireplace and petted Ursus, while Drake lay on a small bed, one leg on, one leg off, and snored softly. Taliesin was left to examine the magical tower, which reminded her of Zarnoc's old home at the ruins of Pelekus. She walked over to a table where a washbasin and pitcher of clean water waited. She took her time to wash her hands and face before she sat at the table and filled a plate with food.

"How long has it been since you had a good, hot meal?" Zarnoc asked, puffing smoke rings into the air. "I could cook a meal exactly the same as what you are eating. While you were dillydallying outside, I made the beds upstairs. It only took a snap of my fingers."

"I'm beginning to wonder about you, Zarnoc. You said I had to clap my hands three times to make the Travel Castle work."

"Oh, that. Obviously, the tower wanted to show off to a *Sha'tar*," the wizard said, grinning. "Next time, I'm sure it will require three claps. Those are the rules."

"I was nearly crushed!"

Zarnoc sniffed. "I saved you, as I recall, and scratched my knees in the process. You might thank me for the meal. Try the milk. It's cow milk. The real thing."

"I don't see a cow in here," she mumbled. She took a sip, found it tasty and cold, and drank the entire glass. Eyeing the eggs, she attacked them with a fork, stuffing her face while making yummy sounds.

"Nor do you see chickens, yet you are eating scrambled eggs." The wizard let out a long sigh and closed his eyes, the pipe still between his teeth as he made tiny clouds of gray smoke pop out of the bowl like tiny bubbles. "Not that I'm telling you your business. You might check the map again to make sure we weren't spotted."

"I already looked at the map."

"Look again, Taliesin. Humor an old man."

Taliesin wiped the back of her hand across her mouth to wipe away the milk mustache from her upper lip. She pushed her plate aside, unfastened her sword harness, and placed *Ringerike* on the table. The sword was the length of the table and let out a soft hum. She gave it a pat before opening the pouch and pulled out the silk scarf which turned into a leather map. It opened on its own and spread out on the table. She grabbed a hot biscuit and took a bite before she checked the map. A Wolf Clan patrol was entering Miller's Wood. She tossed the biscuit onto a plate and licked her fingers.

"This isn't good," Taliesin said. "There are *Wolfen* nearby. Why am I not surprised to see it's Master Phelon? What is he doing here?" She heard the tower door open and close. "Zarnoc?" She glanced at his chair and saw he'd left behind his pipe. She rose and heard *Ringerike* give a loud thump against the table. "What is wrong?"

The sword thumped again, this time harder, clearly giving her a warning. The other magical items in the two bags on the table started moving, knocking over glasses and upsetting the spoon from a bowl of porridge already growing cold. They let out tiny sounds that *Ringerike* silenced with an unspoken command Taliesin heard in her mind. *Ringerike* was clearly in charge of the magical weapons, and they obeyed. She felt a surge of pride as she drew the sword from its scabbard and squinted as it erupted into a blue light that tickled the edges of the blade. She turned toward the door as it swung open and a dark shape appeared.

A tall bearded man in black armor with a long black fur cape stood in the entrance, flanked by two enormous wolves. Her heart leaped in her chest as she recognized Ragnal, the God of War. He looked exactly as he had in the ancient temple, only this time he radiated an intense malevolence that made her clutch the sword tighter. *Ringerike* jerked her arm upwards as a line of blue energy rippled down the length, for it felt threatened as well. She pointed the sword at the massive figure, her eyes flickering to Cano and Varg, who were unchained, as the trio entered the tower. The wolves went to Thalagar's stall, sat down, and licked their chops.

The door slammed shut behind Ragnal, and he smiled, flashing uneven teeth. Taliesin glanced at Tamblyn, holding the cub, and Drake, surprised to find them sleeping. She sensed Ragnal had placed a spell upon them, for when she turned to Thalagar, she found the horse frozen in place, unaware the wolves watched him.

"What do you want?" Taliesin asked, using a stern tone. Fear gnawed at her resolve to stand up to the god, and she knew he tried to use magic to make her lower her guard. "Tell your pets to back off, or I'll cut them down to size."

"Bold words for a mortal," the god replied. He snapped his fingers. Varg, and then Cano, trotted to their master and sat down. He patted Cano on the head. "I did not come here to fight you, Taliesin. Lower your sword."

There was no trust in Ragnal's dark eyes and no hope for escape. Her concern for her friends and horse kept her from running to the door. Taliesin gripped the hilt with both hands and moved back from the table to make room to fight if need be.

"I said before I will not help you."

"You will change your mind," Ragnal replied. He kept his eye on *Ringerike* as he walked to the fireplace and poked the toe of his boot into the flames, his back deliberately offered to her. "Zarnoc cannot help you if that is what you think. He is currently...indisposed." He glanced over his shoulder at her. "Phelon has been tracking you since you left Duvalen. I trust you did not have an unpleasant time in the company of the fairies and *darklings*?"

"Keeping tabs on me, are you?" Taliesin started to pant and realized she had sprouted whiskers. It was what the god wanted, she thought. He wanted her to turn *Wolfen* so he could control her. "The Hellirin won't fight for Prince Almaric. They signed a treaty with the Lorians."

Ragnal's black eyes held her gaze as he turned around. He seemed to grow taller as the fingers of his left hand tapped on the hilt of a wicked sword hanging from his side, nearly two feet longer than *Ringerike*. He wore gloves, and a large onyx ring glittered on his right index finger. Noticing her attention on the ring, he removed it and tossed it to her. She caught it in her left hand and turned it around to look closely. Within the stone, she saw the fairy city, the twinkling lights replaced by flames and a large Hellirin army, comprised of *darklings* of all sizes and shapes, encamped around the exterior wall.

"There is no treaty, girl," Ragnal said. He walked to the table, swung a muscular leg over the bench, and straddled it. "The Hellirin have taken Duvalen. It was foolish of you to steal *Eevhass*. Dolabra assumed Dehavilyn ordered you to do so, and the alliance lasted no more than an hour before she ordered her army to attack." His gloved hand reached across the table for the ring. She tossed it back to him. "Does this news upset you, Raven Mistress?"

"Of course, it does, but I'm inclined not to believe you. As far as I know, you could be lying, and that ring shows me only what you want me to believe."

Taliesin heard movement and swiftly turned as the two giant wolves walked to lie down in front of the fireplace. Ragnal helped himself to a biscuit. He took the time to butter it and slather it with honey from a jar. Only then did she decide to lower her sword and take a seat across from the God of War.

"The Hellirin are devious creatures that Heggen finds difficult, at best, to control," the god said. "It is your fault Duvalen has fallen. Dehavilyn should not have given you sanctuary in her city. Nor should Tamblyn have taken his lute and joined you here." He stared at the bags on the table. "You made off with a good haul, scavenger girl. Another mistake on your part, for you left Queen Dehavilyn defenseless. Without *Graysteel* and a few other prized weapons found missing in the armory, it was not difficult for the Hellirin to take control of Duvalen. The fairies have fled, or been captured, killed, and turned into *darklings*."

"So you say," Taliesin replied. "I have no reason to believe what you say. The Queen, the Augur, and Lorian Magic Guild are powerful magic users. And we didn't take all of the magic weapons, only the best."

Ragnal placed his hand on the table, palm down, and when he removed it, she stared in disgust at his gory, little trophies. Index and middle fingers, severed from a dozen hands, lay on the table. He picked up an index finger. "Do you see these, girl? The Lorian bowmen who fought beside you against the Hellirin will never pull another bowstring," he said, chuckling. "Is this proof enough that what I say is true?"

The image in her mind was horrific as she imagined *darklings* lining up the Lorians archers and hacking off their fingers. *Ringerike* seemed convinced the war god lied to her, for it knew from Korax about the rules of warfare in the Magic Realms, which were the same applied at Black Castle. Visiting royals left their armies outside the walls, and neither side would ever attack the other while discussing terms of a treaty or an alliance. Her sword didn't believe him, so she didn't. She watched as Ragnal tossed the fingers to the giant wolves. Their jaws snapped as they swallowed the fingers and licked their chops afterward.

"Why did you come here?" Taliesin asked. "You can't make me join sides with Prince Almaric. I don't care what you say happened in Duvalen. Nor do I think you caught Zarnoc by surprise. If you think you can come here and intimidate me into doing what you want, then you are trifling with the wrong warrior. My powers have grown since we last met, and I am able to control my wild side, which means you have no power over me, war god."

Ragnal's eyes narrowed as his lips peeled back from his lips in an ugly manner. She expected to see fangs any minute. The god put the ring onto his index finger and stood, and she rose with him. Her panting had stopped, and the whiskers on her face vanished. The two wolves moved closer to their master, watching her intently.

"The Wolf Pack will be at your door soon enough," the god said. "I thought you might need help when they arrive. Join me, and I will make certain you are treated like the princess you are and arrive safely at Almaric's camp. You will wed the prince, and perhaps lead his army in the attack against Padama. What say you? Do you want to command an army like Duchess Dolabra?"

"Wolves are already inside this tower," Taliesin said.

"I will also remove the Hellirin from Duvalen and restore the Lorian king and queen to their thrones. Think of it, Taliesin. The Magic Realms will be your allies. You will sit beside Almaric on the Ebony Throne, as King Korax and his queen once did long ago, and all I ask in return is your...obedience."

Taliesin held his gaze. "Mira would never let Heggen lay claim to Duvalen," she said. "The Goddess of Magic has always protected the Lorians, and I don't believe she would allow their city to fall. If you think I have any intention of obeying you, then you're barking up the wrong tree."

Ragnal puffed out his chest. "You dare oppose me, girl? I am a *god*," he roared. "No mortal has ever spoken to me as you have or refused to obey my command! Not only will you lower your sword, but you will also this instant turn into a wolf. When that is done, you will crawl over here and lick my boot! Do you hear? Obey, mortal, or you will suffer my wrath!"

Taliesin kissed her sapphire ring and stepped back as the red dragon armor appeared on her body. Through the slits in her visor, she caught sight of the giant wolves circling around her. Her sword raised, she placed her back to her sleeping friends.

"Some people can't take 'no' for an answer," she said. "There's the door. Make use of it!"

"Fearless and foolish," Ragnal rumbled. His hand dropped to the hilt of his sword. He started to draw the sword from the scabbard, taking his time at revealing the jagged edges along the curved blade as he stepped forward. "Very well, Raven Mistress. It is time that you met *Gurgala!*"

With a final jerk, Ragnal pulled his sword free and swung it over his head as he shouted a battle cry. The firelight gave the steel a dark brilliance, offset by a silver wolf skull on the pommel's end. It was long enough to require both hands to wield, and Ragnal brought it crashing down. He was surprised when *Ringerike* swung upwards and blocked the blow, and sparks flew as the swords crossed. Cano, a white blur, jumped toward Taliesin. A punch from Ragnal sent the wolf flying through the air to crash into the wall.

"She's mine, boys," Ragnal snarled. "Kill the others!"

The door burst open. A youthful Zarnoc, tall and lean, appeared, blocking the waning sunlight. He clapped, and Thalagar gave a shake of his head and threw out his back legs. His hooves caught Varg in the ribs and spun the wolf through the air. Ursus grew to full size, roared, and slammed into Cano. Taliesin set upon Ragnal with a flurry of sword cuts and thrusts and forced the god to step backward. The wizard lifted his hand, and sparkling lights appeared before Ragnal's face, momentarily blinding him. The god miscalculated his proximity to the bench behind him, tripped, and stumbled into the table. With a roar of rage, he broke the table with his fist and raised his sword high.

"You'll pay for this, Lorian wizard," Ragnal shouted, spittle flying from his lips. "You should not have returned!"

"My house, my rules," the wizard said.

Zarnoc pointed at Varg, scrambling to bring down Thalagar as the horse beat it with his wings, and produced a bolt of light. It streaked across the room and slammed into Varg in an explosion of flames. The wolf howled in pain, and a furry fireball ran out the door. Ursus and Cano continued to bite and claw at each other, drawing blood and breaking furniture as they rolled across the floor. Tamblyn and Drake, now wide-awake, cowered behind a chair.

"You should have waited for Phelon to arrive," Taliesin snarled as she swung her sword at the god. The tip of the blade slid across the front of his armor, leaving behind a deep slash, and his eyes widened in surprise.

"And you need to die, Raven Mistress!" Ragnal shouted.

His counter-attack was fast and brutal. *Gurgala* slashed downwards, and her body was too slow to respond. *Ringerike* leaped forward on its own and knocked the jagged sword aside. The blue blade slipped beneath the god's guard, and the tip pierced the black armor. Blood spurted from the wound as *Ringerike* jerked free. With a roar of fury, Ragnal swung his sword in a sideways arc. *Ringerike* again was there to protect Taliesin. With loud clangs, sparks both blue and gray shot from the two swords each time they clashed together, filling the tower with rumbling thunder.

Gurgala moved with great speed in the hand of Ragnal, and it left behind shadows that moved and twisted around the god, only visible when it flashed in the firelight. Wide and heavy, its edges were as gruesome as the teeth of a *Wolfen*. *Ringerike* was its match in every way, but where the god's sword covered him in darkness, Taliesin remained illuminated in bright blue light. *Ringerike,* in the Raven Mistress's hand, followed every block, slice, and lunge. When the tower was a blanket of black filled with swirls of bright blue, it found its mark.

Ragnal cried out as the sword pierced his armor, and the blue light faded as it slid between two ribs and sunk deep. Blood as red as any human's poured from the god's chest as *Ringerike* jerked free, and its blue light shined on Ragnal's stunned face as he staggered backward, dropped his weapon, and placed his hands over his breastplate. A red glow appeared between his fingers. With a coarse laugh, Ragnal removed his hands to reveal he was healed, while on the floor, *Gurgala* lost its dark glow, and lay still at his feet.

Cano, with a whimpering cry and blood covering his white fur, was thrown across the room by the giant polar bear. The wolf rose to his feet and held a front paw off the ground as he limped out the door to join Varg in filling Miller's Wood with a terrible chorus as they howled in rage.

"My wolves have retreated...never before have they done so, nor have I ever been wounded in battle..." Ragnal spoke as if he couldn't believe it himself. "You have drawn first blood, Raven Mistress, the blood of a god." Thick fingers ran across the two punctures that scarred his breastplate. "How is it a mortal is able to wound the God of War and pierce his armor? How can this be?"

"*Ringerike* is superior to *Gurgala*," she said, "and I'm lighter on my feet."

Tamblyn and Drake appeared beside Taliesin. The boy pointed *Calaburn* at the god, a slender flame hungrily glowing at its tip, while Tamblyn held the claymore *Graysteel* as though trained to fight. As the god staggered backward toward the door, Thalagar snorted, shook his head angrily, and trotted forward.

"I think it's time you left, Ragnal," the wizard said.

Zarnoc swept across the room and stood before the war god, shorter only by a few inches in his true Lorian form, though Ragnal carried an extra hundred pounds of solid muscle. Ragnal gave the wizard a hard look, held out his hand, and *Gurgala* lifted from the floor to float before the wizard. Shame appeared on the god's rugged face.

"Take it, Zarnoc," Ragnal said. "I do not want *Gurgala*, not anymore—it has failed me. There are other weapons at Mt. Helos, and I will find one to defeat *Ringerike*."

"The fault is not with the sword, Ragnal, but with its owner." Zarnoc grabbed *Gurgala* by the hilt and lowered the tip to the floor. "Perhaps this is a sign things are changing and in our favor."

"This isn't over, wizard," Ragnal growled.

The dark weapons in the two bags started to protest as the god turned to leave, demanding he choose one, though he ignored their calls. Taliesin assumed the god thought Zarnoc would soon turn them all into weapons for order and light, and she was relieved when the items fell silent at his rebuff. Ragnal's big frame blocked the waning sunlight as he joined his wolves, and the door slammed shut behind him.

"What a relief," Tamblyn said, lowering his father's sword.

In an instant, the furniture returned to its former, unbroken state, and the feast returned to the table, but it now included ham hocks, a roasted pig, loaves of freshly-baked bread, a bowl of berries, four pitchers of ale, and several bottles of red wine. Zarnoc explained he'd left the tower long enough to purchase food from a nearby inn, the real thing, and would provide the nutrition they needed. Without waiting for an invitation, Drake sat at the table and filled his plate, while

Tamblyn ran to Ursus, sank to his knees, and cradled the bear's head on his lap. The wizard attended to the polar bear's injuries. The bear let out a moan and turned into a cub. As a pint-sized patient, it was easier for Zarnoc to work his magic, and a grateful expression appeared on the prince's face.

"You're going to be fine, Ursus," Tamblyn said. "Isn't that right, Zarnoc?"

"Yes, yes. No serious damage. None at all."

Taliesin sheathed her sword and walked to the door. She opened it an inch, looked outside to make certain Ragnal had left and no *Wolfen* had arrived, and locked it as soon as she slammed it shut. Tamblyn picked up the cub, placed him on the bench, and fed Ursus slices of ham. Taliesin walked Thalagar back to his stall, while the wizard set out a basket of green apples, oats, and hay. She placed her hands on Thalagar's cheekbones and pressed her forehead to his, and the horse snorted.

"You were magnificent tonight, old boy," she said. "No big bad wolf is going to sink his fangs into you. Varg will think twice the next time he takes you on."

"Huff and puff," the wizard said. "All you have done is enrage a mad war god who will stop at nothing to seek his vengeance. Now sit down, girl, and eat your dinner before it grows cold. We have much to discuss."

* * * * *

Chapter Thirteen

The moon lay high in a dark, purple sky, and a mist grew over the creek in Miller's Wood. Taliesin stood with Zarnoc at the top of the tower, wood smoke on the breeze, gazing at the ancient oak tree in the distance. It was quiet, too quiet. Though the tree was miles away, she imagined a yellow lantern left in a window by Minerva, a tradition kept by the women at Raven's Nest, who had always left a light on in an upper window for the Black Wing guards and clan members from a battlefield returning with a large haul. The wagons had rolled through the gate, where more Black Wings stood on top of the wall. Every member of the clan would then gather in the courtyard to help unload the wagons. In her own room, on the second story of Raven's Nest, she had collected unique weapons and banners taken from the dead.

The memory of Raven's Nest lay thick in her mind like the fog. Built around and within the giant oak, it had been a wondrous place, with guard shacks, called 'nests,' and chambers for the women and children cut into the branches high above. Master Osprey had created the Ascender, a marvelous invention, to travel up and down the interior of the tree. A wooden cage attached with thick ropes that thread through an enormous pulley, raised or lowered with counter-weights controlled by a lever, provided transportation to and from the upper platforms. Stairs had curled around the massive trunk, a longer route to the top, though perhaps safer. At mid-way point, there was a section that could be raised, offering additional security at night.

The Wolf Clan had reduced the home of the Raven Clan to ashes in one night, though by a miracle, the giant tree had

211

survived. The map showed the Wolf Pack had returned, sniffing around the tree, though it wouldn't take long for them to follow their noses and arrive at Miller's Wood. Taliesin hoped Ragnal and his nasty pets had returned to Mt. Helos, and as she put away the Deceiver's Map, she caught Zarnoc thoughtfully staring at her. His appearance suddenly changed to that of an old man with a long gray beard in a starred cap and a long blue robe.

"It is strange Ragnal didn't notice the boy, nor sense he is *Wolfen*," Zarnoc said as he continued to smoke his pipe. "The boy seems content. He's made friends of Tamblyn and Ursus very quickly I might add. I don't think Drake remembers his life with the Wolf Clan. He remembers living on his father's farm in Scrydon, and that was more than two hundred years ago."

"Better not tell him how old he is," she said.

Wolves sang in the distance, a frightening chorus that grew louder as the moon continued to rise. The moon, large, full, and covered by a line of reddish-black clouds, gazed back at Taliesin with the face of the goddess Mira. The wizard noticed as well and waved his hand in the air, blocking Mira's eyes with the clouds.

"What we have to say to each other should be kept private," Zarnoc said. "I have no malice for Mira, for she is the kindest of the gods. Sadly, she is romantically involved with Ragnal. It doesn't mean she approves of the *Wolfen* curse, Taliesin. It just means she dotes on the war god. Even so, Mira has the power to break it, only no goddess or god would dare interfere with Ragnal's plans. It is for you to stop him, child. As I said before, I will help you."

"How?"

"For starters, I can restore Wolfgar to his former self," he said. "I rather like the boy. Unfortunately, we can't trust anyone from the Wolf Clan. Wolfgar is fond of you, Taliesin. It's not enough to make him loyal. Given a chance, he would sneak off and return with Phelon and the pack. I think it's best he stays a boy and forgets, don't you?"

"Why didn't you tell me this before? You said I had to do it. I think Drake should have a choice, Zarnoc, and be asked what he wants." Taliesin slid her fingers along the stones, feeling the rough ridges, and felt it radiate with magic. "If you can do that, Zarnoc, then why can't you break the curse and turn us human?"

He smiled. "Enough mistakes have been made by my family and me. It would be remiss of me not to include you in that family pool, for we have both made mistakes. No, I'd rather not tempt fate by helping you make another. Besides, it is forbidden to do so, Taliesin. Many magic users in the past tried using their potions and charms to break the curse. Nothing ever worked, and those who tried, each and every one died at the hands of Ragnal in some nasty manner."

Ringerike started to quiver in its scabbard on her back. With a hand raised to caress the hilt, she stroked it to calm the sword. "I won't ask you to do that, Zarnoc," she said. "I didn't turn when Ragnal ordered it. Bonaparte's blood has helped me control my wild side. How did Lykus become *Wolfen*? I've always wondered. What happened to him? He was a knight. Surely he wasn't always evil."

"Sir Lykus was a proud man, and loyal to Korax. He never told anyone he came upon Varg in the Tannenberg Forest," Zarnoc said. "Soon, I noticed he was invincible in battle, for no wound, no matter how serious, required healing. He was stronger, faster, and frequently disappeared during the night. I suspect Arundel used his magic to help maintain the illusion Lykus was still human. When Korax died, Lykus lost control and turned *Wolfen*. He killed dozens of Tarquin's men, and turned many more before Arundel convinced Lykus to flee into Scrydon. King Titus Draconus searched for him and those he had turned for months before he finally gave up. By then, Lykus had built Wolf's Den and turned innocent country folk into *Wolfen*. Had I been able to cure Lykus, I would have done so, for he was one of King Korax's best friends, and he was my friend, too. That man no longer exists. Over the centuries, his mind twisted, and his lust for blood and power grew stronger.

There can be no doubt Lykus will do whatever is necessary to see the Age of the Wolf comes to pass, for he is truly Ragnal's creature."

"Chief Lykus murdered my clan and fed upon the flesh of my people," Taliesin said, feeling no sympathy for the chief. "I may never have cared for my adoptive mother, but it doesn't mean I don't care Minerva is now his slave. So are Talon and Falcon, and they were such sweet boys." She ran a hand through her hair, sending the curls spilling across her shoulders in an untidy manner. "Maybe I'm wrong to feel compassion for Wolfgar. He wasn't present when it happened, so I can't blame him for what his chief and clan did. I think I can control the boy if he turns, Zarnoc, yet I still harbor hope a cure can be found. You brought Ismeina along for a reason. If she knows of a spell or potion that can cure me, then it's worth angering Ragnal."

"I did not bring Ismeina here for that purpose, child," Zarnoc said, a note of sorrow in his voice. "I brought her with us because I am responsible for her being turned into a harp. Marrying Azniya was not my choice, nor hers. Our fathers arranged the match. I'm afraid I'm too much like Korax. Matrimony never stopped us from enjoying the company of other women. Though my wife and I never consummated our marriage, she remained jealous and spiteful, traits most Lorians share. I am not without fault, Taliesin. Just as she imprisoned Ismeina in the harp, I imprisoned Ysemay in *Ringerike*. What a fool I was for allowing Korax to be killed in battle. It is a mistake I have regretted since the day it happened."

"It was a long time ago, Zarnoc. You're not the same man, either."

The wizard snorted. "Am I not? I am responsible for what happened to Korax, and to everyone at Black Castle, including Ysemay and Ismeina. I've not told you everything," he said, "for fear you'll think less of me. Mira found a way to punish me for abandoning the Raven King to his fate. Many of those magic trinkets I took from Duvalen contain the souls of the royal court from Black Castle, and most were my friends. If I release Ismeina, they all will want out. You saw how the queen and king regarded you with suspicion and blind hatred — they blame you for what is happening. Those whom Mira imprisoned inside the trinkets will blame me for what happened to them. It's better they all stay locked away, at least for now."

"They're Lorians, Zarnoc, and Ismeina was your lover," Taliesin said. "She still cares for you. She must. Ismeina warned us about the palace guards. She helped us escape from Duvalen. I think you should consider releasing her. Just her."

A strange look appeared on the wizard's face. "You know nothing, Taliesin," he snarled. "Leave it alone, lest things are made worse than they already are. I cannot release her! I dare not. Stop meddling, I beg you!"

Zarnoc turned on his heel and departed. Taliesin didn't blame the wizard for being angry, nor for hesitating before he acted on impulse and released Korax's royal court from the magical items. The wizard had centuries to dwell on his guilt, regret, and shame, which was part of the reason he'd chosen to live as a hermit at the ruins of Pelekus. His only friends were his cat, Ginger, and the Ghajar, who had come and gone from the ruins, trading goods for his magic. She knew Zarnoc had saved the life of Shan Octavio, who in turn had saved the wizard and her life in an attack led on the ruins by Captain Wolfgar, no less.

The wizard was the one who had set her feet on the path to her own destiny. He did care about what happened to the world, and she knew Zarnoc also cared for her. Sharing past mistakes wasn't easy for him. He usually told her only what he wanted her to know at that specific moment and many things remained unsaid. Taliesin knew he had his reasons for not wanting to release Ismeina, but she couldn't forget the witch also might know a cure for the *Wolfen* curse, and she wasn't about to let him forget it, either.

Returning to her friends, Taliesin found Tamblyn seated beside the roaring fire in a comfortable chair, boot toes point-

216 | SUSANNE L. LAMBDIN

ed toward the flames, and a sleeping bear cub on his lap. Drake sat on the floor beside the chair and polished *Calaburn* with a cloth. *Graysteel* lay in front of him and waited to be shined next by the mindful boy.

"I'm worried about Ursus," the prince said, keeping his voice low. "He was bitten many times by Cano. The wounds have healed, but not his soul. Ursus is a gentle soul, though many can't see it because, long ago, he was once a general."

"Ursus is no ordinary bear, my boy," Zarnoc said, coming back in. He sat at the table and poured a glass of wine. "His kind is immune to disease, much the same way Taliesin's dragon friend Bonaparte is, so do not worry. He has no disease, not of the mind and not of the soul. Ursus need not worry about a scarred soul or a wounded ego. You should be more concerned about Master Phelon and the Wolf Pack patrol not more than a few miles from here. Ragnal's two wolves made enough noise to arouse the attention of every *Wolfen* within a twenty-mile radius."

"Phelon is at Raven's Nest, for now," Taliesin said, sitting across from Zarnoc. "I have no doubt Ragnal will send him here when he thinks we've gone to bed. I for one intend to stay awake through the night."

Taliesin glanced at Drake, now polishing *Graysteel*. *Calaburn* lay on the table in its Lorian scabbard beside the golden harp, covered by a white cloth. Zarnoc's finger played at the edges of the cloth, though he did not uncover it or talk to the witch.

"I'm sure Ragnal is back at Mt. Helos, sulking," Zarnoc said, at last. "Don't worry about him. Ragnal is not with Phelon, or I'd know. That he came here was a rare event. Ragnal is not a god who enjoys the company of humans, infected or otherwise."

Taliesin spread the map on the table, and her thoughts drifted to Sir Roland. The Knights of the White Stag, with a large army, appeared on the map, on the road to Maldavia. She caught Zarnoc staring at her, wadded the map into a ball, and stuffed it into the pouch on her belt, where it turned into a scarf. Tamblyn placed the bear cub on the rug beside Drake, picked up his lute, and started to strum. His playing had improved, and Taliesin let out a yawn.

"Ragnal and Navenna appeared to me a few weeks ago. I was hunting with my little wolf pack near Ysemay's shack when Navenna found me and led me into an ancient temple in the forest. They said there is a prophecy about two mighty warriors and a *Sha'tar* that will battle for domination of the world. Only, I seem to be all three, and that's supposed to be impossible. Each expects me to lead one of the clans to greatness, but you know I'll only help the Raven Clan. If I didn't have to be *Wolfen* anymore, or a *Sha'tar*, it would make things easier."

Zarnoc puffed on his pipe. In his bright pink robe, fuzzy slippers, and nightcap, he looked far less intimidating than the young Lorian wizard who had fought a war god. In fact, Zarnoc looked quite comfortable in his dotage. *Gurgala*, covered as if it were a child, lay on a blanket at his feet and rested contentedly.

"I already know this, child. There is little that escapes my attention," he said. "You've been bestowed with three gifts simultaneously, though I'm not one to believe in prophecies, other than to say nothing is written in stone. I've always known the three clans would one day wage war and bring about the Age of the Wolf. Being blessed and cursed means you have found favor in the eyes of Stroud. It's fate, not a coincidence, Taliesin. One can imagine Ragnal's surprise to discover you are as powerful as any god in Mt. Helos."

"Are you going to release the witch from the harp, or not?" she asked.

"I already told you I'm not going to." Zarnoc's eyes twinkled as the harp let out a soft sigh. "There is something else you should know, Taliesin. The race of the gods is as old as the Lorians, and not without their share of family squabbles, which you now find yourself in the middle of. Navenna is naïve and more often than not, does what her mother Broa says to do. Mira is Ragnal's lover and wants to please him, and as

218 | SUSANNE L. LAMBDIN

you saw for yourself, he only enjoys bloodshed. The big lummox practically challenged you to go to Mt. Helos to steal their stash of weapons, or didn't you notice?"

"I don't need the weapons in Mt. Helos, and don't you dare mention it to Hawk when we see him in the morning. We have all we need here. Ragnal said the Hellirin attacked Duvalen. Is it true? Did Dolabra break the treaty with Dehavilyn and cut the fingers of the Lorian bowmen and turn everyone into *darklings*?"

"No," Zarnoc said. "Ragnal lied to you. It never happened. The treaty was signed, and the Hellirin returned to Nethalburg. Will Dolabra and Folando fight for Almaric? I cannot say at this time. They would have to be offered something they don't have to go to war, and Dolabra has everything she wants."

"What could persuade them to fight?" Taliesin picked her glass of wine off the floor and took a sip. She found magic wine had great taste, only it lacked potency.

"Oh, they've always had their eyes on Skarda. Talas Kull is the ruler of Skarda and has often fought skirmishes against the Hellirin. I am told Duke Fergus paid the Skardan ruler, quite handsomely in fact, to join the rebels. If Almaric wants to keep his army together, he'll have to think of something else to pay the Hellirin for their help."

Taliesin set aside the glass. "Ragnal left his sword here," she said. "Is there a weapon in Mt. Helos more powerful than *Ringerike*?"

"Yes and no," Zarnoc said.

"Fine. Be that way," she said. "You can at least tell me why Ragnal gave you *Gurgala*? He knows I'm collecting magical weapons. Now he's given us his sword. Why?"

"You won *Gurgala* in battle. I suppose he was trying to insult you by giving it to me when it clearly belongs to you. You're not looking at this the right way. It wasn't only *Ringerike* that bested *Gurgala*. *You* bested a god in combat. Had you been using a lesser sword, like *Calaburn* or *Trueblood* or *Graysteel*, you would have lost." Zarnoc let out a loud yawn.

"Have no doubt you are the true heir of the Raven Clan. However, the future is never certain, and even gods know fear. I believe Ragnal is afraid he may lose this war."

"I should write a song about the duel between the Raven Mistress and the War God," Tamblyn said. He added lyrics that told the story of Taliesin fighting Ragnal to his song. Not a bad attempt, thought Taliesin, and grinned when the bard fell silent in mid-sentence, caught on the name *Gurgala* and finding no suitable rhyme. He fell silent and played without singing.

"Where did *Gurgala* come from? Who made it?" Taliesin asked.

"The Lorians made the sword long ago," Zarnoc said, lifting the weapon in his arms and holding it like a child, still wrapped in the blanket. "In the war between the Lorians and the Maeceni, those you call the 'Gods of Mt. Helos,' he won the enchanted blade by killing my father. Ragnal habitually slices the throats of his enemies, hence the name he gave it. However that is not its true name. This is *Brightstar*, for in battle it lights the way like a beacon and summons all allies into the fray. It has the capability to allow its owner to appear and disappear at will and can take you to another location by simply thinking of it. The blade can cut through anything and heal its owner from any wound. Ragnal gave it to me because he must have something else at home he thinks is better."

"It's a fairy sword like *Ringerike*?" Taliesin asked. The wizard nodded. "You are from the Royal House of Vorenius. It's right you should have *Brightstar*, Zarnoc."

"Perhaps you should touch *Brightstar*, my dear. Cleanse it of Ragnal's foulness for me, won't you? And do the same with *Graysteel* and all the weapons in the bags. It is, after all, what a *Sha'tar* is supposed to do."

Going to Zarnoc, Taliesin knelt on one knee to examine the blade he held. *Ringerike* remained silent as she reached out to place her hand on *Brightstar*. Taliesin felt a strange sensation begin deep inside her stomach, causing her to feel slightly nauseated. She pressed her hand harder on the blade, willing

220 | SUSANNE L. LAMBDIN

it to release its evil until she felt the sword start to tremble. Zarnoc held fast to *Brightstar* and whispered a little incantation. Taliesin felt the sword shake and pulled her hand away. She stood with effort and returned to her seat, aware *Ringerike* was speaking to *Brightstar* in its strange language, reassuring it all was well and as it should be.

"It's your sword now, Zarnoc. *Brightstar* will serve only you. At least, I hope so. Some *Sha'tar* I turned out to be. I lack confidence and imagination, that's what Ysemay told me. I wonder what she's doing without me, and if my little wolf pack is all right. I named the alpha wolf Korax. It seemed rather fitting."

"Company is coming," Ursus said. The polar bear grew in size as he grinned at Taliesin. The sight of so many large fangs was a bit unsettling, and he'd eaten something red that remained lodged between his fangs. "Many riders, in fact."

"Is it the Wolf Pack?" Drake asked.

"The Ghajar have arrived," Zarnoc said, blowing smoke rings. "I see no reason for all of you to get so excited. We have plenty of wine to go around. And I could use the company of adults for a few hours. You children have worn me out."

A pounding on the door brought the group to their feet, with the exception of the wizard who was more concerned about blowing smoke rings. The door burst open, banging on its hinges, and Hawk, wearing tattered black pants and a bloodstained shirt, tumbled inside. His dark hair was damp from sweat, he was barefoot, and he was unarmed. He slammed the door shut and glanced around the room in alarm.

"They're right behind me! You can't let them kill me, Taliesin! It's not my fault!"

"Good to see you too, boy. Already in trouble, and it's been the span of one full moon since I left your company. What now? Did you sleep with one of the Shan's wives?" Zarnoc asked, with a yawn. "One should never sleep with a wife or husband of another. I speak from authority." He winced when the harp let out a minor chord. "And with respect."

MISTRESS OF MAGIC | 221

Hawk ran to Taliesin and grabbed her arms. Sharp nails scratched her arms, and her armor immediately appeared on her body, one scale at a time. He stared at her in surprise, unsure if he was more afraid of what lay outside the tower or of the armored woman before him. He started to speak, stared at the magical swords on the table, and his frown started to turn upwards until he caught himself and scowled.

"No matter what they say, it's not like I wanted to hurt anyone," Hawk said in a complete panic. "I simply couldn't stop myself from...from changing. This is your fault, Taliesin. You shouldn't have saved my life at Dunatar Castle. When your lips touched mine, I must have tasted your saliva. Heggen's Beard! It's happening again!"

"Great. We have another *Wolfen* in our midst," Zarnoc said in a droll tone.

Taliesin noticed the fur sprouting on the tips of Hawk's ears and his facial muscles twitching as he started to turn. It was obvious why the gypsies were chasing him, for the Ghajars' sworn enemy was the Wolf Clan. The gypsies hunted both *Wolfen* and werewolves, relying on silver weapons to get the job done.

"Calm down, Hawk," she said.

"Well, just don't stand there," Tamblyn cried. "Do something!"

Hawk turned *Wolfen*, stuck in the middle of transformation—neither man, nor wolf, but a hideous, terrifying thing to behold. Tamblyn reached for *Graysteel* and pointed it at the young man, shaking hard, while the bear raised on its hind legs, prepared to knock the creature out the door.

"Grand-uncle, aren't you going to help her? Kill the beast!"

"Keep still, boy," Zarnoc said in a stern voice. "Taliesin knows what to do. This is her clansman. She is not going to kill Hawk, but if you don't pipe down, she may have no other choice."

Unable to control his rage, Hawk took one look at Tamblyn, sniffed the air, and charged on his hind legs, snarling and snapping his jaws. She threw her arms around his midsection, arched her back, and lifted him off the ground. Voices raised in anger as axes hacked into the door. The arrival of the Ghajar only increased Hawk's agitation. He howled in fury and struggled to break free, while Taliesin squeezed hard. The wind rushed out of his lungs, and his snarls turned to whimpers. She kept hold of Hawk as she glanced at the door as the axes continued to chop and created a large hole.

"Watch out!" Zarnoc shouted.

A wicked silver bolt from a Ghajaran crossbow spiraled toward Hawk. Taliesin turned her body at the last second and took the hit. The bolt bounced off her armor and dropped to the ground, its tip smashed flat. Zarnoc lifted his staff as two more bolts whizzed through the hole in the door. He deflected each one and sent them upwards to stick into the wooden rafters and lowered his staff. Magical lights shot out of the end of the staff to create a shield.

"Octavio, is that you? It's Zarnoc! Stop shooting, I beg you!"

Taliesin heard a snarl from Hawk. Despite his size, she treated him like a child's toy and shook him until he cried in a man's voice. "You're going to break my spine!"

"Then calm down, you idiot! No one is going to hurt you," she said. "Turn back right this minute, Hawk."

It wasn't a spell, but it worked like one.

Hawk started to tremble in her arms. With a soft groan, his body morphed into a large black wolf. Taliesin tried to hold him. He was surprisingly stronger as a wolf, and matched with his determination to get free, he escaped her grip and fled across the room. The door burst open. Slivers of wood flew in every direction, and the angry voices outside echoed within the tower. Five gypsies charged through the remains of the door. Dressed in beaded vests and baggy pants, crossbows slung over their shoulders, they each held a section of a silver mesh net. Paying no attention to Zarnoc or Taliesin, they launched it toward Hawk. The wolf collapsed under the net, crying out as it burned where it touched his body, and commenced to wither in pain. Reacting in an instant, Taliesin drew *Ringerike* and cut the net from her friend. She placed her foot on Hawk's back and pressed down to keep him from moving. Her sword lifted and pointed at the tallest man in the group while the wolf hid behind her and whimpered.

"Shan Octavio has ordered us to capture this beast," the man said. "Stand aside, Raven Mistress, for we also have orders to subdue any who stands between us and our prey." His companions lifted their crossbows, already nocked and ready to fire.

"You'll do no such thing, Charon!" Zarnoc shouted. He held his arms wide, staff in his right hand. "Send for Shan Octavio, and we'll sort this out! This is my tower, I'll have you know, and you have ruined my door!"

"Apologies, Zarnoc. As the Shan's second-in-command, I must follow his orders. Move aside, and no one else need be hurt," Charon said in an unyielding tone.

The polar bear let out a roar that shook the rafters, his jaws opened wide, and spittle flying through the air. The gypsies crowded together, clearly frightened as they moved back toward the entrance.

"You best do what my grand-uncle says, or my bear will most certainly kill you for trespassing," Tamblyn said. He placed his sword on the table and swung the lute around, strumming a few chords, watching the gypsies' reactions. Charon glared at the fairy prince, while the others yawned and rubbed their eyes.

Movement at the door and a course laugh stiffened Taliesin's spine. She watched as Charon motioned at his men to stand aside as a sixth Ghajaran entered the tower. This man was shorter than his companions, and defiance shone in his eyes as he stood before Zarnoc and slowly removed a blue scarf worn around his face. Taliesin sucked in her breath as she recognized Nash, the Shan's youngest son, a handsome youth with blond curly hair and a cruel smile. Taliesin disliked Nash, and more than once had collided with him in the past. The youth carried a crossbow and glanced between the bear and wolf, undecided on which animal was the greatest threat.

"Did you not hear me, boy? Fetch your father," Zarnoc demanded.

"My father sent me to take care of this matter, wizard," Nash said, contempt in his voice. "We've been chasing this beast for three days. I was just about to give up when I saw it enter this tower. There are more *Wolfen* in the area, Zarnoc. Let us have Hawk, and you may return with us to my father's camp."

"What did Hawk do?" the wizard asked.

"Shortly after my sister and the three Ravens arrived at our camp, one of our patrols returned. They were attacked by Maldavia soldiers," Nash said. "Hawk helped carry an injured man to his wagon. There was a lot of blood, and no sooner had Hawk left the wagon when he started to turn into a werewolf. We tried to contain him, but he was too strong and injured a dozen people, including my father. You know as well as I do that once bitten by a werewolf, this beast must be killed to free the others of the curse." He glared at Taliesin. "Jaelle told us that the Raven Mistress is the one who infected Hawk. If you want to save Hawk, my father, and our people, Zarnoc, then Taliesin must die."

More Ghajaran, wearing scarves on their heads, beads, and colorful vests, and each carrying a bow nocked with a silver-tipped arrow, arrived to support Nash. The men pressed inside the tower, which grew in size to accommodate them. No women rode with the Ghajar, and they stared at Taliesin with hate and fear in their eyes.

"Neither Hawk nor Taliesin were bitten by the Night Breed. They are not werewolves, Nash. They are *Wolfen*," Zarnoc said. "If I can see Octavio, perhaps I can help him. Those infected will not turn—they never turn—unless they succumb to their wild side and taste human blood. A daily dose of apple wine will subdue that craving, so give it to your father and to your people. This is a priority, boy. You should go at once, while I see to the care of Taliesin and Hawk."

"We will do things my way, wizard," Nash said. "For too long, my father has risked our clan's safety by harboring you and now your Raven friends. Under Caladonia law, as well as our own, we have every right to string you up and burn you alive. If you want to avoid the flames, old man, move aside, or we will kill more than two wolves this night."

Taliesin knew nothing about the effects of apple wine. She assumed Zarnoc had made it up in order to get Nash to return to his father's camp in all haste. The stubborn youth did not intend to leave the tower, not until he exacted his revenge. She motioned for Ursus to stand down. Tamblyn and Drake had picked up their magic swords, and stood behind her, keeping Hawk from view. Zarnoc looked so furious, she thought steam would burst out of his ears and he'd used his staff to pound Nash into the ground. She gave Zarnoc no opportunity to do so and walked over to the young man.

"Jaelle knows I'm not one of the Night Breed," she said. "Your sister knows what happened. Killing us will not cure your people or your father. It doesn't work like that, Nash. I'm sorry about what happened, but you're not helping things. Return to your father and tell him we will figure out a cure. Zarnoc has a friend who may be able to help us."

Nash flashed his teeth as he pointed out the entrance where a wagon outfitted with a silver cage waited along with more mounted gypsies. They were a nervous lot, Taliesin thought, as they glanced in every direction as distant wolf howls rose and fell.

"Come with us willingly, Raven Mistress, and we'll spare Hawk," Nash ordered. "We will determine what manner of wolf you are, and deal with it according to our laws. If our healer says you are a werewolf, then you will be killed. If you are a *Wolfen*, you will agree not to turn and will remain our prisoner until Zarnoc arrives with a cure. If he fails to do so, then you must pay for what Hawk has done."

"Taliesin isn't going anywhere," Zarnoc said. He held up his hand, snapped his fingers, and *Brightstar* appeared in his grip. Armed with staff and sword, the old man seemed to grow in size until he challenged Charon as the tallest male in the tower. "I doubt Shan Octavio gave instruction to threaten my guests or me. At first light, we will come to the Gorge of Galamus and meet with the Shan. If you desire wolf blood this night, Master Phelon is at Raven's Nest, convinced Taliesin is hiding in a nest high in the limbs above. While they are occupied trying to find a way to the top of the tree, I suggest you go and kill them."

"Very well. You have until we return to find a cure, old man. Use your time wisely, for we will not return home empty-handed." Nash lifted his arm. "Come! We ride to Raven's Nest!" He turned on his heels and marched out the door, followed by the rest of the gypsies.

Zarnoc pointed his staff at the splinters of wood, and a wave of his staff repaired the door. "As good as new," he said. "Now, why don't you give Hawk a bowl of apple wine and brush his tail. Once he has calmed down, he can turn into a man and tell us what happened. Drake, your tongue is hanging out of your mouth. Tamblyn, pour wine for everyone, and I'll smoke my pipe and come up with a plan."

"You used magic to throw Phelon off our scent?" Taliesin asked.

"Something you could have done if you were able to make better use of your magic," the wizard said. "I'm sure Ysemay told you that you must focus and visualize what you want to happen or to recite a spell. Your lack of confidence in magic and a propensity to resolve your problems with a sword has led us here."

"She also told me if I could combine the two that I'd be more powerful than even the gods," Taliesin replied, feeling unjustly accused. "You're the one who should be training me, not that old witch. I suggest you release Ismeina and together figure out how to break the curse."

Taliesin turned to find Hawk where he crouched behind her. She sheathed her sword, her mind swirling with the strange events of a very long day, and sat in a chair, motioning the wolf to come to her. As she kissed her ring, the dragon scale armor and helmet vanished, and Hawk placed his head on her boot. Tamblyn brought a bowl of apple wine and placed it beside Hawk, wrinkling his nose, clearly not convinced Zarnoc spoke the truth about it being a soothing tonic for a *Wolfen*.

"It will be alright, boy," Taliesin said, scratching Hawk behind his ears. Drake sat on the floor beside Hawk, turning so he could lay with his back against the wolf, and stretched out his legs. Ursus remained a full-grown bear and lay by the repaired door, sniffing the floor as if to memorize the scent of the gypsies.

"What are we going to do?" Tamblyn asked. He poured wine for everyone, including the boy, before he sat at the table. He snapped his fingers and the fireplace sparked to life, and the prince offered a proud grin at Zarnoc. "I have not met any gypsies before. Nor has Ursus. I can say, with certainty, they are not friendly. Is it my imagination, or am I the only one Nash didn't threaten to kill?"

"Nash is a despicable little rodent," Hawk growled. "I hope Phelon eats him."

"Calm down," Zarnoc said. He grabbed a piece of meat off a plate and tossed it to the wolf, chuckling when he swallowed it in one bite. "Well, it seems I have no other choice. I must comply with your request, Taliesin. The White Witch will most certainly know how to de-fang you three *Wolfen*."

"Can I really turn into a wolf, if I want to?" Drake asked, turning to throw his arms around Hawk's neck. "I don't know why those gypsies wanted to kill Hawk. He hasn't tried to hurt us. If I hadn't seen him turn into that other thing, I wouldn't believe it possible, Uncle Zarnoc."

"Boy, I am not your uncle, and you'll kindly remember that in the future and address me as Master Zarnoc, Zarnoc the Great, or Your Grace."

Taliesin frowned. "He'll do nothing of the kind," she snapped. "Let's get to it, Zarnoc. I'm anxious to speak with Shan Octavio and resolve this matter. I don't know why Jaelle told her father I'm a werewolf. She knows the difference, and I'm insulted she'd lump me in with those mindless monsters."

"I am sorry," Hawk said in a broken, pitiful voice. He spoke clearly, though he was unable to turn back into a human. "Nash told the truth. The man I helped had been stabbed, and I must have gotten his blood into my mouth. I couldn't control what happened next, and now Wren and Rook are prisoners of the gypsies."

"Are they?" Zarnoc asked. "Boy, open the door. Put your feet to use."

Taliesin grinned and thought Zarnoc certainly liked secrets as much as he liked surprises. Drake scrambled to his feet, ran to the door, and removed the plank to open it to reveal Wren and Rook. Both carried backpacks and held the reins of their horses, looking confused as Zarnoc laughed. Wren had dyed her hair black and outlined her eyes with charcoal like the gypsy women. She ran to Taliesin and threw her arms around her middle, hugging her tight.

"I'm so glad to see you," Wren said, out of breath.

"Perfect timing," Taliesin replied, glancing at the wizard. Zarnoc had an annoying way of keeping secrets. "We'll take care of Hawk. Don't worry. Come and sit down." She led Wren to the bench and turned to Rook. "Please don't be angry with me, I didn't mean for Hawk to get infected or for anything bad to happen to you."

"We're not angry with you, Taliesin," Rook said. The young man from the Isles of Valen wore his hair in dreadlocks and the colorful garments of the Ghajar. He led both horses inside, while Drake closed the door, and placed them in the stall with Thalagar before tossing their bags onto the floor. "I can't say the same for Shan Octavio or the rest of his people. We decided it was time to leave, stole two horses, and spotted Nash on his way to Miller's Wood. We hid until he left and nearly couldn't find the tower since it's invisible on the outside. I doubt if any of us will be welcome back at the gypsy camp."

"Didn't Jaelle defend us?" Taliesin asked.

"Not really," Rook said as he shrugged his shoulders. "She didn't want to come with us, Taliesin, even though I told her she is still a Raven and the Service Oath, once taken, is a lifetime commitment."

"Don't blame Jaelle," Wren replied. "Her father was furious when he found out she took the oath. I think she was scared more than anything else, especially after Hawk bit the Shan. You should have told us you were cursed, brother. Shame on you."

"Is that shaggy beast Hawk?" Rook asked as he spotted the black wolf beside the fireplace. "Why didn't you turn into a wolf instead of a monster?"

"Yes, it's me," Hawk said, annoyed. "And I talk too, Rook...like you do."

Hawk rose and walked to Rook, his tail between his legs. He whined as he sat before the young man and let his friend scratch behind his ears. Wren immediately walked over, knelt beside Hawk, and wrapped her arms around her brother.

"You poor darling," Wren said. "Zarnoc, isn't there anything you can do for him and Taliesin? You are the most powerful wizard in the world. After you left us in Garridan, Taliesin, I hoped you'd find a cure. That is why you left us? Because you turned into a beast and nearly bit Jaelle?"

"Yes," Taliesin said. "I didn't mean to be gone for so long."

The wizard waved the group silent. "Let's be quick about introductions," he said. "The boy was Captain Wolfgar and is now Drake, a member of the Raven Clan. This handsome young man is my grandnephew, Prince Tamblyn, and his furry companion is Ursus." He removed the white cloth from the golden harp. "And this beautiful lady is Ismeina of Duvalen. I think it's time I released her from the harp, for if anyone can help us, it is the White Witch."

* * * * *

Chapter Fourteen

Zarnoc stared at the harp, annoyed nothing had happened after he'd recited a dozen spells to free the White Witch. He slumped on the bench, his face in his hands, and shook his head. "I have no idea why I can't release Ismeina," he said. "I thought after you touched every item in those bags, Taliesin, as well as the harp, that I'd get results. Apparently, my wife's spell is more powerful than I thought."

"It's not that," the harp replied. "The clouds have moved away from the moon, my love. Master Phelon has figured out you tricked him. He is on his way here with his Wolfmen. We need to leave before they reach us."

"Where should we go?" Taliesin asked. "We can't join the gypsies, not now." She rose from the table, creating a stir of panic on the faces of her friends as she drew her sword. "Just how does this Travel Castle work, Zarnoc? Can we leave people and items inside it? Or not?"

"Not in their human forms," Zarnoc replied. "And I'd rather not turn everyone into a spoon and leave them here. Gilhurst Abbey is nearby, and it's abandoned."

"It's a ten-mile ride straight south," Taliesin said. "We can fly there, Zarnoc, if you give each of the horses' wings, and the riders double up. Tamblyn, you take the boy on Ursus. Rook, you will take everyone to the abbey. I'll be right behind you. Zarnoc? Are you listening? Put wings on their horses, please."

The wizard had not heard a word. He tried another spell and cursed when the harp strings started twanging off-key. Rook and Wren were already on their feet, had gathered their gear, and headed to their horses. The polar bear and the wolf ran to the door, growling and wanting to go outside, while Tamblyn and Drake grabbed their cloaks, the bags of magical items, and prepared to leave with haste. Thalagar trotted to Taliesin and nudged her as she sheathed her sword and rapped her knuckles on the table to get the wizard's attention. Finally, the wizard looked up, clearly frustrated.

"Yes, yes, wings," Zarnoc said, as he stood.

The wizard turned to the horses and thumped his staff on the ground. Wings appeared on Rook's and Wren's horses. They laughed as they led the horses to the tower door and opened it. Already familiar with how to ride a horse with wings, Rook and Wren climbed into the saddles. Zarnoc held out his staff lengthwise and blocked Tamblyn who carried his lute over his shoulder, Drake, and Ursus from existing.

"Tamblyn, don't you dare leave without *Graysteel*," he said, placing his staff on the table. "It's your sword now, so don't leave it behind. Boy, you are responsible for *Calaburn*, so put it on and be quick about it. Take only what you need and leave everything else here. Go to the abbey. Yes, it will be safe there."

Zarnoc turned into a raven and flew out into the night, leaving his sword and staff inside. General panic stirred the group as things were forgotten and chairs knocked over as the polar bear, with Tamblyn and Drake on his back, charged out the door. Hawk, on all fours, dashed after them, joining Rook and Wren mounted on their horses. Taliesin glanced at the fireplace as it grew dark, and not one ember glowed hot. She kissed her ring so her armor would appear and tapped the small gold scale on Thalagar's forehead. His gold armor appeared and with a snort, he trotted out the door and waited for her. Satisfied everything in the tower was secure, she walked outside and clapped her hands three times. The tower shrank into the familiar chess piece, which she picked up and stuck in the pouch. She climbed onto Thalagar's bare back, and the horse galloped forward, wings beating to gain altitude, and then they were flying over Miller's Wood.

Taliesin doubted she'd be able to see Master Phelon and the Wolf Pack in the trees below. She could see flecks of white through the forest as the polar bear sped toward the abbey. Tucking low over Thalagar's neck, she urged him to fly faster, and soon sped past Rook and Wren, and then the black raven. She flew straight to the abbey, able to see it in a large clearing, and arrived before her friends. Thalagar landed gently on the ground and pranced as Taliesin drew her sword. No blue light shone from the blade, and it remained calm as she approached the open iron gate.

Gilhurst Abbey lay two miles south from the village of Sansurt, built five hundred years earlier by its benefactor, Sir Walter Gilhurst. The knight had given the abbey to an order of Stroudian monks who had taken their vows of silence seriously and quietly tended to their fields of potatoes. The monks had left the abbey 20 years ago under mysterious circumstances, never to return. The Raven Clan had used the abbey to hide goods they were unable to sell on the black market and had treated the abbey like a regular smuggler's inn. During the last year, they'd stopped storing goods there for fear the citizens of Sansurt were aware of their nefarious activities.

On the west end of the church was a tall bell tower, the bell intact; a gargoyle statue guarded every corner of the roof. A porch covered the main entrance, and the heavy wooden door was closed and chained shut. The chapter house ran along the east side, and storage buildings were in good condition. There was a cloister in its center, and a covered walkway bordered the inner garden, all of which Taliesin knew quite well from previous visits. Weeds grew along the wall, and the nearby woods provided a tangle of branches, thorns, and thick roots. It was called the "Wild Wood" for a reason, and no *Wolfen* would be able to get through, forcing anyone attacking to come across the field or along the road. The gate was the only access into the abbey. The wall stood high enough to protect the occupants from an attack by the Eagle Clan or Wolf Clan, and as long as guards were posted to raise an alarm, they wouldn't be caught by surprise. The stained-glass windows depicting the Gods of Mt. Helos were dark, and she noticed a few were broken as she rode back toward the entrance.

At the loud clamor of whinnies and shouts, Taliesin wheeled her horse around and saw Rook and Wren's horses land within the wall. They pointed at the gate as the polar bear arrived. Tamblyn and Drake hung onto the bear's back, laughing like kids, with Hawk trailing close behind. Taliesin didn't see the black raven wing its way across the wall, and assumed Zarnoc lingered to scour the Wild Wood, making certain they hadn't been followed. She rode back to the gate, sheathed her sword to dismount, and used brute force to push it shut.

"Any trouble getting here?" Taliesin asked as she rode back to her friends.

"None," Rook said, smiling wide. "I'd forgotten how much I love flying. When we escaped from Dunatar Castle, Zarnoc had us leave our horses back, minus their wings, so Sertorius couldn't make use of them. All he did was snap his fingers, and we vanished and reappeared at Shan Octavio's camp."

"It's not half as fun as flying," Wren said with a giggle.

Hawk ran to the door and sniffed the ground and iron chains. Drake jumped to the ground, and showing no fear of Hawk, also ran toward the door and sniffed the air. The boy might not remember anything about life as Wolfgar, but his animal instincts remained. Drake stood at attention at Rook's approach, clearly in awe of the man with his tattooed arms and strange, ragged locks. Tamblyn took Wren by the arm, doting on her, and remained under the porch beside the polar bear and warily glanced toward the Wild Wood over the wall. It was Tamblyn who showed concern when Taliesin didn't dismount.

"What's wrong, cousin? Is this not the place you wanted to take shelter in?"

"Yes, yes, of course. I thought I'd fly over the wall into the cloister and make certain the church isn't occupied. When you get the door open, take the horses into the church and secure the area. Don't explore until I join you. I won't be long."

"I've been here before," Hawk growled. "Stop worrying."

"I'll stop worrying when Zarnoc arrives," she replied.

Thalagar ran a short distance and jumped, beating the air with his wings, sailing over the old garden, and curled around to make a pass over the abbey. Taliesin peered at the cloister below and saw a statue of Stroud, the All-Father, covered with an abundant layer of moss and wildflowers. She saw no lights and no sign of activity. Thalagar, responding to a tap to his flanks, flew across the tiled rooftops and landed in the garden, coming to a running stop just short of the statue. Taliesin threw her right leg across the saddle and slid to the ground as the horse sidestepped to counter-balance her descent. She immediately drew her sword. A soft blue light burst from the tip of *Ringerike* and lit the cloister and the gardens, which at second glance, seemed to be well-tended and produced fruit and vegetables as well as a wide variety of fragrant flowers.

Someone was here, she thought. She'd been right to be cautious. The echoing roar of Ursus within the church certainly notified whoever was present they were inside, and she focused on the doors to the different parts of the abbey. Her *Wolfen* nose detected the slight odor of fresh bread, along with the discernable odor of humans, which lingered in the air and came from the east where the kitchen and dormitories were located in the same building. A door to the cloister opened, and she turned, expecting to see Rook or Tamblyn. Instead, she stared at a monk in a dark brown robe carrying a lantern. His potbelly jostled as he walked along the path toward her, and beside him walked a small, one-eyed dog with white fur that barked at Thalagar as it ran to nip at his heels.

"A ferocious beast," Taliesin said, smiling crookedly. She sheathed her blade and kissed her ring, and her armor and helmet vanished. With a tap to Thalagar's flank, his golden scales vanished, and the monk gasped aloud at the strange sight.

"My apologies, madam," the monk said. "Minsky has a mind of her own. She doesn't like horses. I can't say I've ever seen a flying horse. Are you lost, or here to light a candle at the altar for a deceased family member?"

"Neither. I'm Taliesin, the Raven Mistress, and my clan is with me. You must be a Stroudian monk, though no longer sworn to silence. None lived here when my clan used this place as a hideout. Why return now? Only a few families live in Sansurt, and the city of Bernlak has a new church, so no one comes here anymore."

"Some call me 'Father Jorge.' Once I did pray to Stroud, but no longer," he said, in a robust voice. "I now pray to whoever will listen, though I can't say any of the Mt. Helos gods listen to my prayers. If you have come for sanctuary, it is freely offered. Minksy, leave that horse alone, you little she-devil, or you're going to get trampled."

"Thalagar won't hurt her. You said others are here. Would they be Ravens, Father Jorge? I left home a few months ago, right after the Wolf Clan attacked Raven's Nest and forced my clan to go to Wolf's Den. Chief Lykus killed my clan in cold blood. If any escaped, this is where they could go since our home was burned to the ground."

"I'm well aware of the plight of your clan, Raven Mistress. Sad times are upon us all," he said. "Sad times, indeed."

The monk was more interested in his dog than in Taliesin and grabbed Minksy before Thalagar accidentally stepped on her. Father Jorge walked right up to Taliesin, acting almost too friendly for a hermit. His eyes were brown and warm, matching his smile, and she detected his body odor, which smelled like two-day-old bread. Pointing toward the open door, Father Jorge set Minsky on the ground, and she ran inside, barking loudly.

"Master Osprey was a friend of mine," Father Jorge said with a sigh. "It might surprise you to know I took the Raven service oath after my order left this place. I, too, lived at Raven's Nest. I do recognize you. You were a child when they called me 'Black Rooster,' on account of my hair." He motioned with his hands above his head. "It rather stood up on end and turned every which way, and over the years it fell out. I felt the calling to be a monk, so Osprey allowed me to leave to come here. I have been at the abbey ever since, and when my brothers left, I remained to take care of this garden."

"How many people are here with you?"

"Quite a few actually," he said. "Many villagers came here after Raven's Nest was destroyed, and several Black Wings are in residence. I'm sure they will be glad to see you, Taliesin. Bring your horse inside and meet my flock."

A door from the church opened and Rook, holding a silver Erindorian spear, stepped out. Everyone had been someone else before they joined the Raven Clan. Rook was born on the Isle of Valen, and his mother was a slave, and his father was Duke Dhul Fakar of Erindor. The duke was not a kind man, and Rook had fled from the palace and joined Hawk and Wren, and they had found their way to Raven's Nest. Rook and Wren planned to marry, for though it didn't show, she was pregnant, and Taliesin assumed the young man did not care to bring a child into the world out of wedlock. Whatever happened at the palace had deeply affected Rook. When he first arrived at Raven's Nest, he had never talked and pretended to be deaf, though he'd eventually put his past behind him. His deep voice now filled the cloister.

"We've secured the church, Raven Mistress. When you didn't return, I thought it best to come and find you. Is everything all right? Who is this man?"

"Some call him 'Father Jorge.' The Raven Clan knew him as 'Black Rooster,'" Taliesin said, vaguely remembering a man by that name.

Nicknames were used to protect those who joined the Raven Clan, criminals who ran from the law, people who had fled from unpleasant family situations, or those who simply wanted a fresh start. Most names were reused after people died and were preferably names of birds or ones that reflected personality quirks. Sir Roland had been called 'Grudge' for his surly temperament, and had he been present, the Black Wings would have greeted him warmly, for he'd been their captain. As for the man known as 'Black Rooster,' she recalled a big fellow who often brought barrels of ale to Raven's Nest. It was hard to recognize him without his hair. *Ringerike* believed he was who he said he was, so she didn't doubt his sincerity.

"I was about to introduce Taliesin to those who have come here for sanctuary," Father Jorge said. "I'll wake the men and bring them to you."

"Wake the women, too," Taliesin said, firmly. "And the children, if there are any, Father Jorge. The Wolf Pack is near-by. I also spotted Eagle legionnaires." She didn't add she'd spotted the Eagle Clan on the Deceiver's Map to avoid questions. "Everyone can return to their beds after we properly secure the church and post guards. Leave no one behind, including your dog."

With a nod, the monk entered the door behind him, while Taliesin took Thalagar's reins and followed Rook as he led her into the church. The interior was drafty. The wind flowed through the broken windows and stirred candles lit on a stone altar. The ceiling was forty feet above her, and the cedar beams were home to pigeons and owls. Bird droppings covered the pews and floor. Her friends were settling down to rest behind the altar, where Rook and Wren's horses were placed. Thalagar trotted to the horses and nibbled at a mound of fresh grass someone had brought inside. Drake, covered by a cloak, slept in a pew beside the wolf. Tamblyn lay on the next pew over, the lute cradled in his arms, and the bear cub was curled on a blanket on the floor.

"Do you trust the monk?" Rook whispered.

"Yes, but I'm worried about Zarnoc. He should be here by now. Wake Tamblyn and have him go to the top of the bell tower to watch for him."

Rook did as ordered and roused Tamblyn, who sat up and rubbed his eyes. The Lorian prince took his lute, leaving Ursus sleeping, and dragged his feet as he walked toward a side door that opened to a winding staircase into the tower. Wren, hearing voices in the cloister growing louder, hurried over and picked up Ursus. She wrapped the blanket around the bear and held him as if he were a child, keeping his white muzzle hidden. Led by Father Jorge, people of all ages entered the church; a collection of ruffians and thieves, country folk, three Black Wings wearing frayed dark green cloaks over their leather armor, orphans, and widows. Taliesin felt like it was a homecoming, for these were her class of people.

"Taliesin!"

The familiar voice was Hillary's, the Raven Master's former advisor and friend, who pushed his way through the crowd. The old man wore a clean tunic, and his thin, blond hair was combed over to one side of his head. Mrs. Caldwell, a heavyset woman with curly dark hair who had cooked for the Raven Clan as well as kept the old man warm at night, was at his side. Both were dear friends, and Taliesin was shocked to see they were still alive. She ran to them, laughing and crying at the same time, a reflection of her conflicted emotions, for too few had survived.

"Bless my soul. Here you are, flown back to us," Hillary said. "No longer a young chick, but grown into a strong, handsome woman. Master Osprey would have been so proud to see you now. I cannot believe my own eyes. Hug me, child, so I know you are flesh and bone."

"I am here, old friend," she said.

Taliesin threw her arms around Hillary and hugged the old scoundrel, hearing his sobs as Mrs. Caldwell's sturdy arms wrapped around the pair. Her massive breasts crushed against Taliesin's back, comforting her, and, for a moment, she remembered her childhood at Raven's Nest. To have those days back was a cherished fantasy. Now that Hillary and Mrs. Caldwell had returned to her, it was more than she'd ever dreamed possible.

"Our young chick has come home," Mrs. Caldwell sobbed.

A group of mostly new faces, with eyes full of hope and relief, gathered around Taliesin, eager to meet her. The three armored men shook Taliesin's hand and glanced over her shoulder at the pale girl and the tall, tattooed man.

"Look, it's little Wren and Rook," a Black Wing guard called out.

The guards hugged Wren and Rook. Mrs. Caldwell clucked her tongue against the roof of her mouth, gathered Wren into her arms, and smothered her head between her bountiful pillows. Laughing through his tears, Hillary took Rook by the arm and pressed his head to the young man's shoulder, shuddering hard from his emotions. Rook quietly embraced Hillary, moved by his show of affection, while Wren pushed the older woman back and gasped for breath. A smile hovered on her face as tears stained her cheeks.

At the sound of a low growl, Mrs. Caldwell pushed Wren behind her and shook her fist at the large brown wolf. One of the Black Wings drew his sword as the country folk cried out in alarm and gathered behind the rotund figure of Father Jorge. The screams and shouts grew louder as Ursus grew to full size, and his big body knocked over two pews as he rose to his feet.

"Do not be afraid! These are my friends. They will not harm you," Taliesin shouted.

"It is my brother," Wren said and threw her arms around Hawk. "Please don't hurt him! He means no harm!"

The other two Black Wings drew their weapons, the country folk wielded knives and blades, and Father Jorge brandished a spoon he pulled from the folds of his robe. Taliesin placed herself in front of Hawk and Ursus, and red-scaled armor appeared on her body, along with the dragon helm, which shadowed her face. *Ringerike* let out an audible hum, and an aura of blue light seeped from the scabbard. Voices quieted, along with Ursus' rumbling and Hawk's growls. A clamor from the stairwell brought Tamblyn bursting through the door and into the church.

"Zarnoc comes!" the Lorian prince shouted. "The Wolf Pack gives pursuit!"

"Everyone stay inside. I shall go out and greet them," Taliesin said, drawing *Ringerike*. "Rook, you're in charge of the defense of this church. Tamblyn, back to the tower and play your lute. Drake, go with him and keep an eye out for Zarnoc. Wren, go with Hawk and Ursus into the cloister to make certain none gain access through the back door. You other three Black Wings stay here and guard these people."

"What about weapons for the others?" Rook asked. He held his silver spear in both hands and eyed the women and children with concern.

Hillary took one look at the broadsword, knew at once what it was, and sank to his knees beside Mrs. Caldwell, who pressed a hand against her heart and let out a soft cry. "We need no weapons," he replied. "Not when Taliesin is armed with the Raven Sword and wears dragon armor and brings such powerful friends to fight for us."

"Barricade the door behind me!" Taliesin ordered.

The Black Wings opened the doors and gazed at the moon on the road and the riders coming fast as Taliesin mounted Thalagar and rode outside. A shield appeared on her arm made of the same scales that covered her body. The warhorse gave a snort as golden armor covered his body from head to rump as he passed under the roof of the porch and trotted toward the gate.

Forty Wolfmen, dressed in armor and riding lathered horses, rode toward the abbey, hard pressed to reach it as another group of mounted soldiers gave pursuit. One glance at their golden flags told Taliesin they were Eagle Legionnaires. She had to make a choice. Fight the Wolfmen or let them in and together fight the Eagle Clan soldiers. She hated both clans, and she recalled Navenna's words, *'Be careful whom you trust and whom you give your heart. Those who call themselves friends are not always true, and your enemies may become your allies. Rely on your instincts.'*

Ringerike glowed bright blue, and Thalagar swept his wings wide. Taliesin sensed the sword was prepared to fight for her, either way, but if she chose the Wolf Clan, she was fighting for Ragnal and Prince Almaric. If she fought against them, she was helping Mira, though why a goddess of magic protected King Frederick, known for his hatred of magic and magic users, made little sense to her. The Eagle Clan wanted magic restored, though they supported the king. Since Lord Arundel had been the one to kill Prince Tarquin, she didn't want to assist the Eagles. Nor did she want to help King Frederick, whom she considered a murderer.

She had to decide. Which clan did she hate the most? Who had done the Raven Clan the most wrong? The Eagle Clan, with all their intrigue and secretive activities carried out in the shadows, had allowed the Wolf Clan to destroy the Raven Clan, and in so doing, they were as much at fault. It was Chief Lykus and the bloodthirsty Wolfmen who killed her people, ate their flesh, soaked in their blood, and hunted her across the realm. What was the right thing to do? Should she let the wolves in, or let the Eagle Clan kill them? If the opposing clans were wise, they'd join forces to attack Gilhurst Abbey and take her hostage. Perhaps that's what they intended. Make the wrong move, and she'd invite death into the church. Make the right one, and she would be one move ahead of the enemy in the game for power.

"Navenna," she whispered, "help me decide what to do!"

But no voice answered. She had to decide on her own.

* * * * *

Chapter Fifteen

The moonlight on the road seemed bright as day as Taliesin imagined taking hold of the silver brightness and using it to build a higher wall around Gilhurst Abbey. *Ringerike* let out a whine in warning as a strange swirl of silver light appeared at the gate and blocked the Wolf Clan from entering. It was Mira who answered her and not Navenna. In a cloud, Taliesin spotted Mira's face and silently thanked her for her help.

The Wolfmen turned their horses toward the potato field and its far border, the Wild Wood. The golden-armored legionnaires charged after Phelon's men and shouted war cries into the night. The Wolf Pack jumped from their horses and either turned into wolves or *Wolfen*, shedding their armor as they ran for the tangle of trees and sharp thorns. The riderless horses broke from the race, turned from the woods, and headed toward the silver light at the abbey's entrance. The gate shimmered and allowed the horses to run through it as if it did not exist and turned back into iron when they were safely inside.

Taliesin set her heels to Thalagar's flanks and sent the horse climbing into the air under the pale glow of the moon. She soared across the potato field and watched the Eagle legionnaires confront twelve *Wolfen* who chose to remain behind to help give the pack time to escape. The larger *Wolfen* dragged riders and horses down and savagely ripped them apart. A larger group of men in gold attacked the wolves unable to escape through the Wild Wood. With silver swords and spears, the Eagle legionnaires slaughtered the wolves, leaving behind the corpses of dead, naked men.

244 | SUSANNE L. LAMBDIN

As Taliesin flew lower, she spotted a single red wolf of medium size trapped in the thick bramble and whimpering loudly, trying to get away. "It's Phelon," she shouted. "Land, Thalagar! We must help him!"

The horse set down with wings spread wide. The howls of wolves and *Wolfen* and the cries of men filled her ears as she jumped out of the saddle. Landing on her feet, she ran toward the red wolf, caught him around the middle, and jerked him free from the thorns. Phelon immediately turned into a man, naked and bleeding from numerous scratches and cuts. He offered no resistance as she gathered him into her arms, ran toward Thalagar, and threw him over the saddle. As she caught the bridle to mount, eager to leave the battle, a large, furry form appeared in front of the horse and swiped at Thalagar's nose with a clawed hand. The horse let out a snort and reared to ward off the *Wolfen's* attack. Taliesin was quick to intercede, stepped between them, and took a hard blow to the side of her helmet that nearly knocked her to the ground.

"Thalagar, go!" Taliesin shouted. "Return to the abbey with Phelon!"

Taliesin drew *Ringerike*, which moved of its own accord and stabbed the beast through the chest. Two more *Wolfen* raced toward her from different directions as Thalagar flew into the air and headed toward the abbey. Aware the beast on her left had lunged, intent on bringing her to the ground, she raised her shield and knocked it aside. The second *Wolfen* rose on its hind legs and offered a large target. She swung her sword, cut through thick muscles, and separated the head from the beast's body.

Wolfen and men on horses fought around her. The Eagles were prepared, each armed with silver, and the beasts they killed did not heal nor return to the fight. Taliesin noticed two wolves managed to escape through the Wild Wood, and another raced through the battle, reached the road, and vanished. The Wolf Pack had lost this fight, and by the time she reached the abbey wall, it was over. Not one member of the Wolf Clan remained alive. The only prisoner was Master Phelon, who she assumed was now in the hands of Rook and the Black Wings.

Taliesin returned to the entrance and watched as the gate turned into silver light to allow her to enter. The moment she passed through, it returned to iron. The silver glow remained and spread across the wall, an additional barrier against the Eagle legionnaires. Rook, the Black Wings, and the farmers stood in the yard as boys herded the horses to the far side of the church. Hillary and Mrs. Caldwell stood nearby, armed with pitchforks. Thalagar waited under the porch, while Phelon was bound at the feet of Father Jorge. Things were in order, at least on one side of the wall and as she turned, she found mounted warriors waiting on the opposite side. The silver light started to fade as she stepped forward, holding *Ringerike* at her side. White faces beneath golden helms stared back at her with open hatred.

"Who is your commander?" Taliesin asked in a loud, commanding voice.

The riders jostled as a large man rode forward. Taliesin assumed he was a knight since he wore silver spurs, which he apparently used too often on his horse, for its flanks were slick with blood. The big knight slid from the saddle with effort, and his horse bolted to the side, its reins caught by another man. Annoyed at the cruel treatment of the horse, Taliesin imagined the bridle slipping off its head, and watched, surprised when it actually happened. The horse broke free and bolted across the field. The Eagle commander cursed angrily, pulled off his helmet, and revealed a harsh face with a scar across his left cheek and eyes so gray they did not look human. She sensed magic coming from the commander and felt a tug on her sword.

"You give sanctuary to Master Phelon," the knight said in a hoarse voice. "Turn him over to us, and we will leave. Keep him, and we will lay siege to claim him."

"I am Taliesin, the Raven Mistress, and by the laws of our clans, I have the right to take Master Phelon as prisoner. This church lies inside the Tannenberg Forest, which belongs to the

Raven Clan, as well. Consider this place Raven's Nest, for it is so while I am in residence, and as such, I am not subject to Eagle law. I will not turn Phelon over to you, nor have I invited you in. Have you a name, or just bad manners?"

"Sir Cerasus," he said. "Commander of the Eagle legionnaires. Remove your helmet, so I may confirm who you are, for, as far as I know, there is no Raven Clan left to speak of, and certainly no Raven Mistress to give me orders."

Taliesin rubbed her forehead, and the helmet vanished, though the armor remained. She gave a shake of her long red hair, flipping it over her shoulders, and lifted *Ringerike* higher. Blue light spread across the length of the blade. Its glow cast upon the knight's face and his eyes momentarily turned the same shade. The soldiers, recognizing what she held in her hand, started whispering, and the commander's scowl deepened.

"So, you have recovered *Ringerike*," he said. "I heard as much but didn't believe it to be true. You say your name is Taliesin? You are the *Sha'tar*?"

"Raven Mistress, *Sha'tar*, and *Wolfen*," she said, smiling wide. "I think that gives me even more reason to keep Master Phelon as my prisoner. He is, after all, the one who turned me." She felt no reason to add Wolfgar to the mix, for technically Phelon had seen that she tasted human blood.

"Then you fight for Prince Almaric?"

"I killed Wolfmen tonight. I do not fight for the rebel prince, nor do I fight for your king. I am the Raven Mistress, as I said, and I fight for my clan." Taliesin glanced across the field as fresh troops arrived. She counted more than three hundred legionnaires. It was no mere patrol, but an army. "You've done your job, Sir Cerasus. Take your men and go on your way."

"I'm a King's Man. We all are. The king wants Master Phelon."

"Careful now," she said. "You've had your fill of blood. Leave before I turn you into something very small and nasty. A slug, I should think, would suit you well."

A raven flew out of the sky at that moment and landed up-on Taliesin's armored shoulder. She knew without looking it was Zarnoc and continued to stare into Sir Cerasus' strange fluorescent eyes.

"Do you have any idea who I am, Raven Mistress?"

"Yes, you're Sir Cerasus. You have limited magic ability. I sense you are a magic user of the lowest rank."

"He actually is a sorcerer," Zarnoc whispered.

Taliesin turned her head, keeping her eyes on the knight. "Do you know him?" she asked.

"Yes. Tread carefully. He means to do you harm."

"Does he?" she asked, angrily. "Well, I wish he'd just go away and stop bothering me."

The moment the words were out of her mouth, another ill-made wish, Taliesin tried not to panic and focused on the knight's strange eyes. His will was strong, and so was his magic, but it was not his night. A strange look appeared over his face. Sir Cerasus blinked his eyes several times, his jaw hung slack, and he turned toward the nearest man. Cerasus waved his hand. The soldier fell from his saddle and dropped to the ground, and the commander took his horse. The soldier reached to his companions, shocked when they refused to help as they wheeled their horses and rode from the abbey.

"Come here," Taliesin said.

She lifted her hand and summoned the stranded soldier to her. She wasn't prepared for him to vanish and reappear next to her. She'd actually brought the Eagle soldier to her side, needing no spells or assistance from Zarnoc. At least she didn't think the wizard had intervened, and it was *exciting*, for it was her first big step in controlling magic and using it for the benefit of others. She was even more surprised when the soldier took a knee before her and bowed his head.

"This is unexpected," Zarnoc said, mirroring her thoughts. "I think you have a new recruit, Raven Mistress."

"My name is Vestus. If you will have me, Raven Mistress," the man said, "then my sword and life are yours to command.

I renounce the Eagle Clan and curse the day Sir Cerasus was born."

Zarnoc flapped his wings. "Get ready," he said. "It's coming."

Taliesin watched the retreating commander in the distance, for a greenish cloud, in the likeness of a hand appeared, and its fingers curled inward as it was denied the death of the soldier. The cloud faded away, along with the hoof beats of the Eagle Legionnaires. No sooner had they vanished, then the forlorn cries of the wolves that slipped through the Wild Wood pierced the night. Without a second thought, Taliesin summoned them to join her and was amazed when dark forms appeared in the potato field, yellow eyes focused on her.

One after another, six wolves ran toward her, jumped through the wall, and gathered around her. Each wolf wagged its tail and whined softly as she reached out and touched their heads. Behind her, Phelon called out to his friends by name, "Adalwolf. Bardalph. Bleddyn. Ulmar. Toralu. Farkas. Do not listen to her, my brothers. Help me. Free me from these chains, or my father shall hear of this and punish all of you." The wolves ignored him, interested only in Taliesin and wanting to be touched by her. As she stroked each bloody muzzle, the wolves turned into naked, dirty, bearded men. They remained on their knees and gazed at her with something close to awe.

Zarnoc gave a soft chuckle, and his beak brushed across Taliesin's cheek. "Make them take the service oath, while they are mesmerized. Act quickly," the wizard said, "while the moonlight gives you power, girl."

Taliesin shivered. She was relying on her magical gift as a *Sha'tar* to bind men from two clans to her own. *Ringerike* tingled in her hand and confidence surged along her arm. The sword wanted her to act *now*, while she had the upper hand. No matter the consequence, she knew it was now or never.

"All of you stand. I assume you know the Raven Service Oath," Taliesin said, looking at each man. "Pledge yourselves to me this night and join the Raven Clan or join the dead in the field. If any lie, or are not sincere, *Ringerike* will tell me. In that case, I will remove your tongue before I remove your head, for there is no sword more powerful than the Raven Sword, and I am the Raven Mistress."

Seven men, only moments before fighting to the death, in unison placed hands over their hearts. *Ringerike* glowed bright blue as she held the sword aloft and its light shined upon each face. At the last man, the one named Farkas, it started to tremble, and acting on its own, the sword suddenly jerked Taliesin's arm forward and plunged through the man's chest. He made not a sound as he toppled to the side, dead before he hit the ground, and the sword returned to Taliesin's side. The remaining men didn't glance at the dead warrior, nor did they turn and run away or offer any accusation at the swift, brutal justice of the Raven Sword. In one voice, they each gave the oath.

"*We come from nothing, say nothing. We swear to protect the Raven Clan, brothers and sisters, eggs, nest, and tree. Family first or comes the grave.*"

The moment they spoke the words, something about their eyes altered. They didn't look upon her merely with awe. There were respect and reverence in their expressions. Where once their hearts, as sworn enemies of her clan, had been against her, now they truly belonged to her, heart, body, and soul. She started with the man formerly named Vestus and thought how quickly he'd come to her with an open heart, followed by the five Wolfmen. She judged them all by their appearances and gave each a new Raven Clan name.

"From now on, your pasts no longer matter, and I will hold you to your vows on pain of death. You belong to the Raven Clan. As such, each will be given a new name. From now on you will be known as Earnest," she said, looking at the former Eagle, "and you are Hornbill, Trogon, Kingfisher, Petrel, Condor, and Robin."

Taliesin relished in the moment. She alone ruled her clan, as Master Osprey had before her, and one hundred and fifty-eight raven masters before him. The former Eagle had no magic powers, and the five others were still *Wolfen*, and she wanted to make it clear what she expected of them.

"I too am a *Wolfen*," she said. "I have learned to control the animal within, and so must all of you. Ravens are a family, not a pack. You will not turn into wolves unless I command it, nor harm another and in so doing cause them to turn. The penalty will be a slow and painful death. Master Phelon is no longer your master. I am your mistress, and you will do as I order at all times, and in return, you will be respected, protected, and loved."

"Well done," Zarnoc said.

Earnest smiled at her. "Thank you," he said. "I have long waited to find a commander worth my sword and life, and it is you, Raven Mistress." The other six new recruits agreed with him, each wanting to offer their gratitude.

"All of you are most welcome. As for you," she said to Zarnoc, "I expect you to take the oath as well. Everyone in this church will join the Raven Clan. Afterward, you will free Ismeina from the harp and see if she can help you remove the curse on those inflicted with it."

"Must I? Must I?" he screeched at her.

"You most certainly will," Taliesin said. "And so will Ismeina!"

Zarnoc flew off her shoulder, and before he landed on the ground, turned into an old man dressed in dark blue robes with a conical hat on his head. He stood beside the seven men, a hand on his heart, and offered the service oath in a solemn voice. Before he finished, Drake, Tamblyn, and the entire group of country folk stood behind her. Even Father Jorge repeated the service oath, which meant he'd taken back his former name of Black Rooster. As the jumble of voices recited it, word for word, *Ringerike* sparked brightly. When the group grew silent, the sword singled out one man, with a black beard and black eyes, dressed as a farmer. The sword jerked forward, intent on killing the man who let out a scream of fear, raced across the path, and tried to scramble over the wall. Earnest and Hornbill ran after him and dragged him back to Taliesin.

"He is a newcomer," Black Rooster said. "I know no more than he came from the east and claimed to be hunted by Prince Almaric's men, so I took him in."

"He's one of us," Phelon snarled.

Rook dragged the Wolf Clan heir forward by a silver chain fastened to a silver collar. Taliesin didn't have a clue where Rook had found it in the church. The silver restrained Phelon and kept him from escaping over the wall. This time Phelon did not call out the trapped Wolfman's name. As heir to the Wolf Clan, Phelon had no interest in joining the Raven Clan, and he looked away when Earnest turned and drew his sword, a Mandrake silver blade. Taliesin realized then the former Eagle joining them was no mere coincidence, not when he carried one of her father's swords. He plunged it into the farmer's chest and said, "He was a Wolf spy." The body hit the ground, and he jerked his sword free.

With a glance skywards, Taliesin noticed Mira's face had vanished in the cloud, along with the last remnants of the silver glow on the wall. Mira had helped her. It surely was a sign Mira did not do what Ragnal said; in fact, she had helped Taliesin by convincing Ragnal's own followers to join her clan. Perhaps it was possible to serve both Navenna and Mira, she thought.

"Come inside," Black Rooster said as if he knew what she was thinking. "The moonlight is upon us, and too many eyes watch from the forest. Our enemies have seen far more than they should this night, and what we do from now on must be done in secret, Raven Mistress."

Taliesin sheathed her sword and motioned to Rook. He stepped forward, a look of curiosity mixed with concern on his handsome face as she took Phelon's leash from his hand, gave a hard tug, and brought the Wolf Clan heir to her side. Phelon was furious. Fur appeared on the tops of his ears and whiskers on his cheeks; otherwise, he maintained his human appearance.

"Captain Rook," Taliesin said, promoting her friend to the commander of the Black Wings, "post your guards and secure the horses. You may select among the country folk those most suited to be guards. It is now your duty to defend and protect the Raven Clan, and as captain, it is your right to choose your own officers."

"It will be an honor," Rook said, giving the ground a smack with the end of his silver spear. "Earnest, you and your new brothers will guard the wall. The rest of you men are now Black Wings. We'll see later about finding cloaks and armor for you. For now, take care of those horses."

Leaving Rook to the business of defending the abbey, Taliesin dragged Phelon inside. She was joined by Black Rooster, Zarnoc, and Tamblyn. Every man remained outside with the new captain, including a few of the young farm girls who looked strong enough to fight. Women with young children and Mrs. Caldwell were exempt from the Black Wings, as was Hillary who was too old and frail. Drake, along with Hawk and Ursus, bolted out the door, with Hawk in his wolf form. His inability to change weighed heavily on Taliesin's mind. She noted Tamblyn was sulking, visibly upset he had not been selected as a Black Wing when he was capable of fighting.

"By right I should be made captain, for I am of royal blood," Tamblyn muttered to the lute, for no one else listened.

Drake appeared in the doorway, shoved two fingers between his lips, gave a sharp whistle, and motioned for Tamblyn to join him. "You're to be a Black Wing, too," the boy shouted with great enthusiasm. The pair went out the door together and closed it behind them.

"Taliesin, is everything all right?" Wren asked. "The children were very frightened. You weren't hurt, were you?"

"We're fine, for the time being, and so am I," Taliesin said. "I'll start looking for a new place for us to live. Not until the war is over do I dare rebuild Raven's Nest. And since I refuse to pick a side, I guess that means we are on the outs with everyone."

"Let them think what they will of us. We're family."

Wren didn't mention she'd also been scared. Taliesin knew her well enough to know the girl preferred a quiet garden to the chaos of a battlefield. Lit candles filled the church with a golden light where Wren stood near the altar and allowed Taliesin to notice a flush to Wren's cheek and the slight rise of her stomach beneath her gypsy blouse. Mrs. Caldwell stood at the back door as mothers, their children, and a few elderly Ravens returned to their rooms in the adjoining building. Zarnoc, Hillary, and Black Rooster sat in a pew in the middle of the church and talked in soft tones, growing quiet when Phelon shook his chains, which Taliesin had wrapped around one of eight slender pillars near the altar. Wren's relief at once turned to anger as she noticed the red-haired Wolfman, and she quickly hurried past him to stand next to Taliesin, who fished in her pouch for the chess piece.

"Our clan is growing by leaps and bounds. I think Master Osprey would be surprised to see all our new recruits," Taliesin said. "The only person we are missing is Jaelle. I'll figure something out to set things right with Shan Octavio. She's a Ghajar, not a Raven—at least in his eyes."

Wren frowned. "You already sent the Shan's eldest son to serve as Sir Roland's squire," she said. "And the Nova brothers went with Tamal. When he let Jaelle accompany us on our quest to find *Ringerike*, he didn't mean for her to remain with us. After Tamal learns humility and honor, traits he lacks, he is supposed to return home too, Taliesin. When he does, the four Nova brothers will go with him."

"Jaelle is a fierce fighter, and one of the bravest people I ever met," Taliesin said. "If she returned, Rook would make her a Black Wing."

"Hawk didn't mean to hurt anyone. I'm sure he's upset you didn't pick him to be your captain, though I'm delighted you chose Rook. The only reason both you and Hawk are *Wolfen* is because of that dreadful little man over there. It is believed among the gypsies if you kill the *Wolfen* who bit you, you can break the curse."

"That's actually a falsehood," Taliesin said. "Nash doesn't know what he's talking about. He said the same thing and threatened to kill me. Don't worry about Phelon. No Wolfman can break through silver chains. Silver drains their strength and makes them easier to handle. Besides, Phelon isn't the one who bit me. It was Captain Wolfgar. I'll figure something out. I want Jaelle with us as much as you do, Wren."

The girl smiled. "I know Jaelle cares for you. She only did what her father expected of her. Don't be upset with her for breaking the oath."

Taliesin saw no reason to discuss the details of Jaelle's feelings. She knew Jaelle romantically cared for her, and it was a little embarrassing, especially since she didn't feel the same. "I'd appreciate it if you checked on the children and women," she said. "With all the stories told about the Raven Clan, I don't want them to think they've joined a band of thieves, even if the rest of the world will view us as such. Please reassure them they've made the right decision and don't need to be afraid anymore."

Wren gave a nod and slipped past Mrs. Caldwell as the older woman walked down the aisle, swaying her massive hips. She nodded at the three men and joined Taliesin. From her apron, she withdrew a bone from a stew she'd made earlier and tossed it at Phelon. Meat still clung to the bone. It was hardly a meal worthy of the Wolf Clan's heir, but he accepted it gladly and started to gnaw on the end.

"You did a good thing this night," Mrs. Caldwell said. "Though I can't understand why the Wolfmen and Eagle soldier took the oath. I saw everything from the doorway. Your magic is growing stronger, Taliesin. Master Osprey would have been proud of you. I dare say I am proud of what you've accomplished so far—you have found the Raven Sword. Normally, we would celebrate with a grand feast and drink countless barrels of ale after your father renamed new members of our clan. All I fixed for supper is a hearty mutton stew and fresh-baked loaves of country bread. Black Rooster has a stock of ale in the basement, only I don't think it would be wise for our small group to drink this night."

"Not so small. We have forty-eight new members, Mrs. Caldwell. Of course, I am counting the ten children. They'll grow up fast enough."

Taliesin sat on a pew, held the chess piece in her hand, and wondered if she set it down, just how large it would grow. It was probably best to set the tower in the cloister in order to give Zarnoc access to the magical harp. She could decide later which Ravens deserved magical weapons, and which ones to bestow based on their personalities, skills, and worthiness. She smiled as Mrs. Caldwell sat beside her.

"Naming new members wasn't quite as difficult as I imagined," Taliesin said. "There is one thing I've always wondered, Mrs. Caldwell, and that is how you came by your name. I know 'Hillary' means cheerful, which he certainly is, but he was once the infamous thief called the Red Bandit. Why did Osprey call you 'Mrs. Caldwell,' when customarily no one is allowed to use their former names?"

The woman, clearly amused by the question, snorted and smoothed her apron across her lap. Taliesin had never thought Mrs. Caldwell graceful. Even when Taliesin was a child, Mrs. Caldwell looked just as she did now. She was a large, formidable woman, with a mop of brown hair and stern features, though her laughter was contagious. She had defended Raven's Nest with a broom or rake more than once, usually fighting off foxes after chicken eggs or rowdy children trying to sneak cookies out of the kitchen. Yet, it was graceful when she moved her hands to straighten her clothing, belying her extra pounds and the wrinkles on her face.

"Master Osprey had quite the sense of humor," she said. "Thinking how I must have looked back then, with my belly swollen as a harvest pumpkin, two black eyes, and wearing nothing but a potato sack dress, he assumed I'd run away from an abusive husband. But it was Duke Andriel Rigelus I ran from. Osprey had a way of judging people by their looks or personalities. He was usually right on target, and when he took one look at me in my pitiful condition, the old codger smiled and said, 'Mrs. Caldwell, I'll have chicken tonight for my supper,' and in an instant, I became the new cook."

Taliesin laughed with delight. "That sounds just like him," she said. "You were married, Mrs. Caldwell?"

"I was born and raised in the dukedom of Thule, grew up in a local brothel outside Acre Castle, and made my living there," she replied. "I was a pretty thing, then. Unfortunately, Duke Andriel Rigelus was not a kind man, and rumors fly on fast wings. I'd heard of the Raven Clan and sought safety there, but our son didn't live long after he was born. Poor thing. Not long after, the Red Bandit made his appearance at Raven's Nest. Oh, you wouldn't think to look at Hillary; he'd once been handsome and strong. The tales of the Red Bandit's exploits were known to every Raven, and he arrived on the back doorstep one night with a bag filled with the Bavolian duke's family jewels, seeking a place to hide. He took one look at me and never left."

"Hillary is the best of men," Taliesin said.

With a chuckle, Mrs. Caldwell gave a wink. "Truth to be told, I've always thought it was my cinnamon buns that kept Hillary at Raven's Nest, but he joined the clan, and we've been together ever since."

"I have something to ask you." Taliesin held the chess piece in her hand and turned it this way and that. "What happened on the road to Eagle's Cliff? Secretary Glabbrio and the Eagles were your escorts. Wren saw it all in a vision. She has the gift of sight, and I know what happened to Osprey and the clan. How did you and Hillary manage to escape when everyone else was taken to Wolf's Den?"

"Hillary is the Red Bandit now, isn't he? Never been caught. Never will be."

A snarl from the pillar brought their attention to the Wolf Clan heir. Phelon wiped a hand across his mouth and licked his fingers. He'd finished the bone.

"Pure luck," Phelon said, butting in. "Only a few ever escape the Wolf Pack. Had the old hag and her skeleton lover been captured, I assure you, Raven Mistress, they would have made a delicious meal. Just like your father. I imagine now your mother is mending my father's shirts and emptying his bedpan, while those little brats shovel horse manure. Don't think anyone else survived, nor that my men won't return for me. You may have tricked those idiots into joining you, but when the Wolf Pack comes for me, and they will, we'll take our time peeling the flesh from their traitorous bones and will eat their livers while they are still alive. And then we will eat every last one of the Ravens."

"I guess that means we aren't friends anymore," Taliesin said. This was the Phelon she'd known at Dunatar Castle and not her companion on the road, and she was glad she had not given such a thankless wretch the Draconus sword. "Mrs. Caldwell, keep your eye on this filthy dog. If he talks again, you have my permission to beat him with a broom handle until he shuts his yap. I've something that needs tending to that can't wait any longer." She stood, clasping the chess piece. "I should have let Bonaparte eat you. Give Mrs. Caldwell any trouble, Wolfman, and I'll summon the dragon and let him finish the job."

With a nod to Zarnoc, Hillary, and Black Rooster, Taliesin waited for them to stand and join her in the cloister. She placed the chess piece on the ground, clapped her hands, and watched as it grew into a full-sized tower. The monk and the old man were stunned. Zarnoc merely laughed and beckoned everyone to join him inside. It was time to release the White Witch, thought Taliesin.

* * * * *

Chapter Sixteen

Sinking into hot, soapy water, Taliesin relaxed for the first time in weeks. She'd chosen the room on the third floor with a window open to let in a breeze that swept across the Wild Wood and brought the scent of earth and rotting vegetation. It wasn't that unpleasant. The bath salts added to the water assailed her nostrils with the scent of lavender, her favorite. Zarnoc remained inside the tower, still casting spells to release Ismeina, a task that proved daunting and lasted into the morning. Taliesin had finally excused herself and made herself at home. Black Rooster tended to the clan's needs, Mrs. Caldwell baked fresh bread, and Taliesin could hear the Black Wing standing guard duty — their voices carried on the breeze. Rook had Phelon under guard, and the new recruits were working out quite nicely. There were no incidents to report, no enemy troops spotted, and the morning was turning out wonderful.

The door opened, and she smelled dog. Her keen senses told her it was Hawk. She heard him pad across the room and then saw his black furry head at the end of the tub. He sniffed at the water, soap bubbles appeared on his black nose, and he sneezed.

"Turn into a man, and you can join me," Taliesin said, teasing him.

"Tell me how, and I'll gladly do so, Raven Mistress." Hawk glanced at the bed with an old brown blanket and a soft pillow. Two of the three bags of magical weapons lay on top with several jeweled hilts visible. Zarnoc had kept one in the tower, a collection of miscellaneous items, which were Korax's royal court. He licked his chops and turned back to her. "Promise me one of those magical swords is mine. I'm not always going to be a wolf. Phelon says the trick is concentration. If I think hard enough, he said I'll be able to turn back."

"Don't listen to Phelon."

"He was good enough company for you after you left us in Garridan," Hawk said, his tone stern. Even as a man, he'd hardly ever smiled and found amusement only in making money or stealing it. "The weeks spent as Prince Sertorius' prisoner was unpleasant and being hunted by Shan Octavio's men twice as bad. You missed all that while you were dallying with dragons and fairies and *darklings*. Drake tells me you had quite the adventure in Duvalen. I like him better than Wolfgar. He can't remember what a shit he used to be. For all your magic, you can't turn the boy back into a man, and you can't do the same for me. And then you went ahead and made Rook captain, not me when I'm clearly the one for the job."

For all her determination to spend the morning in reflection and soaking in the tub, Hawk's sour mood ended her respite. He wanted her to feel sorry for him. Apologizing yet again was not going to happen. She had said she was sorry far too many times, and Hawk was starting to wear on her nerves. Sitting forward, Taliesin wound her wet hair on top of her head.

"Not while you're a wolf," she said. "It doesn't take concentration to turn. You simply have to want it badly enough, Hawk. Personally, I think you're more attractive as a wolf — it suits you. Now, if you're done complaining, go away."

The wolf placed his paws on the edge of the tub, and his big head lowered as he gave her an intense look. His red tongue hung out of his mouth, and he panted as he closed his eyes. He was trying far too hard to turn. Whatever Phelon had told Hawk was not to his benefit, and she imagined the Wolf Clan heir lied about a great many things. Though Hawk's plight wasn't funny, not in the least, she splashed soapy water at her friend. His eyes opened in surprise, and his fur and muzzle vanished, replaced by a human face on the body of a wolf. Feeling slightly annoyed at herself, Taliesin splashed Hawk again, and wet the floor and his entire wolf body in the process. The fur faded and revealed white skin and a muscular human body. Hawk fell onto his backside and laughed as he ran his hands over his human form. Then he grew quiet, eyed her, and without a word, slid into the tub with her.

"What are you doing?" Taliesin cried, splashing him harder.

"You said I could get into the tub if I turned into a man. Phelon said you spent one night in his arms, so I guess you can do the same for me. I am your friend, after all."

"For your information, I didn't sleep with him."

"Just a dragon."

"I only kissed Bonaparte," she said. "And I have no intention of staying in this tub and playing patty fingers with you, Master Hawk!"

Taliesin sprang out of the tub, grabbed a nearby towel and wrapped it around her body. Hawk sank into the water and stared at her. Despite how handsome he was, she cared for Hawk like a brother, and the very idea of kissing him was simply far too strange to contemplate.

"Stop sulking. Wash off the dirt and do something about your bad breath. I'm going to put something on and sort through these weapons. Behave, and you may get a present. Try something like that again, and I'm going to geld you."

"You're a mean old mother hen," he grumbled. "It doesn't matter how much I try to please you. That's all I want to do — please you. My heart is filled with longing, and you think of me like a brother. Well, it's disgusting, that's what it is. You love Roland, and I know it. He's the only one you ever loved. I don't want you, anyway. You're disgusting!"

"Shut up before I cram that soap down your throat, you odious little toad!"

Hawk sank beneath the water with a snarl and blew bubbles like a child. Taliesin went to the window and angrily gazed across the inner courtyard at the black tower. Sparks the color of the rainbow shot out the top of the tower into a pale blue sky as magic scattered on the breeze. Whatever spells Zarnoc was using to release the White Witch weren't working.

"Can I trust you here with the magical weapons?" Taliesin asked, quickly putting on a pair of leather britches, a clean undershirt, and her boots. "That crazy old wizard is going to blow himself up. Don't touch one thing. I mean it, Hawk. There's liable to be a weapon or a trinket inside those bags that will give you warts or turn you into a demon. Be curious and ignore my warning, and you'll be sorry."

A pair of eyes appeared above the water, and long black hair floated atop the suds. Two hands, clasped as if in prayer, appeared holding the bar of soap as he submerged beneath the foam. He hadn't answered, although he'd damn well heard her. She toweled off her hair, left it long to dry, and finished dressing. She put on the red leather sword harness, gave a quick adjustment to the sword so it hung at the proper angle on her back, grabbed the cords to both bags, and marched out of the room.

No weapons, no temptation, she thought.

Taliesin ran toward the black tower as a loud explosion shook the very foundation of Gilhurst Abbey. The moment she entered the inner courtyard, she ducked as red, yellow, blue, purple, and green sparks showered the lawn and landed on her skin with sharp bites. She opened the door with a screech and ran into the tower to find Zarnoc seated on the floor with black soot covering his face, his long white beard, and his yellow robe. The hair on top of his head appeared singed, and his eyes watered as he repeatedly sneezed without covering his mouth with his hand.

"Bless you, you mad old fart! What are you doing? Seriously, Zarnoc, just how hard can it be to counter the Augur's dark magic without blowing us up in the process?"

"Well, I...I don't have to explain myself to you. Argumentative and surly, that's what you are." Zarnoc wiped a hand across his face and caused the black soot to smudge the entire length as he gave an exasperated huff. "I have been too long away from my cat Ginger. I need my familiar. If you had any sense, you'd stop fooling around with Hawk and go visit Shan Octavio. If the Ghajar decide to attack us, we'll really be in a pickle."

"You already are," she grumbled.

Taliesin walked to where the golden harp sat in the middle of a table and slid her fingers along the strings without plucking. A ripple of music filled the tower. Zarnoc stood, brushed off his garments as the yellow material turned dark purple, and the smoke filtered out the open door as he retrieved his wooden staff. He joined her at the table, gave the harp a dubious look, and let out another violent sneeze. This time he turned his head aside, and the harp started to laugh with a rich, warm female voice, which caused the wizard to chuckle.

"Ismeina, I'll remind you I am still the man of the house," Zarnoc said. "Or rather, the wizard of the tower, such as it is. This is not a bad place to set up shop. I won't turn you human if you're going to laugh at me."

"Just turn into a woman, Ismeina. It's what you are. You're a powerful witch," Taliesin said, "one who uses white magic—the magic of light and goodness." She gripped the gold soundboard, shaped in the likeness of a beautiful lady, and heard Ismeina groan. "Darkness turn to light. Harp turn to human. I release you."

"That's not going to work," Zarnoc said.

"Oh, yes, it will!"

Taliesin felt the harp shudder and lowered her hands. The harp turned into a beautiful woman seated on the table. Long white hair draped across her shoulders to hide her nudity. Zarnoc's mouth dropped. Taliesin wondered if it was seeing the harp turn into a woman or because the woman was lovely. If he was pleased she had broken the Augur's curse without the need of a spell or wishes, he didn't say. His surprised expression made Taliesin laugh. Ismeina laughed as well, a carefree, happy laugh, and a gown of sparkling silver appeared on her with a clap of her hands. Her hair curled at the ends, framing a lovely face unaged through the centuries, still as beautiful as ever. She climbed off the table and hurried to Zarnoc, eager to kiss him.

"Do you two need time alone?" Taliesin asked, amused.

"Not at all. Stay right here, Taliesin," Zarnoc demanded. "Woman, cease your folly! It's been ages, I agree, but now is not the time or place, and we have much to talk about."

"After, after," Ismeina moaned. "Privacy, please, Raven Mistress—it won't take long."

"I resent that remark, madam!"

Before Taliesin, eager to leave, made her way to the door, the wizard caught Ismeina's hands and jerked them to her sides. She pressed against him, head on his shoulder. Zarnoc remained in the appearance of an old man, his disguise meant to keep the witch from smothering him with kisses, and with difficulty, he managed to place the table between them.

"The intent here, Ismeina, is not to renew our love affair. It is to find a way to cure Taliesin, Drake, Hawk, and those Wolfmen who have joined the Raven Clan," he said, firmly. "At one time, you were considered the most promising witch in the realm. I want you to tell Taliesin the truth. Can you, or can you not, cure her with a spell or potion?"

Ismeina's eyes opened wide, and a hand rose to curl at the side of her mouth as she looked upon the wizard as if he'd grown horns. Frightened at his demand, she turned, wrapped her arms around her slender body, and gave a shake of her head.

"No, it's impossible," she said. "I wouldn't dare try it. Not again, Zarnoc."

"It won't be like the last time, dearie. I'm here to help."

"Then there is a way," Taliesin said, wanting an answer. "I'm willing to do whatever it takes, Ismeina. Allowing *Wolfen* into the Raven Clan has never been done before. Surely, with three magic users, there is a solution to the problem."

"Dangerous, yes, it's dangerous," Ismeina said. "Zarnoc, you must explain to this girl there are always side-effects when such powerful magic is called upon. She's primarily a sword handler, not a *Sha'tar*. Untrained, a natural witch can cause great destruction, but an untrained *Sha'tar*...I can think of nothing worse. Mira came to her aid last night, and Mira will want compensation. In truth, Mira is still with her, or the girl wouldn't have been able to turn me into my normal state."

Taliesin placed her hands on her hips. "Now look," she said, "this isn't about my magic abilities, it's about keeping Ragnal from winning. If we can stop the Age of the Wolf from happening, and if that means turning me human, then that's what we must do. Maybe there are side effects we need to consider, so if you're worried, then try it on Phelon. Once human, he must not be able to be turned again. The cure must be permanent or, at the very least, binding."

"You're prepared to risk his life to cure him?" Ismeina asked.

"I don't care if he has to wear a magical collar for the rest of his life. You can make one for all of us. I don't want to be *Wolfen*. I intend to make the Raven Clan great again, and I've brought enough magical weapons to make that possible. Balancing Navenna and Mira's demands is something I can do, for they coincide with my own. Now that Ragnal keeps popping up, demanding that I join him, something must be done. I don't want him visiting again...."

Ismeina gasped. "The War God has visited you? Personally?"

"And Navenna," Zarnoc said. "Ragnal has visited Taliesin twice in as many days. Cano and Varg were with him. The gods have taken an interest in this young lady, for she possesses magic and royal blood, and she is *Wolfen*. If something isn't done, Ismeina, and Taliesin and the *Wolfen* in this clan decide to grow fangs and eat people, we only enable Ragnal to bring about *Varguld*. Doing nothing isn't an option. I know you are frightened, as am I, but this is a desperate situation."

"I can inventory the items we took and see if any will help," Taliesin said. "Sometimes a magic sword or flute has more power than any curse. It's why they're so coveted, especially with magic on the verge of a rebirth. The Age of Magic, not of the Wolf. No, the 'Age of the Raven;' now that sounds much better."

While Ismeina and Zarnoc talked, Taliesin took out her father's spell book and lined up the swords and weapons on the table, double-checking which ones she had and if any had the power needed to break the curse.

"It will take some time," Ismeina said. "Time to reflect on which spell is strong enough to break the curse. And time to plan on which night and hour to cast the spell. None of these weapons are able to break the curse. Weapons are made for war, my dear, so we can't rely on them. After all, Ragnal is the God of War, so it's entirely inappropriate to use any of them. I may be able to pair a few enchanted trinkets, which will do the job quite nicely, but again, these things take time." She glanced at Zarnoc. "My time as a harp may be well worth the lost years. Never did I imagine to find an heir of King Korax still living. The resemblance between them is uncanny. She has Korax's eyes, mouth, and red hair. She's also stubborn like him."

"There are a few differences," Zarnoc replied. "She's set her heart on one man, and one man only, Ismeina. Others have tried to win her heart. I can honestly say she has found the right match in Sir Roland Brisbane."

The witch smiled. "Good for her," she said. "I knew at once Taliesin wasn't the type to rest until she gets what she wants. It's interesting to learn she also freed Ysemay. The old crone repaid her debt by training her. I can only do the same by helping her break the curse."

Taliesin was not pleased the two ancient Lorians spoke about her as if she was not in the room. They also read her thoughts as if they floated overhead, easy to catch like butterflies. It was a little rude, she thought. Lorians lacked the social graces found amongst even the lower class in Caladonia, including those considered of lesser quality like Master Osprey's Raven Clan. The one person who had disliked her the most was her adopted mother, Minerva, and she had never spoken about Taliesin in front of her, preferring to direct any comments to her face, or behind her back.

"Provided we are able to do so, my dear, what do you intend to do after your debt is paid?" Zarnoc lifted a scraggy eyebrow. "What then? Will you return to Duvalen or travel the world?"

"I have not yet decided. I may stay with the Raven Clan or go on a long sabbatical. There's so much I want to see, so much I've yet to do," the White Witch said. "Yet, I may be precisely where I am most needed. I was always fond of Korax, even when he was a boy. Does this girl know what she's doing any better than he did?"

"Korax had his faults, and so does his heir," Zarnoc muttered as his gold eyes flickered toward Taliesin. "Now, where is that Book of Moon Spells? You know the one I had, tied with string?"

The wizard and witch continued talking about Taliesin and many other things. Their laughter filled the tower, blending harmoniously, and their hands brushed together. Zarnoc seemed smitten. A former flame was precisely what he needed to rejuvenate his spirits, for though gradual, he started to grow younger. They stood before a tall bookshelf laden with magic texts and scrolls, jars of unusual items from animals, vegetables, and minerals, five human skulls, and a jar filled with broken and mended wands with crystals tied to their ends. The items hadn't been in the tower when Taliesin arrived. Whatever Zarnoc and Ismeina discussed of a magical origin appeared in the tower along with a vapor cloud that slid from between the pages of manuscripts when touched.

Taliesin eventually turned her attention to the magical weapons. *Ringerike* continually warned the weapons not to communicate with her or try to control her. When every ax, sword, compound bow, spear, and dagger were placed side by side, Taliesin stood back and rubbed her temples to still the yammering in her head.

"Wait your turn," she said to a pair of lovely rapiers. "I know your names and what you can do in battle. For now, I am sorting and will get to you in a moment. Now be quiet!"

She reached into the bottom of the first bag, after twenty-two weapons were placed on the table, and set the smaller magic items above them. A wooden doll, a hand mirror, a box of nails, a spool of gold thread, and a green glass frog all generated friendly magical auras. A wooden box inlaid with tiny tiles, one boot, and a necklace of human teeth all gave off negative energies, but worst was the rage coming from a sealed jar of four sets of eyes that watched her every move. A mummified arm with a hand tightly holding a silver dagger required her immediate attention, for she instinctively knew being together might be dangerous. She tickled the back of the hand, and the fingers opened, allowing her to snatch the dagger and set it among the weapons.

"Oh, nice," Ismeina said, appearing at the table. She picked up the spool of gold thread, the box of nails, and the inlaid wooden box and brought them to Zarnoc. "This is not thread. It is a golden strand of hair from the goddess Broa, which can be used for binding spells. The iron nails, used to subdue an enemy, belonged to Ankharet the Wise, and the box contains the essence of Jesmond, one of the Ruby Sisters, who is the only witch bitten by a *Wolfen* and able to use magic to neutralize the curse. I noticed a bag of gold coins, too. You know they contain the souls of the returning Raven Lorians who were imprisoned by Dehavilyn?"

"Mira told Dehavilyn to do it to get back at me," Zarnoc said. "Do you really want the entire royal court here, my dear? Taliesin is not yet crowned, and they'll only obey her if she is."

"*Ringerike* obeys her," the witch said. "So will Korax's royal court."

"First things first, woman. Fetch the silver dagger of Lothar to cut Broa's hair, and then we'll tie a nail and sprinkle a little Jesmond onto each strand. Binding necklaces should temporarily subdue the *Wolfen's* bestial natures. That gives us more time to find the right spell."

"And to be together," Ismeina said.

Trying not to listen to their conversation, Taliesin went down the line of weapons, starting with the five silver swords made by her father, though she was unable to touch silver without burning her skin. Her own sword, *Wolf Killer,* was not among them. She'd left it sticking out of a rock near the Cave of the Snake God, and until she was cured, returning for it had to remain at the bottom of her 'list of things to do.' Three swords were made by Falstaff, a swordsmith alive during the reign of King Korax, and though not Lorian himself, possessed magic bestowed upon them by the wizard Zoltaire. The double-bladed ax, *Dark Blood,* had a dragon-bone handle wrapped in black snakeskin; it was able to cut through rock and grew more powerful the more lives it took. The twin rapiers, *Sting* and *Fang,* she intended to give to Hawk, once he was able to use silver. Most of the magical weapons were listed in John Mandrake's book, an illustrated guide, with stories about each weapon, including the twin rapiers, which stabbed whatever they were thrust toward.

There were weapons created by famed smiths like Gregor, Rivalen, and Falstaff, and all contained magic. Queen Dehavilyn had very good taste, acquiring the weapons of heroes, knights, and noblemen. With new recruits, Taliesin would eventually be able to track down every sword shown on the Deceiver's Map. For the moment, she had enough weapons to hand out to those of her clan who proved themselves worthy in battle and in intelligence. She imagined how excited Master Osprey would feel if he'd been alive to witness the moment, knowing his clan had the most magical weapons in the realm, and soon would reclaim their former glory.

A knock on the door preceded Wren poking her head inside. The girl looked distraught. Makeup stained her face from shed tears, and her dress was in tatters. She staggered inside and sank to her knees, her sobs drawing the attention of Taliesin, Zarnoc, and the witch. Zarnoc was first to reach her side and appraise the situation. He offered his hand to draw Wren to her knees at the same moment a gut-wrenching scream arose from the chapel.

"It's Hawk," Wren cried. "He's...he's gone wild!"

"Quickly, Taliesin! Go check on Phelon before Hawk does something we'll all later regret," Zarnoc ordered.

Taliesin ran out the door, hand on *Ringerike's* hilt, able to hear more screams and shouts, and what sounded like furniture being broken and glass shattering. She entered the back of the chapel to find it in shambles, with two Ravens on the floor, moaning in pain, and a broken main door. Phelon was no longer chained to the pillar. Someone had broken his chains with an ax and left large cracks in the stone. Shouts from outside the front door brought Taliesin scurrying through the broken pews. She reached the door as a furry bottom wiggled over the top of the wall and vanished on the opposite side.

"They're getting away! Stop them!"

Rook's shouts carried to Taliesin on the breeze. She ran to where the young captain stood behind a barricade newly built at the entrance, a silver spear still in hand. His reaction time not fast enough to throw it at Phelon who led Hawk and Drake through the potato field. The Black Wings fired arrows from their positions on the wall and on every roof. Phelon's red fur was as bright as her hair. The larger Hawk, black and sleek, ran right behind him. The small blond wolf followed, yelping as an arrow sliced open his ear.

"Stop firing," Taliesin cried. "You'll kill Hawk or Drake! Cease fire!"

Taliesin waved her arms at the Black Wings, furious they'd fired at Hawk and Drake. She didn't care about Phelon, not after he persuaded her two friends to join him, but it was far too risky to shoot at him and risk injuring one of their friends. A loud voice ordered the guards to stop shooting. Rook ran along the line of guards toward Taliesin, angrier than she'd ever seen him.

"Something has to be done, Taliesin. Hawk attacked two of my men. The boy turned the moment he saw Phelon and Hawk change shapes," Rook said. He lowered his spear, the tip pointed to the ground. "By the time I realized Drake turned, he was already over the fence."

"What about Hornbill and the other Wolfmen? Did they turn?"

"No. They're still here," he said. "They're Black Wings, *true to the beak*."

Taliesin hadn't heard the old cliché in ages and looked where Rook pointed at the roof. Hornbill, his large nose defining his name, stood on top of the church with his feet braced and a bow in his hands. A man with two tufts of hair behind his ears, Kingfisher, stood nearby. Petrel, Robin, Condor, and Trogon were at the wall with the rest of the guards. The new recruits hadn't turned *Wolfen* or tried to escape with Phelon. She felt it was nothing short of a miracle.

"It's possible Drake remembered he used to be Wolfgar," Taliesin said, unsure what she wanted to do at that moment. "My inclination is to go after them, only I fear Sir Cerasus remains in the neighborhood, and I don't want to run afoul of him. I know Wren won't understand my reluctance, Rook. I have to go with my gut feeling. It doesn't feel right to go after them."

"You suspect more Wolfmen are in the forest. I do as well."

Taliesin gave a nod. "Phelon is crafty," she said. "I've no doubt he hopes I'll follow. You know it's a trap, and so do I."

"I'll explain the situation to Wren," Rook said. He made no attempt to hide his emotions, and his dark eyes glittered from unshed tears. "Whatever Zarnoc and the witch are doing, it better be soon. Two guards were bitten by Hawk."

"They won't turn unless they taste human blood."

"Hawk is my best friend, Taliesin. I blame Phelon for what happened, but they were my responsibility. I offer no excuse for my failure to subdue them. If you want to choose another captain, I understand and will comply with your order."

Taliesin smiled. "That won't be necessary," she said. "This is on me, not you. I'm the one who brought Phelon here. I should have let Sir Cereus have him."

A loud whinny from Thalagar caught her attention. The black stallion was mingling with the horses left behind by the Wolf Clan. *Ringerike* smacked her leg, wanting to go after their friends, not agreeing with her decision.

"I counted heads, and we have twenty-three Black Wings," Taliesin continued. "I have magical weapons I can hand out just as soon as these farmers know the difference between a pitchfork and a magical blade. Your spear, by the way, is magical. It's one of Rivalen's spears. I guess you already figured out it never misses its target." He gave a nod. "Until I can find us a better place, let's make certain we can defend the abbey against any outside force. We can use the tower to fall back to if need be."

"Take a look at the Deceiver's Map," Rook said. "Find out where Hawk is going, so I can let Wren know. I assume my father will take the King's Road to Padama. Erindor fights for King Frederick. Sir Cereus commands the 1st Legion. The Eagles have six legions, with twenty thousand men in each legion, and I'll feel better if I know they do not intend to stop at this abbey."

"I know Wren is pregnant, Rook. *Ringerike* told me. I'm not going to let anything happen to her. If I can rescue Hawk, you know I will."

"Wren comes first," he said. "Check the map."

Taliesin removed the scarf from her pouch, gave it a hard shake, and it turned into a square board printed with the Deceiver's Map. Taliesin thought of Hawk, and he appeared on the northern border of the Tannenberg Forest, with Phelon and Drake. They appeared to be heading toward Scrydon, and it would take days for them to reach Prince Almaric's army.

"Hawk is headed toward Wolf's Den," she confirmed. "Duke Dhul Fakar is approaching our position from the south. He comes with Lord Arundel and their combined armies. This is strange. The Ghajar are also on the move. They are headed west into Thule."

"Thule fights for King Frederick, according to Black Rooster," Rook said. "I know the Shan said he wouldn't pick a side unless forced, and Taliesin, he leans toward the current king. So does Sir Roland, and if he and his Order do, then so does the Shan's son Tamal. Not all of Maldavia supports Duke Peergynt, and many of the small towns remain loyal to the king."

Taliesin gazed at the map. The king's banner appeared beside Duke Andre Rigelus. The Duke of Bavol and the Knights of the Blue Star were trapped in Scrydon, fighting the Wolf Clan, with heavy casualties on both sides. Sertorius' fleet from Garridan appeared on the map, despite the fact they were moving along the western coastline of Caladonia, heading south. She suspected they'd land in Thule and take the King's Road as well to Padama. The map did not reflect whether he fought for his older brother or father.

"The dukedoms of Aldagar, Maldavia, and Scrydon have joined Almaric," she said catching his gaze. "Black Rooster is right. Duke Andre has sided with the king. Why am I starting to think you want to help the king, Rook? I suppose you mentioned Roland's name for a reason. Have you heard from him?"

Rook shook his head. "I know you are thinking about Roland. He didn't betray you, Taliesin. He is loyal to his king and did what he thought was necessary to secure *Ringerike*. Wren told me you still love Roland. Is this true?"

She merely nodded, for a lump in her throat made it difficult to speak.

"Then it makes sense for us to support King Frederick," Rook said. "I know you have a good reason to hate the king, Taliesin. Just hear me out. Frederick Draconus could live another 20 years. During his reign, there has not been a war, until now. He didn't start it. Almaric did, and now Sertorius appeared to have joined his brother. I don't know the other three princes. I imagine they are no better than the rest of the litter."

"Prince Galinn was sold to the Skardans by Almaric years ago," she said. "I don't remember Dinadan or Konall, so I can't say what they're like. All I know is that Frederick had my father killed, and he sent my mother to an abbey."

"You know who your mother is?" Rook asked.

"I'm not ready to tell anyone who she is. Not yet."

"Then we won't go to Padama and ask for sanctuary. What about Shan Octavio? If you could make amends with him, Taliesin, we would be safe with the gypsies. Nash is a problem, granted. All we have to do is avoid him. Plus, Jaelle is there." Rook fell silent as she put away the map. They strolled toward the horses' corral. "Shan Octavio may be strict, but he loves his people. He's only doing what he thinks is best for them and Jaelle. Tamal sent word to his father that he has chosen to remain with Sir Roland, for now, and the Nova brothers are with him. If you want to know my opinion, then yes, I think we should send word to Sir Roland that we will help King Frederick. Shan Octavio and the Ghajar may also be needed to win this war, Taliesin."

"Roland is surely angry with me," Taliesin said, feeling the sting of regret. "I didn't want to leave him. I love Roland."

"Then what is the problem? I'm sure Roland loves you."

Taliesin kicked a stone off the path. "I might as well tell you why I'm really reluctant to join Roland and the king," she said. "Roland knew my mother was Princess Calista, King Frederick's younger sister, but he never told me. I learned about her while I was in Duvalen. My parents married in secret, only the king found out and sent my mother to Talbot Abbey, where I was later born. She died giving birth to me, and I was returned to my father, only the king suspected I inherited magic from my father. That's why Frederick killed my father, Rook. John Mandrake was a warlock and the Raven King's last surviving heir. When he was killed, Zarnoc sent me to live with Osprey and the Raven Clan. Roland only joined us because he wanted to find out whether or not I also had magical abilities. How can I be with a man who would hide the truth or serve such a cruel king? I'm not saying Roland isn't a man of honor, for he is, but he chose his king over me. If he loved me, truly loved me, he would have told me what happened to my parents."

Rook accepted the news with his usual stoic expression. "I think you should give Sir Roland the opportunity to explain, Taliesin. True love only comes along once in a lifetime. You may love others, though it will pale in comparison."

"You think I'm being too hard on him."

"I think you are being too hard on yourself," Rook replied. "Roland took an oath to serve the King. If he was ordered not to tell anyone the truth about your parents, then as a Knight of the White Stag and a King's Man, he could not break it, not even for you. I'm quite certain Roland regrets not telling you, Taliesin. What happened to your parents is not his fault. Forgive him. If you don't forgive him, you will regret it the rest of your life."

The former Eagle Taliesin had renamed Earnest approached carrying *Calaburn* wrapped in his cloak. He presented the sword to Rook. Taliesin pushed aside thoughts of Roland and looked to the guard for an explanation.

"The boy dropped this in the potato field," Earnest said. "I thought I should bring it to you, Captain Rook."

"Well done, Earnest. That will be all." Rook removed the material from the sword. "It was foolish of Drake to leave this behind. This sword belonged to Prince Tarquin Draconus. I recognize it from drawings Wren showed me in a book. I assume you felt Drake was loyal or you would never have given it to him."

"I was wrong to give it to Drake," Taliesin said. She smiled when *Ringerike* gave a soft whine. "The gift was meant to strengthen the bond between us. Apparently, there is no bond. It takes a stronger personality to use this sword. This is why I am not ready to hand out magical weapons to the clan. I have to be careful to whom I give magical weapons, Rook. Each weapon has special gifts as well as side effects, and in the hands of weak-willed men or women, they can cause great harm."

Rook stroked *Calaburn's* blade with his fingers. The blade glowed red, producing heat, and he jerked his hand away to suck on a singed finger. He offered the hilt of the sword to Taliesin. She sensed *Ringerike's* immediate annoyance. *Calaburn* wanted to return to her, wanted it desperately. She made a decision, placed her hand on Rook's shoulder, and met his gaze.

"You have a strong personality, Rook."

"The blood of the Draconus kings runs in your veins, Raven Mistress. Not only are you King Korax's heir, but you also have a right to claim the Ebony Throne of Caladonia." Rook took hold of *Calaburn's* hilt and held it aloft. "Had Prince Sertorius proven to be an ally, he might have been suited for this blade. He may be your cousin, but he is an enemy of the Raven Clan."

Taliesin smiled. "You are my captain, Rook. I chose you because you are dependable and loyal." She removed her hand from his shoulder, aware he was unable to look away from the magical sword. "If you think you are strong enough, then I'd like to present you with *Calaburn*, for in truth, Ringerike does not want me to keep it."

"I am honored, Raven Mistress. I shall treat this sword with respect; I swear it." Rook removed his own sword, handed it to a guard standing near the horses, and slid *Calaburn* into the scabbard where it fit snugly. "Are you certain your mother is dead?"

She stared at him. "Why would you say that?"

"Talbot Abbey is a two-days journey from here, at least on Thalagar," he said. "Zarnoc told you she was dead; yet, I am inclined to think he only told you this so you wouldn't go looking for her. You know he likes to keep secrets."

"Has Wren had a vision?"

Rook shrugged. "Perhaps," he said. "Wren can see many things, Taliesin. Not only about the present and future, but also in the past. I knew before we meet you in Miller's Wood that your mother was a princess. Wren saw your birth. She said Zarnoc and several nuns were present. The wizard took you back to Padama and gave you to John Mandrake. Zarnoc considered giving you to Master Osprey to hide from the world. He returned you to Mandrake because he felt it was his duty to do so. I don't tell you this to cause trouble between you and the wizard. He is your friend, as I am, and I know he is worried about your future."

"What are you saying, Rook?"

"If I didn't want you to claim the throne or had reservations about what you might do with so much power, I too might hide the fact that your mother is alive," Rook stated. "I might pretend Princess Calista is dead, for only she can legitimize your birthright. Otherwise, you are only the heir of the Raven Clan, and not so much of a threat to King Frederick or his sons, even with *Ringerike*."

Taliesin turned toward the abbey, wondering what Zarnoc and Ismeina were doing at that moment. She didn't want to jump to conclusions about her mother. She suspected Wren had seen far more than her birth and had given Rook instructions not to tell her everything. Things were complicated, that was certain, and for whatever reason, those she loved best went to great lengths to keep the truth from her.

"Before you say anything else, Raven Mistress, I suggest we find somewhere else to make our nest," Rook said. "I know the perfect hideout too. Master Osprey always said when in trouble, head to higher ground, and he didn't mean in the upper branches of *Mother*. Penkill Castle is in ruins, and only our clan ever went there, and it's not far from here. It would be easy to defend the castle against anyone who opposes our clan."

"I'll check it out then," she said, glad he'd suggested it. "I'll return as soon as I can. Until then, you're in command, Captain Rook."

The young man saluted, his hand slightly curled as he gave a quick tap to his forehead; her first salute as Raven Mistress.

Protocol did not require the Raven leader to respond in kind, but it was far too tempting, and it was *her* clan.

* * * * *

Chapter Seventeen

At Taliesin's whistle, Thalagar cleared the corral fence with a mighty leap and trotted toward her. He wore neither bridle nor saddle. She grabbed a fistful of black mane and placed a foot on the root of his wing, careful not to press too hard as she slid her leg over his back. They would fly faster without their armor, so she did not touch the Draconus ring or make his dragon scales appear. The horse pranced forward as she gripped his sides with her legs. Her muscles tightened as he galloped forward, fanned his wings, and sailed into the air. They flew away from Gilhurst Abbey in the direction of the Gorge of Galamus.

An overcast sky provided tendrils of sunlight that escaped through the cloud, and as they headed toward the deep ravine, they flew 20 miles along the lower southern section of Maldavia. The gorge ended at the border of Thule and opened to a wide valley, where the gypsies had gone. The ruins of Penkill Castle, built 400 years ago by an ancestor of Duke Regis Peergynt, stood on an escarpment that overlooked the valley and gorge. The only way to reach the castle was along a steep road cut into the side of the cliff. No one had lived in the castle in the last century, due to the lack of fresh water. The waterfall that once fed the Snake River had long since dried, though the river that ran through the gorge into the valley remained. In the spring, it was at its highest, and in the fall months, it was nothing more than a thin creek, bordered by weeds.

"Let's fly lower," Taliesin said as she leaned forward. "I want to make certain Shan Octavio has left." She'd learned from experience the map didn't always tell the truth. With the Eagle 1st Legion in the area, as well as the Wolf Pack, it

279

seemed only prudent to make certain the gypsies had moved on.

Thalagar dropped into the gorge, its sandstone walls appearing yellow in the sun's glow. A large shadow cast by the winged horse appeared on the bottom of the gorge, and she concentrated on searching for movement as they flew over the narrow river. Weeds and cattails grew along the banks, home to a variety of birds, and tall birches soaked their roots in the water. She saw no signs of the Ghajars. When traveling, young boys, called sweepers, used wide brooms to wipe away tracks left by their wagons and horses. The gorge bent and turned like a snake, which was how the river got its name. Smaller shadows moved on the side of the gorge, dipping and rising, and then vanishing as they sailed around a rocky finger that stuck out of the right side of the gorge. Deadman's Finger, she thought as she lifted her eyes to the sky.

Ten black vultures circled over the gorge up ahead, signaling something was dead and ripening in the sun. With Penkill Castle visible on the horizon, her curiosity demanded a closer look at whatever caught the vultures' attention. Her heart thudded in her chest as she imagined what they'd find waiting for them. *Ringerike* gave a sudden quiver on her back.

"Trouble," Taliesin said. "Let's check it out, boy."

Thalagar sped across the tops of river birches and dropped lower as a yellow wagon appeared, stuck in the mud of the shallows. Two horses, still harnessed and shot full of arrows, lay dead in the river. Taliesin clearly saw the golden fletchings of arrows used by the Eagle Clan. Thalagar landed on the bank and trotted toward the wagon, and she drew her sword, wary of an ambush.

"This wagon belongs to the Ghajar," she said. "They never leave their dead behind, not even their horses. What do you think, *Ringerike*? Sense anything?"

The sword let out a soft whine.

"You want me to check it out? Very well."

Taliesin slid out of the saddle. The sword picked up no trace of the living, which meant if the Eagle 1st Legion had been there, they had moved on and used magic to hide their footprints. It made no sense why the clan attacked the gypsies. This was not Eagle land, it was Maldavian land, and the Ghajar were neutral. Opening the back door of the gypsy wagon, she peered inside and found it undisturbed. A table, chairs, a bed, and pots hanging from the oval ceiling looked tidy. She backed out, closed the door, and walked around the wagon. There were no prints in the soft sand other than her own, another sign someone had taken the time to remove all tracks. As she approached the dead horses, she noticed flies had started to gather to feed on the blood, which still trickled down their sides. Both the blood and recent arrival of flies suggested the horses had been killed a few minutes before her arrival, and if that was the case, and the footprints only recently cleared away, it meant the killers were close.

Thalagar let out a loud snort at the same time *Ringerike* started to rise from the scabbard. Loud cries filled the gorge as riders in brightly colored vests appeared from the west riding toward her. She counted more than thirty Ghajar warriors as she ran back to the wagon and drew her sword. Silver-tipped arrows struck the carriage and the sand on either side near her position. Taliesin let out a groan as her horse jumped the creek and ran in the opposite direction. There was only reason Thalagar would leave her, and she knew he'd been struck by an arrow. Fearing for her own safety, she entered the wagon, glad for its wooden walls and roof, and shut the door. Her sword knocked aside pots as she knelt beside a curtained window.

"There is no place to run, Raven Mistress," Nash shouted.

Arrows slammed into the wagon, and she immediately smelled smoke. She pulled the curtains aside and peered out the window as the riders circled the wagon, their red vests and silver beads in their long hair visible in a cloud of dust and black smoke. Taliesin spotted Nash riding a buckskin horse. He turned in the saddle to shoot an arrow at the window. She ducked as the projectile hit a pot hanging overhead.

It fell to the ground as flames appeared, lapping at the curtains.

"Kill the wolf," the men shouted.

Taliesin held *Ringerike* in both hands and pointed it at the floor, covered by a colorful rug that now burned on the far side. She pictured the river in her mind, summoned it to rise and douse the flames, and heard an answering rumble in reply. The wagon shook as water rose through the floorboards, flooded the cabin, and soaked her boots and knees. She'd called on the water, wanting only to create a wave to put out the fire, but hadn't counted on it filling the interior of the wagon.

"This is not what I imagined," she muttered.

Taliesin stood, waded through the water, and kicked open the back door. Water poured out of the wagon and joined the rising river, which now flooded the gorge as a wall of water more than 40 feet high appeared in the east. The shadow cast on the ravine brought a cool breeze, a spray of water, and a thunderous roar. She waded through the creek, now at knee level, and spotted the gypsies whipping their horses as they turned and rode in the opposite direction. Horrified, she sheathed her sword and cupped her hands around her mouth, shouting for her horse.

"Thalagar!"

No sign of the winged horse appeared as the wall of water approached. Taliesin sheathed her sword on the run toward the gorge wall. It was steep and offered no footholds, leaving her no way to climb out of reach of the enormous wave. She tried and failed to make it vanish with a simple thought. Droplets of water hit her face as she turned back, the roar of the wave in her ears, and prepared to be submerged. At a loud whiney, she saw Thalagar, an arrow embedded in his shoulder, land nearby, and he raced to reach her as the curl of the wave towered over her.

Taliesin grabbed a handful of mane and threw herself onto Thalagar's back while the horse kept running and beating the air with his large, black wings. Each time she attempted to throw her leg over his back, his wing stroke slammed her against his side, making it impossible to straddle the horse.

"I'm slipping!" Taliesin shouted.

The black stallion lowered his left wing, caught her legs, and pushed her onto his back. She swung her leg over, clamped her legs tight around his body, and with his thick mane in her face, she felt her stomach lurch as the horse flew into the air. A quick glance at the gorge made her gasp as the wave swallowed the trees and swept over the wagon with a loud roar. The wave overtook the Ghajar riders and crashed over horses and riders, dragging them beneath the murky water. She spotted Nash and his buckskin as they vanished in the churning water and then one lone rider trying valiantly to outride the flood. Horse and rider charged out of the gorge as the waves smashed against either side of the rocks and flowed into the valley. The rider's long hair and shrill, female voice reached Taliesin's ears. She tapped her heels to Thalagar's flanks. The horse flew lower, moving ahead of the thunderous rush of water as it swept across trees and boulders, and caught up with the rider. Jaelle glanced at her and lifted an arm, her face filled with fear and hope.

"I...got...you," Taliesin said as she caught the girl's arm. She pulled Jaelle over her lap as the wave took down the girl's unfortunate horse.

Beneath them, the water continued to flow out of the gorge and spread outward, losing its momentum as it created a large lake. Thalagar struggled to stay aloft, the arrow in his side now broken in half and the wound bleeding. He headed toward the shoreline, descending at a fast rate, and landed, still moving at a gallop. Jaelle let out a scream as she slid out of Taliesin's grip and hit the ground. The horse bucked and sent Taliesin toppling over the side and smacked her with his wing. She fell backward and slammed into the ground, flopped onto her stomach, and tasted a mouthful of dirt as she skidded to a halt. The horse ran on with a loud, angry whiney as Taliesin struggled to her feet. The water flowed toward her. She stood and waded toward Jaelle as the girl vanished beneath the churning flow, and she managed to grab her arm as the girl swept past her. Jaelle screamed in pain as Taliesin caught hold of her broken arm. The water was at their waists, requiring Taliesin to drag Jaelle behind her as she swam toward the shoreline.

"Let go of me, wolf girl!"

Taliesin dragged the angry, screaming girl onto a boulder, watching the water rise until it lapped at the sides. She spotted Thalagar racing along the shoreline, trying to escape the water, and turned back to the gorge. The water continued to pour into the valley as if a dam had broken. Raising her hands, she willed the water to stop and sank to her knees. With a splash against the rocks, dousing them both, the rush of water ended and flowed into the new lake. She spotted Thalagar on high ground, and glanced at Jaelle, furious to see the hatred in the girl's eyes. She lifted her hand, prepared to slap the gypsy girl, and paused. One arm hung broken at Jaelle's side, and she looked away from Taliesin, sobbing.

"Nash is dead, and it's your fault," Jaelle said.

"Unless you want to drown, then I suggest you stand up," Taliesin said. "Let's hope that arrow shot at Thalagar hasn't crippled him. He has to carry us to Penkill Castle. Now stop crying. We have to get out of here!"

Thalagar flew into the air and back to the boulder. He landed and spread his wings to remain balanced. Taliesin used his wing as a stepping stool to climb onto his back and held out her hand for Jaelle. The girl's movements were awkward, and she lost her footing on Thalagar's wing. Grabbing the girl's vest, Taliesin pulled Jaelle across her lap as the horse used wing-power to lift off the boulder. He snorted several times as they lifted into the air, struggling hard to remain aflight. The weight of both Taliesin and Jaelle made it difficult for him to fly, and she quickly reached out to touch his neck, willing his injury to heal.

"We're going to drown," Jaelle cried.

Beating his wings double-time, Thalagar flew upwards. Taliesin patted his neck, able to see the arrow work itself out of his shoulder and fall away as the injury healed. He flew across the lake and entered the gorge. The Snake River continued to flow, with no sign of subsiding, into the valley. Taliesin lifted her eyes as Thalagar headed for the ruins of the castle. He sailed over a low wall and landed in the courtyard, trotting forward until he slowed to a halt. Taliesin released her hold on Jaelle, wanting her off her horse, and shouted in a loud voice, "Get down!" She gave a little shove, and Jaelle cried in pain as she scrambled off the black stallion. As soon as she moved to the side, Thalagar spun around, and reared on his hind legs, angrily lashing the air with his front hooves. The gypsy girl flew behind a fallen pillar, seeking refuge from the horse, while Taliesin patted his neck, trying to calm him. With a snort, Thalagar lowered and folded his wings. Easing off his back, Taliesin checked his shoulder and found it had healed without leaving a scar.

"I'm sorry," Taliesin said, stroking his nose.

"Apology not accepted!"

"I wasn't talking to you, Jaelle." Taliesin turned to find the girl clutching her broken arm against her chest. Jaelle looked frightened and continued to gaze around the castle ruins, clearly looking for a way to escape. "Consider yourself my guest, for the time being. You might say thank you. I did save your life, Jaelle Alvarez."

"You're a werewolf. I don't owe you a damn thing," the girl shouted. She turned away and found a stone to sit on. "It's your fault Nash is dead. If my father hadn't moved our caravan, they would be dead, too."

Taliesin moved away from Thalagar. The horse trotted over to the long grass growing around a block of stone fallen from a crumbled tower. He started to nibble, more concerned about his appetite than their surroundings, while Taliesin decided not to respond until Jaelle calmed down. Jaelle's remark had only angered Taliesin. She never would have summoned a flood if the Shan and his tribe had been in the gorge. She didn't feel she owed Jaelle an explanation, especially since the girl had tried to kill her. As far as she was concerned, Jaelle not only needed to explain her actions, she needed to apologize about a thousand times before Taliesin would ever consider forgiving her.

Taking a moment to calm herself, Taliesin decided to examine the ruins and make certain they were suitable for the Raven Clan. She left the girl to sulk and walked around the courtyard. Three of the original four corner towers remained, but only the north tower was in good condition. The stones appeared weatherworn, eroded over time, and a large hole on the north side enabled her to see the hills surrounding the flooded valley. Weeds filled the courtyard, and a layer of green mold covered the east and west walls, hit hardest by winds that swept through the gorge. Most of the stairs leading to the battlements were in disrepair. Access into the castle was still available on the east side through four narrow towers and a large door with faded blue paint. Apart from the keep, there were no other buildings. The walls remained, 10 feet wide, and were also used for sleeping quarters and storage. Chimneys were visible on each side of the castle, and a flight of stairs led to the upper level of the keep. Most of the windows retained stained glass, although a few were cracked. She heard the trickle of water and glanced at the well, now overflowing, as water started to seep across the courtyard.

"Enough water," Taliesin shouted.

With a wave of her hand, the water on the ground dried and the trickle ceased. She'd been lucky. While she was pleased she had stopped the overflowing well and healed Thalagar's injury, the flood had not been what she wanted. For some reason, her magic had gone amiss, and she didn't know why, and now the gorge and valley were underwater. Zarnoc would have been disgusted with the results. It was going to take a lot of work before she knew how to control her magic. Being a *Sha'tar* wasn't easy, but then, perhaps it wasn't supposed to be.

"Heggen's beard," she grumbled. "I didn't ask to be blessed and cursed. Why me? Why can't I just return to Raven's Nest and rebuild my life? Why do I have to save the world and everyone in it? It's not fair. It's not what I want."

"Who are you talking to?" Jaelle asked. "If you're talking to me, I could care less what you do with your life." She pushed wet, black ringlets out of her face. "Nash was right about you. You have lost your mind."

"You took the Service Oath, Jaelle. I suggest you mind your tongue," Taliesin snapped. She stomped over to the girl. "Only a few weeks ago you told me how much you loved me. Now you and your brother tried to kill me. And for what? You knew I was *Wolfen*, that's why I left Garridan. When I need your help, what do you do? You sided with your brother against me. I bet you were at the Traveling Tower when Nash and his men tried to capture Hawk. Did you know your brother threatened to kill Zarnoc as well as me? Of course, you do. Well, your little ambush failed, Jaelle. I'm not sorry Nash and his men are dead. Just be glad I saved your life."

"When it comes to love and war, there are no rules," Jaelle said.

"Yes, there are, you stupid girl! You don't go around stabbing the people you claim you love in the back, and that's precisely what you did. Turning on me is one thing. Hurting Thalagar is unforgivable!"

Jaelle lifted her chin in defiance. "What are you going to do with me?"

"I want an explanation, Jaelle. Did your father order you and Nash to kill me?"

"Hawk bit my father and quite a few other people," she said. "It's our custom to kill the werewolf responsible, but my father said...."

Taliesin held up her hand. "Before you say another word, Jaelle, I want you to know the only reason I stopped at the wagon was to look for you. I was worried you were inside that wagon. I thought the Eagle legionnaires had killed you. You know Hawk and I are not werewolves. It's an insult to every *Wolfen* to be called one. You knew Wolfgar and Phelon bit me. You knew that and lied about it. And now Hawk has run off with those two mongrels!"

"Hawk has joined the Wolf Clan?" Jaelle sounded shocked.

"So, you do admit we're Wolfen and not werewolves."

"I told my father what I saw. To my people, there is no difference between the two breeds of monsters," Jaelle said. "When you didn't come to our camp, when you made no attempt to make amends to my father, I thought you didn't care about my people or me." She angrily wiped away her tears. "All you had to do was talk to my father, and he would have forgiven Hawk and allowed me to return to you. After Rook and Wren left without saying a word to anyone, Nash suspected they were coming to join you. Nash said you tried to kill him. What was I supposed to think? He's my brother!"

"You could have trusted me," Taliesin replied. "I have no other choice and must free you from your oath. As far as I'm concerned, you are no longer a member of the Raven Clan. If your father feels the same as you and Nash, then there's no reason to talk to him. As long as your father doesn't drink human blood, he'll never turn, and that's the difference between a *Wolfen* and a werewolf. I'll heal your arm and take you home. After that, I never want to see you or your people again."

Jaelle struggled to stand. She gritted her teeth in pain as she approached Taliesin. Her tears were plentiful, too many to wipe away, nor did she try.

"My father didn't order Nash to kill you," she said. "He didn't know I went with my brother and Charon to set an ambush. Please understand, Taliesin. I didn't know Nash was going to try to kill you. He said we were going to capture you and take you back to my father to stand in judgment for Hawk's crimes against our tribe. I thought I was doing the right thing."

"You chose your people over the Raven Clan. I understand why, Jaelle, and this is why I release you from your oath." Taliesin crossed her arms as *Ringerike* let out a soft whimper, aware the sword wanted her to forgive the girl. "You can't serve my clan and your father at the same time. Zarnoc will try to break the curse. He's working on it, and I'm sure he intends to visit your father. Now let's fix your arm and get you home."

Taliesin avoided the girl's eyes, raw with emotion. She placed her fingertips on Jaelle's broken arm and *willed* the bone to mend. As it had with Thalagar, energy, warm and generous, flowed from her fingers into Jaelle's arm. She heard a welcome sigh of relief from the girl and stiffened when Jaelle smiled.

"You did it," Jaelle said, laughing. She wiggled her fingers and bent her arm. "You mended my arm. How can I ever thank you, Raven Mistress?" She threw her arms around Taliesin and tried to kiss her. "Please. Forgive me, Taliesin. Don't you know I'd do anything to be with you? Don't throw away our friendship. Please."

Taliesin remembered a shared kiss in the Ghajar camp months ago. The situation was similar, for then, Jaelle had tried to kill her to defend the honor of her older brother Tamal. Her brother served as squire to Sir Roland to redeem his honor for a past crime against the knight. Taliesin had forgiven Jaelle then. She would not do so a second time. She pushed Jaelle away.

"Why are you so cruel? You know I love you," Jaelle said, her cheeks turning a bright red.

"I'm sorry. I truly am. I can't give you what you want. I never could."

A look of hatred flashed in Jaelle's amber eyes. She raised her fist and prepared to strike Taliesin, passion driving her every motion. Taliesin sidestepped the blow. The girl flailed her arms like windmills, screaming, as she charged forward in frustrated rage. Not wanting to hurt her friend, Taliesin reached out with her hand to hold her back. Jaelle slammed into her hand and fell backward. Shocked and angry, Jaelle stared up at her in disbelief.

"Why did you hit me?" Jaelle shouted.

290 | SUSANNE L. LAMBDIN

"Hello? You attacked me! I was only protecting myself," Taliesin said, disgusted with the entire situation. She made no move to help Jaelle to her feet, wanting her to stay on the ground where she'd put her. "The last thing I want is to hurt you, Jaelle. It's why I left you in Garridan. It could have been you, not Hawk, who I turned *Wolfen*. I am unable to be with anyone who is not of my own kind. Even if you were Roland, I couldn't share a kiss with you. Not while I'm cursed."

"It's Roland you love. It's always been Roland," the girl snarled.

"Yes, always."

Taliesin watched as Jaelle turned from her, cursing at her in Ghajaran. She had no idea what to say to the girl to mend the rift between them. Jaelle had said a great many things, but she had not apologized for her actions. At the arrival of a black raven in the courtyard, Taliesin felt ashamed Zarnoc had discovered her in an emotional scene with Jaelle. The raven turned into an old man dressed in a drab brown robe. Jaelle glared at the wizard as he held out a necklace to Taliesin.

"This is made from a single strand of Broa's golden hair," he said, "wrapped around an enchanted iron nail. I want you to put it on."

Taliesin stared at the necklace, hesitant to touch it. "I assume you know what happened to Nash?" she asked, aware Jaelle watched them.

"Dreadful," Zarnoc said. "Nash paid the ultimate price for his lack of good judgment, and it seems you have learned what unharnessed magic can do. I came as soon as I could. This necklace, I think, should help keep your inner beast in check. I also instructed Rook to bring the clan here."

"This necklace will keep me from turning *Wolfen*? Are you sure it works?"

"Oh, it does, fear not. I have already collared Hornbill and the other *Wolfen* Black Wings," he said. "I've brought the Traveling Tower with me. The weapons are all inside. I think it best if you keep them safe. Now let me put the necklace on you, child."

Taliesin lowered her head allowed Zarnoc to slide the gold strand of hair around her neck, and at once felt its subduing power. The strand of hair was as strong as a chain of iron, and the nail held no heat, only magic, though it glowed red-hot. Her anger faded in an instant, replaced by a great sense of regret for what happened in the gorge, and she was aware of an ache in her heart from the loss of Jaelle. She could forgive Jaelle, but she didn't want her with the Raven Clan, not anymore. There was no cure for betrayal, other than the healing of time and distance placed between them.

"How do you feel?" Zarnoc asked.

"Much better," Taliesin admitted.

"It's a temporary solution, not a cure," Zarnoc said, with a chuckle. He gave her the chess piece and a small pouch. "Inside are necklaces for Hawk and Drake. There are more necklaces in the pouch, in case you manage to wrangle Phelon, though I suggest you don't bother. Ismeina and Black Rooster will make certain the Raven Clan arrives. I'll take Jaelle home and explain what happened in the gorge. It's not your fault, Taliesin."

"I doubt the Shan will see it your way. I killed Nash."

"I'll be glad to explain, my dear. Octavio is an understanding man."

An image of Shan Octavio, a proud, handsome man, appeared in her mind. He was husband to eight wives and father of more than forty children. She didn't want any bad feelings between her clan and the Ghajar. The Shan had been friends of Master Osprey, and she didn't need more enemies.

"Tell the Shan both Hawk and Nash have done their part in the last few days to damage the friendship between our people," Taliesin said. "For this reason, I have released Jaelle from her service oath to the Raven Clan, and it is with a clear conscious I send her home." She paused, wondering what Zarnoc was thinking, for a wistful expression appeared on his wrinkled face. "Say I desire the Shan's friendship and remain as such. If something else should be said, then you say whatever he needs to hear. I trust you."

292 | SUSANNE L. LAMBDIN

"Ah, trust," he said glancing at the gypsy girl. "So few can be trusted these days."

"Jaelle thought she was doing the right thing. Her actions made it clear she's not a Raven. Take her home, Zarnoc, and return here as soon as you can. I guess I'll be going after Hawk."

"Home is where the wagon rolls," Zarnoc said. "I'll grease the wheels of friendship with soothing words but won't apply it too liberally. It is best for a ruler to be feared, more than loved. You did what was necessary to stay alive. I think it far better for the gypsies to fear you than to think you're weak, my dear."

"I leave it to you, then," Taliesin said.

She walked to her horse, thoughts filled with doubts. She had a feeling Zarnoc wasn't talking about her leading the Raven Clan and meant the day she sat on the Ebony Throne as Queen of Caladonia. If he wanted this, then she wondered why he had told her Princess Calista had died in childbirth. And she thought about King Frederick. Fear must have guided his hand when he exiled his sister and murdered her father. Frederick was a weak king, and his princes scrambled over each other like unruly puppies fighting over a bone, proof no one loved him. Queen Dehavilyn and King Boran were tyrants, feared more than loved. Master Osprey had been loved *and* feared by the Raven Clan, but he hadn't been a king, and he hadn't been cruel.

"Farewell, Raven Mistress," Jaelle said in an unpleasant tone.

Taliesin nodded at her, thinking about Sir Roland, who had told her long ago to 'never trust a gypsy,' and though it seemed prejudiced and wrong at the time, she now understood why he had warned her about the Ghajar. Their ways were not her ways, and though Shan Octavio had given her no reason to doubt his friendship, she couldn't help wondering if he'd receive her message well. She knew Zarnoc would handle things as he saw fit. After all, he had served as King Korax's chancellor and could do the same for her. Even that knowledge offered little comfort, for the wizard had betrayed his king in the end, and his helping her now, she suspected, was only due to wanting to make amends for past wrongs.

Perhaps she couldn't trust her friends, not completely, she thought, wishing she'd said something kinder to Jaelle. She turned to say farewell and found the wizard and girl had vanished. Magic hung thick in the air, and the smell of burnt feathers lingered. It was an odd smell not associated with the wizard, and a tingle of magic spread along her arms. Worried it was a bad omen, she kissed her ring, and the red dragon scales appeared. She then touched the tiny scale on Thalagar's forehead, watching his gold armor appear, and wondered if she'd ever see Jaelle again.

* * * * *

Chapter Eighteen

Returning to Raven's Nest was not the wisest decision on her part, and Thalagar showed great reluctance to land in the remains of the village. The Wolf Clan had not left a single structure standing, though *Mother* looked as she always had, with green leaves on every limb that defied the passage of the seasons. The large hall had burned to the ground, and the vegetation consumed what remained. Weeds grew on the blackened timbers, vines crept over vacant windows, and late summer flowers sprouted from the ashes. The big red barn and the storage sheds were rubble. Wolfmen had used axes to chop down the log fence that once protected the village and left the tree-trunk posts where they fell, now covered by thick vegetation that one day would completely hide the skeletal remains of her former home.

The forest always reclaimed its own, thought Taliesin. Seeds turned into trees, trees were cut down and over time rotted to become soil for the seeds. It was the same for every living thing on the planet; the cycle repeated—birth, growth, death. She mourned the loss of Raven's Nest, but she could rebuild it, along with her clan. This was something she wanted to do and felt it was her purpose in life.

"Hawk!"

Taliesin's voice echoed through the forest as she dismounted. She drew her sword and left Thalagar in the courtyard to enter the remains of the hall. Her room had been on the second floor, with the flags she'd collected and the non-magical weapons she'd found on battlefields left on the walls to be burned or melted in the great fire. The upper rooms and guard posts in the limbs of the giant tree still existed. The Ascender, designed by Master Osprey, had been destroyed, along with the outer staircase, so there was no way to reach them. Flames had spread along the trunk of the giant ancient oak, leaving scorch marks on its lower half, but it would heal, in time.

"Hawk, I know you're here! Come here, boy!"

Returning to the courtyard, she checked on Thalagar who looked perfectly able to take care of himself in his gold dragon scale armor. She again left him to walk along the path toward the garden, strewn with blackened vegetation and debris from the hall. Her nose picked up the ripe scent of wolf. Resolute not to lose any more friends that day, she relied on *Ringerike* to point the way, aware the sword was tense and ready for action. The sword led her around the ancient oak tree, where she paused, able to hear a sharp whine of an injured wolf. Her clan often set traps for the Wolfmen, who were infrequent and unwanted visitors at Raven's Nest, and she'd thought nothing more about the traps, nor did she remember their precise locations. Pitfalls, snares, and large iron traps with jagged teeth were commonplace for capturing wild animals, including Wolfmen. She came upon a large pit with the remains of more than forty Wolfmen slain months ago by Sir Roland, then known as Captain Grudge, and the Black Wings. White bones were mixed among black ashes where nothing grew—not a single weed. The whine grew louder, carried by a strong breeze that also brought the scent of wolf and blood.

"Hawk? Drake?"

Quickening her pace, Taliesin kept to the well-worn path and circled the pit, able to see movement in the bushes. The whine turned to snarls as the prey smelled her as well. She lifted *Ringerike*, pushed aside the bushes, and gasped to see Master Phelon lying on the ground, one leg caught in an iron trap. There was no sign of Hawk or Drake. They had left Phelon in the trap, and before he'd turned into a man, the fool had gnawed at his own leg to try to get free. Phelon was in severe pain. When he spotted her, he turned from man to wolf to *Wolfen* in time to the beating of her own heart. When human, she saw only a naked, red-haired man with a bloody limb. She took pity on the wolf, hating to see any wild animal suffer. Only when he turned *Wolfen,* the monstrous and ugly shape — caught between man and wolf — did she feel anger.

"Another trap. You should have been more careful," Taliesin said as she approached him. "You need to calm down, Phelon. I want the trap off just as much as you do. Let me help you. I can heal that wound. Try to stay human, will you? I don't want you to bite me."

"The pain..." Phelon groaned as a man. The wolf whimpered when it appeared, and the *Wolfen* snarled with ferocity and continued to chew on the flesh around his femur, trying to get free.

The sound of a wagon and the gruff voices of men spun Taliesin, searching the trees for the source of the noises. Thalagar appeared near the pit, looking more like a dragon than a horse. He shook his head, worried, and flew across the pit, intent on reaching her before the strangers arrived. *Ringerike* let out a responsive whine — she was in danger.

"I can't leave Phelon," she whispered.

The sword tugged her toward the horse, insistent they leave, as the voices of the men grew louder. Taliesin made a quick decision, knowing Phelon was bleeding out, and erred on the side of caution. She could do him no good if captured by whoever approached. She climbed onto Thalagar's back, her sword raised, and watched warily as a small group of Maldavian trappers appeared. A large, bald man pulled a cart filled with wolf pelts. A young boy followed, holding the reins of a pack mule. Two more men armed with spears and swords dragged a black wolf caught in a net behind them. The captured wolf was quiet. Its eyes were bright yellow and filled with hate for its captors. She knew at once it was Hawk, still unable or unwilling to turn back into a human.

"Ho, there," Taliesin sang out. "This is Raven land, and I am the Raven Mistress. That means whatever you caught belongs to me. No poaching is allowed."

The trappers stopped at the edge of the clearing. The big man pulling the cart smiled, revealing black-stained and rotten teeth, while the boy continued forward with the pack mule, a dim-witted look on his face. It was pure luck the two men with spears dropped the net, raised their weapons, and crept forward. Hawk turned human and quietly removed the net, vanishing into the bushes.

"This here is free lands," one of the spearmen said. He wore a black cloak, and his dark and greasy hair hung past his shoulders. A layer of mud covered his worn boots and ragged pants. "I'm Connor, and these here lads work for me."

His companion, a man with gray hair and eyes and stubble on his jaw, pointed his spear at Taliesin as he started to circle around her. The boy suddenly stopped and stared at Taliesin in disbelief as the mule started to tug in the opposite direction.

"Dra...dragon," the boy said, pointing.

"Be a dragon for sure," the gray-eyed man said. "But a small one, and curious looking, at that. It has legs growing from its side, two heads, and its different colors. Seen one like that before, Connor?"

"No, Big Bud, I have not," the man in black said. "Billy, go see if it's a dragon."

The boy shook his head. "Not me. Tell Jake to do it."

Jake, the other spearman, took a step forward. He had a slack jaw, and his hands quivered on the spear, making the tip bounce.

"Did you hear what I just said?" Taliesin asked. "You can clearly see I am not a dragon. Nor do I approve of trappers. Connor, tell your men to leave the cart and furs, and I'll let you leave with your lives. That is as much as I will do for you."

"A talking dragon," Jake said. "Connor, can we kill the dragon?"

"You will do as ordered," Taliesin said. "Leave at once!"

Hearing only laughter, she wheeled her horse and pointed her sword at the black-cloaked figure as he charged her. Connor was the bravest and the most foolish. She stabbed him in the chest as Big Bud left the wagon to attack from behind Thalagar. He received a kick in the chest that knocked him to the ground. Taliesin spotted Jake as he jabbed his spear at her. She knocked it aside, cutting it in half, swung the sword back, and effortlessly removed his head from his shoulders. As the body toppled, Big Bud jumped to his feet and threw his spear at her back. It rang as it bounced off her armor and fell to the ground. The boy, Billy, took a final look at the 'dragon' and ran off screaming into the night. He didn't get far before she heard the snarls and vicious snaps of a wolf and knew either Hawk or Drake had finished off the boy.

"Now there's only you, Big Bud," Taliesin said.

Big Bud ran to his wagon and removed an enormous spiked mace. As he advanced on Taliesin, holding the rusty weapon, she heard snarls as Drake, a small blond wolf half the size of Big Bud, charged out of the underbrush. Drake jumped onto the giant's back and sank his fangs into the man's neck, producing a fountain of red blood. Taliesin jumped off her horse and stabbed the man in the chest to end his suffering.

"That'll teach you to hunt wolves," she said. "Drake, let him go. He's dead."

As the blond wolf continued to maul Big Bud, Taliesin sheathed her sword and opened the bag containing the necklaces. She pulled three out and watched as Hawk walked out of the trees. His face, covered in blood, made him look gruesome when he smiled. Taliesin placed the necklace over his head. Hawk looked momentarily confused at his surroundings and the situation he found himself in. His smile faded, and he leaned over to throw up bits and pieces of Billy onto the ground.

"There, there," Taliesin whispered as she approached Drake.

With one hand, she tossed the necklace around Drake's neck like a lasso, letting the enchanted iron nail fall against his furry chest. No sooner was it around his neck than the small wolf went into convulsions. He flopped on the ground and whined piteously, while Taliesin watched in horror, unsure how to help. After a moment, Drake grew still and with a shudder, turned from a wolf into an adult man with long, blond, shaggy hair.

"Are you all right...Wolfgar?"

"What? How...how did I come to be here? This is Raven's Nest."

"I brought you here. Don't you remember?"

"Not a damn thing!"

Wolfgar stood, naked and covered in blood, his gaze transferring from Hawk to Taliesin. He recognized her and was furious, his memory restored along with his adulthood. The Wolfman rushed past Taliesin without another word, and vanished into the bushes, going straight to Phelon.

"That's gratitude for you," Hawk mumbled.

Hawk tugged off the dirty pelt Big Bud had worn as a cape and wrapped it around his waist like a tunic, covering his lower extremities. He gave a thankful nod, decorum satisfied, at least in his mind, and hurried after the Wolf Pack captain.

"Thalagar, keep close. There may be more trappers," Taliesin shouted.

The horse gave a snort and watched as she joined the two men in the bushes. Wolfgar knelt beside the blood-covered iron trap. Phelon was no longer there. If Phelon had bitten off his own leg to get free, it would only reattach, and he'd left running or walking. *Wolfen* healed quickly, and Phelon was far enough away Taliesin couldn't hear him moving through the forest. Hawk looked squeamish as Wolfgar stuck his fingers into the blood and drew five lines along his own cheek. Wolfgar's brief stint as a boy had left him angrier than usual.

"You didn't help Phelon? Why not?"

"I meant to," Taliesin said. "The trappers arrived before I had a chance. He's already healed. *Wolfen* heal quickly, as you well know, so there's no need to be angry."

Hawk sniffed the air and Wolfgar stared at him as though it was the first time he'd ever seen the man. The two men stared at each other and bristled, both trying to intimidate the other by their glare.

"Forget about Phelon and come back with us," Taliesin said. She didn't know why it mattered, but she didn't want the Wolf Pack captain to rejoin his pack. "You're a Raven now, Wolfgar—you took the Raven service oath. You are part of my clan. Phelon is no longer your master, nor is his father. Freedom. It's what you wanted."

Wolfgar caught at the iron nail, immediately reacted as if his fingers were burned, and dropped his hands to his side. His face was lined with concentration as he tried to morph into a wolf or *Wolfen*, and he made a disgusted snort, unable to change.

"I'm not a Raven. I'm a Wolfman. Now take this necklace off me," Wolfgar said. "It's hot on my skin. Nor can I change into a wolf and go after Phelon with this on. You've no reason to enslave me, Raven Mistress. I do not belong to you. Let me go."

"I thought we were friends."

"Nothing of the sort," he said. "I may not remember much since being captured by the Lorians, but as I'm now at Raven's Nest, it's obvious you are to blame. You used magic on me. Whatever you think happened between us in Duvalen ends here. I'm not your friend. We're enemies, and I must rejoin my pack."

Taliesin sheathed her sword, and remembered the day, months ago, when Wolfgar arrived at Raven's Nest to take her to Chief Lykus, claiming she was a witch. The Black Wings had sent him away, only he'd returned with the Wolf Pack and burned Raven Hall to the ground. While his pack had run down the Raven Clan on the road to Eagle's Cliff with Secretary Glabbrio, he'd chosen to trail after her, Grudge, Rook, Wren, and Hawk. His long hunt had brought him to Garridan, to the Cave of the Snake God, and it was there Wolfgar, following Phelon's instructions, had repeatedly bitten her. She hadn't blamed Wolfgar for turning her *Wolfen*, or for obeying his master, but after their time in Duvalen, she'd thought he'd changed.

For whatever reason, which she dared not examine too closely, it was harder to let Wolfgar go than Jaelle. It was foolish, however, to try to convince the captain to stay with her clan when it was so evident he wanted to leave. Being a Raven wasn't what Wolfgar wanted, and whatever he'd been searching for during the last few weeks, the part of his soul stolen when he'd been turned *Wolfen*, had been rediscovered during their time together. Wolfgar belonged to the Wolf Clan; heart, body, and soul. She had to let him go.

"Remove the necklace and let the ungrateful wretch go after his master," Hawk said with his usual sarcasm. "I, for one, am glad I can't turn into a wolf. The bottoms of my hands are calloused, and I have fleabites where I shouldn't have bites. If you want to go after Phelon, then go, Wolfgar. I'm not stopping you."

"You're *Wolfen*, too," Wolfgar said. "Did she bite you?"

"She breathed life into my lungs after I nearly drowned. Saliva, remember? Bodily fluids turn anyone, same as a bite."

"Only human blood can make a man become a wolf. When did you taste it?"

Hawk frowned. "It's really none of your business," he said.

"You don't belong with the Raven Clan," Wolfgar growled. "Come with me, Hawk. You'll bring Taliesin only harm if you stay with her clan."

"Hawk is a Raven, true to the beak," Taliesin said.

"But I am not," Wolfgar said with a sad smile. "I swear I will not harm either of you nor try to stop you from leaving. In the morning, if Phelon orders me to find you, I will not hesitate to find you, Taliesin. Take your friend and go, and don't come back here. This is now Wolf Clan territory."

Taliesin placed her hand on Wolfgar's chest near the iron nail and saw it was leaving a scar where it touched his skin. Interesting, she thought, for it was clearly having an adverse effect on him, though not on Hawk. It could only mean Wolfgar wasn't her friend, or it wouldn't harm him. A red dragon scale was attached to his flesh under his nipple. She pulled it off and stuck it onto her arm, where it blended in with her armor. She lifted the iron nail in her hand to remove the necklace and watched as the flesh on his chest healed.

"The next time we meet, I may be forced to kill you," Wolfgar said.

Taliesin felt a lump in her throat. She understood then why it was difficult to say good-bye. In a way, by letting Wolfgar go, she was saying farewell to her own wild side.

"Is this truly what you want?" she asked.

"This was always my destiny," Wolfgar replied. "Prince Almaric and his army will soon march on Tantalon Castle. Stay out of the way, Taliesin. Be wise for once and let men do what they will do without trying to interfere. This isn't your fight, mistress of magic."

"Of course, it is."

His eyes narrowed. "Then you have decided to side with King Frederick. I knew you'd reach that decision, sooner or later. When you see Sir Roland again, be sure to tell him that you could have been mine, if you'd stayed wild."

With a dip of his head, Wolfgar leaned in and kissed her. His face was bloody and stuck to her skin, yet a shiver slid down her spine. Going on the defensive, Taliesin pushed him back and ended the bittersweet kiss, disturbed she'd reacted so intensely. His laughter only confused her. Taliesin bit her lip, wanting to say more, and found she couldn't find the words as she placed the necklace into her pouch.

"You would have made a fine Raven," she said.

An eyebrow lifted. "I've always been a wolf, Raven Mistress. Always."

Wolfgar turned, morphed into a large blond wolf, and raced through the trees after Phelon. Taliesin turned to find Hawk no longer behind her. She found him in the clearing with Thalagar standing beside the cart and unable to look away from whatever was in the back. A horrified look hung on his handsome face. Curious, Taliesin went to see what had her friend so upset. When he'd moved aside the wolf pelts, he'd found a pile of human bodies. The trappers not only killed animals, but they also hunted the Wolf Clan and made no differentiation between the species. From the smell, the kills were fresh.

"I didn't realize the trappers were using silver weapons. Of course, they'd have to, or they wouldn't be able to kill Wolfmen," Taliesin said. "Their weapons and trap are covered with old, dried blood. That's why I couldn't see the silver."

"They're not trappers. They're bounty hunters," Hawk replied in disgust.

"Murderers," she said. "I don't know why it upsets me so much, but it does."

"No doubt the king hired these bounty hunters. We should burn the bodies and the pelts. I'll toss them into the old pit. We can use the donkey and the cart to haul their filthy weapons and the trap—no reason to leave good silver behind," Hawk said. "It stinks. Let's be quick about it and return to the abbey."

"Penkill Castle. I sent everyone there. It's safer for the clan." Taliesin thought of Jaelle and wanted to tell Hawk what happened between them. Hawk had cared for Jaelle, though she had not felt the same.

"Good choice for a new Raven's Nest. I was going to suggest it myself."

"Well, I'm glad you approve," she said, her tone sarcastic.

Hawk grabbed the cart, pulled it to the pit, and dumped the load of bodies and pelts into the black hole. Thalagar led the donkey, holding its lead rope in his square teeth, though the smaller animal seemed quite content to be with the proud, black stallion.

"This is such dirty work," Taliesin grumbled. "Some things never change."

Taliesin found a long rope, tied it around the legs of the three dead men, and dragged them across the ground like dead birds. She arrived at the pit and rolled the bodies over the edge. They fell onto the remains of the Wolfmen, among which were women and children. She hadn't realized the Wolf Clan had encroached on Raven land, and the map hadn't revealed this information. Perhaps they'd hoped to rebuild Raven's Nest to use as a headquarters while the Wolf Pack laid siege to Tantalon Castle. It seemed probable Prince Almaric was already in Maldavia. Phelon and Wolfgar would soon rejoin Chief Lykus and the rebel prince and go to war. As soon as they arrived at the castle, she'd look at the map to confirm the Wolf Prince's location.

"We need kindling to start a fire," Hawk said. "Want me to gather wood? It won't take long. I'd forgotten how much I dislike this type of work."

"No. I've got this," Taliesin said.

She tapped her left wrist, and the red scales vanished, revealing her leather tunic and britches. Sparks shot into the pit when she clapped her hands together, and a fire started in the center, burning bright. Soon flames consumed the bodies and pelts.

"Can you turn the donkey into a horse with the same ease?" Hawk asked, impressed. "I didn't think you knew how to use your magic. How did you become so skilled in such a short time?"

"I'm not at all," Taliesin admitted, truthfully. "It's a knack, I suppose. We need to find something for you to wear since you can't turn back into a wolf. Neither can I. It's rather nice to be wearing human skin again. Permanently. At least while we wear the necklaces."

She concentrated on the donkey, wanting it to grow larger. At her very thought, the donkey grew into a much larger version, though it was certainly not a horse. Thalagar snorted and gave a shake of his wings as the donkey brayed loudly. It wasn't quite what she'd imagined. She tried again, and with a sudden shimmer, the donkey changed into a horse. She glanced at Hawk, her confidence growing, and imagined him in the clothing he'd worn when he first came to Raven's Nest nearly a year ago. In an instant, he was dressed in a white ruffled shirt, black pants, and tall boots, resembling a pirate. Hawk and Wren were pirate captives before they joined the clan. Hawk seemed quite content to be wearing familiar clothing, and a smile appeared on his face. She couldn't recall a time when Hawk actually smiled, for he usually frowned, and it set well on his features. He climbed onto the back of the former donkey, needing no saddle or bridle.

"You're too modest, that's what you are," Hawk said. "You've turned into a fine witch, Taliesin. I don't suppose we really need the cart or the bounty hunters' silver. The gorge is a way off. Can you wish for a pair of wings for my horse?"

"Using magic is exhausting, Hawk. I'm not sure where magic even comes from, or why I'm sometimes able to make things happen, and sometimes things turn into a disaster. Zarnoc says I'm never to make any wishes, it's a bad thing to do, so I have to be careful."

"You're only twenty-six years old. You are strong. Give it a try, Taliesin. I bet you could rebuild Raven's Nest with a wave of your hand. Seriously, do you even know what you can do?

"Not really. I'm still learning."

Taliesin slid onto Thalagar's back. She wanted to head toward the abbey to make certain her clan was on the road to the castle. When Hawk's horse brayed instead of whinnying, she realized the donkey merely looked different. It was still a donkey on the inside. She was too nervous to give it wings and find out they didn't work. Zarnoc and Ismeina were tried and true magic users, while she was an untrained natural. It made her nervous not to use spells that were binding and lasted forever. She had given wings to Rook and Wren's horses, and they'd not vanished in flight. It was surely possible to do the same for Hawk's mount with the same results.

"I can't promise your horse will fly once I give him wings," Taliesin said. "If you trust me, I'll see what I can do."

"I trust you," he said.

Taliesin closed her eyes with a deep sigh, imagined wings on Hawk's horse, and heard him laugh. The sound was warm and rich. Her eyes fluttered open, and she stared at a pair of dragon wings that grew from the sides of his horse. Maybe she'd thought about Bonaparte one too many times that day. They were bright gold, and larger than the raven wings on Thalagar. With a snort, Thalagar's armor appeared. The warhorse wasn't about to be outdone by the newcomer and had figured out how to summon the armor on his own. Taliesin peeled off a scale from her arm and handled it to Hawk.

"What's this?" he asked, holding it up.

"A dragon scale. You may need it. Just place it on your arm and tap it."

Armor appeared on Hawk when he followed her instructions. He peeled a scale away as he'd just seen her do and placed it on his horse. A bray came from the startled animal as it turned into what appeared to be a small-sized dragon, at least in comparison to Bonaparte. Taliesin was almost afraid of what she'd created. Hawk pressed his heels to his dragon-donkey with a cry of delight, and it flapped its wings, getting used to the feeling. It then ran forward, gained altitude, and flew past the giant old oak.

"Come on," Hawk shouted. "Let's have an adventure!"

* * * * *

Chapter Nineteen

Thalagar spread his wings, reared, and lifted into the air. The large black wings carried horse and rider around the giant oak, gliding under a large limb with the remains of a guard nest. Hawk, on his fake dragon, joined her as they sailed over the remains of Raven's Nest as a procession of Eagle legionnaires arrived. Taliesin spotted Sir Cerasus beneath her, mounted on his warhorse. He angrily shouted for his archers to open fire, and a wave of arrows flew into the sky and dropped short of their targets. Hawk laughed at their failure. He shook his fist at the knight as they sailed past.

"Remind me to knock that guy in the jaw when we see him next," Hawk shouted. "Right now, I just want to feel the wind on my face and enjoy the ride. We're like ravens!"

Taliesin found it difficult to hear with her helmet on. The jubilant look on Hawk's handsome face told her all she needed to know. He was happy, and they were safe among the clouds. At least, she assumed that was the case. She'd never given the Eagle Clan credit for having magic users among them; she hadn't met any until she encountered Master Xander, the Eagle heir, in the Salayan Desert, and now Sir Cerasus. An Eagle Magic Guild existed. It was news Sir Roland would find quite interesting, and she wondered if it would turn the king against Lord Arundel Aladorius and his clan. As she glanced at Hawk, she spotted a convocation of eagles, giant-sized at that, headed in their direction. Sir Cerasus was certainly dedicated to revenge, she thought.

"Hawk! We have company!"

Pointing at the eagles flying toward them from the south, Taliesin leaned across her horse's neck and set him on a fast track into the clouds. Hawk's mount stubbornly resisted flying harder, proving it retained the mind of a donkey. The screech of the giant eagles pierced the air as the clouds folded around them like large, fluffy arms. Taliesin was armed. Hawk, however, had failed to grab one of the bounty hunters' weapons and attempted to vanish within a cloud. She drew her sword, Hawk's defense on her mind, and turned in the saddle as the first wave struck.

The eagles came from all directions and attacked in pairs. Their talons scraped across the armor worn by horse and rider, causing no harm. Taliesin swung her sword and sliced through bodies as they flew through the clouds. She saw no sign of Hawk. There was no time to search for him as the eagles regrouped and flew toward her. This time, instead of clawing, they used their bodies to slam into her in an attempt to knock her from her horse. The birds were as large as ponies, and ten times stronger, and she tightened her legs against her horse, aware the scales of her armor had joined with those worn by Thalagar, fusing them together. She continued to swing her sword, keeping the eagles from pecking at the horse's head as he sped out of the clouds, and swooped toward the trees, gaining speed and distance. As they neared the forest, Taliesin noticed black smoke coming from the Wild Wood and suspected the Eagle legionnaires had set fire to the abbey.

"To Gilhurst!" she shouted.

Thalagar glided over the trees, still pursued by the giant eagles. Taliesin glanced down and gasped to see a long line of armored men marching on the main road through Tannenberg Forest. Eagle legions marched beside Erindor soldiers in red turbans and capes, headed toward the royal city of Padama. The abbey appeared in a blaze of fire and black smoke. A large group of men cut down the trees of the Wild Wood, while soldiers built catapults. More men stood outside the wall that surrounded the abbey and watched the church burn. Taliesin hoped her clan had made it out of the abbey and found the desecration of a church unforgivable.

"Damn you, Lord Arundel! This is my land! My forest!"

As she circled the abbey, Taliesin spotted the eagles flying toward her in a straight line. They were persistent creatures, and far too numerous to kill by hand. The Eagle Clan and Wolf Clan seemed adamant to kill her. If both clans wanted a war with her, then she'd oblige and give Lord Arundel and Chief Lykus a reason to fear the Raven Mistress. She was no man's fool. After the last few days and their continued harassment, she considered it a personal vendetta to exact her own revenge.

Directing her thoughts toward the eagles, she imagined the birds turning into large stones and falling from the sky. In an instant, every eagle morphed into stone and plummeted to the ground. Men fell beneath the stones, crushed and pulverized. A volley of arrows soared into the sky. Thalagar flew higher, but she kept him circling, not yet done with the Eagle legionnaires. At a simple thought, the fire jumped from the abbey like a red flaming monster and attacked the soldiers at the wall. Men encased in armor erupted like lanterns, and their screams reached her ears. Another stream of arrows flew into the air, this time turned by the Eagle's magic users into fiery missiles she cast aside with a wave of her sword and sent spiraling toward their soldiers.

As more bodies crumbled to the ground, Taliesin immediately regretted her actions. In her anger, she'd actually helped Prince Almaric and his god, Ragnal, by lessening the number of the king's army. By no means did she desire to help the rebels nor bring about the Age of the Wolf. She'd only wanted to teach the Eagle Clan a lesson, and in so doing had surely labeled herself an enemy of the crown. Now she'd never be able to join Sir Roland in Padama, and her heart ached at the miserable turn of events.

"Zarnoc, where are you?" Taliesin shouted. "I need you!"

Taliesin didn't pause to look over her shoulder as she flew away from the abbey and considered herself fortunate the Eagle magic users had failed to unhorse her. She wanted to put distance between herself and the legion, so she headed toward the Gorge of Galamus. Assuming Rook and the Raven Clan left the abbey while she fiddled with Jaelle, they should be traveling along the upper pass toward the castle. Hawk had left on his flying donkey while she was pursued by the eagles and should have made it to Penkill Castle, unless he'd taken a detour along the way. The Deceiver's Map, neatly tucked into the pouch on her belt, was the only thing other than Zarnoc that might tell her where her friends were; however, the wizard was nowhere in sight. She didn't want to open the map while in flight and risk losing it and knew she'd have to wait to look at it later. As they approached the gorge and flew between the high cliff walls, she noticed the Snake River was flowing fast, still fed by her magic.

It seemed there was permanency to her magic, a comforting thought, even if the submerged valley near Penkill Castle remained a lake. "Raven Lake" had a nice ring to it, she thought, as she studied the landscape for signs of her clan. Her heart pounded as she spotted a line of riders traveling single file along a ridge toward the castle. A dark figure she knew to be Rook was in the lead. She was able to see his dreadlocks and the tattoos on his arms as she flew over her clan. People waved and shouted beneath her. She flew toward the castle, able to see the main door was open. Hawk stood in the threshold and waved at her.

"Thank Navenna he's safe," she whispered to the wind.

Dropping into the courtyard, Taliesin slid off Thalagar's back and touched his side; his armor vanished. He trotted to the well where Hawk's winged horse drank. A tap on the ring removed her armor, and she sheathed *Ringerike*. The mountain breeze was cool on her skin, and dried her hair dampened by sweat. Her stomach growled as she ran toward Hawk, joined by Rook at the entrance. Wren and a Black Wing guard rode through followed by the rest of the Raven Clan.

Hawk turned toward Taliesin, a broad smile still on his face. "What a day this has been," he said. "How did you manage to get away from those giant eagles?"

"Turned them into stones and dropped them on the heads of Lord Arundel's men. They've burned Gilhurst Abbey to the ground. I was afraid Rook and the others were still inside. There were magic users among them, Hawk. They tried to bring me down and failed."

"I'm not at all surprised," Hawk said.

"Everyone is safe and sound, thanks to you," Rook stated. "You know, it's going to take some hard work to repair the hole in the wall, unless you use your traveling castle and patch it, good and true." He nodded at her. "I'll see that everyone is situated and will post guards. Come see me later, Hawk." He hurried after Wren.

Hawk eyed the sword at Rook's side with envy. He turned to Taliesin, his arms crossed over his chest and a frown on his face. "Maybe now you'll give me one of those magical weapons you have inside the tower," he said. "With this armor, my winged horse, and a magical weapon, I'll finally be a great warrior."

"You already are, and much more," she said. "Hillary was Master Osprey's right-hand man. Now that your inner beast is subdued, I think you're perfect for the position. Will you be my chancellor, Hawk?"

"What about Zarnoc?"

"He's my advisor."

"No, I mean, he's not here," Hawk said. "Where is he? I don't see him."

Riders continued to come through the gate, and Hawk had apparently been counting heads. A slender white form appeared on the path. Ismeina glided toward Taliesin and Hawk who immediately stood at attention. The witch was far lovelier than she remembered, and a great deal more worried than Taliesin had left her.

"Hasn't Zarnoc returned from his errand?" Taliesin asked.

"No, he has not," Ismeina replied. "The Eagle Magic Guild were in force today at the abbey. It required every bit of my magic to disguise the clan so to ensure they reached this castle safely. Zarnoc said my magic would grow stronger by being around you. I believe him. However, I'm not a clairvoyant like Wren, nor am I able to know everything that's going on like Zarnoc. I know enough to tell you with assurance he is in trouble."

Hawk rolled his eyes. "Just where did you send the old fart?"

"To take Jaelle back to her father," Taliesin said. "I might have failed to mention the Ghajar ambushed me in the gorge. The Snake River is high because I called on it to drown Nash and his men. Jaelle was with them, Hawk. Even though she tried to kill me, I thought returning her to her father would make amends for what you did."

"Zarnoc was taking Broa necklaces to the gypsies," Ismeina said, concern etched on her face. She placed a hand on Taliesin's shoulder. "I am able to protect the clan from the Eagle Magic Guild. Once this door is closed, no one will be able to get in, and no Eagle legionnaires will be able to break through my protection spells."

"That means you have to go after Zarnoc," Hawk said. "You won't mind if I don't accompany you. I should have known Jaelle couldn't be trusted. Never trust a gypsy, for they will invariably turn on you."

"I thought you loved her."

"Me? You've got me all wrong, Taliesin. What I love is gold and flying," he said. "Maybe I also love a good adventure. Correct me if I'm wrong but visiting the Shan's camp is more like...suicide."

Taliesin reached into her pouch, removed the chess piece, and handed it to Hawk. He looked surprised she'd given him the magical item and then nodded, as if accepting his new position as chancellor.

"Place it where you want it, Hawk. Clap your hands three times, and it will appear. Don't go inside to retrieve the magical weapons until I return, not unless it's necessary, and then only upon threat of death. Ismeina, you are responsible for keeping the tower door closed. I'll see everyone is given the right magical weapon when I return. We might even see about freeing the rest of the Lorian royal court."

"When you return with Zarnoc," the witch added.

Taliesin nodded. "That's right."

"Then I'm in charge?" Hawk asked.

"Rook is the captain of the Black Wings. You replace Hillary, which means as my chancellor you work together, along with Ismeina, to defend Penkill Castle," Taliesin said, hoping she'd done the right thing. It felt right, and Hawk was her best friend. She removed the map, willing it to remain as soft leather, and spread it across Hawk's back to get Zarnoc's location. Many names and armies, all converging on Tantalon Castle, appeared on the map, but she only wanted to find Zarnoc.

"Hillary served you muffins. I'm not doing that," Hawk said. "I'm a warrior."

"What? Muffins? Why are you talking about muffins, Hawk?" Taliesin asked, distracted, as she glanced up from the map. "Let Rook know his father's army is nearby. If Duke Dhul Fakar knows we are here, the Erindorians might try to take this castle. He fights with a magical scimitar called *Tizona*." She heard Hawk snort and felt *Ringerike* quiver on her back, not at all impressed with the Fakar family scimitar. "Shan Octavio's caravans are well within Thule and not far from Acre Castle. They have Zarnoc. I'll bring him back. Just take charge, Hawk, and damn the muffins."

"As long as we're clear on the subject," he muttered.

"Be careful, Taliesin," Ismeina said.

"Don't worry about a thing," Hawk said, holding the chess piece in the air. "I'll take care of everything!"

Taliesin whistled to Thalagar as she walked to the well. The clan was busy unpacking their horses and carrying baggage and supplies inside the keep. She took a moment to drink from the well herself, aware many eyes watched. There were far more people present than she'd thought were staying at Gilhurst Abbey. She wondered if more country-folk had joined their group on the road, only she didn't have time for a report from Captain Rook. She climbed onto Thalagar's back, already feeling spent as he spread his wings and charged across the rocky turf. Gold-scale armor appeared on the horse as they flew into the sky. Anyone spying on the castle would think two gold dragons were in residence and under her control. Not a bad thing, she thought, as she headed across the flooded valley toward the setting sun to deal with a problem she should have sorted out days ago.

It was her fault Zarnoc was a prisoner of the Ghajar. In her defense, she reminded herself the Shan had been the wizard's friend for many years. Any recent turn of heart seemed entirely unjustified and unfair. Zarnoc hadn't caused injury and had gone to their camp as her emissary. Any reasonable person should accept an apology if sincerely given and not expect a penalty of death to settle the score every time an offense was committed. Nash and his men had attacked her, not the other way around, and she had saved Jaelle's life despite the girl's traitorous behavior. Someone had to pay, and better her than her very own great-great-great...whatever Zarnoc was and however far removed, uncle.

The sun began to set as the horse headed toward Acre Castle. Their path crossed green hills and farmland, where farmers harvested crops of wheat, and dozens of people rolled the hay into bales, pausing to watch as they sailed past. Taliesin was able to see tiny lights from several small Thulian towns and castle towers along the way. Troops sent by wealthy nobles to Padama to fight for the king marched along the main road. Traveling at dusk made it harder for enemy spies to know their numbers, and, from high above, Taliesin was able to see their family banners and the heraldry of the knights. A great battle was impending, and everyone in the dukedom apparently wanted to be present. Several knights, not knowing who she was, waved at her, and it seemed only polite to wave back.

Such niceties would not be shown by the Ghajar, she thought.

When Taliesin had fled Raven's Nest with Grudge, Wren, Rook, and Hawk, they found Zarnoc living at the ruins of Pelekus Castle. A skirmish with Captain Wolfgar and the Wolf Pack had ended with the arrival of Shan Octavio and the Ghajar. The gypsies had driven away the wolves, welcomed them to their camp, and it was there that Taliesin had learned Grudge was really Sir Roland of the White Stags. After Tamal, the eldest son of the Shan, accused Sir Roland of raping a girl, who turned out to be the knight's own wife, they'd been expected to fight to the death. Only because of Taliesin's intervention, both men had been forced by the Shan to drink *baju*, a filthy-sweet concoction that acted as a truth serum, whereby Tamal admitted to his actions. It was not rape. Roland's wife was less than faithful and seduced Tamal, only to accuse him of rape when her husband unexpectedly arrived home.

However, the Shan was not tolerant of lying, and again at her request, Tamal became Sir Roland's squire. The four Nova brothers, Sirocco, Simoon, Khamsin, and Harmattan had left with Tamal and now defended Tantalon Castle. Had she learned from Tamal's mistake, she would have known Shan Octavio would not receive Zarnoc well and would side with whatever nonsense Jaelle told him.

All sorts of thoughts and images popped into her head during the miles covered. She imagined Zarnoc splayed on the ground, hands and feet tied to spikes as women tortured him with knives. Forced to drink *baju,* she could see him spilling all of his secrets—that wasn't so bad. Another scenario pitted Zarnoc in a fight against the Ghajars' best fighter or, the wizard tied between two horses and pulled apart. As twilight turned to night, she made it a point to still her thoughts as she noticed the glow of a hundred fires and untold numbers of gypsy wagons. The Shan's new camp was enormous, spreading across a mile, and apparently, many more tribes had joined him. A large number of men had gathered around a huge bonfire, and the thumping of drums reached her ears.

"This is it, boy," Taliesin said. "If things turn ugly, you are to leave me behind and return to Hawk. I won't have you harmed. Is that understood?"

The horse snorted as he landed at a gallop and approached the wagons. The Ghajar were a suspicious lot, who believed dark magic present in every shadow and misdeed of every person even before that soul had imagined doing them. When they saw the arrival of a winged horse covered in scaled armor, they naturally assumed it was a dragon. Weapons were drawn, and the crowd closed around Taliesin and Thalagar. She slid from his back and held her hands before her, feeling like an unjudged criminal.

Charon, the Shan's second-in-command, stepped forward, catching Taliesin by surprise. She had thought the tall, broad-shouldered gypsy had drowned along with Nash and his men. His long black hair and thick beard hung in braids, adorned with silver beads. He carried a silver ax and scrutinized her until she lifted her visor. He caught her gaze and flashed his teeth.

"It's the Raven Mistress, not a dragon," Charon announced. "We've been expecting you. Come. Shan Octavio would speak with you."

A dozen armed men circled Taliesin with their spears lowered and forced her to walk to the bonfire. Thalagar's whinny of alarm created a great commotion as men tumbled in all directions. The horse flew into the air, circled the camp, and vanished, leaving behind a few cracked skulls and men with bloody faces.

"The Raven Mistress rides a dragon," a child cried out.

"Be careful," someone muttered. "She's dangerous."

Taliesin strode toward the Shan, though her confidence wavered, for he had gathered thousands of Ghajar, and their leaders stood forward, each more impressive than the next. She hoped she presented a formidable image in her dragon armor, for she noticed silver knives flashed in the firelight and men grumbled in their native tongue. Their tone made their words plain enough to understand. She was in danger, and

Ringerike whined in protest and emitted sparks of blue from the end of the scabbard. The quick intake of breaths and additional muttering produced the results she wanted—they feared her, and that fear kept the men from laying hands on her.

"Where is Shan Octavio?" Taliesin asked.

Charon turned. "Keep walking, mistress," he said in a gravel-hard voice. "The tribes have all gathered here at his command."

"Armies are marching on Tantalon Castle. I am used to men at war."

"You do not bring the accused with you?"

"No, I did not bring Hawk. I come alone."

"Werewolf," voices whispered among the warriors.

Charon waved the tribal leaders away, for many stepped forward for a closer look at Taliesin, only to be pushed aside. Her concern grew as deadly threats continued on a louder scale. "Kill the werewolf! Burn the witch! Slay the dragon!" She might have laughed at their confusion if she had not been frightened for Zarnoc. Unable to see the wizard, she feared the gypsies had bled him dry and he lay somewhere in the dark, slowly dying. A few men tried to tap her armor with their spears, a type of bravery that won the successful a hearty cheer from their comrades. Charon lifted his weapon, shaking it at the men, and they fell back. She assumed his rise to the Shan's second was a hard-won battle. Thankfully, the men respected him, for they stopped trying to tap her and let her pass unharmed.

"Bring the Raven Mistress here," a loud voice ordered.

The Shan, a handsome, older man with gray hair and beard, wearing a dark-blue shirt and red balloon pants, waited, seated in his chair. The tips of his boots curled like the ends of his mustache. His dark eyes rested upon Taliesin as he toyed with the ends of his beard with jeweled fingers. Octavio held a riding whip. As she stopped in front of him, guarded by Charon, she noticed flesh and blood matted on his whip, and her heart fluttered in her chest.

"Greetings, Shan Octavio. I came as soon as I could," Taliesin said in a loud voice. Whenever she was frightened, she always maintained a confident demeanor. Her armor hid the fact she trembled, and to maintain the appearance of bravery, she met the Shan's gaze. "I sent Zarnoc here with your daughter this morning. Have they arrived?"

"Greetings to you, Raven Mistress," the Shan replied. He tapped the whip on his knee. "This morning, you say? That is strange, for they have not yet arrived. Nor has my son Nash and his men. Charon returned yesterday with news of their encounter with you in Miller's Wood, which is why we moved our camp here. You were lax in not coming to see me sooner. I should not have needed to send my son to fetch you. Is there a reason my son and daughter have not returned? My daughter assured me you would arrive and give amends for Hawk's transgressions. I begin to believe she placed too much faith in you. Of course, she left with Nash against my orders. It seems she has picked up bad habits from the Raven Clan."

Taliesin was surprised to learn Jaelle had spoken on her behalf. She felt even worse about their quarrel at Penkill Castle. Had Jaelle told her the truth, and admitted she'd defended Taliesin and then disobeyed her father to come after her, she wouldn't have been so hard on her nor tossed her out of the clan. Jaelle had too much of her father's pride, and now Taliesin was faced with sorting out the terrible misunderstanding.

"My enemies are many, Shan Octavio. I took the time to kill them before coming here—including Nash and his men." Taliesin heard gasps from the crowd. "I spared Jaelle's life. She said it was Nash's idea to kill me. He set a trap and nearly succeeded. Again, I ask. Where is my wizard? He and your daughter should be here, yet you say they have not arrived."

"No, they have not, Raven Mistress. Can you explain why?"

"I can only speculate," she replied. "Ismeina the White Witch said Zarnoc was in great danger. If he is not here with

Jaelle, then I suspect the Eagle Magic Guild is behind their abduction and must go look for them."

Octavio stood tall and imposing and commanding absolute silence. Seven of his wives stood behind his carved, wooden chair and clung to their children seated before them. Five hundred or more armed men had gathered in a circle around the bonfire. Taliesin felt her heart leap in her chest as Octavio walked toward her, smacking his whip on his leg until he halted with his legs braced apart.

"Werewolves in dragon armor are something we don't usually encounter," Octavio said. "You will remove your armor and sit with me so we may discuss how to best handle this matter. Your Wolfman wounded many of my people when he turned into a beast." He lifted his hand to show her fang marks. "I had no choice and killed the cursed ones, including my youngest wife. Many of my chiefs desire your blood for their blood. It is our way, and I have promised them justice. You will drink *baju* and tell me how Hawk came to be cursed, and then I will decide your fate."

"Didn't you hear me? I said Zarnoc is in danger. That means Jaelle is, too."

"That is not my problem," he said. "My daughter disobeyed me yet again. I have no choice but to exile her from my tribe. When one female shows disobedience, others will follow, and I cannot allow this to happen."

"Lay one hand on me, and I'll lay low your entire tribe."

"You dare threaten me?"

"I am the Raven Mistress," she replied, her temper getting the best of her. "I don't have to make threats. Nor do I care if I am outnumbered, Shan Octavio. I tell you Jaelle and Zarnoc are in danger, and it is not from Hawk or the Raven Clan. Both the Eagle Clan and Wolf Clan would see me dead and all Ravens destroyed. Can we not go somewhere else to talk?"

A smile played upon his handsome face. "In private then?"

"Yes, in private," she hissed. "I'll tell you everything if you come with me now. We've not much time. Not if your daughter and Zarnoc are prisoners of the Eagle Clan. You should send out your best riders and try to find them."

Charon, heeding Taliesin's warning, stepped forward. The Shan turned to speak with him. His second gave a nod, lifted his hand, and held up five fingers. Fifty men followed as he headed away from the bonfire, and soon they were riding from the camp.

"How did Nash die?" Octavio asked.

Taliesin hesitated. "You said we could talk in private."

"We have no secrets here, Raven Mistress. Speak."

"Perhaps it's best if I show you...."

The Shan made no move to leave his men, forcing her to take drastic measures to get his full attention. She took a step back and reached for *Ringerike*, aware the gypsies were muttering angrily and pointing their own weapons at her. She pulled her sword from the scabbard, grateful when it burst into a bright blue light and brought shouts of alarm from the crowd. Even the Shan looked amazed and shielded his eyes from the glare. Women and children knelt, while the men lowered their weapons. To see their reactions told her they were fully aware she held the Raven Sword, and what that meant, for only the heir of King Korax could wield the legendary blade. Once, the Ghajar bent a knee to the Raven King. Taliesin was no queen, so the Shan merely placed his hand over his heart and inclined his head.

"*Ringerike*," he whispered. "You found the Raven Sword."

"Yes, at great cost. It was at the Cave of the Snake God I was bitten by Captain Wolfgar. I do not turn *Wolfen* while I wear this magic iron nail," she said. "Zarnoc and Ismeina the White Witch found a way to suppress the transformation. I have more necklaces with me, Shan Octavio. Had you waited, I had the means to keep your people from changing. Hawk now wears a necklace made from the hair of the goddess Broa and a nail enchanted by Zoltaire the Great. One day I will find a way to end the curse of the Wolf Clan. However, you asked about Nash. Since we last met, I have learned how to use my magic, Shan Octavio. It's how I raised the Snake River, and how I killed Nash and your men."

"She admits she killed Nash," an angry man shouted.

"Ghajar law demands justice," another called out.

"Silence! This is the Raven Mistress, heir of King Korax, and as such, our laws do not apply to her. Hear me, people." The Shan, furious at the interruption, lifted his hand and glared at the crowd. When he turned to Taliesin, he placed his hand on her forearm in a possessive manner. "You will treat her as a guest and not question my authority. I speak for everyone here, and should anyone say otherwise, my guards will bring silence by the tips of their swords."

"Yes, great Shan," a man with hair dyed bright red said. Taliesin assumed he was the Shan's third in command, or at the least, one of the chiefs of another gypsy tribe, for no one else spoke afterward.

Unsure of what Octavio expected from her, she sheathed *Ringerike*, knowing the sword remained on guard, and her thoughts briefly turned to Thalagar, hoping he'd reached Penkill Castle unharmed. She kept her armor on, nervous when his hand slid down her arm and grasped her hand. He held her fingers in a tight grip as he led her past his chair and through the circle of gypsies toward a large red wagon where men stood guard. The door was opened. The Shan drew her inside after him, released her hand, and sat at a table. She joined him, no longer feeling threatened, and realized the Shan still considered her as a friend.

"What has happened, Taliesin? I want to hear everything."

"It's too long of a story," she said. "I think we should locate Jaelle and Zarnoc. I have Zoltaire's Deceiver's Map. It will show me where they've gone."

"Then show me," he said. "I'll pour us glasses of wine. We will drink in friendship as we have done in the past."

"I'll drink from the same glass as you do, Shan. Jaelle did try to kill me."

"And you think I'll do the same. If I wanted you dead, Taliesin, I would not have brought you inside my wagon.

Chief Toman spoke on your behalf. He is the eldest of the chiefs and my younger brother." The Shan smiled. "All the chiefs are my brothers by birth. No one will raise a sword against you. Your horse need not have left—Thalagar would not have been harmed."

"I told him to leave if there was trouble," she said. "He did as I asked."

"And I give you my assurance you are safe, Raven Mistress."

It was a matter of trust, yet again....

Taliesin tapped the ring, and her helmet and armor vanished. She reached into her pouch, eager to look at the map, and spread it upon the table. In the candlelight, the material remained soft, like leather, but Zarnoc and Jaelle did not appear as she had hoped.

"The Deceiver's Map is being difficult for some reason," she said. "It's possible Lord Arundel and his magic users have used a spell against me. They are a far greater threat than I am, Shan Octavio. I am your friend."

"Let us drink to that...friend."

The Shan placed a goblet on the table, took a sip, pushed it toward her, and leaned over to gaze at the blank piece of leather. He seemed disappointed he was unable to see what she did—an outline of Caladonia with moving stars that represented enemy troops. She raised the glass to her lips and sniffed. The gypsy wine smelled like fresh blackberries, which she did not like. Thirst overcame her dislike of the berries, and she lifted the goblet, accepting the risk it was poisoned, and took a sip. It was sickly sweet. Disgusted, she placed the goblet on the table and licked it off her lips.

The Shan's soft chuckle made her feel embarrassed. "I'm not trying to poison or to trick you," he said. "Why can I not see the map? It's nothing but a piece of leather."

"Because it's magical and needs a magic user to read it. Even then it can be tricky," Taliesin said, feeling her stomach gurgling from the blackberries. She grimaced as she gazed at the map, fearing she might belch, and with a lean finger, traced Thule and a road that led into Erindor. "Earlier, the map showed Jaelle and Zarnoc were in Thule. That's no longer the case. They are now on the road to Erindor, hostages of the Eagle Clan. I fought their magic users at Gilhurst Abbey. Another reason why I was late coming here, Shan Octavio. It wasn't out of disrespect or fear."

"You came for Zarnoc. I know this, Taliesin. Not for Jaelle or for me."

Taliesin nodded. "The map can show me whomever I want to see, but as of late it has been lying," she said. "Zarnoc *was* coming here to help you. If he has been taken prisoner, it must be by a powerful sorcerer. Who is more powerful than my great-uncle? Is Lord Arundel more of a threat than I gave him credit?"

"The Eagle Clan has long since harnessed the powers of darkness," he said. "It is common knowledge among my people that sorcerers and sorceresses who use the black arts reside at Eagle's Cliff. It would require more than one magic user to take Zarnoc hostage. Had I suspected Eagle magic users were at the Gorge of Galamus, I would have sent Nash to hunt them down, not you. His orders were to capture you, Taliesin. As for Jaelle, she loves you, and the love of a gypsy is passionate and deep."

"I know I hurt her," she said. "I'm sorry."

"The apology is not owed to me. Nor is it necessary to offer one to Jaelle. She has disobeyed us both and as a result is now a prisoner of Lord Arundel." The Shan sat back in his chair and crossed one leg over the other. "The Eagle lord is far more dangerous than you realize. Zarnoc must have told you that Arundel lived during the age of King Korax and always plotted behind his king's back, which he now does with the Draconus kings. My people are coming here from all over Caladonia. Duke Andre has opened his borders to us because I once saved his life, and he owes me this favor. The young duke intends to go to Tantalon Castle to fight for his king. What are you going to do?"

326 | SUSANNE L. LAMBDIN

"About the king, nothing. About Zarnoc and Jaelle? Go after them."

"On your own? You will not stand a chance against the Eagle Clan's black magic, Taliesin. I know you have *Ringerike*, and I know of the sword's greatness. It will take more than *Ringerike*, a flying horse, and a little white magic to defeat their dark guild."

"Then I'll take the Black Wings with me," she said. "My clan is growing. People are leaving their farms and flocking to Penkill Castle. Most want protection. The dukes are all headed toward the royal city, prepared for war, and people are afraid."

"If you are going to Eagle's Cliff, you will need more than a handful of guards."

Taliesin decided to tell the Shan everything. His support was crucial, especially since he commanded thousands of Ghajar warriors, and she might have need of them one day. Unlike the citizens of Caladonia, the Ghajar valued magic and hid many magical weapons in their wagons. As gypsies who lived a wandering life, they paid little creed to the King's Law, and as such were considered outsiders, which meant the laws did not apply to them.

"I took most of the magic weapons from Duvalen," Taliesin said. "The Lorian queen and king might be related to me, but they are extremely hostile. They've signed a truce with the Hellirins. You know as well as I do that this civil war will spread to all four corners of the continent before it is over, Shan Octavio. The Magic Realms are already involved. Queen Dehavilyn thought I was dangerous and locked me in a prison cell. My cousin, Prince Tamblyn helped me escape and has joined the Raven Clan. The Hellirin's ruler, Duchess Dolabra, was the sister of King Korax and King Boran. It amazes me to think that at one time each of the Vorenius children had a kingdom of their own, but it was Boran and his wife, Dehavilyn, who plotted against Korax and brought about his demise."

"I'm well aware the fairies and *darklings* are treacherous beings," he said. "Perhaps your magic has grown strong enough to defeat Arundel's magic guild. Have you ever been inside Lord Arundel's home before? It is like no other castle you have ever been inside, for it's a labyrinth, built to keep prisoners from ever escaping the Eagle mountain."

"No. Never. It can't be any worse than the Cave of the Snake God."

Taliesin let out a soft cough, aware her throat was dry, and took another sip of wine. The moment the sickly-sweet liquid trickled down her throat, she realized it was *baju*, which explained why she felt the need to tell Shan Octavio everything. The Shan offered a knowing smile and chuckled at his own deception. He reached out to take hold of her hand. She felt a tingle of excitement and felt a blush creep up her neck.

"You are very brave. None can deny that," Octavio said. "I have been to Eagle's Cliff before. It was a long time ago, when I was a young man, but I doubt it has changed since I was a guest of Lord Arundel. His son, Xander, is eight hundred years old. Some say their family crawled out of the ocean and they are not humans at all."

"Is it true?"

The Shan chuckled. "I cannot say for certain. I believe they walk on land as men, and in private return to their natural state in water," he said. "Eagle's Cliff has deep wells, Taliesin, and some run straight to the ocean. Lord Arundel may have once served King Korax as a knight and been a loyal friend, but through the ages, he has turned evil. So has his son, Xander. If the Eagles now march on Tantalon Castle, I do not think it is to side with King Frederick or to help Prince Almaric take the throne. Arundel wants the Ebony Throne for himself. He has always coveted the throne and will kill anyone who stands in his way, including my daughter and our friend Zarnoc, for he also wants *Ringerike*. If you go after them, know that it is a trap."

The sword gave a heavy sigh, confirming the Shan was right.

"The map can turn into a floorplan and show me the details of Eagle's Cliff, including the precise location of Zarnoc and Jaelle's prison cells," she said. "It can even tell me the names of everyone in the Eagle Magic Guild if I ask it to. As long as Arundel's magic users don't try to tamper with it, the map does work."

"A guide will suit you better, my dear. I will take you there, Taliesin."

"It will be dangerous. Extremely. Your people need you. It's not worth the risk."

"My daughter would think me a coward if I did not go." His fingers brushed across the iron nail hanging from her neck. He tested the strength of the golden hair with a gentle tug and found it unbreakable. "At such an auspicious moment, when life and death have only a strand of hair to set them apart, I find it pleases me to face such danger at your side. For now, Raven Mistress, you must rest. I insist you use my wagon."

"I'm not tired," she said, unable to suppress a yawn.

"I admire your spirit. Your body says otherwise."

His deep chuckle gave her goosebumps, and he smelled like grass and sky and smoke from the fire. When he dropped the nail and leaned back in his chair, she reached into her pouch and removed one of the Broa necklaces, sliding it to him across the table. He placed it around his neck and stood.

"I thank you for the gift," he said. "Of course, I will sleep elsewhere. You're far too beautiful, Taliesin, and I would prove to myself I can resist all forms of temptation."

"Break of light, wake me."

Octavio tapped his hand to his forehead. "But of course, mistress," he said, leaving her to sleep in a bed that smelled exactly like him.

* * * * *

Chapter Twenty

Morning brought Taliesin the sight of Thalagar waiting outside the wagon as the sun, angry and red, seeped along the horizon. The horse wore a saddle and bridle as if he'd come out of the barn to find her. He had not come alone. Hawk had brought Captain Rook and the Black Wings. The Black Wings gathered beside her wagon, dressed appropriately in black cloaks and not the dark-green cloaks her clan used to wear.

"We rode all night to reach you," Hawk said. "The witch figured out Zarnoc is in Erindor. Not that it was difficult for her to do so. The old fart managed to send a message through a friendly pigeon, though how it got through the eagles circling our castle seems to be the miracle of the day. Zarnoc said to stay out of his affairs, which clearly is a cry for help, so Rook decided to come looking for you and well, here we are."

Rook bowed his head. "Raven Mistress, my blood brother is far too enthusiastic this morning to realize the danger he personally is in. I asked him not to come with us. Our horses are too exhausted to ride any further. We pushed through the night and rode until we saw the campfires. They're in no shape if we must take flight."

"It's alright," Taliesin said. "Everything with Shan Octavio is as smooth as the fuzz on a baby chick. I explained Hawk has been tamed, and Shan Octavio now wears a necklace as well. He has also expressed a desire to come with us to Eagle's Cliff. Since you roused me before he did, I'm sure we have time for breakfast." She was surprised when Hawk handed over the small chess piece. "You brought the Traveling Tower?"

"Ismeina thought you might need it," Hawk said. "If we're going after that old wizard and Jaelle, we will need magical weapons. Maybe it's time you handed them out. I mean, you did give Rook the Draconus ancestral sword, so surely, it's not too much to ask. As for the other weapons, you can give them to whomever you want...."

Rook placed a hand on *Calaburn's* hilt. As Hawk continued to prattle, Taliesin considered herself quite fortunate she'd selected Rook as her captain. He was silent and thoughtful, and showed the respect due the leader of his clan, not buying into the nonsense that flowed from Hawk's lips. Rook was younger than Hawk by at least seven years yet seemed a man in comparison. Earnest, Hornbill, Kingfisher, Trogon, Petrel, Robin and Condor seemed quite proud to be wearing the cloaks of the Black Wings. At the approach of Shan Octavio and the thirteen men chosen for the journey, Captain Rook stepped forward to introduce himself. Twenty-three Ravens and fourteen Ghajar seemed a suitable number of warriors to assault Eagle's Cliff, and Taliesin found several young men among the chosen gypsies who shared their father's dark, good looks. The Shan wore black, as did his men, a color Taliesin had not seen used by the Ghajar. She thought the somber shade befitted their clandestine mission.

"Good morning, Raven Mistress," the Shan called out. "As your Black Wings are here, we can prepare to leave for Eagle's Cliff. First, you must eat."

A young woman appeared from nowhere, bringing Taliesin a cup of strong java and a plate of raisin scones. She selected one from the tray and raised an eyebrow at Hawk, her thoughts on muffins. Hawk took one look at Shan Octavio and hid behind Rook. Not wanting to spoil Hawk's preconceived notion he was about to be slaughtered by the gypsies, Taliesin sipped her coffee as she walked from the group and placed the Traveling Castle on the ground. She snapped her fingers, instead of clapping, and the tall black tower appeared, causing quite a stir among the Ghajar.

"What is this marvelous tower?" Octavio asked. "And where can I get one?"

"Just wait and see," Taliesin replied.

Rook, Hawk, and the Black Wings remained to have breakfast with the Shan while she entered the tower. She placed her cup on the table and found the weapons precisely aligned where she'd left them. Nothing was out of order nor a chair out of place. Magic was wonderful at its best, she thought. Hawk was first to enter the tower.

"The rapiers I mentioned have basket hilts, Hawk. They're twins," she said. "My father told me about the twin rapiers, *Sting* and *Fang*, when I was a little girl. They were made by Falstaff for a great swordsman known only as 'The Ghost,' who fought many duels and never lost. It was his jealous wife who finally brought about his demise, with an iron skillet to the skull."

"Anyone can see they were made for me," Hawk said, puckering his lips and making kissing sounds as he walked toward the table. "Come to daddy."

Hawk lifted one rapier at a time and kissed both. Since they were exact duplicates, Hawk didn't know he'd kissed *Sting* until the sword spoke to him—an intimate imprint passed from the sword to its owner upon acceptance. The bond was also forged the moment he kissed *Fang*. Hawk was unaware of the drawback, for, without equal affection, they'd both turn on him. However, every magical weapon came with a side-effect, she thought, some were simply worse.

"Thank you very much, Raven Mistress!" Hawk's laughter filled the tower as he strode into the sunlight and branded his new blades.

"Send in the Black Wings," she called after him.

Hornbill was the first to enter. Neither he nor any of the Ravens would know the significance of what weapons selected them. Names mentioned held little meaning, for only a prolific reader or someone prone to listening to actors and poets in taverns or on stage with traveling minstrel shows would ever know the names of the legendary weapons. Taliesin stood alongside Hornbill. The former Wolfman was fast becoming a favorite of hers, with his big nose and big toothy grin.

"It's easiest to let the weapons pick their owners," Taliesin said. "Otherwise, I'll be at this all day, picking and choosing who goes with whom. Place your hand out, Hornbill, and walk along the table. You could hear a whine, a squeak, or a shrill note. If a weapon talks to you, it wants you. If two shout out, I'll help you pick between them. If no weapon makes a sound, just stand to the side and wait until everyone else goes through the line, and then we'll find something suitable."

Hornbill gulped as he lifted his hand and walked slowly along the length of the table. A Mandrake sword wanted him, one of five on the table, all made for the Caladonian princes. It seemed odd a sword of silver made by her father wanted to be used by a Wolfman, and stranger still when he picked it up and was not burned. The Broa necklaces worked, and silver no longer hurt the Wolfmen-turned-Ravens. Nor was she surprised when a Mandrake sword picked each Wolfman turned Raven. Robin, however, arrived too late for a Mandrake sword. A Rivalen ax whined at him, and he eagerly grasped it, lifting it to feel its weight.

"I like it," Robin said, moving aside for Earnest.

The former Eagle looked delighted when a longbow, engraved to appear wrapped in ivy, chimed in, wanting to be claimed. He grabbed the bow, along with a quiver filled with arrows with purple fletchings. And so, each weapon, from spear to ax, longsword to dagger, chose an owner. No one was turned away.

At last, the Shan and his men appeared in the doorway.

"One weapon remains," Taliesin said. "*Dark Blood*, a legendary curved sword used by the Lorian hero, Cul'Hagan, in ages past. It is said the sword grows more powerful the more lives it takes. It's taken hundreds and is able to cut through any metal or rock. I don't imagine Eagle legionnaires' armor is all that thick, even if magical." She motioned Shan Octavio to come forward, taking delight in the fact he seemed almost shy about accepting a weapon among so many Black Wings.

"I do not think I should have a weapon, mistress. They are meant for your clan."

"You once gave *Moonbane* to my companion, Sir Roland. In return, I now give you *Dark Blood*. Try it out. Let's see if the sword likes you, Shan Octavio."

"*Dark Blood* is a jealous sword," Octavio said. He slid his hand along the blade, and a red glow appeared on the metal beneath his fingers, clearly some type of bonding ritual between them. "I know about this particular sword, Raven Mistress. Moreover, I could tell you many stories about the legends and lore of the heroes and villains of this land, and beyond. Clearly, *Dark Blood* wants me."

"Must be true love," Taliesin said. "She didn't glow for anyone else."

"Then it is settled. I accept the gift, Raven Mistress."

As Octavio's hand closed around the hilt, the blade turned blood red with traces of lighter red appearing like veins pulsating beneath a transparent layer of magic. A womanish moan, faint but audible, came from *Dark Blood*, and the Shan's expression changed as if he experienced a pleasurable satisfaction from merely holding the curved sword. Side effects were always unusual in nature. Some were serious, even dreadful, and others were comical or beneficial. However, the Shan's wives would certainly discover their husband had little desire for them, for he'd unknowingly forged a type of marriage with the magical sword.

"*She's* very jealous," Taliesin said. "In every story told about Cul'Hagan, he never married and spent his life traveling the world, saving and rescuing damsels, as well as a few tender princes. *Dark Blood* never let the hero fall in love with another and remained at his side until the very end—a cold, steel mistress, this one." She offered a smile, but this powerful man needed no reassurance, for confidence oozed from his pores as he studied the weapon. "I wouldn't dare give it to anyone else," she continued, "as it can consume a weaker personality. I know you can control *Dark Blood*."

"I'm possessive as well, Taliesin. And married many times over. Why a weapon has a gender is beyond me. I know *Dark Blood* is one of a kind. It's a match well-made and will suit me later in life."

"As long as you know what *Dark Blood* is, there can be no surprise."

The Shan smiled at her. He slid the curved sword under a bright purple sash worn around his middle and adjusted his maroon vest, covered with silver beads, so the weapon was shown off to its best advantage. The silver blade sparkled in the light and pressed against his thigh as if it wanted to be as close as possible to its new owner.

"Let's discuss how we are going to save my daughter and that crazy old wizard," the Shan said with affection in his voice as they walked out of the tower. "We can't simply ride to Eagle's Cliff and knock on the door. They've seen your flying horse and will be expecting you on the King's Road. However, they won't expect us to come at them from the west, across the marshes. Deception is key, Taliesin. As long as the Eagle Clan suspects you remain with my people, we have a chance at surprise. Someone who wears your armor and has a winged horse should stay here." The Shan pointed at her new chancellor, who was swinging his swords outside the tower to impress the gathered women.

"Hawk won't mind having all the attention for once," Taliesin said. "If you can guarantee his safety, then I'll ask him to remain and play decoy." It meant riding to Eagle's Cliff without armor for herself and her horse. Hawk's horse had gold armor when he first arrived, and since Hawk already had a red dragon scale, both he and his mount might fool the enemy.

"Chief Toman will be ordered to protect your friend with his life. My word is law, Taliesin. None will touch Hawk. Toman will do what I say, or he knows upon my return I will inflict such pain he will beg for death."

This was not a threat, he meant what he said, and it meant a great deal to her when the Shan stuck out his hand. It was a Caladonian custom, not a Ghajaran one, to shake hands. His grip was firm, promising his full support, without which she felt far less optimistic about their chances. She knew the Shan was putting a great deal of faith in the Broa necklace.

One of the Shan's sons approached — a young boy wearing silver hoop earrings. He listened as his father whispered in his ear, ran off, and returned moments later with the eldest chief, Toman.

Taliesin waved Hawk over and explained the plan to him. "It means you'll need to stay in your armor at all times, as will your horse, except at night. No one must suspect you're not me," Taliesin said. "Chief Toman will ensure your safety. I am sure he does not want to experience the wrath of the Raven Mistress."

"No," Chief Toman said in a deep voice. "I do not. I will keep your man safe."

"The Raven Chancellor, for that is what Hawk is, is a position of great respect in my clan," Taliesin replied. She clapped her hands three times, and the tower shrank. The boy with the silver earrings picked it up and ran over to place it into her hand. In turn, she handed it to Hawk. "King Korax's royal court is inside this tower, Hawk. Safeguard this tower with your life."

"I will not let you down." He bowed low, and when he straightened, he wore the red-scale armor, with his helmet winged as hers had been. His height matched her own, and at least from a distance, he would fool any spies.

Taliesin laughed when the boy handed Hawk a braid of hair dyed right red. Hawk looked as if he had no idea what to do with it. The boy tapped Hawk's arm and motioned for him to tuck the braid under his helmet. Hawk placed her hair under his helmet and let it fall across his armored shoulder — the final piece to add to the deception. Taliesin walked to Thalagar and peeled off the golden scale on his arm, startled to find it turned into a shield. She handed Bonaparte's scale to Hawk and motioned for him to put it on his own horse. As he did as she asked, she tucked her hair under a black scarf and tied it around her head. She slid into a gypsy coat with padded shoulders, blue as the sky. The Black Wings removed their cloaks and gave them to Ghajar volunteers who, after giving their vests and coats to the Ravens, placed the black cloaks around their shoulders.

"Of all our brothers, Toman, you are the only one I trust," Octavio said. "Look after Hawk as you would one of our people, and make sure Payton stays out of trouble." He ruffled his son's hair with an affection not commonly shown by adult males, clearly favoring the boy. "And you, son, show this Raven what it means to be a Ghajar."

"I shall father," Payton said with pride in his voice.

"You may rely on me, brother," Chief Toman said, offering a thin smile. He was a hardened warrior. He shared neither his older brother's good looks nor his charm. If the Shan failed to return, he would assume the position as the great leader of all the Ghajaran clans. "Be wary among the Eagles, for they have hearts of stone and souls dark as night."

Within the hour, the group, mounted on fresh horses, rode from the large Ghajaran camp. One of the Shan's sons, wearing a bright red jacket, rode in front on a white stallion. The Eagle Clan was cunning as well as prudent, and spies were surely watching. Taliesin and the two women selected by Rook to join the Black Wings were dressed as men and stayed in the center of the group. She'd covered Thalagar with a dark purple blanket, despite his protests about hiding his glorious wings. Anyone watching from a distance would see only gypsy warriors. It would take four days of traveling on the main road to reach Eagle's Cliff since discretion was required as they crossed five hundred miles of open hill country.

Taliesin felt uneasy as Thule troops appeared along the road, hoping they wouldn't insist her group join them, for the king needed as many soldiers as possible if he was to win the war. The gypsies kept on the move and gave the soldiers no cause to stop them, and soon the fluttering banners and bright armor were no longer in view. Ahead was a hard ride through rugged terrain, with few towns and castles between them and the border of Erindor. As the morning slid into the afternoon, she was tempted to gaze at the map to reassure herself Zarnoc and Jaelle were still alive; it was starting to become an obsession. Relying on experience and instinct had worked for years, and she didn't want to lose her independence by relying on the Deceiver's Map. Nor did she want to spend time guessing if it was accurate or lying, so she refrained from looking and tried, instead, to focus her attention on the landscape and the wildlife.

In the past, she'd always been able to anticipate what was ahead of her by the types of birds encountered. A flock of ravens settled into a large cornfield, one of Thule's main crops, unconcerned about scarecrows placed within the tall shocks or the passing gypsies. Most considered ravens a bad omen, but she found ravens comforting. Several white cranes winged their way over the group, which meant fresh water was nearby. A lone hawk circled overhead, hanging on a wind draft while searching for rabbits. Nothing was out of the ordinary. The farmland gradually turned into rockier terrain, dotted with patches of dense trees. She listened instead of relying on her eyes and heard the doleful cry of an owl in the distance. The elders in her clan had thought it the song of death. To others, it meant murder was about to be committed, and some believed it was a sign of ill-boding at the birth of an infant. She found the song lonely and haunting and imagined Zarnoc and Jaelle sitting in dark cells wondering if anyone was ever going to rescue them.

"Do you hear the barn owl hoot?" Rook asked.

Taliesin rode beside her captain, who had a bright orange scarf tied around his head, covering his lower face. He had every reason to be as cautious as her about revealing his identity. When they crossed into Erindor, his dark complexion would blend in with the populace; that didn't bother her. She was worried the duke's eldest illegitimate son might be recognized. This apparently wasn't on his mind, for he continued to talk about the bird.

"Some say barn owls are friends of the gods," Rook said.

"They do say that. I don't believe it."

"You should. I know Ragnal visited you in Miller's Wood. When the gods walk among mortal men, it is time to take heed and notice when winged messengers appear."

"I don't think it's anything to worry about, Rook. Nor do you need to worry about Wren. Ismeina and the clan will look after her."

"They said if you lay the heart and right foot of a barn owl on anyone who is asleep, he must answer whatever you ask of him. But a warrior who carries its heart will be strengthened in battle."

"And if you place it over the heart of your loved one," she said, "he must admit whether he loves you or not. They are simply stories, Rook, nothing more."

Rook glanced toward the trees as the wind picked up, and the owl quieted. They rode on, passing a rock formation that reminded Taliesin of a sleeping giant. At least, no wolves would be in their area since they kept to the forest. She again felt the urge to look at the Deceiver's Map. She wanted to know if Sir Roland and the Knights of the White Stag had arrived at Tantalon Castle, where the armies of the eight dukedoms now headed, while they rode through the country.

"Roland does love you, Taliesin." Rook glanced at her. "He did come to Dunatar Castle, and his knights defeated the Wolfmen. I know he hoped to find you there. Before he left, I told Roland you would never wed Prince Sertorius. I told him that you loved him, only sometimes you can be stubborn. I can't say he was convinced when he left that you love him or wouldn't marry that snake."

"A snake who just happens to be my cousin, so it's a good thing I didn't marry him," she said. "Thank you for saying those things to Roland. I hurt him, Rook, and I fear when I see him again that he may no longer love me." She swallowed a knot in her throat and quickly changed the topic. "You know, if you want to be strong in battle, you need to carry a peacock feather."

"Whenever you grow melancholy, your brows knit together, and that only happens when you're thinking about Sir Roland. I'm sure he loves you, Taliesin. I told you before that true love is special. Wren and I feel that way about each other, and one day soon, I will make her my wife. Maybe one day you'll marry Roland."

"Maybe," she said. "Let's hope we both survive to rejoin our true loves. This is bandit country, you know. We need to keep our voices low."

A look of concern crossed his face. "You've been here before?"

"Many times," she said.

"Did you meet the Duke?"

Taliesin thought of Mrs. Caldwell and her sad story. She didn't share this information. "Yes, I met him, and his son," she said. "Duke Andre's father enjoyed going to war for just about any reason. He made war with his lords and with the Erindorians. The old duke was battle-hungry, and our clan made a profit off those slain by his army. Andre Rigelus, however, is not like his father. Not at all. Andre has treated the Raven Clan with respect and allowed us to enter his lands to collect weapons and armor off the battlefield whenever there was even a minor skirmish. He always insisted his nobles buy whatever we had to sell because he liked Master Osprey. It's because of the bandits I was only allowed to come with the clan twice to this dukedom. Captain Leech and the Black Wings never lost any wagons or loot. His boots are large to fill, Rook."

"I have very big feet."

Rook's laughter brought a smile to her face. It faded at a sharp whine from *Ringerike*. As she turned to the captain, the world around her seemed to move in slow-motion. She heard the whiz of an arrow and was able to see it slowly travel through the air and strike a gypsy rider, yet it took a long time for the man to fall from his horse. Her own movement was unaffected, however, and as she rode past the group, she was able to see bandits positioned among a rocky escarpment. They took no notice of her, and her own group seemed unaware they rode past.

"What magic is this?" she whispered.

Taliesin rode around the bandits, frozen in place like statues, mouths opened and arrows in flight that moved not an inch. It felt as if she stared at a painting of a battle, and she caught a whiff of burnt feathers and noticed an eerie fog roll in from the east. A blanket of white covered the Black Wings and the Ghajar. When it reached the rocks and the bandits started to vanish into the dense cloak, she gave a shout and rode in the opposite direction. The frantic hoof beats of her horse were the only sound as she rode across the tended fields, only to find the fog moved faster until she and her horse were completely enveloped.

"*Taliesin!*"

The ghostly voice that called her name came from out of nowhere. With a snort, Thalagar pawed at the ground, and *Ringerike* let out a soft whine. She drew the sword from its scabbard and held it aloft. A bright blue glow permeated the fog, and a castle, surrounded by a great forest, appeared. To the south of her position, one tree stood taller than the rest, *Mother*, where Raven's Nest lay, though it looked younger, and no watch nests appeared on the upper limbs. There was no wind to stir the tree limbs, nor even a single bird in flight. The fog moved away from a well-worn path that led to a black fortress with eight differently-shaped towers. A yellow light glowed in one slender tower that seemed to beckon to her.

"Careful," Taliesin said to Thalagar. "We've been brought here. I don't know by whom or for what reason." She tugged the blanket away from his wings and dropped it on the ground, finding no reason for disguise in this strange, silent place.

Part of her knew she was gazing upon Black Castle — she'd seen pictures in a book, and it could be no other place. Yet, the Tannenberg Forest, a wild place that spread over hundreds of miles, was far larger now than in her own time. The city of Padama did not exist, not yet, and no one else was on the road. She headed toward the castle and held the sword high, able to see ghostly forms that made no sound floating along the border of the fog bank. The echoing *clip-clop* of Thalagar's hoofs on the path created the sound of a herd approaching the castle. She watched, transfixed, as a large drawbridge lowered over a moat filled with green water. The light in the tower grew stronger—a beacon in a world of dreams—and a trumpet blared, announcing her arrival as she crossed the bridge.

Every door opened, and figures wearing elegant and brightly-colored Lorian apparel emerged. A long line of soldiers in black armor streamed through the gate, materializing from the fog as if they'd been there waiting and watching. Taliesin lowered *Ringerike*, aware people stared at the sword, confused she was in possession of the Raven Sword. Knights surrounded her horse, and among the armored men, she spotted the familiar faces of Chief Lykus and Lord Arundel, though far younger than she remembered. It seemed impossible yet, somehow, it appeared she had been removed from her own timeline and returned one thousand years in the past—for this was the age of King Korax Sanqualus.

She doubted everything she saw, heard, and smelled. Maybe she'd fallen from her horse and hit her head. It was possible she'd been struck by a bandit's arrow, dead before she hit the ground, and this was the Underworld, ruled by the god Heggen.

Convinced she was in a dream, she trembled at the arrival of the Raven King and his chancellor, Zarnoc the Great, both looking young and handsome as they emerged from the crowd and approached. She slid off Thalagar and kept close to him as the king and wizard came to a halt in front of her. King Korax was tall, powerfully-built, and extremely handsome, boasting bright red hair, a thick beard, and eyes as green as her own. *Ringerike* was belted at his side. Zarnoc stood next to him, young, beardless, and his eyes full of questions. He held his familiar plain staff, though it looked freshly-cut, and the carved mystical symbols stood out; in the future, they were worn.

"Be wary, my lord," Sir Lykus growled.

"She may be a sorceress. That's *Ringerike* she holds," Sir Arundel said.

"I shall be the judge of that," Zarnoc replied. He came closer. "We mean you no harm, child. I sense I should know you, yet we have yet to meet. Yes, yes. It is in the future I know you. My lord, this is Taliesin Sanqualus, your last surviving heir. I met her in a dream. It's all coming back to me now. She is the Raven Mistress."

"I am King Korax. How do you come to be at Black Castle?"

"I don't know," Taliesin said.

"And how do you come to possess *Ringerike*?" The king placed his hand on the hilt of his sword. Both *Ringerikes* gave a sharp whine, clearly recognizing each other. "There is no need to be afraid of me, Taliesin. Put away your sword and let me take a closer look at you."

"No," she said in defiance. "Stay right where you are, Your Highness. Zarnoc? Explain why I'm here."

The wizard cocked his head to the side and studied her intently. He said not a word, watching, waiting, while the Raven Knights moved forward to surround her.

"So, she does know you, wizard," Sir Lykus said. Dark-haired and bearded, he looked as sinister as he did in the present world. She sensed he had yet to be bitten by Varg and was human. He stood beside his king. "Tell us why you are here, girl? Have you come to harm our Lord? For you reek of magic, and your gaze offends me."

"Then don't look at me," Taliesin said angrily. She sheathed *Ringerike*, regretting her actions when she found the knights blocked her from Thalagar. There was only one person she looked to for answers, and she again asked, "Explain why I am here, Zarnoc. I know you. You are my friend. However, Lykus and Arundel are my enemies, and the king...the king is dead."

Korax frowned and crossed his arms over his armored chest. He wore a black tunic with the heraldry of a raven, a twig in its beak and resting on a human skull, on a field of silver. His green eyes locked with hers, and she felt her knees buckle. She sank to the ground and heard Thalagar whinny in distress as Sir Lykus and Sir Arundel reached her. Each grabbed an arm and yanked her to her feet. They felt solid enough, and their grips were strong and bruised her flesh. Her armor appeared in an instant and covered her as the two knights fell back, alarmed, and reached for their swords.

"Hold," King Korax ordered. "This is dragon armor she wears, which means she is under the protection of one of the old ones. Vargus the Dreadful is a black dragon, though the scales, when worn by humans, turn to the color they favor. It could be the scales from Shavea, or Klakegon, or even Malagorigaz."

"It is Huva'khan's scales, that devil of a red dragon," Sir Arundel whispered.

Taliesin hadn't expected King Korax and his Raven Knights to be afraid of dragons, and out of loyalty to Bonaparte, she did not mention his name. She noticed Ysemay the Beguiling among the women watching her. It was instinct, not appearance that alerted Taliesin to the witch's identity. The witch was beautiful, there was no denying the fact, but she didn't seem to recognize Taliesin. Only Zarnoc seemed unafraid of her, though he was perplexed as he motioned Lykus and Arundel aside and held out his hand to her. Rings adorned each finger, and not a wrinkle marred his skin. She took his hand, felt a ripple of magic exchanged between them, and hoped the fog would clear and she'd find herself back with her friends. It was not to be.

"Welcome to Black Castle, Taliesin," the wizard said, offering a knowing smile.

* * * * *

Chapter Twenty-One

"Who shall guard this beast?" Sir Lykus waved his arms in the air. First of the Raven Knights, he was in command, followed by Sir Arundel, and drew his men toward Thalagar. Taliesin thought the man mad to be afraid of her horse when there were dragons in the country, and they knew about *darklings* in the Magic Realms. "If ever there was a foul beast that crept from the crypts of Heggen's underworld, it is this winged black devil."

A young knight stepped forward and caught Taliesin's eye. There was something familiar about his face, and he called out in a clear voice, "I, Sir Rigelus, shall guard the horse of the Raven Mistress. Come, Sir Garridan and Sir Aldagar. Our captain seems to think this horse will snort smoke from his backside."

The knights chuckled. Apparently, Sir Rigelus was a favorite, and his good humor cut through the tense atmosphere as the two knights with names of dukedoms in her time-line stepped forward. Taliesin wondered if knights with the names of every Caladonia dukedoms were among the Raven Knights. It was quite possible, she thought, even likely, and with a quick caress to Thalagar, she left him in the company of the three knights. The other knights, led by Sir Lykus, formed a line to accompany King Korax, Zarnoc, Ysemay, and Taliesin into the enormous keep.

Taliesin watched King Korax as he strode through the door, long legs carrying him quickly into the throne room. Strong body odor and perfume, mingled with a strong scent of incense that burned in golden trays set upon small gold pillars, and the horse dung covering the knights' boots assailed

346 | SUSANNE L. LAMBDIN

her nostrils. She expected to find the war god, Ragnal, around every corner, laughing at her for falling into his trap. There was no sign of any of the ancient gods in physical form nor featured in any of the tapestries upon the walls.

Black banners with the Raven crest hung from the rafters, and silver shields and gold swords were arranged on the stone walls. The only statue was that of the Stroud, the father of the gods, which stood twenty feet tall in the corner of the enormous chamber and guarded over the equally impressive Ebony Throne. The chair, cut from obsidian, was large enough for two to sit in comfortably. King Korax sat upon it and gazed at Taliesin with disapproval.

"Come forth, girl," Korax said in a deep voice.

The Raven Knights stood in line on either side of the throne, with Sir Lykus and Sir Arundel at the front positions. Zarnoc stood to the right of his lord and master, and Ysemay, in a gown of bright yellow, to the left. Both wizard and witch scrutinized Taliesin, and she felt a tickle in her brain as they tried to read her thoughts. She imagined a bucket of worms and focused on it, keeping her thoughts clear, and saw Zarnoc smile.

"I suggest you allow me to question her, sire," the wizard said. "All magic guilds forbid the use of magic for time-travel. I do not think her powers strong enough to create a portal into our world, though I sense she is a natural-born witch. A *Sha'tar* to be exact."

"They are not allowed in my court, Zarnoc," King Korax grumbled.

"Yes, I know, Your Highness. I do not sense the girl is lying, and I am quite certain that is *Ringerike* she carries, proof she is of your line. Ardea made the sword for you, and if this one did not have Lorian blood, she would not be able to carry it. Nor do I think Ardea duplicated the sword, so it must be she comes from the future."

Korax crossed one leg over the other and lifted his hand as a male servant stepped forward, holding a tray with one silver goblet. The king did not reach for the goblet but waited until the servant lowered the tray and maneuvered it so it brushed against Korax's fingers. Only then did Korax grasp the goblet, sniff the contents, take a hearty drink, and wipe his mouth with the back of his hand.

"Question her, Zarnoc. Find out what she wants and why she is here."

"Certainly, sire," the wizard said. "Taliesin, did you open a portal, or did, by chance, *Ringerike* bring you here? Leave nothing out of your description and start at the beginning. What were you thinking when you first awoke this morning? What was the color of the sky? Were the clouds red? Is it close to the summer or the winter solstice? Come, girl. Do not be shy."

Taliesin wavered, uncertain what the wizard was after. She knew she needed to be careful about what she said, for not only were they judging her, she didn't want to alter the future. A Lorian trait seemed to be holding every stranger in doubt and forcing them to prove their valor and honesty. It wasn't a bad idea, she thought, considering how many enemies King Korax had among his own people and in his siblings' courts. It was not a trait Master Osprey had shared, for he'd taken in every criminal in the realm and allowed him or her to join the Raven Clan, forgiving all their sins the moment they took the service oath. Her delay caused a stir among the royal court and knights. Their chattering ended as a young woman, dressed in a gown of gold that matched her hair, appeared in an arched doorway behind the throne. A slender silver crown set with sapphires, matching the color of her eyes, sparkled on her brow. On closer inspection, Taliesin realized her eyes were luminescent, a Hellirin trait, and, like a chameleon, assumed the colors of the vaulted chamber.

"Ah, Queen Madera is here," Zarnoc said. "Did you send for her, sire?"

Korax's frown marred his good looks. His visible hostility toward his Hellirin queen surprised Taliesin. He was reportedly a ladies' man. He freely slept with whomever he chose among the women in his court, be they the wives or lovers of

348 | SUSANNE L. LAMBDIN

friends and nobles, or common serving girls. Taliesin felt pity for the young queen, for she was pretty and behaved timidly and shyly amongst the older Lorians. She couldn't help but wonder how an undead queen could give a living king an heir and assumed black magic was used.

Taliesin couldn't remember reading anything about Queen Madera in history or in the poems and ballads of famous poets and bards. The Raven Clan knew nothing about the queen. No one had spoken about her in Duvalen either, and Zarnoc, at least the wizard she knew, even less. Taliesin wondered why Queen Madera was not liked. The queen sat quietly on a footstool before her husband, though there was room enough on the Ebony Throne for her to join him. Korax ignored his wife, as did his court. Taliesin's disappointment only grew stronger, for Korax was nothing like she'd imagined. He was cold, arrogant, and uncharitable, and his indifference toward his queen bordered on abusive.

The young queen seemed to sense her distress, and her eyes turned red to match the color of Taliesin's armor. It was a little creepy and reminded her of the same morbid calmness shown by the Eagle Clan whenever they went to a Gathering—when the three clans met at a battlefield. The Eagles always stared at the dead before they decided which of the slain to remove and return to their grieving families. Taliesin hadn't taken a good look at General Folando, the Hellirin general and Duchess Dolabra's consort. She assumed the general had the same eyes and graveside manner. The moment she thought about the general, the queen's eyes widened, leaving Taliesin to wonder if the two Hellirins were related by birth.

"The goddess Mira sent this girl here, my lord. I am almost sure of it," Zarnoc said, glancing toward Ysemay. The witch nodded in agreement. "The Gods of Mt. Helos have clearly taken an interest in Taliesin. Not only is she your heir in the future, sire, but she is also from the same bloodline as Tarquin Draconus, the barbarian prince of the north. Her thoughts are guarded, yet I know she has been tested by Ragnal. Twice in fact, and both times she refused to join him. This I saw in her mind, thick as a quagmire, and just as murky. Ragnal must believe Taliesin will bring about the Age of the Wolf. She worships Navenna, yet Mira sent her here. I know not why. Perhaps Taliesin will tell us more."

The king toyed with his goblet. "How can you be so certain Mira sent her to Black Castle, uncle?" He finished the contents and held up the goblet. The servant placed the tray beneath the goblet as it was set down, bowed low, and scurried out of the way.

"Can you not smell the odor of burnt feathers? That is Mira's smell. I would know it anywhere," Zarnoc said, his eyes glinting sharply.

"Her reluctance to talk is annoying. Ask her how she comes by *Ringerike*."

"I found it in the Cave of the Snake God," Taliesin blurted. She winced as the royal court started to whisper, and remembered most were in the Traveling Tower, turned into magical items. Perhaps Mira didn't want her to release the royal court in the future. If this was Mira's way to warn her to keep the Lorian nobles locked in the tower, then Taliesin was inclined to agree with her. She caught Ysemay staring at her, and pictured worms crawling in a rotten apple, blocking her thoughts. The witch scowled.

"The girl speaks when she is not addressed," Korax said. His tone was sharp.

Zarnoc smiled with tolerance. "Perhaps, sire, it is because...."

"Because I am related to you, and Zarnoc, and like all Lorians, I am overly proud," Taliesin said, enjoying the king's look of indignation. "I am perfectly capable of answering your questions, Your Highness. However, I fear it is not wise to tell you too much about myself or about the future. If Mira brought me here, it must be to learn something that will help me in my own time—I can think of no other reason. Can you?"

"She asks me a question. Such impertinence."

"Perhaps she is distantly related to us, sire," the wizard continued. "I do not think it wise to traipse through her thoughts. It is unwise to meddle in the future, and her being here puts us all in danger. What might be, could change, and what might never be, could now happen. It cannot be safe to have two *Ringerikes'* this close together, any more than it would be prudent for you to face yourself in the past. I cannot be sure of the outcome since it's never happened before, though I am certain it is not for your betterment that she is here."

"The girl should be sent home at once," Ysemay said. "I sense violence in her nature. You saw how she drew her sword the moment she felt threatened. Like a wolf, she is quick to react and bare her teeth. There is no reason to believe a word she says. Zarnoc, tread carefully. She smells of wolf."

Taliesin bristled. It wasn't the witch who angered her, nor the king's rudeness, but Zarnoc's behavior. She reminded herself that the wizard wasn't her friend, not yet. Ysemay slid her fingers along the king's arm, and he tensed. Though Zarnoc didn't see the exchange, Taliesin noticed. She glanced at Sir Lykus and Sir Arundel and caught them whispering. The queen, poor thing, was as clueless as Zarnoc that the king and witch were lovers. Taliesin ignored the whispers among the royal court and focused her attention on Madera, the one person no one thought of any consequence, and history seemed to have ignored, though she must have given the king a child. Taliesin didn't know if Madera gave birth to a son or daughter, for that too was a part of the story missing from history. Nothing else was said of the queen and her child after the king died, mainly due to Queen Dehavilyn turning the royal court into magical instruments and items when they returned home. Taliesin wondered if the goddess had brought her to the past to show her why she'd ordered the Lorian queen to carry out her command. She sensed Queen Madera knew more than anyone else, including Zarnoc, and looked to her for answers when others did not.

"I'm Taliesin, Your Highness. Are you...are you with child yet?"

A smile grew upon the queen's lovely pale face, and she nodded. The court grew silent, not expecting a conversation to break out between their queen and Taliesin. She walked to the queen, bowed her head, and knelt, flinching as her armored knee clanked on the floor. It was more respect than Taliesin had paid to the handsome, arrogant king, and far more attention than anyone apparently ever gave Madera, for the queen suddenly laughed. Korax cleared his throat, stunned, while Zarnoc and Ysemay whispered to one another.

"You are not quite as fearsome as they all think, Taliesin," Queen Madera said, her voice light and airy. "Your eyes remind me of Korax's, though I think you have my brother's chin. It gives me comfort to know my unborn child will live. And yes, magic must be used for a Hellirin to have children. You guessed, of course, that Akyres is my older brother. Is he still alive?"

Taliesin nodded, not sure why the revelation delighted her. "Your brother and Duchess Dolabra are alive and well, Your Highness," she said. "I met Queen Dehavilyn and King Boran a few days ago. They failed to mention you by name, and I've always wondered who married King Korax. As for me, I never knew my own mother, and only recently discovered she is Prince Tarquin's descendant. History is always about men, which is hardly fair or proper."

"I like you," Madera said, giving Korax a shy glance. "My brother brought me to Black Castle two years ago. It was an arranged marriage, you see. Dolabra was visiting Korax at the time, and when they met, it was love at first sight. She never returned to Duvalen and went with Akyres to Nethalburg. Everyone blames me for what happened next, for Dolabra took her own life to be with Akyres. Since I am Hellirin, all assume I am evil like my brother. He's no more evil than I am. We Hellirin are in many ways far kinder than the Lorian, for we do not send anyone into exile, and all are welcome in the halls of the underworld."

"That's like the Raven Clan in the future," Taliesin said, aware Zarnoc had moved closer to try to overhear what they discussed. "If you don't mind, Zarnoc, I'd like to talk to the queen in private. Tell the king I want to speak privately with his queen. I will tell her why I am here and no one else."

"Very well," Zarnoc snapped. He turned to the Raven King.

Taliesin stood and held out her hand. The queen looked at no one else and placed her hand on Taliesin's as she rose to her feet. It was obviously something no nobleman or knight, nor even the king, had ever done before, and the queen took advantage of the attention, almost preening as they walked past the armored men and stopped in front of the tall statue of Stroud. The god was depicted as a strong, older man with a long beard, holding a large staff crowned with a human skull. It seemed rather grotesque, for, in her time, Stroud's statues showed him with arms crossed over his chest. She noticed King Korax had turned in his black throne to watch them, while Zarnoc and Ysemay seemed hesitant to approach.

"Who was your father?" the queen asked.

"I was going to ask you the same thing. My father is John Mandrake; however, I was adopted by Master Osprey of the Raven Clan," Taliesin said. "I fear if I say too much about the future, Your Highness, it may make things worse."

"My father is a cobbler in Duvalen, and my mother came from Nethalburg. She was Hellirin royalty and sadly, died when I was born," Madera said. "The dark magic used for my kind to have children often kills the mother, and that is why it is forbidden in the Magic Realms. This is the first time I have ever challenged my husband by speaking to someone in private right before his own eyes. There is something about you that makes me feel not so afraid to be here. No one takes any notice of me—Korax least of all. He only married me because he believes our child will unite the Magic Realms. He wants very much to heal the wounds with Boran and Dolabra. Does it work?"

"I cannot tell you."

"You have told me already. I can see it in your eyes," the queen said, saddened. "I am sorry you did not know your mother, Taliesin. If she is alive, you must go to her. I will pray to Mira you find her well, and she will be happy to see you."

"Then, you pray to Mira?"

"Yes, of course. And you?"

"I'm not sure to whom I pray anymore," Taliesin said. "You see, I didn't know the gods were Maeceni until I visited Duvalen. I was told they were an ancient race of immortals. It doesn't make any sense to pray to the Maeceni. They're not gods."

"They are a formidable race and far more powerful than the Lorians and Hellirins. We both waged war against them. The Maeceni won and over time became known as gods and goddesses. We are immortal as well, Taliesin, only the Magic Realms are constantly at war against each other. The barbarian tribes of the north will one day come here. Zarnoc has already told us this, and that is why my husband fears Prince Tarquin, the Lord of Skarda, also known as the Lord of the North. The prince sailed from another continent to this place, wanting a kingdom of his own. Skarda is not enough for him. Tarquin wants a warmer climate, so they say, and has his eyes on Caladonia."

Taliesin raised an eyebrow. Here was something interesting. "The Lord of the North doesn't call himself 'king,'" she said. "Skarda remains a barbaric world in my time. They have no royal court and no titles. They are an untamed people and remain in the frozen wasteland far to the north."

"Tarquin is a prince because that is what the fairies and *darklings* call him," Madera said. "He is a king in his own right. He refuses to take the illustrious title until he conquerors Caladonia. There are whisperings in Nethalburg that Tarquin is building a great army and will come here to fight Korax for that right."

"Tarquin will sit on the Ebony Throne one day, Your Grace, but he does not rule for long," Taliesin said, noting a shrewd gleam in the queen's eyes. Zarnoc and Ysemay started toward them, obviously wanting to end their intimate chat. "I've said too much, I fear. Thank you for listening, Your Highness. I will not let history forget you."

"Do not misjudge the Hellirin as these fools do," the queen whispered. "Among them, you may very well find allies, Taliesin. My brother is a powerful man. Remember this and accept my gift. Give it to no one else, for it will help you command the Hellirin army one day, and you may have need of it, Raven Mistress."

The queen turned toward the wizard and witch. Madera seemed strangely at ease, and Taliesin wondered if her presence had anything to do with it. The queen was not a *Sha'tar* but a witch, and Taliesin sensed her magical powers grew stronger while she was present. She felt cool fingers glide across her hand, and something small and round was pressed into her palm by Madera before the queen stepped forward. Taliesin didn't dare look at what she'd been given, but it felt like a ring. She quickly placed it into her pouch before anyone noticed.

"Queen Madera, your husband wishes you to sit with him," Zarnoc said. He looked none too happy with Taliesin. "As for you, girl, you will come with us. You have displeased the king, and he has asked for you to be removed from his throne room."

"I was planning to leave anyway. I have learned what I need to know," Taliesin said. She bowed as the queen glanced at her one last time before walking toward the throne. Taliesin felt less inclined to dislike Korax when he moved over and allowed Madera to sit beside him.

"What is this?" Zarnoc asked. "My nephew has never let the queen sit with him before. Yes, it's time you left Black Castle, girl. Already you have started to change our traditions. Cause and effect. Alterations are dangerous. Ysemay, I am reluctant to keep her here any longer, despite the king's orders to place her in a deep, dark dungeon."

"No prison can keep me," Taliesin said, glaring at the wizard. "Stand aside, old man, and keep that ugly witch away from me. Don't make the mistake of thinking you can use magic on me, for I am far stronger than you realize. I am leaving, and there is nothing you can do about it. I suggest you keep the queen's child alive or history will certainly forget about you and your unfaithful lover."

Ysemay gasped when Zarnoc gave her a sharp look. Taliesin seized the opportunity to slide out the door the queen entered through and found herself in a hallway with one window high above. She didn't know what made her pull the Broa necklace off and put it away. She turned *Wolfen* as anger filled her mind, and her armor accommodated the growth spurt. A shower of colorful lights fell upon her as she jumped into the air, crashed through the window, and landed in the courtyard. Zarnoc and Ysemay had used their magic against her. It had no effect on her, none at all, though anyone within twenty feet of her fell unconscious.

"She's getting away!" Sir Rigelus cried.

Heart pounding, Taliesin ran to the three knights guarding Thalagar and growled as she pushed them aside as if they were little children. The knights fell to the ground, weapons clattering on the cobblestones, and she leaped onto Thalagar's back. With an angry snort, the black stallion spread his wings wide and galloped across the courtyard, scattering knights in his wake.

"Get us out of here, boy," Taliesin said. "Take us home!"

She slid the Broa necklace back over her head and felt her body change, turning human, as the horse beat the air with his black raven wings and flew into the sky. Sir Rigelus, Sir Garridan, and Sir Aldagar stood, swords in hand, and shouted for assistance. Knights streamed out of the keep and ran across the courtyard to stop her. Thalagar flew over the wall and into the fog, rapidly leaving Black Castle far behind. He soared into the moist air, unafraid, and almost at once the fog started to fade, revealing a blue sky and green crops below.

Tiny figures appeared on the horizon. Taliesin recognized Shan Octavio's large frame and orange scarf, riding beside his son Joaquin. Rook and the Black Wings were with them, though their number was greatly diminished from the battle against the bandits. She wondered if the magical weapons had been picked up and given to the Ghajars, though it was something to ask later, out of respect to the Raven dead. Despite her absence, they had continued their journey toward Erindor.

Rook spotted her and called out to the others as Thalagar descended from the clouds. Heads turned and looked upwards as Thalagar dropped to the ground and tucked away his wings as he galloped alongside Rook's horse. Taliesin rubbed her Draconus ring with her thumb, and her armor and helmet disappeared, and her long red hair blew freely in the wind.

"Where have you been?" Rook asked. "We thought you'd ridden ahead of us."

Her little adventure had changed many things about how she saw things, including her feelings toward Navenna and Ragnal, for it was Mira who protected her, and to whom she now felt she owed her allegiance. Magic came first, then her clan, for without magic, she had no hope to rebuild her clan or claim the Ebony Throne for herself, and she knew the Raven Sword felt the same. She felt no anger toward Zarnoc, only a greater need to rescue him and return Jaelle to her father.

"It's a strange story," she said, "and one I'll gladly tell you when we make camp for the night. I do not think we will have any more trouble on the road, Rook. I left feeling unsure and afraid, and I return knowing precisely what needs to be done."

Joaquin, rolling his tongue across the top of his mouth, gave a shrill cry that carried through the group. Every gypsy gave the same cry, welcoming her back as they galloped through tall grass with the sun high overhead. Their cries startled a flock of white pigeons as they flew overhead. It was a sign of good luck, she thought.

Slipping a finger into the pouch hanging from her belt, Taliesin felt Queen Madera's ring at the bottom. At her touch, it slid onto her left index finger, to offset Tarquin's sapphire ring, which was on her right index finger. While his was massive, set with a beautiful sapphire, the queen's was a dainty, silver band engraved with tiny dragons and set with a moonstone that picked up the colors of nature, turning it into every possible shade. She wasn't aware of the ring's magical abilities, yet instantly her pride in her Hellirin heritage grew stronger and somehow balanced her anger toward the proud Lorians. Being born a combination of every race and clan now made more sense, for she had the ability to heal old wounds and prejudices as well as restore magic and peace.

"Mira," Taliesin whispered. "I am one with nature. I am all things, and none shall stand in my way. I am a Raven. See me soar."

"Let's ride, sister. For the sun is high, and the fog has lifted," Rook said, his voice warm in her ears. "We can forget our cares and worries, at least for now."

* * * * *

Chapter Twenty-Two

T he crackle of the small campfire, with its tiny pops and sparks, along with the scent of burning pine logs helped calm Taliesin's frayed nerves. She rested on one elbow, her legs extended on a blanket, with the sword harness and *Ringerike* in its red leather scabbard at her side. The Black Wings and Ghajar, seated on horse blankets around the fire, shared a meal of rabbit and hard-crust bread. Their company, along with the still of the night and a waning quarter moon, felt soothing. She chewed on a sliver of jerky provided by Joaquin instead of partaking in the cooked meal, content to listen to the drone of voices while she replayed what had happened at Black Castle.

For some reason, Mira had felt it necessary to send her to the past, though not once had the goddess paid a visit. It seemed a more thoughtful move on Mira's part and far less aggressive than Ragnal had acted, or as shrewd as Navenna had behaved in the ancient temple. King Korax and his royal court were as inhospitable and unpleasant as the Lorians in Duvalen, and she was left with the impression most fairies were selfish, full of pride, and prone to suspicion and acts of cruelty. Though she'd not been harmed and had escaped with no real difficulty, the king's neglect of his wife and the court's refusal to show Queen Madera any respect or compassion pressed on her mind.

She lifted her left hand to gaze at the Moon Ring as she thought of it, for the white stone appeared milky with a splash of red in the firelight. It was cast in a reddish glow that reminded her of the moon the night Ragnal had visited the Traveler Tower in Miller's Wood, yet its magic lacked malice. She felt connected to Madera, being part-Hellirin, and wondered what had happened after she had vanished. Madera had said her mother was of royal blood, a Lorian, possibly related to the Vorenius family. Korax's intentions had been honorable, and by marrying a Hellirin, he'd meant to create harmony in the Magic Realms, only he had allowed his own sister to be taken to Nethalburg, where she had taken her own life to become a *darkling* and remain with Akyres. Madera never should have married King Korax, for by trying to do something right, he had set in motion his own downfall. She doubted Boran or Dolabra cared Korax was dead, yet she sensed Madera had cared for him. Korax had not loved his wife, that was obvious, and for her to have a child meant either Zarnoc or Ysemay or perhaps both had used dark magic to allow an undead woman to carry a child to full term. Madera's mother had died in childbirth, so she wondered if the same had happened to her, leaving the Raven heir with human foster parents. Prince Tarquin had eventually destroyed the Raven Clan, and his death had prompted Mira to order Dehavilyn to enchant Korax's court into the magical items now carried inside the Traveler Tower in her pouch.

After what she'd seen, Taliesin was no longer eager to free them, and perhaps this was why Mira had sent her there. Yet, she had returned with the Hellirin ring, solid proof she had been in the past, and she could summon General Folando and his army if needed. She also had *Ringerike*, a dragon at her command, and *Calaburn*, if she wanted to take it back from Rook. She even had *Graysteel*, for Zarnoc had left it inside the Traveler Tower, though Hawk now had it in his possession. Three powerful swords that had changed history now belonged to her clan. If she wanted the Ebony Throne, she had the means to take it, only she no longer thought she wanted to be a queen. Not after she saw how miserable it had made Madera, how bitter Dehavilyn had become, and what Dolabra had sacrificed for power.

Knowing the precise events that led to the destruction of Black Castle and of the stories surrounding the deaths of King Korax and Prince Tarquin provided a guidebook for what she should not do or let happen. If power could corrupt people who started out with good intentions, it certainly wasn't in her clan's best interest to seek the crown. Did she really want to restore magic? She could always leave Caladonia, Taliesin thought, and go far away. Then again, maybe it had nothing to do with her and had everything to do with how people used magic and magical weapons. King Magnus Draconus had outlawed magic two centuries ago, perhaps for the very reasons that now troubled her, for people did bad things when they had too much power, and magic offered power with too much ease.

For magic to be restored, and for good and darkness to remain balanced, there had to be peace between Caladonia, the Magic Realms, and Skarda. It seemed an impossible task, especially since the people who had been a part of Korax's world remained in power. Boran, Dehavilyn, Dolabra, Folando, Arundel, and Lykus still schemed and plotted. Even the Gods of Mt. Helos had their little game, and the threat of *Varguld* seemed more real than ever. War was already upon the land, spreading into the Magic Realms and into Skarda since they had sided with Prince Almaric. Despite how many times she twirled the ring around her finger, wondering how to handle the situation, the only way to end war meant people would die. Did it mean Zarnoc had to die as well? He was a different man from the one he had been in the past. She didn't want the wizard to die, nor Ismeina or poor Ysemay, yet it felt like the playing board had to be cleared if both magic and peace were to co-exist together.

"A copper piece for your thoughts," Shan Octavio said.

Startled, Taliesin watched as his large frame sank onto the blanket beside her. Without the orange scarf on his head, long black-and-grey hair hung down his back and fluttered in the breeze. He placed *Dark Blood* across his massive thighs and used a cloth to polish the silver blade as he watched Taliesin from under his thick eyebrows. Her guards sat or lay on Ghajar blankets with colorful patterns while the gypsies stood guard. The horses, tied to a rope that ran from a walnut tree to the closet oak, nibbled on tall grass. Thalagar seemed content, and she wondered if he'd already forgotten the past, something impossible for her to do.

"It's only worth a copper piece," she muttered.

"Come now, Taliesin. You've not spoken to anyone since you returned from wherever it is you went during the battle. I'd like to know what happened, and it looks like you need someone to confide in. Must I give you *baju* to make you talk?"

Taliesin took a deep breath, about to confide in a man who only yesterday had considered killing her for being a *Wolfen*. Octavio Alvarez didn't need at truth potion to make her talk, showing far more experience as a leader, for he'd known she needed to talk and offered a compassionate ear.

"Mira transported me through time to the court of King Korax," she said. "I met Korax and Zarnoc and the royal court. More importantly, I met his queen, Madera, who was a royal Hellirin on her mother's side, and her father was a commoner in the fairy court. Madera was pregnant with Korax's child. I could tell she was unhappy, for Korax chose to ignore his wife, and I felt sorry for her. She told me her mother, like most Hellirin women, had died in childbirth. There's something else I've been reluctant to tell anyone. My mother is Princess Calista Draconus, and my father was a commoner. Of course, we know John Mandrake was descendant of Korax Sanqualus, and in truth, he had every right to marry Calista. I can't help wondering if Madera's child was raised by foster parents, like me, or if my own mother is alive. Zarnoc said she died in childbirth. Madera said she may be alive, and she also gave me this ring. It's supposed to control the Hellirin army. She didn't really tell me much about it, and I had to leave in a rush. Korax was a cruel man, and Zarnoc was no better. Arundel and Lykus were also there. Have you ever heard about a magical Hellirin ring? Do you think it can control the undead?"

The Shan leaned toward her when she held up her hand and gazed intently at the moonstone. *Dark Blood* let out a sharp whine, jealous its new owner sat so close to a woman, and its blade turned a deep red. The Shan placed a large hand upon the blade, and the magical weapon quieted as the red shine on the blade faded.

"I have never heard any stories about a Hellirin ring of such immense power," he said. "Have you been visited by the gods before, Taliesin?"

"Ragnal twice, Navenna once, and Mira has helped me several times. Each wants something of me, only the sisters want the same things I want—to restore the Raven Clan, to end the war, and to bring back magic. Since I left your company, I have met nearly everyone involved in the death of the Raven King and the Draconus prince. Things that happened then seem to be repeating. I don't want to make the same mistakes, but I don't know what to do."

"My advice is to resist all temptation and stay true to your own heart," Octavio said. "If you want to restore the Raven Clan to its former greatness, then that is what you must do. You do not have to be a queen to accomplish this goal. However, you are of royal and magical blood. If Arundel managed to capture you, and I'm not saying he will, he could bend you to his will and make you do terrible things in order to finally sit on the throne."

"Is that what he wants?"

"It's what they all want, and you are the one person who can bring this about, my friend." The Shan pointed at the sapphire ring on her other hand. "You wear two magical rings, carry the most powerful sword ever forged, and wear dragon armor. Not any dragon, mind you. The red dragon Huva'khan terrorized this land for ages. No one knows what happened to him or the other dragons. We tell their stories around the campfire at night; tales about Vargus the Dreadful, Shavea and her brother Klakegon, Malagorigaz, Tagallagon the Black, and the blue dragon Ūerdraine. Something happened to them, for once there were many, and now there is only Bonaparte, who still resides in the ruins of Ascalon. I have always suspected it was dark sorcerers who killed them, for what else could kill a dragon if not magic?"

She smiled. "I know Bonaparte. He is my friend."

"Now that is interesting," Octavio said. "One would think a higher force, and not those who live on Mt. Helos, is in control of your destiny, Taliesin. My people pray to the wind, the sun and the stars, and the ground beneath our feet. We believe a force of nature made all things, and it's Nature itself we worship. You do not have to decide tonight what you are to do with your gifts and natural born powers. Remember who you fight for, and why, and let the rest fall into place."

"You think Nature controls my destiny. Does that mean it's an entity like a god or goddess? Is this entity more powerful than the Maeceni, the ancient race my people call the gods of Mt. Helos?"

"Yes, but this god has no name and no gender and no voice other than the wind," he replied with a wistful smile.

The Shan drank from a flask of water, swirled it in his mouth, and spat into the fire. The flames sparked and sizzled. Across the fire, Captain Rook studied them, reflective and choosing not to converse with the Black Wings next to him. *Calaburn*, content to be with a strong-willed man with a good heart, lay at his side, as *Ringerike* lay at hers. Long ago, Wren had dreamed of Taliesin seated on the Ebony Throne with a child in her arms. Taliesin had always thought the child belonged to Wren and Rook, for marriage and motherhood were things that seemed so far in the future she didn't dare dwell on them. Her mind turned to Roland. She wanted to discuss these same things with him before she decided what to do. He had a way of seeing matters more clearly and took no action until he'd thought it through to reach the right decision. It had been foolish of her to mistrust him, and now she never thought she'd see him again or tell him how she felt.

"King Frederick is your uncle, and it is your cousin who fights him," the Shan said, handing her the flask. "You are a princess of the royal blood from three powerful royal houses. Once we rescue my daughter and Zarnoc, I suggest you ask him about your mother. If she is alive, Taliesin, I think you should seek her out. A king and four princes stand between you and the throne. Almaric is supported by Sertorius, for now. Dinadan and Konall fight for their father, and Galinn remains missing. I do not think he is dead. There are rumors Talas Kull made Galinn an advisor after the prince was sold into slavery by Almaric. I have no dealings with the Skardans of the north, so I do not know if this is true. The barbarians were paid to help Prince Almaric in this war. Who can say if they will keep to the bargain or not, for Talas Kull does not think like ordinary men. He does what he wants when he wants, and that makes him a most dangerous man. If Galinn *is* alive, it may be he has convinced Talas Kull to help him lay claim to the throne, and the treaty with Almaric is nothing more than a clever ploy."

"The Skardans have never come this far south," Taliesin said. No one went into Skarda, and if they did, they did not return, just like her cousin Galinn. When she was a girl growing up in Padama, she had met all five princes. She could not place a face to Galinn and knew nothing about him. As for Talas Kull, it was a name every child feared, as well as adults.

Rook buckled on *Calaburn*, rose, and vanished into the trees with his silver spear in hand. Annoyed he'd left without telling anyone where he was going, she found herself distracted. The Shan stared in the same direction as she did, and his fingers closed around the hilt of his sword.

"Do you see something in the woods?" the Shan whispered.

Taliesin nodded, picked up *Ringerike*, and stood. "Stay here," she said. "I want to check on Rook. I won't be long."

She left the Shan at the fireside and noticed the moon shining on a tall walnut tree where Rook had vanished. The tree was old and majestic, with thick bark and large limbs spread across a wide area. The moon had turned the leaves silver, and they seemed to tinkle in a whispering wind. She walked softly as she made her way through the tall grass and found no sign of Rook on the opposite side of the tree. Pausing, she sniffed the air and caught a trace of his scent. She followed her nose and headed to a wooded area to the north of their camp. Walnut trees produced a floor of broken shells left by squirrels that crunched under her boots, and she came to a halt, listening to the chirp of crickets, wondering if her young Erindor captain had met foul play.

A short walk through the trees brought her to a glade where she spotted a hunter's shack that had seen better days. She crept toward the shack, gazed through a hole in a window, and spotted Rook, spear beside him, crouched on the floor and talking to the dark fireplace. There was no fire, and she saw no one else inside. Curious, she waited a few minutes, watching Rook and listening to him muttering about Penkill Castle and the number of commoners gathered there for protection.

Movement within the shack lifted the hairs on the back of Taliesin's neck. She noticed a fleeting shadow glide across the far wall and caught a strong whiff of an unwashed woman. There was no doubt in her mind a magic user had brought Rook to the shack, and she knew the culprit by the odor.

"Ysemay," she whispered.

A fire appeared in the fireplace and cast a yellow glow upon Rook's tall form. The shadow shifted and grew solid. Ysemay, still wearing the same clothes Taliesin had last seen her in, took a seat upon a stool and ran a hand through a tangle of gray hair. She handed Rook a small item, which he lifted to his mouth. Before he could consume whatever the witch had given him, Taliesin tapped Tarquin's ring. Armor appeared at once, and she slammed her fist through the window, startling both occupants.

"What are you doing here, Ysemay?"

The witch shrieked, and the flames grew larger. Rook dropped a piece of dried bread on the dirty floor, turned toward Taliesin, and glared at her with wild eyes. He grabbed his spear, stood swiftly, and walked to the window. Taliesin stepped aside as the spear jabbed through the window, caught the shaft, and jerked it out of his hands. Taliesin dropped the spear, ran to the door, kicked it open, and drew *Ringerike*. The sword blazed bright blue as it dragged her inside the shack, its first impulse to kill the witch. Ysemay ducked behind a rickety table as Rook spun to face Taliesin. Under the witch's enchantment, he was unable to resist a silent command to draw *Calaburn* from its scabbard.

"You will not harm the witch," Rook snarled.

In response, the Draconus ancestral sword burst into flames that climbed up Rook's arm and seared his clothes and flesh. He screamed and ran out the door into the night, releasing the blade, which hung in the air and spread fire throughout the shack. There was no helping Rook at the moment, for *Calaburn* flew to Taliesin's other hand, and armed with two swords, one in red flames and one shining bright blue, she advanced on Ysemay. The fire spread throughout the shack, hungrily jumped onto the table, and streaked toward the witch as a blue glow surrounded Taliesin. Taliesin held *Calaburn* aside, but the sword refused to stop spitting flames. Sparks showered the witch as she tried to move out of its reach and backed into a corner.

"It's your fault Zarnoc turned on me," Ysemay shouted.

"What do you want with Rook? Has he been spying for you?"

"Yes," Ysemay answered. "The pure of heart are the easiest to prey upon. Rook led me here, and here you will die, Taliesin of the Raven Clan!"

The witch threw out her hands, and an invisible barrier pushed the flames across the table toward Taliesin. In dragon armor, nothing could harm her, especially fire, and she used her hip to push aside the flame-engulfed table to reach Ysemay. The roof caught fire and flames lapped at the walls, filling the room with smoke. Inside the blue orb produced by *Ringerike*, Taliesin didn't smell the smoke, nor feel the heat of the fire. Sections of the roof fell, and a large beam fell on Ysemay, knocking her to the floor.

"Help me!"

"This is not my doing," Taliesin said, backing away. "You brought this on yourself, Ysemay. As King Magnus once said, 'Burn, witch. Burn to ash!'"

Taliesin stepped outside the shack as flame engulfed the witch, and the roof collapsed on Ysemay as she screamed in agony. Taliesin gave a hard shake to *Calaburn* and silently commanded the sword to cease its destruction. Its flame subsided at the same time the blue light faded from *Ringerike*. She glanced at the Draconus sword and offered a silent apology for giving it away yet again. *Calaburn* gave a soft whine and let her know it would obey only her. Rook's silver spear lay in the grass, and she left it as she searched for her friend, finding him lying in a blackened heap not far from the burning shack.

"Taliesin! Are you all right?"

Shan Octavio and his men, followed by the Black Wings, ran out of the trees and gathered around the still form of the burnt body. Taliesin sheathed *Ringerike* and stabbed *Calaburn* into the ground as she knelt beside Rook and placed her hands on his side. He was still alive and in considerable pain. Without help, she knew Rook would not live through the night.

"What happened?" Octavio asked, waving at the Black Wings to stand back. He took a knee beside her. "Did Rook start that fire?"

"No, it was Ysemay the Beguiling. Something must have happened when I went to the past. She blamed me for what Zarnoc did to her, and she came for revenge. She used Rook to do her bidding by feeding him magical bread. He tried to defend her, only *Calaburn* wouldn't let him harm me, and it burned him and then killed the witch."

"The boy will die unless you can save him."

Taliesin calmed her thoughts, formed a picture of Rook as he had looked earlier that night in her mind, and placed her hands on his body. She willed his body to heal, as she had done with Thalagar and Jaelle, and noticed moonlight playing across Rook's ravaged body. A ripple, like the brush of the wind across her arms and hands, coursed from her fingers into his body. All her love and appreciation of his friendship and devotion added to the flow of energy. She felt it, strong and pulsating, and her confidence in her abilities grew as she heard Rook suck in a lungful of air and slowly exhale. Within seconds, his appearance altered, and, fully restored, he opened his eyes.

"What happened?" Rook asked in a hoarse voice.

A cry of surprise from the gathered men and women brought a smile to Taliesin's face. With Octavio's help, they both helped Rook sit upright, and Joaquin appeared with a flask in hand. Joaquin removed the cork, squeezing the flask just enough for water to spit from the opening before he handed it to her. Taliesin lifted the flask to Rook's lips and poured water into his mouth.

"Someone fetch Rook's spear," she said.

Hornbill ran toward the burning shack, returning with the spear, while the female Ravens gathered closer. The two young women touched Rook's unsinged dreadlocks and handsome face and marveled at the sight of his unmarked skin. As Rook gazed at Taliesin, the guards started pushing and shoving, holding out scraped hands and minor injuries, everything from missing teeth to old scars, and demanded she heal them with her touch.

"Stand back," the Shan said in a gruff voice. "Give the Raven Mistress some breathing room. Let's get Captain Rook to his feet." He slid an arm around the young man and hauled him to his feet without Taliesin's assistance. "Steady, lad. There's no reason to guzzle the entire contents of the flask. We have plenty of water."

"What happened?" Taliesin asked as she pulled *Calaburn* from the ground. She did not offer the sword to Rook and walked beside him and Octavio back to camp. The guards followed, and Hornbill hung onto the silver spear.

"I'm sorry, Taliesin. I can't tell you when Ysemay first contacted me, for I don't remember, nor do I know how she controlled me," Rook said. "All I can remember is an urge to walk into the woods. I tried to resist the witch. There's no way for me to know what I told her."

"She's dead," Taliesin said.

"Maybe she was working for the Eagle Magic Guild," the Shan said.

Taliesin glanced at him. "I hope that's not the case," she replied. "She wanted me to kill Zarnoc, I know that, but I refused to do it. She obviously blamed me for her misfortunes. *Calaburn* only did what it was made to do, and that is to kill anyone who tries to harm a Draconus. You're my blood brother, Rook. It's not your fault Ysemay forced you to attack me. However, I can't let you keep *Calaburn*. I never should have given it to you or Drake."

"You're a Draconus," the Shan said as they walked out of the trees. "That's right, Rook. Her mother is Calista, King Frederick's younger sister. Your Raven Mistress is a Draconus as well as a Sanqualus and a Hellirin. You are fortunate this night. Her magic restored you to full health."

"Thank you," Rook said. He turned to look over his shoulder. Hornbill stepped forward and handed him the Erindor spear, and together, they walked to the camp.

"I should have known Ysemay was not done with me yet," Taliesin said as she fell into step beside the Shan. "Now that I know I can heal all injuries, I guess I should tend to our warriors."

"Perhaps you should," Octavio said.

As soon as they arrived at camp, Earnest and several men, each wanting to be healed, traded blows as they tried to stand in front of Taliesin. She noticed a Black Wing with a blind eye—white and the iris barely present. Blindness was something she hadn't tried to cure. She touched the man's brow and watched, amazed, as it healed. Earnest stepped forward. The Shan waved him aside, caught her arm, and pulled her behind him to keep the crowd from harassing her further. Joaquin stepped forward, holding Rook's empty scabbard, and offered it to her.

"For *Calaburn*, Raven Mistress," Joaquin said. "I'll give Rook one of the other magical swords we took from our slain comrades. Five were slain, and five weapons need a new owner."

"Thank you, Joaquin. Keep a sword for yourself and hand out the others to your men. Consider it a gift from the Raven Mistress."

"You are far too generous," the Shan said. "I think it would be wise to explain to those with magical weapons what to expect from them. Rook was not cautious enough, and it nearly cost his life."

"My father taught me to respect magic," Joaquin said.

Taliesin faced the group. "What happened to Rook is a lesson to us all that even with the magical weapons I have given you, another sorcerer or witch can still use magic against you," she said in a firm voice. "Since I can't be sure how your weapons will respond in battle, I think it best if we take the time to train you properly tonight. When we face the magic guild at Eagle's Cliff, you will need to know you can trust your weapon, and it can trust you." She caught the Shan looking at her with approval.

"The guild knows we are coming," Earnest said. Dark bangs covered one side of his face. He flipped them back with a toss of his head. "There are at least ten magic users at Eagle's Cliff, though I cannot tell you their names, for they seldom walked among the common soldiers. My former commander, Sir Cerasus, once said he was a warlock, and it was the lowest rank among magic users. He uses a magical sword. I think it's a Gregor blade, though I don't know its name. I have seen it level trees when he waves it in the air."

"That would be *Faller*," Taliesin said. She still carried John Mandrake's book in her saddlebag. He had been thorough about listing every magical weapon ever forged and paid special attention to swords. Taliesin doubted many people in Caladonia knew the names of the magical weapons. Having Earnest as a Black Wing, with his knowledge of the Eagle Clan and Eagle's Cliff, made him indispensable, though she wondered why he'd waited to tell her about Arundel's guild. Since *Ringerike* found Earnest to be loyal to her, she wanted to make certain the man stayed alive.

"Earnest, I'll start with you. Show me your weapon, and let's teach you how to use it to avoid future calamities. It's not enough for a magic weapon to want to be with you. First, you must discipline your mind as well as your body to be able to call upon its power and not be consumed, quite literally."

"Will this take long?" Earnest asked.

Her eyes lifted to the moon and, for a moment, she thought she saw the face of Mira smiling back at her.

"Not if you trust me and pay close attention. Now let's get to work."

* * * * *

Chapter Twenty-Three

Eagle's Cliff appeared, bathed in moonlight, a mighty, grim fortress upon a sheer cliff of granite. The lack of lit fires or torches made the castle appear dark and foreboding. Taliesin stood beside Shan Octavio in a ravine, gazing up at the castle, spinning the queen's ring on her left hand. She wore her red scale armor and felt high on excitement. A hard two-day ride had brought them into Eagle country earlier than expected. She'd spent both nights training the Black Wings and Ghajar with their magical weapons and found most caught on well. The sound of footsteps crossing the rocky terrain revealed Earnest and Hornbill, carrying ragged Eagle legionnaires cloaks. The once-gold material looked dull under a layer of grime and mold.

"Where did you find those?" Taliesin asked. There was a foul reek to the material, which suggested it had been beneath the ground, and she realized the two had raided the Eagle graveyard. She wrinkled her nose in disgust. "No, don't tell me. I already know where you've been, Earnest. See everyone is given a cloak."

"The castle shouldn't be this dark," Earnest said.

"I suspect they know I've arrived. Magic has a certain scent of its own. I could wallow in horse guts, and they'd still know I was here," Taliesin said. "That's why I'm sending you in first through the secret passage you mentioned. You know the labyrinth within that mountain, Earnest, better than anyone else. The Shan hasn't been here in years, and my map...well, it is not helpful. I'm giving you the responsibility to locate Zarnoc and Jaelle. Can you do it?"

"I was only a foot soldier under Sir Cerasus' command, with no access to the lower levels," he said. "It will be touch and go, Raven Mistress. There are more than human prisoners in this place. As a traitor to the Eagle clan, if I am caught, they will strip the flesh from my body and hang me out to feed the vultures."

"That's not what I asked you."

Earnest gave a nod. "Yes," he said, "I can lead the way, mistress."

"Then see to it, and there will be a promotion for you," she replied.

Earnest, looking more worried than when he'd started out that evening, joined Hornbill, and together they handed nasty-smelling cloaks to the entire group. The horses remained hidden behind a large mass of boulders, guarded by the two female Black Wings. Taliesin had said she needed her best to guard the horses. In truth, she was afraid the women would get killed trying to prove they were worthy of fighting beside men. The rest of the group gathered close to where Taliesin and the Shan stood and waited for instructions. The graveyard was well within sight and lacked markers of any kind. Mounds of dirt revealed the shallow-dug graves, excavated by Earnest and Hornbill, of Eagle warriors from ages past. Disturbing the dead was taboo among the Raven Clan. For centuries, they'd made their living taking armor, weapons, and personal effects from among the dead left on the battlefields. What was above the ground was their legal right to take, but what was below, especially what belonged to the Eagle Clan, was strictly forbidden, and if caught, every single one of her people and the gypsies would be flayed alive.

"Landing in the courtyard of that castle is a bold move, Taliesin," the Shan said as he lifted the filthy cloak and took a sniff. With reluctance, he put it around his shoulders. "A diversion is needed, or you won't get far, and nor will we, even with Earnest leading the way. That's a labyrinth we're entering, while you will be up against ten magic users with far more years of experience."

"Are you trying to talk me out of it?" Taliesin asked.

"I am just reminding you *who* you are up against. Earnest says the entrance to the tunnel is close by and leads to the dungeon. I know what manner of prisoners Lord Arundel collects. Magical creatures, cowards among the legionnaires, and noblemen whose families are unable to pay their ransoms, all left to rot in those damp cells. Once we get Zarnoc out, I'll send him to help you and make certain our warriors make it out of the ravine. I'll even provide the diversion."

Every inch of her skin tingled with magic. It was in the air and in the rocky ground beneath their feet, and it permeated the massive cliff and castle. She felt a nudge from Thalagar against her armored back. He was nervous. The warriors gathered beside Earnest as he pointed out the dark entrance, with stairs barely visible in the moonlight.

"I am the diversion, Octavio," she said, feeling familiar enough with the gypsy lord to forgo the use of his title. She was weary of titles and noble lords, and he didn't seem to mind her familiarity. "I'll keep them busy. Just get Zarnoc and Jaelle out of that dungeon and go directly to Penkill Castle. Don't wait for me."

"Brave men, or women, die as quickly as cowards," he replied.

"As long as the moon is bright, I have the advantage. I'm strongest when the moon is out, even a crescent moon as it is now." Taliesin removed her necklace and slid it into the pouch on her sword belt. She noticed the Shan tense before he took a step back.

"You go as a *Wolfen*?"

"I'll need to use all of my powers, Octavio, especially my wolf-side. I realize now it's an added defense to what I already have, and I need it. Go join your men and be careful. Arundel will likely have booby-traps set for you."

Taliesin thought of Phelon, caught in the silver trap, and placed her hand on the Shan's arm. She imagined a protective shield around his body and those of his men and the Black Wings. Her eyes widened as Madera's ring sparked to life and a soft silver glimmer came from the ring. She saw a look of

376 | SUSANNE L. LAMBDIN

amazement appear in the Shan's eyes and then noticed her hand was no longer visible on his arm. The ring gave her the ability to blend in with everything around her and made her nearly invisible to the eye, which she tested by walking around the Shan. He turned, trying to listen to her footsteps to guess her location. His face turned ashen as she rounded him, and he slowly drew *Dark Blood* from its place in his sash.

"What is it?" Taliesin asked. "Not impressed with my magic?"

Her gaze turned toward the graveyard where fog had risen unexpectedly, and through the blanket of white, she noticed movement. A hand, with decayed flesh hanging from white bone, thrust upwards from the ground, and another breached the soil, sticking out like a branch without leaves. All around, at every grave touched by Earnest and Hornbill, the Eagle dead were rising. Taliesin pushed the Shan toward the tunnel entrance, ran to her horse, mounted with one leap, and drew her sword.

Armor appeared on Thalagar's body, the same red scales as her own, and then he vanished from sight, hidden by the Hellirin ring's magical camouflage.

"Quickly! All of you inside the tunnel," she shouted. "I'll hold them off!"

A piercing scream rent the night air as a creature dragged a Black Wing beneath the ground. Panic ensued among the guards and gypsies as they ran toward the tunnel, only to find their way blocked by the living dead. Each corpse carried a weapon covered with a layer of slime and climbed from its grave with an eagerness Taliesin knew was instilled by dark magic. With a shout, she rode to the graveyard and slashed her sword at the skeletal forms as they took the bait and headed toward her. She caught sight of the Shan and the warriors fighting at the mouth of the tunnel, the magical weapons in their hands gleaming bright and filling the night with a colorful display of fireworks.

The dead continued to rise from their graves and stagger toward Taliesin, their numbers growing as the ancient joined the fresher corpses. The fog grew denser around Thalagar's legs, and the horse reared as bony hands clawed at his dragon armor. Taliesin twisted in the saddle and chopped a head filled with maggots from the shoulders of a soldier. Her nostrils filled with the scent of decay and rot. The warhorse charged forward, head lowered, and knocked over a line of soldiers with rusty helmets. She held her sword out and cut through blackened flesh and yellowed bones, hearing the crunch of the corpses beneath Thalagar's hooves.

Twenty undead soldiers turned into two thousand and still grew in number as they advanced toward Taliesin, as if drawn toward the Hellirin ring. Graves directly beneath Thalagar opened as hardened cracks appeared and bones penetrated the surface. Countless generations of Eagle dead stirred from their shallow graves and filled the ravine, their whispered groans turning to a cacophony as they came at Taliesin from all sides. She quickly glanced at the tunnel as Hornbill closed the iron grate behind the warriors to cut off the undead. Five of the warriors, left for dead on the rocks beneath the grate, started to twitch and came to life as they lifted their weapons from the ground and joined the horde that surrounded Taliesin.

"Into the air," she shouted. "Quickly, Thalagar!"

Black wings spread wide as he beat the air, scattering the skeleton soldiers. Thalagar whinnied shrilly as the ground opened beneath his feet, and his heavy body lifted off the ground as 100 bony hands reached toward them. As they flew up, the dead toppled over, the dark magic that gave them life cut off as someone in the Eagle Magic Guild redirected it toward her. A hard gust of wind came from the fortress and blew Thalagar head over hooves through the air while Taliesin clung to the armored saddle and gritted her teeth in terror.

"Mira, help us!"

At Taliesin's cry, moonlight surrounded the horse, the wind subsided, and Thalagar managed to right himself. The black stallion flew head down toward the fortress against a gale-like wind and managed to climb higher over the rocky escarpment toward Eagle's Cliff. The structure was enormous, never having fallen in battle, and was as impregnable as it was imposing, for guards in golden armor were posted in each tower; north, south, east, and west. A thin layer of magic lay over it like a black shroud, which cracked like an egg as Thalagar descended toward the courtyard. The queen's ring glowed brightly as the black stallion drifted over the 40-foot-high wall with a magical wind howling in their ears.

The courtyard was smaller than expected, flanked by three sets of stairs that led to the battlements, and was engulfed in a fog that flowed from an open door to the keep. A male magic user in a dark purple robe, covered with celestial symbols, stood in the threshold holding a staff. The fog swirled around him, pushed by a wind created by his rod that made his long gray beard blow to the side. Though he searched the night sky, Taliesin assumed he could not see her or her winged horse. Thalagar landed on the flagstones without making a sound, and the magic user sniffed the air, alerted by a sudden increase in magic.

"The Raven Mistress has come!" the man shouted.

Taliesin remained in the saddle, holding *Ringerike* at her side, which refrained from showing its bright blue light as the Eagle Magic Guild filed from the keep into the courtyard. Witches, warlocks, wizards, and sorcerers, wearing colored cloaks to signify their ranks, fanned out on the stairs. Some held staffs and others wands. None seemed to notice where Taliesin remained perched on her horse. Guards gathered at the battlements and gazed toward the courtyard, unable to see Taliesin, despite the glow from their torches. A witch lifted her wand, and torches set around the courtyard came to life, producing a bright golden light that bounced off Taliesin's dragon armor and momentarily revealed her position.

"There she is! I see her," the sorcerer in purple said. He used his staff to point in her direction, and from the tip, a red light appeared.

Ringerike went into action as a bolt of fire shot toward her. A blue orb surrounded Taliesin and Thalagar, acting as a shield that deflected the bolt and sent it flying into a tower. An explosion created a shower of hot flames into the sky, scouring the courtyard with falling stones. Guards standing nearby were struck by the flames and incinerated on contact, and the gust of wind the explosion created toppled several more over the battlements. The magic users combined their powers to send an arsenal of death in her direction, either deflected by the blue orb or by *Ringerike* as it reacted on its own, making her arm swing in every direction. Despite this being her first battle against a magic guild, she felt strangely calm, aware moonlight shined directly upon her. The ten magic users banded together, with wands raised and staffs held before them, hurling spells, hexes, and curses, all of which slammed into the blue orb and were sent sputtering into the wind.

"Your magic is strong," the man in purple shouted. "Not strong enough, for I am Karnok the Magnificent, and this is my guild! Coming here was foolish, Raven Mistress, for you are outnumbered and will not leave here alive."

"Ysemay the Beguiling is dead," Taliesin replied. "Abducting Zarnoc and Jaelle was a mistake. This is *Ringerike*, and despite what you throw at me, in the hands of a *Sha'tar*, it is a deadly weapon!" She felt *Calaburn* tremble against her leg, wanting to be of service, but she did not draw it.

Ringerike let her know Karnok and the guild members were among the most notorious magic users found in legends, ballads, and poems. They stared at her from the stairs, ancient magic users who long ago turned their minds toward harmful and malicious practices and used dark magic to control and manipulate the world and people around them. Zarnoc had never resorted to this type of magic. Nor did he lust for power or allow greed and conceit to motivate him.

"Your secret guild has remained hidden in Eagle's Cliff for centuries," Taliesin said as her horse pawed at the stones with his front hoof. "And here you will die, for I do not intend to allow any of you to live one day longer."

"If you have heard of me, then you know you are too late to save Zarnoc," Karnok said. "Lord Arundel believes you and your pet wizard are a threat. My old adversary sinks further into the Great Well with every minute that passes. At midnight, he will drown, along with the gypsy girl. Unless...."

Taliesin pointed her sword at Karnok, aware guards had started to filter into the courtyard from every direction. "Bartering? Like commoners? That's not the Eagle way," she said.

"Ysemay told us you are unable to control your magic," Karnok lashed back. "It was foolish to come here alone, Raven Mistress." He pointed his staff at her. "Remove your dragon armor and surrender. Your life for that of your friends. That is what I offer."

Taliesin felt her temper rise. Fangs slid out as she snarled, "I do not accept your offer, Karnok. Nor am I powerless. All I need do is leave and tell King Frederick that Lord Arundel has defied his law by keeping alive your magic guild. All Arundel has worked for will be taken away, and all of you will burn at the stake!"

"Careful, *Sha'tar*," Karnok said. "I can cover the moon with clouds at a snap of my fingers and end your moment of glory. It will take more than the ring of Queen Madera to protect you and the Raven Sword. The two are opposed to one another, yet you come baring *Calaburn* as well. Don't you realize you are nothing more than a mutt? Your royal blood is tainted— you are *Wolfen*!"

Taliesin gave a tap to Thalagar, and he rose on his hind legs as she waved her sword at the guild. "There stand the Ruby Sisters—Isueda, Jesmonde, and Vivian," she said. "Risen from the dead is Grangwayna of the Lake, and though you've brushed off the dust on the sorcerers Tembol and Vatan the Black, and even Hescariot the Bold, the lack of magic war-craft has left you all weak. I challenge you to a duel of magic! I win, and you release Zarnoc and Jaelle. I lose and, well, that's just not going to happen."

"Mira sent her to the past, Karnok," a Ruby Sister said. "She thinks we don't know where she goes and what she does, but we do. Let the Raven Mistress see what befell Queen Madera after she left."

The green mist rose as high as the castle walls and blocked the magic guild from view, though not the moon. The color changed to a pale green, and an image of the throne room in Black Castle formed before her. There, head upon a block of stone, lay Queen Madera, with an executioner standing behind her holding a large-handled ax. King Korax, Zarnoc, the Raven Knights and the royal court had gathered to watch. A baby, the Raven heir, only three weeks old, lay bundled in Ysemay's arms. As the ax lifted, Taliesin sensed what the guild showed her was a lie, and she turned away, refusing to watch the grizzly execution.

"No more tricks," Taliesin said.

"Your great-uncle, seventy-times removed, is not your friend, Taliesin," Karnok said. "He allowed Queen Madera to die. Why? She was Hellirin! It is Zarnoc who lied to you. He should have been King of Duvalen, for he was the eldest, not Xerxes, yet he let his brother's son, Boran, take the throne and dragged Korax south to stake his own claim. Your mentor pitted brother against brother and brothers against sister. He turned the Lorian against the Hellirin. It was he who buried Korax in the Cave of the Snake God, along with *Ringerike*, and then waited through the centuries for one such as you to be born. Zarnoc has plans for you, but it's not what you think, not at all."

"I do not believe you, Karnok! You are nothing but a liar!"

"Zarnoc wishes to bring about *Varguld*, for he is tied to Ragnal, made blood brothers by the darkness of their souls and their love for war. It is what Zarnoc has always wanted. Lord Arundel is doing you and the world a favor by killing the wizard." Karnok lowered his staff and stepped forward. "I offer you something else. Do nothing and let me kill him, and I'll give you the gypsy girl. You may restore her to Shan Octavio and remain here, our welcomed guest, and learn how to use your magic. We will see King Frederick remains on the throne. What say you?"

"Sounds horrible," Taliesin said. "I won't lift a finger to help Arundel. Zarnoc is my friend, and he would never betray me."

"Korax said the same thing," the guild replied in unison.

Taliesin felt an itch in her head as the guild tried to read her thoughts. She formed an image of Karnok burning at a stake and let them all see it, feel his pain, and imagine his screams. It was Grangwayna of the Lake who reacted first. She waved her wand and attempted to breach the grisly image and probe her thoughts, and for a moment, she managed to slip through Taliesin's defense and found a surprise waiting. Taliesin thought of Grangwayna as Glabber the Glib, an Eagle playwright, had written in a story about the witch. She repeated the words of Glabber's play: '*And the witch of the lake, chained and gagged, rocks tied to her legs, was thrown into the lake. Knights and soldiers watched as she sank to the bottom, and stayed at the bottom, trapped in her watery grave, forevermore.*'

The witch merely laughed, until the glow of the queen's ring spilled upon the Granwayna's face. Her true appearance was revealed, hideous and scarred like something that had crawled out of the Eagle graveyard. With a screech, the witch turned away, hiding her face behind her hands.

"She sees into my mind!" Grangwayna cried.

"Trickster, that's what she is," the Ruby Sisters said in unison.

Tembol, eyes as dark as his robe, laughed. "Give her a taste of steel, Karnok," he said in a deep baritone.

Taliesin sensed an archer on the battlement take aim and heard *Ringerike* whine as the sword jerked her arm and knocked an arrow aside. It clattered to the ground. Taliesin never looked to see which man had fired but imagined the culprit flying over the side of the castle and plummeting to his death on the rocks below. The other archers held their fire as one of their comrades sailed over the wall, his screams piercing the night.

"So stubborn," Karnok said. "Allow me to show you the future, child." He spread his arms wide and an image projected from the folds of his purple robe. The symbols from the robe floated over his head and turned into a future timeline with the planets precisely aligned above Tantalon Castle.

Taliesin saw herself within the royal castle, just as Wren predicted, seated upon the Ebony Throne with a crown on her head. Rook, dressed in armor, stood beside her. Wren and the foreseen child were not present. Her friend wore a look of sorrow, and she knew Wren had died in childbirth. Outside the castle walls, the city of Padama lay in rubble, and the dead filled the streets, their bloated faces and the sores on their skin was a sign of the plague. An army of barbarians, led by Talas Kull, wearing a horned helmet, advanced upon the castle from the north. King Frederick and his five sons were dead. Zarnoc, Sir Roland, and the Knights of the White Stag were dead, as were the Shan and the Ghajar, and of the Raven Clan, a mere 100 Black Wings survived. The guards stood at the battlements and watched heavy siege equipment roll forward. It was an illusion, she knew and refused to believe what she saw.

"Enough of your games, sorcerer," Taliesin shouted. "What you have shown me is the defeat of the Wolf Clan, as well as my own. I somehow don't think Ragnal would take it kindly that you predicted a future where he doesn't win. I do not fear the Skardans. But you should fear me!"

Taliesin caught the flip of a wand and smelled burnt feathers, and knew the witches secretly used magic to try to sway her to their side. Karnok acted as if he wasn't aware what the Ruby Sisters and the lake witch did, and Tembol smiled. Vatan twiddled his thumbs and stirred a small cloud, as if attempting to create a tornado, while Hescariot the Bold had removed a notepad from his robe and used a magical quill to write down everything said, recording the incident for the Eagle records.

"We have another prisoner of noble blood in our dungeon. One you know and might desire to release instead of that Lorian fool and the gypsy assassin." Karnok smiled wide and revealed tea-stained yellow teeth. A woman wearing a dirty nun's habit appeared before Thalagar.

"I don't know who this is," Taliesin said, leaning forward in the saddle. "One beggar looks very much like another. You've a dungeon full of the forlorn and the forgotten. Be charitable and let her go. In fact, let them all go, Karnok, and I will spare your life!"

"Come now, Raven Mistress. Do you not recognize your own mother? This is Princess Calista, the king's younger sister, a Stroudian nun," the sorcerer said. "Is it the habit that blinds you? The king's sister has taken her vows. She is the spiritual wife of the god Stroud. Still, she is your flesh and blood."

"Now you've gone too far with your filthy illusions," Taliesin snarled.

Ringerike saw through the deception and throbbed in Taliesin's grip to warn her it was not her mother in disguise. As she imagined the magic guild turning into pebbles, the Ruby Sisters used their wands and muttered a spell the old-fashioned way to move clouds across the sky to block the silver rays of the moon. Taliesin pointed her sword at the sky, and the clouds formed into a giant dragon and swooped to the earth. The startled magic guild lifted their wands and staffs as the dragon roared, sounding exactly like Bonaparte, and opened its great jaws as it landed before them.

Taliesin jumped from her horse and swung her sword, sending blue streaks of flame spiraling toward the guards on the battlements, blinding them as she reached the woman's side. Instantly, the nun turned into a hideous beast, with twelve tentacles and a beak in the middle of its head. Taliesin swung her sword at each tentacle and severed them. Her footwork spun her around on the stones, and she struck off its head. Green blood spread across the ground, tentacles flopped, and Taliesin turned into a *Wolfen*.

"We are done negotiating," Taliesin said as she lifted her visor and bared her fangs. She drew *Calaburn* for good measure and attacked the guild.

While *Ringerike* warded off spells and flame arrows, puffs of deadly gas, and the ghostly form of a skeleton reptile she'd met in the Cave of the Snake God, *Calaburn* fired bursts of flames at the guild. The Ruby Sisters, touched by the fire, lit like torches and screamed as they ran across the courtyard and dropped to the stones. The three wizards launched a ball of flame at Thalagar. *Ringerike* lifted its blue barrier and sent it flying across the courtyard, to strike a tower and knock it off its base. The tower fell with a crash, sending guards tumbling from the wall as the armored horse trotted out of the way.

"Kill her," Karnok ordered. "Wands and staffs! Strike at her heart! Kill the Raven Mistress!"

"*Ringerike!*"

Taliesin roared the sword's name as it cut through the barrier, and with *Calaburn*, she stabbed Tembol's tall body. The wizard let out a shriek as he burst into flames and fell onto his back, thrashing until nothing was left but ashes. She struck again and broke through a protection spell combined with a sleep spell, feeling only a mild head rush and a fierce need for blood before she impaled the red-haired Isueda with both swords. *Ringerike* jerked free from the body, while *Calaburn* burned its prey, and swung back toward Jesmonde, barely missing her as the sorceress fell to the ground, hands covering her head. Taliesin caught Vivian trying to run down the stairs and sunk her fangs into the woman's shoulder, tasting hot blood rank with black magic.

"Mira help us," Grangwayna of the Lake cried. She waved her wand like a child with a stick and shot colorful sparks from the tip. Wave after wave of deadly missiles struck Taliesin's armor and bounced off harmlessly with *plonks*. With a piercing scream, she fell beneath *Ringerike's* fierce blow.

Vatan the Black turned into a giant gold dragon and flew into the air, to be met by Thalagar, who flew upwards and fought him over the heights of the castle.

Hescariot the Bold joined Karnok, and they pointed their staffs at Taliesin. A bolt of energy struck Taliesin in the breast, and she staggered back two steps. She retaliated with two quick sword thrusts. Hescariot, cleaved down the middle by *Calaburn*, toppled to either side, in flames, while Karnok, his chest cut wide open by *Ringerike*, ran inside the keep. The door closed behind him, and Taliesin turned her attention to the dragon fighting her horse. Pointing *Ringerike* at the black beast, she imagined the blue light from her sword turning into a deadly lance and watched it fly into the air. It struck the dragon in the chest and pierced through its magical scales.

With a roar, Vatan the Black spiraled like a comet and crashed into the roof of the keep. The heavy body smashed through the timbers and ignited the wood with a bright blue fire that spread rapidly across the castle, engulfing the outer buildings and garrison. Guards hidden within came rushing out, screaming in pain and terror as they burned alive. Taliesin held her swords to either side and walked toward the center of the courtyard, filled with vengeance and hate.

"*Thalagar*! Come here!"

The horse descended to the courtyard and gave a shake of its mane. Taliesin tapped *Calaburn* on the ground, dousing its flame before she slid it into the scabbard. With *Ringerike* still in hand, she climbed onto Thalagar's back and urged the horse into the air. She pointed the Raven Sword at the north tower and brought it crashing down. She did the same to the south and east towers, tasting victory, until she spotted Zarnoc as he appeared in the courtyard, holding Jaelle draped over his arms. As the fire hungrily reached for Zarnoc and Jaelle, the wizard turned into a giant raven, Jaelle clutched in his talons, and flew into the air.

Taliesin took one last look at Eagle's Cliff and the destruction she'd caused. Her hatred and anger faded, leaving her horrified at what she'd done in a moment of madness. Her *Wolfen* form turned human, and her armor returned to its original appearance. She continued to stare at the fire as Thalagar flew from the castle and headed after her friends, afraid for the first time of the consequences of her actions.

* * * * *

Chapter Twenty-Four

The black stallion sailed through a sky thick with smoke. A heavy rumble from the burning castle echoed through the ravine as she flew lower to search the area for the Shan and Rook, hoping they had made it out in time. Taliesin glided closer to Zarnoc and glanced at Jaelle dangling from his talons, not moving, and felt a lump in her throat at the thought her friend was dead. As her horse descended behind the giant raven through the layer of smoke, she gazed at the ground, able to see the remains of the Eagle soldiers, white bones under the moon, lying where they'd fallen. Not one arm or finger twitched. Not a sound was made. The dead should be quiet, and again she looked at Jaelle, fearing the worst.

"Do you see Rook and the Shan? They went inside to find you," Taliesin shouted.

"No," Zarnoc squawked. "A fine mess you made of things, Raven girl!"

"Keep looking!"

"I fear your *Wolfen* wrath has taken its toll," the wizard said. "I told you not to remove that necklace. Not everyone inside was evil, and every prisoner is now dead as well as the magic guild and Eagle legionnaires. Put on your necklace and put out the fire, I beg of you!"

Taliesin slid the necklace over her winged helmet, heard the iron nail strike her armor, and felt an immediate sense of guilt at her own rashness. It was a monstrous thing she'd done, so dark and twisted that she imagined Ragnal laughing at her from Mt. Helos, for the deaths awarded to him only brought the world one step closer to *Varguld*. Hot tears fell onto her cheeks as she willed the fire to end with no results, for it continued to spread and wreak havoc. By the time Thalagar landed in the ravine, she was in tears. Zarnoc gently placed Jaelle's limp body onto the ground and turned into an old man.

"What are we to do?" Taliesin asked, frantic.

"There is nothing to be done. Jaelle is dead," Zarnoc said. "Had you controlled your anger, had you used your head and not your swords, this might not have happened."

Taliesin sheathed *Ringerike* and sank beside her friend. She was a *Sha'tar*. Her magic was strong, so why not use it to restore her friend's life. Taliesin placed her hands upon Jaelle's still chest, closed her eyes, and willed life to flow from her into her friend's body. Nothing happened. Zarnoc's hand dropped to her shoulder, and she heard shouts but refused to open her eyes or break contact as the Black Wings and Ghajar arrived.

"Guards, stand watch," Rook said. "Two of you, check on the horses."

"What happened to my daughter? Is she alive?" the Shan asked, his voice choked with emotion.

Taliesin continued to fill Jaelle's body with her own life essence and felt the energy flow from her fingertips into the still body. She felt a twitch in the girl's leg and a brush of fingers upon Taliesin's thigh, which gave her hope. Without opening her eyes, she sensed the Shan knelt beside her and placed his hand on Jaelle's brow. Taliesin felt his energy first disrupt the flow of life, and then a push as he unknowingly added his own essence to that absorbed by Jaelle. Taliesin begged the gods, each and every one, to help her, and summoned every bit of strength as she willed Jaelle to live.

"Zarnoc, this is dark magic Taliesin calls upon," the Shan said. "I feel strange, my body aches, and I grow weary." His hand jerked away, and the energy piping into Jaelle's body ebbed. "The dead cannot be resurrected. You know it is not allowed by my people. Tell Taliesin to stop. My daughter is gone. Let her rest in peace."

"Jaelle drowned. I was not able to save her," Zarnoc said, his tone angry. "Taliesin is trying to start her heart with magic. It is not dark magic, but it is ancient. Give her a moment."

"We looked all over for you, Zarnoc." Rook was shaken by what he'd seen, and Taliesin opened her eyes, distracted by her captain. "The Eagles kept many Ravens as hostages, and for weeks starved them. I will not tell you about those we found tortured or what we found living inside a deep well."

"Be still, boy," Zarnoc said. "Let Taliesin concentrate."

"Do not let her die," Octavio whispered as he pressed his daughter's hand to his face. "Take all of my energy, Taliesin. Take my life, if it will restore Jaelle's heartbeat. She is not cold to the touch—there is still warmth."

"Please, Mira, restore her life, I beg of you." Taliesin paused in her prayer, uncertain if she felt Jaelle move until she heard Octavio breathing heavier in excitement. "Please, Mira. I'll do anything you ask, just give her life."

"Anything?" Zarnoc asked. "That is a vow she will hold you to, child. Enough. Let Jaelle go and move aside. I have indulged you long enough. Move, I say."

Taliesin cried out as Jaelle started to move. The girl raised an arm, and her fingers opened wide. With a cry of relief, Shan Octavio pulled his daughter into his arms. Sobs of relief shook his entire body. Taliesin glanced toward the group of men. Two men returned with the horses without the female Black Ravens. Only three gypsies and Earnest and the former Wolfmen had survived.

"Joaquin?" Taliesin asked, catching Earnest's gaze.

"He didn't make it," the Black Wing said.

"I lost a son," the Shan said, "but you have restored Jaelle to me. My dear, sweet girl. Your father is here. I am here."

A finger tapped Taliesin's shoulder. Her gaze lifted as Rook took her arm and helped pull her to her feet. Before she could say a word, the captain threw his arms around her, exhibiting a rare display of emotion as he hugged her tight.

"I didn't think it possible. You saved Jaelle," Rook said. "Master Osprey would be so proud of you, Taliesin. So would Grudge...I mean, you know...Roland."

Taliesin caught Zarnoc gazing at her, his expression that of relief and regret all rolled into one and sprinkled with a fine layer of anger. The wizard pushed Rook aside and shook his finger at her.

"Never take off the Broa's necklace again. Your wild side is too strong in the moonlight," Zarnoc scolded. "There is so much darkness inside you, Taliesin. Hellirin and *Wolfen*. Draconus and Lorian. And being a *Sha'tar* makes you deadly. I don't know whether I should thank you or put you in a cage."

Taliesin tapped the sapphire ring to remove her armor and helmet and tried to get a glimpse of Jaelle's face pressed to her father's shoulder. Zarnoc blocked her view. He was angrier than she'd ever seen him before, and she was quick to take offense.

"If it wasn't for Mira, I don't think I could have stopped the magic guild. Believe me. I gave them every opportunity to let you both go, Zarnoc. They tried to deceive me, to get me to join them. I didn't want to kill them. I didn't want bloodshed this night. Not until they tried to trick me with an image of my mother. I know she is alive, Zarnoc. I just know it."

"You just *know* it," the wizard said, clicking his tongue against the roof of his mouth. "If you can't learn to control your power, Taliesin, it may yet destroy you and everyone around you. I tried to convince Karnok he was in serious danger. Had I known what you were capable of doing in the moonlight, I would have tried harder. By bringing down the Eagle magic guild and Eagle's Cliff, you have made Lord Arundel your most hated enemy. He will not rest until you are destroyed."

"I'm sorry."

"Are you? Really?" Zarnoc gave a shake of his head. "Stop thinking you are the most special person in the world and try to learn something about life before you get us all killed. You are a *Sha'tar*. There's no disputing that. Only you, because of your heritage, are capable of using *Ringerike* and *Calaburn*, two swords that never should have joined forces, for what they did together was evil. I expect you to uphold the rights of all people and beings, no matter race, or kin, nor king. Be better than the rest. Make something of yourself. In the meantime, don't forget what you do affects everyone around you, for better or worse. Tonight, it was for the worse."

"I said I was sorry," Taliesin replied, aware everyone stared at her. "I'm tired of it, Zarnoc. Tired of being judged and feared and hated. When does it end?"

"When you sit on the throne or lie in a grave, I suppose. Then it's over."

"You are under a moon curse, my friend," Rook said, in a soothing voice. He held his silver spear close to his body, leaning on it for support. "Everyone knows Mira and Ragnal are lovers. Navenna has no reason to work against the Raven Clan, so it's Mira who allowed the magic guild to capture Zarnoc and Jaelle. And it is she who gave you such dangerous power to use this night. It is the moon goddess whom you must guard against, she and her wolf lover."

Shan Octavio let out a cry of pain and suddenly pushed Jaelle away. The girl's eyes were open. They were opaque, and blood covered her face. She bared her teeth at her father as she crawled toward him, snarling like a beast.

"Something is wrong! This is not right. Taliesin! What have you done? My daughter is one of the undead," the Shan cried. He stood, protected by his three men, as he tore a strip of cloth from his cloak and pressed it to his cheek.

"You brought her back, Taliesin, only we did not take into account it was done in a graveyard," Zarnoc said as he approached the gypsy girl. "That ring on your finger, the one with a moonstone, I know it is Queen Madera's ring. Where did you get it? I cannot read your thoughts this night. It is possible the Moon Ring has turned Jaelle into a mindless *darkling*."

"A *darkling*," the Shan whispered.

Octavio and his men turned away and talked amongst themselves, the words growing heated. With a wave of his hand, the Shan pushed through his men and headed toward the horses. The three gypsies ran after him. He gave no instructions on how Taliesin was to deal with his daughter, which had to mean Shan Octavio Alvarez no longer cared what happened to her. His daughter, in his eyes, was dead, dead like his son Joaquin. The gypsies were in their saddles and riding out of the ravine as Jaelle stopped before Taliesin. She gazed at Taliesin with gray eyes and opened her mouth to snarl. *Ringerike* gave a hard twitch, demanding Taliesin draw it from its scabbard. She reached for the hilt, reluctant to act as Jaelle crawled toward her.

"I can't bear to watch," Rook said, with a sob. "I'm sorry. I just can't."

The captain and the seven Black Wings mounted their horses. They took the extra horses by the reins and rode after the Ghajar, leaving Zarnoc, Taliesin, and an undead girl in the Eagle graveyard while the castle burned.

"Gypsies fear the dead and undead," the wizard said as if this was enough to explain the sudden departure of their friends. "Either give her the Moon Ring and hope it restores her mind or kill her. Decide fast. She's hungry."

Jaelle reached Taliesin and clawed at her boots as Zarnoc turned away. A human skull appeared in the dirt close to Taliesin. Jaelle seized it, rolled it in her hands, and studied it as she quieted and hummed an unfamiliar tune. Taliesin was reluctant to give her the ring without first knowing everything it could do. She didn't want to make things worse by turning Jaelle completely into a *darkling*, and hoped, somehow, she might be able to make her human again.

"I don't understand why I couldn't bring Jaelle back as she was," Taliesin said. "Octavio gave me his life energy, and I used it. We both fed Jaelle until I felt her heartbeat. What went wrong?"

"The rules that apply to the magic guilds are the same that apply to every independent magic user, charlatan, jokesters or magician. In essence, we are all children of magic," Zarnoc said. "Our power comes from the same place, the earth itself, and it is that power the goddess Mira and the gods on Mt. Helos have harnessed. It's what you must harness, Taliesin. If you're going to use magic, then learn the simple rules. You will read a play or a sonnet, but you refuse to read books on magic, written by folks who have been at this a lot longer than you."

"What are they? Just tell me."

"Cast away vile speech, thought, and manners. Keep your own, and your fellow magic users' secrets. Use magic against another magic user only in self-defense. Use your magic to do good, not evil. Show mercy to the poor as well as the rich if they are in need of your help. Avoid excess greed, gluttony, lust, envy, and sloth. And, above all else, respect your magic gifts."

"I saw you," Taliesin said, as she slid her fingers around the Moon Ring. "I saw the man you used to be in Black Castle. Mira sent me to the past, and I saw how you all treated Madera. Karnok wanted me to believe Korax beheaded his wife because she was Hellirin. I realize now the Hellirin dabble in necromancy, and that's how they restored life to the dead, a half-life, and this ring is extremely powerful. If I gave this ring to Jaelle, she would have control over the Hellirin army."

The poor girl tossed aside the skull and sat staring at Taliesin and Zarnoc. She worked her jaw, trying to talk, only the words wouldn't come out. The wizard went to her, careful not to excite her, and motioned for Jaelle to stand. He made no move to help as Jaelle struggled to rise, unsure of how to work her muscles, giving the impression of a broken puppet with clipped strings.

"It's not in our domain to restore life," Zarnoc said, gesturing toward Jaelle. "Giving and taking life is what the Gods of Mt. Helos do. The Maeceni did not come into power overnight, nor did they assume their role as gods without bloodshed. Too many Lorian and Hellirin died fighting them for supremacy ages ago. Part of the surrender terms requires the Magic Realms to respect the gods and never use our magic to resurrect the dead, for that is their domain alone. I should have stopped you from saving Jaelle. In truth, I didn't want her to die any more than you. Nor could I help you, though I don't care to explain why. As I said, give her the ring or kill her."

Taliesin stared at him. "Did you dabble in necromancy?"

"You saw King Korax at the Cave of the Snake God and saw what he'd become. I am the one who turned him, Taliesin. I went to the cave without Madera, thinking I was strong enough to bring him back from the dead. When he rose as the living dead, I placed him in his coffin and sealed it shut. Madera was furious of course. She told me to leave her child with foster parents and returned to Nethalburg. I have not seen her since. Jaelle is what Korax was, a zombie, and unless you place that ring on her finger, she will continue to rot and feed on the living and the dead."

Taliesin heard a quiver in his voice. "And? Is there another way to save her?"

"You could take her to Nethalburg," the wizard said. "Dolabra and Folando would certainly know what to do with her. Jaelle would never be able to live above ground, but she could have a life there, and you can keep the ring."

"Maybe I could talk to Madera. I liked her."

"Well, you are not a good judge of character, my dear. All anyone has to do is smile or compliment you, and you think they're honorable. Madera wore a lovely mask. I assure you, her heart is not filled with milk and honey. You'd have to understand the Hellirin history to know precisely what I mean, but we don't have the time to sit here and talk. Your little friend belongs with the Hellirin. Take her to them but close your visor so she doesn't try to eat your face."

"I'll find another place for Jaelle. Someplace where she'll be safe." Taliesin closed her visor before she pulled Jaelle to her feet. The girl snapped her teeth and snarled.

"Safe? There is no place safe. Shall I tell you why Korax was afraid of you?" Zarnoc stepped in front of Thalagar, preventing Taliesin from helping the girl into the saddle. "I remember you paid us a visit. How could I not? When you chose to speak to the queen and not to Korax, I thought the boy might burst a blood vessel. He was furious you favored the Hellirin over the Lorian, and with good cause. That ring you wear summons darkness, Taliesin. You can't keep it, not unless you desire to live among the shadows, for over time, it *will* change you."

"And if Jaelle wears it, her memories will return, and she'll be more like Dolabra than a ghoul," Taliesin said. "Why didn't you just say so, instead of filling my ears with reprimands and rules no magic user pays any attention to? I think the queen knew what she was doing when she gave me the ring. Madera must have known I would need it."

"I'm sure not for the reason you think. It's meant for you, not Jaelle."

"You just told me to give it to her, Zarnoc. That's what I'm going to do." Taliesin removed the moonstone ring, caught Jaelle's arm, and slid it onto the girl's finger. "Now we'll just have to wait and see if it works or not."

Zarnoc crossed his arms over his chest. He frowned when a section of the castle wall collapsed into the ravine, lowered his arms, and gave Jaelle a vicious slap.

"Let's speed things up. I'd like to leave," he said in a stern tone.

With a blink of her eyes, Jaelle gave a shake of her head. Her eyes widened, and she started to breathe in shallow breaths. She raised a hand to her throat and leaned forward. Working her jaw, the girl tried to speak and made a curious bleating sound that reminded Taliesin of a goat.

"Better Jaelle live in the shadows than rot in a grave," Taliesin said. "If Madera was so horrible, why did Korax marry her? Why have a child with her?"

"Korax married Madera because it was arranged to unite the Lorians and Hellirin, but that is not how it worked out.

Madera was never the same after you left. She grew cunning and secretive and sent messages to her Hellirin family, plotting against Korax. I suppose she told you the Hellirins would help you. If you try to use that ring to control General Folando, you will make an enemy of Queen Dehavilyn and my nephew. There is no telling what Dolabra will do to you."

"Were you the eldest son or not?"

"No," Zarnoc said. "Xerxes was two years old than me."

"Is my mother alive?"

He sighed and gave a nod. "Yes, yes, she's alive."

"Just know that I serve neither the Folando family nor the Draconus family. Nor do I serve the Sanqualus or Vorenius lines. I was born 'Rosamond Mandrake,' but I am the Raven Mistress," Taliesin said. She shuddered as Jaelle reached out with ice-cold fingers to touch Taliesin's face. "Well, it's an improvement."

Zarnoc stepped out of the way. "The Moon Ring not only restores life to its owner but can raise the dead," he snapped. "Or didn't you realize you're the one who summoned the Eagle dead tonight? That wasn't Karnok. It was you. Even now, you have no idea what you can and can't do. What you need is training, though I fear I'm not the one to train you, for you won't listen to me."

With a snort, Thalagar stepped forward and nudged Taliesin in the back. She climbed into the saddle, caught Jaelle by the arm, and with a hard tug, yanked her across the front of the saddle. Thalagar spread his wings to help put Jaelle into the saddle, and she managed to swing a leg over and dig her hands into his mane, all the while laughing like a mad woman.

"Where are you going?" Zarnoc asked as he turned into a raven. "You can't take a *darkling* anywhere but to Nethalburg. It's not allowed. Do you hear me?"

"You and your secrets! I'm sick of them, old man. And I'm sick of your little insights into your shady past," Taliesin said, her nostrils filling with the odor of smoke and death. The horse pawed at the ground, anxious to leave. "And to answer your question, I'm going to see my mother, and I'm taking Jaelle with me. Are you coming or not?"

"Absolutely not," he snapped, equally angry. "I'll collect Hawk and the Traveling Tower and return to Penkill Castle. Personally, I'm tired of watching you make mistake after mistake. You're just like Korax—you never learn. Go see your nasty old mother. I have no doubt you'll be very disappointed. Some things are better off forgotten, and believe me, she's one of them."

Taliesin snarled. "Don't you dare insult my mother!" She watched as the raven flew into the air and shouted. "I suggest you start making amends for the crimes you committed in the past! I'll do what I think is best for the future! Oh, and you're welcome I saved your life!"

A large section of the fortress tumbled off the cliff and slammed into the ravine as Thalagar sprang into the air. Two towers toppled over and closed the far entry into the ravine. Zarnoc flew away with an angry squawk and vanished in the thick smoke that hung over the castle ruins. The moment he was gone, Taliesin regretted their quarrel and wondered what she'd find at Talbot Abbey.

* * * * *

Chapter Twenty-Five

"We'll be there soon," Taliesin said. She didn't say how soon, nor did Jaelle ask, and they'd traveled for two days and nights, resting only for a few hours, to reach Talbot Abbey, located on the western coastline of Thule. The morning sun was hot on her back, despite the fact she did not wear her armor, nor did Thalagar. She kept one arm around Jaelle and the other wrapped in the horse's mane, doing her best to keep them both on board.

Jaelle pointed at a brown hawk that floated beside the horse.

"Pretty," she said and giggled. "Pretty bird. Pretty bird."

"You must stop," Taliesin groaned. She was equally weary of the nonsense that came from her friend's mouth. Jaelle hadn't said one intelligent thing since they left Eagle's Cliff. "It's my fault you're like this. I'm going to get you help. I promise."

The wizard had seemed adamant her mother, Princess Calista, was the last person she needed to visit. Taliesin regretted losing her temper and the cross things she'd said to Zarnoc. She loved him and didn't like it when he scolded her. What Zarnoc failed to understand was how much she wanted to meet her mother. Calista was alive! At last, they would be together, and her mother might be able to put things in perspective about a great number of things. Most importantly, Calista might provide insight into what steps Taliesin should take to heal the realm. The abbey would hopefully offer a better sanctuary for Jaelle than the half-dead that lived within Hellirin.

As she fretted, she failed to consider the exhaustion of her horse or her own state of mental and emotional fatigue. Somewhere among the clouds, Taliesin drifted off to sleep,

400 | SUSANNE L. LAMBDIN

barely aware Jaelle kept her in the saddle. Not until she heard a crunching sound did her eyes flutter open, to find herself prone upon a soft bed of grass and the stallion within eyesight eating grass. Taliesin pushed herself onto an elbow, felt a soft wind on her face, and smelled the sea. She no longer wore her armor or helmet, though the Draconus ring remained on her finger, and felt grateful it had vanished so she wouldn't sweat in the hot sun. The rolling waves crashed upon rocks, and water sprayed her face as she sat forward, knees curled under her, and stared at the expanse of blue water.

"Good eats," Jaelle said. "Daisies, cornflowers, little black crickets."

Taliesin turned her head and spotted Jaelle crawling along a ridge, stuffing her mouth with whatever she found. The girl no longer wore clothes, her skin, pulled tightly against her ribs, appeared deathly pale. Her clothes lay on the ground not far from Jaelle, and her leather boots looked gnawed on. Seeing the Shan's daughter in such a pitiful condition brought Taliesin to her feet. She picked the garments off the ground, sniffed them, and wrinkled her nose at the sickly-sweet odor of death. As she approached Jaelle from behind, her friend came to a halt. Her thick mass of hair was wild, covered by grass and flower petals, and as she spun around, she held up a handful of crickets. Jaelle shoved them into her mouth.

"Stop that!" Taliesin ordered. "Are you listening to me, Jaelle? Go put on your clothes. We need to go to the abbey. Now."

"Crunchy."

"Fine. Eat what you want," Taliesin said. "Just stay where I can see you."

Taliesin sat in the grass, removed the Deceiver's Map, and searched for Talbot Abbey. It was no more than three miles north along the rugged coast. However, when she thought of Princess Calista, the name didn't appear on the map. She thought of Zarnoc and found him with Rook and the Black Wings at Penkill Castle, while the Shan was close to his large camp. That was good news. With a sigh, she thought about Sir

Roland, and he appeared at Tantalon Castle, now surrounded by the armies of the dukes of Maldavia, Scrydon, and Aldagar. Duke Andre of Thule, whose dukedom she was currently in, had gone with his army to fight for the king. The only duke missing was the late Duke Richelieu de Boran of Garridan. In his place, Prince Sertorius and a large fleet were following the coastline along Thule. She assumed he'd land on the southern tip of the dukedom and take the King's Road, the fastest route to the royal city.

"Why is my cousin coming to Thule? He could just stay in Garridan and keep his nose out of his big brother's business," Taliesin grumbled. "Jaelle, get dressed. You've grass in your teeth and bugs in your hair. My mother is going to be terrified."

With the map put away, Taliesin whistled for Thalagar before she gathered Jaelle's clothes and attempted to dress her. It was a battle, for Jaelle had completely forgotten how to put on a skirt or button her blouse, and it was well past noon by the time Taliesin managed to clothe her. The sun was high overhead, and while Taliesin had no idea about the practices of nuns in abbeys, there certainly would be prayers and daily chores to attend, and at some point, they'd close their doors to visitors.

"Let's go see my mother," Taliesin said. "Thalagar, come here!"

The horse gave a snort and trotted off a short distance, refusing to cooperate. After several minutes of coaxing and shouting, Taliesin finally grabbed Jaelle by the hand and dragged her down a path along the shore toward the abbey. She heard Thalagar following and smiled, though she didn't turn around since he was in a stubborn mood, and she didn't want him running off. The gypsy, beautiful even for an undead girl, seemed content to hold her hand and laughed every time a dragonfly or bee flew past. She grabbed a handful of flowers, stuck them in her mouth despite Taliesin's look of disapproval, and happily trudged down the path. Between Jaelle's constant need to eat something and Thalagar's lollygagging, the short walk turned into an hour hike, and Taliesin was close to losing her temper.

"That's Talbot Abbey," Taliesin said, pointing.

The abbey, of modest propriety, was built alongside a cliff overlooking the Pangian Sea and had a two-story chapel, arched windows filled with stained glass, and a garden set beside a graveyard. Moss covered the gravestones and obscured the names. Taliesin was relieved not to see any fresh mounds of soil. During plagues and wars, people from the country flocked to churches and faraway private religious facilities such as Talbot Abbey. More often than not, the daughters of nobles, who for whatever reason were no longer needed in society, were tucked away inside, along with the young women who lacked a fortune or a future. She knew some women wanted a quiet existence and arrived willing to spend a lifetime serving their gods.

The garden was cluttered, and the vegetables were left to rot on the vines. There were holes in the roof and cracked windows in the front face of the church, making Taliesin wonder if Talbot Abbey was abandoned.

"King Frederick is surely to blame for the utter lack of consideration to the religious sector. Someone should be tending the garden and at least thatch the roof," Taliesin muttered as she tugged Jaelle's hand. "You will behave yourself inside. Try not to talk or eat spiders or do anything to upset the nuns, especially my mother. I've never met her before, and I want to make a good impression. Can you do that for me, Jaelle? A nod will do."

Jaelle nodded and popped a captured fly into her mouth. At the door to the church, Taliesin released Jaelle's hand and finally looked back at Thalagar. The horse no longer wore armor. His black coat and wings glistened in the sunlight as he bent his head to nibble at tall grass. With a shake of her head, Taliesin used the brass knocker to announce their arrival. She waited for several minutes before the door opened, and a weathered old woman in a habit peered out with cold, blue eyes.

"There's no food here for you and your servant. Go away," the woman snapped.

Taliesin put her foot in the door before it was shut. The old nun gave her a dirty look, then she glanced at Jaelle as the girl stuck a finger in her nose.

"I'm here to see Princess Calista. She's my...my mother," Taliesin said in a rush. "I only learned my mother was alive a few days ago. I was an orphan adopted by the Raven Clan. We never keep our former names and leave our old lives behind when we take the service oath. Please, won't you help me?"

Sharp eyes peered at Taliesin as the woman gave thought to the name. Taliesin was shrewd enough to know it struck a chord. Whether to protect her mother or to investigate her story further, Taliesin did not know. The nun folded her hands across her stomach and looked directly into her eyes.

"There is no one by the name of Princess Calista in this abbey. We too put aside our former names when we take our vows and commit our lives to serve the god, Stroud," the nun said. "I'm sorry, child. I would like to help you and your friend. As you can see, the nobles no longer send their youngest daughters here, and the abbey is badly in need of repairs. We barely scrape by selling oysters and carrots to the locals who come here to barter. I imagine we can feed the two of you and your horse, and then you must be on your way."

"Perhaps she is known by another name, ma'am. Before I was Taliesin of the Raven Clan, I was Rosamond Mandrake and lived in Padama. My father, John Mandrake, was a swordsmith by trade. He met Princess Calista, they fell in love, and later secretly married. The king sent his sister here when he learned she was pregnant with me. Surely you remember twenty-six years ago, when a wizard named Zarnoc came and fetched me from the abbey. As you can see, my friend needs help, and I have no one else to turn to."

"The girl is among the slow-witted?" the nun asked, her voice sympathetic.

"Jaelle is the daughter of Shan Octavio Alvarez of the Ghajar, and met with a grave accident a few days ago," Taliesin said, wincing when her voice cracked with emotion. She felt a tear slide down her cheek and quickly wiped it away. "I've done what I can, but her father doesn't want her anymore. I thought my mother might be the one to help us. Please. If the princess is here, at least tell her I have arrived."

"Oh, child, your desperation breaks my heart," the nun said as she opened the door wider. Her eyes watered as she wiped away her own tears with a gnarled hand. "I cannot pretend I do not know whom you are talking about, for Sister Constance is my dear friend, child. We have shared many secrets over the last twenty-six years, and the story of John Mandrake is one of the saddest I ever heard."

"Then you believe me?"

Taliesin felt her heart pounding as she waited for the answer. Connections to a noble fairy king, a *darkling* queen, and a barbarian prince in the ancient past made her who she was, and everything that justified what she was doing now with her life seemed to weigh upon the nun acknowledging her mother gave birth to her.

"You do resemble the princess when she arrived here so long ago," she said. "I can't say for certain if you are little Rosamond. A wee thing she was when born, with a cap of red hair that was the same color as her mother. Sister Constance is what we call her now. Oh, we doted upon that child. For a month we kept her birth secret, fearing the king would send a knight to take her life, for he never forgave his sister for marrying beneath her. Never. When the old wizard came late at night to steal the child away, Sister Constance begged him to hide her from the world. The babe was returned to her father, and we never heard about her again."

"I'm that babe," Taliesin said. "After my father died, I was taken by Master Osprey to Raven's Nest. I am Rosamond Mandrake!"

"Yes, yes," she said. "It is possible you are Rosamond. Quite possible. Your mother was afraid for your life and for his. When word reached us that John died, she cried for weeks and refused to eat or to take care of her own needs. It wasn't until six years later Zarnoc returned to tell us he'd hidden you among the Raven Clan. Even then, your mother feared for you. I wish she'd been here to see you, child. I'm sorry, but you have arrived too late, for she is no longer with us."

A lump formed in Taliesin's throat. "My mother is dead," she whispered. "I'm too late. Too late to meet her and tell I have always loved her."

The old woman opened the door wider, allowing Jaelle to run inside ahead of them, laughter spilling into the chapel as she spotted a mouse running along the corridor. Taliesin was nudged from behind as Thalagar, eager to find shade under the high ceiling, pushed her through the door. Taliesin took the old woman's arm and held her steady as the horse barged inside and headed straight to the bowl of holy water to take a long drink. The nun said not a word and closed the door.

"When did my mother pass?" Taliesin asked.

"Sister Constance didn't die, child, not yet, Stroud willing," the old woman said. "It was men in armor who came for her, sent by the king, they were. His son, Prince Konall, took her away only three days ago. He is a fine-looking man with a clean-shaven face and hair as yellow as straw. She didn't want to go with him and said she wanted no part of the king's troubles. I think she knew you were coming, for every night since spring first arrived, she set a candle in her window to guide you to us, and now you are here."

"The realm is in the middle of a civil war, ma'am. Prince Almaric has taken up arms against his father," Taliesin said. "If they are on the King's Road, they are heading straight into a battle. Every duke has sent his army to Padama. Is this where my cousin took her?"

"I do not know," the nun said. "Prince Konall told us the war was coming and to avoid taking in strangers. He too might have suspected you were coming. There are eight of us left. No, nine, and I am Sister Henrietta. Mother Superior died last year of a cough that brought blood to her lips. No praying could save her, and through it all, Sister Constance refused to leave her side."

The nun drew Taliesin toward a modest chapel lit with candles. A statue of Stroud, no more than a knee high, stood on the floor, hands pressed across his stomach and head bowed, glowing in the candlelight. His expression was peaceful and made Taliesin think of Black Rooster and Gilhurst Abbey. Stroud was a god both feared and loved. Though Taliesin had never prayed to him, her mother had spent her life in service to him. As c took a match and lit a candle at the altar, she said a silent prayer to Stroud for her mother and felt her worries fade as the flame appeared.

"For my mother," Taliesin said. "Thank you, Sister Henrietta. We have come a long way. Perhaps there is something I can do for you in exchange for taking in Jaelle, not forever, just until I'm able to find a…a cure for her."

The old woman guided her to a pew and sat down with her, while Jaelle chased after the mouse. Thalagar stood in the aisle, causing no trouble, and snorted when he caught Taliesin's gaze.

"You are tired and hungry, child. The prince paid us in gold and gave us a wagon filled with provisions and several casks of red wine to last through these last summer days. I'd invite you to stay with us, Taliesin, but two soldiers remained behind. I fear they are here for you. Men are not allowed inside the abbey, so they have made camp at the shoreline. My sisters are there collecting fresh oysters for our dinner and will return shortly."

The old woman noticed Jaelle eating the mouse she'd caught, rose stiffly, and moved slowly through the pews toward her. Taliesin started to stand, afraid Jaelle might try to bite the old nun. Her legs gave out, and she sagged in the pew, watching as Sister Henrietta tapped Jaelle on the shoulder. The gypsy girl looked up, startled.

"No, child. No," the nun said. "Spit that vermin out of your mouth. A warm bowl of potato soup is a far better meal than a mouse."

Jaelle opened her mouth, and the nun pulled the mouse, still wiggling, out by its tail. She placed it in her pocket, where it stayed, and drew Jaelle to her feet. A shy smile appeared on the gypsy's face.

"What is wrong with this child?" the nun asked.

"Since the accident, Jaelle has been on the fringe of death, sister. I had hoped my mother might know how to help her," Taliesin said, unable to tell the truth, but unwilling to lie. "I have done all I can for her. As long as you don't wave a finger near her mouth, I don't think she'll bite. It's because of her strangeness that her father has rejected her. This seemed the best place to take her, and I was coming here anyway."

"In the past, many people left their children here. There are only nine of us, just nine, and a tenth sister would be helpful," Henrietta said, guiding Jaelle toward the pew. "I'll give her your mother's old room. It's very tidy and has a window that looks to the ocean. Perhaps the sea will calm her. Fresh air, sunshine, and the sea can be quite healing."

Taliesin stood, swords clanking against the seat, as the odor of fresh manure drifted to her nose. Her horse had made a mess. The nun did not look concerned. Nor was she worried about Jaelle and her strange condition. Sanctuary was provided even for mice, and one had found a cozy home in her pocket, so taking in an unwanted orphan surely provided no hardship.

"I'll come back for her," Taliesin said. "Jaelle is a dear friend, and I don't want anything else to happen to her. The ring she is wearing, it's...it's mine. You must not take it off, sister. Not for any reason. It keeps her...alive. Over time, it may cure her."

The nun nodded. She patted Jaelle on the head.

"You are a good child and such a pretty one, too. Such lovely hair. I will brush it out for you after a hot bath, Jaelle, and give you a bowl of soup and a glass of wine. Yes, my sisters and I will take care of you, as we took care of Sister Constance. Three times a day we say our prayers to Stroud. Yes, we do, child. Prayers will bring you comfort."

"Prayers," Jaelle said, smiling with green teeth.

Four nuns appeared in the cloister, carrying baskets filled with oysters gathered from the shoreline, which they placed upon the floor. The front door opened, and the rest of the nuns entered, looks of concern on their faces, and gathered around Sister Henrietta. Jaelle smiled as the old nun introduced her to the sisters, a group of unimposing gentle elderly women. Not one appeared bitter or ill-natured or acted suspiciously. How odd, Taliesin thought, to find such compassion among the Stroudian nuns. They made a fuss over Jaelle as if she was far younger than her years, and it helped Taliesin feel less guilty about leaving her. She considered telling the women she left them with a *darkling.* Jaelle laughed, the sound of a normal human girl. The gypsy seemed content with the old birds, and sniffed at the baskets of oysters, rousing a chuckle from a rosy-cheeked woman built like a bricklayer with sparkling blue eyes and a layer of three chins.

"Who is the tall warrior on our doorstep?" A thickset woman asked, setting her eyes on Taliesin. "Two swords and a horse with wings, now that's a first, and oyster girl over there has glazed eyes. You know what that means? Connie was right—magic has found its way to Talbot Abbey. I haven't seen a *darkling* in more than thirty years. Gives me the jitters, but if you want to help her, Henry, then we'll help her."

"Sister Samantha, I've told you before not to speak in such a manner and using male names to identify our sisterhood goes against all traditions. Stop talking, and I'll tell you who has graced our convent," Sister Henrietta said. Everyone turned to look at Taliesin. "Believe it or not, sisters, that's Sister Constance's baby girl, come to see her mother. Never mind about the magic—we see nothing, we say nothing."

"And you think those two turtle heads outside are going to say nothing when they see a warrior female with two swords and a big, beautiful black stallion with raven wings?" A hearty chuckle came from Sister Samantha. "By Stroud's beard, sisters, this is one for the archives. We have us an hon-est-to-gods Black Wing standing inside our abbey."

"Raven Mistress," Henrietta corrected her. "Of noble blood, no less."

"Related to that king with a dark soul," Samantha said. "Girls, we need to use our heads and not sit on our hands like we did the other day. Now listen up...."

The nuns turned to Sister Samantha, clearly the leader, and they fell into a discussion in hushed voices. At the sound of clanking armor outside the door, the nuns fell silent. Taliesin rose to her feet and headed for Thalagar. At a tap of her ring, her dragon armor materialized, and in response, the horse's dragon scales appeared. Sister Samantha, huffing and puffing, trotted over, stepping over a pile of manure.

"Good for the garden," she said. "What I need is a weapon to clout those two turtles over the head with." The nun re-trieved a gold candlestick from the altar, large and heavy enough to do damage. "This should do nicely. All of you, find something to use, and let's deal with these rascals! Henry, away with the little gypsy girl. Hurry now."

Sister Henrietta whisked Jaelle into another room, leaving the others to deal with the guards. The women assembled be-hind Sister Samantha and headed for the front door armed with candlesticks, brooms, and shovels.

"Listen, honey, your mother was taken by Prince Konall to Dreskull Castle," Sister Samantha whispered. "I heard a guard say the castle is on the southern tip of this very dukedom. If that's where they are taking Connie, they mean to lock her in prison, for that's what that dreary place is—a prison. Before you say anything, child, just listen. Your friend is safe here. Leave the turtles to us, and you fly south and rescue your mother. Just don't come back here with her, for she deserves a better life."

Sister Samantha didn't explain what she meant by "tur-tles." Taliesin assumed it had to do with the helmets worn by the royal guards, which were round with a visor. The big nun pushed the sleeves of her robe to her elbows, exposing massive arms.

"Now, I'm going to open this door," Sister Samantha said to the group. "We're marching out there to give Taliesin time to get away. You mount your winged horse, sweetie, and ride out the door. I've wanted to box their ears since I caught them stealing biscuits from the kitchen. Sisters?"

"We're right behind you, Sam," a slender nun with a wart on her chin said.

"That a girl, Billy," said their leader. "Weapons to the ready! Let's go!"

The nuns, led by Sister Samantha, filed out the door. Taliesin climbed onto Thalagar and waited until everyone was outside before she tapped her heels to his flanks. The horse bolted out the door, spread his wings wide, and leaped into the air. As Thalagar flew into the sky, Taliesin smiled to see Samantha and her sisters beating the guards about their heads and chasing them toward the shoreline. A triumphant cheer came from Sister Samantha and her sisters. They waved their weapons in the air as the guards climbed into a rowboat tied to a rock and cut the rope. With their round helmets and hunched backs, they very much reminded Taliesin of turtles as they rowed hard to the south.

* * * * *

Chapter Twenty-Six

Evening found Taliesin flying along the coastline through a sky filled with pink clouds and a soft sunset over the sea. In a quiet harbor, where the peninsula curled like a tail, she counted forty anchored ships, flying the Garridan flag. The nearby fishing town of Sway looked like most coastal towns; it had rows of two-story houses painted white with blue clay-tiled roofs. Fishing nets draped overturned boats, pulled to shore for the night, and soldiers disembarking from their ships filed along a stretched pier. Prince Sertorius and his army had finally arrived to march on his father's capital.

"Clever little snake," Taliesin muttered.

Coming from the south behind the Erindor army and Eagle legionnaires was a brilliant strategy, for that penned them between the walls of Padama and Prince Almaric's army. Any duke still approaching the royal city, not yet within the walls of Tantalon Castle, need only join Almaric and Sertorius to avoid a battle, capture, or death. Among his brothers, Sertorius was clearly the most intelligent, and his marriage to Duke Richelieu's only daughter gave him control of the largest, wealthiest dukedom. He'd said he planned to land in the south, but it had taken weeks for him to arrive. Like the dukes who arrived at Padama late, Sertorius could certainly change his mind at the last second and fight for his father or try to take the throne himself.

"Prince Konall is at Dreskull Castle," she said, as her horse's ears pricked back to listen. "Best we get a move on, Thalagar."

The black stallion picked up speed and streaked across the fishing port, taking a direct line to the prison. Prince Sertorius' forces most likely spotted her horse in the sky, and he'd know she was within reach. Taliesin didn't remember Konall. Was he strong or weak of character? Did he love his father and mean to protect his aunt? Or was he being nasty and cunning like Almaric and Sertorius?

Taliesin spotted riders wearing sea green cloaks, the sea serpent banner fluttering in the breeze, on the narrow road running along the coast. She counted thirty soldiers and a Knight of Chaos. Taliesin leaned forward to make herself as small as possible and allowed the wind to rush over her back as her horse left the riders far behind. The setting sun faded behind storm clouds, and droplets of rain hit her face as a strong gust of wind suddenly pushed Thalagar inland. He lowered his head, headed toward bright lights in the distance, fighting his way to reach Dreskull Castle. As they neared, Taliesin spotted a small army on the rocky field outside the castle.

With three round towers and a high wall, Dreskull stood high on a cliff with its back to the sea and the only access being a narrow causeway. The Garridan army had the causeway blocked, forcing Konall to remain within the castle while the enemy built siege equipment. The soldiers cleared timber in a nearby wood, and hammering continued despite the arrival of night and bad weather. Campfires started to appear, which enabled Taliesin to get a better look at five catapults and a great many more Knights of Chaos, drinking and laughing under black and red pavilions.

"Thalagar, land in the courtyard," Taliesin shouted into the damp breeze. "Let's hope Konall is desperate enough to want our help."

A cry came from the battlements of Dreskull Castle. Men with longbows and spears stood in two ranks, and their excitement spread to the inner courtyard where additional troops prepared for battle. All they saw was a winged form with scales, not a rider, and Taliesin felt tempted to draw a sword when she heard their shouts.

"It's a dragon! A dragon!"

As expected, a volley of arrows flew into the air. A wave of her hand returned them to their quivers. The stunned soldiers lifted their shields for dragon fire that failed to strike. Figures rallied into a defensive line as Thalagar landed in the court-yard with a clatter of hooves. Taliesin slid out of the saddle as her horse pranced behind her and snorted angrily. Spears lowered as an officer shouted orders. Prison guards, as well as the king's soldiers, ran forward and circled her. No one ad-vanced, nor was an order given to attack. She tapped Tar-quin's ring, and her armor vanished, a sign she hoped they took to mean she was willing to trust them, and in return, they might do the same. Konall's troops were the very men who had gone to Talbot Abbey to take her mother into custody.

"I am Taliesin, the Raven Mistress. I would speak to Prince Konall or your commander. My only desire is to see my moth-er, Princess Calista, the nun taken from Talbot Abbey who goes by the name Sister Constance."

A Maldavian knight in dark blue stepped forward, sword in hand, one of Duke Peergynt's men whom she assumed re-volted against his master to join the king. Such changes in al-legiance did not surprise her, not in a civil war. The knight removed his helmet, handed it to a squire, and pushed back the chain mail coif. Thick black hair fell to his shoulders, and he bowed his head.

"Sir Rikard of the newly-formed Royal Regiment, at your service," he said in a rich voice. "One of you find Prince Konall and tell him the Raven Mistress is here."

A soldier broke from the line and took to a flight of stairs, running hard and shouting for the prince. Sir Rikard dis-missed the soldiers and remained beside Taliesin while the soldiers at the battlements turned to face the enemy. The knight glanced at Thalagar who remained armored with his wings pressed to his sides.

"We heard about a warrior who rides a winged horse," Sir Rikard said. "The Knights of the White Stag sent word they'd seen you flying over Fregia. I've never seen such a horse, nor ever met a magic user." He held up his hand, quick to add,

"His Majesty has ordered you are not to be harmed. The ban against magic users has been lifted, at the request of Lord Arundel. Is it true you are a *Sha'tar?*"

"I am many things, Sir Rikard. More importantly, Prince Sertorius' forces have arrived in mass and more march from Sway to this castle. They have five catapults and a battering ram. From what I could see, it appears the entire Garridan army has landed. You only have a few hundred men against twenty thousand in the field."

"Your magic will be needed," the knight said. He glanced at two soldiers moving toward the armored horse. "None of you get too close to her warhorse! Leave him alone and see to the castle defenses." He glanced toward a tall knight in dark purple drinking a goblet of wine. "Best be at it, Sir Malachi. Hot oil and flame arrows ought to keep that battering ram from reaching the gate."

Sir Malachi handed his goblet to a servant, his gaze on Taliesin, and with a nod, he left with an assembly of two knights and five squires to join the soldiers at the wall. A young squire, hair cut short and helmet tucked under his arm, stood beside Sir Rikard. Taliesin caught his gaze, and he smiled in a friendly fashion.

"What is your name?" Taliesin asked.

The squire stood straight. "I am Zachary, my lady."

"Who are your people?"

"I'm from Aldagar. My...my father was a knight. I do like your horse."

At Taliesin's nod, the squire took a step toward Thalagar. The horse gave a snort, sniffed the young man's extended hand, and allowed him to stroke the end of his nose.

"He's a good lad," Sir Rikard said. "So was his father, Sir Mortimer. He'll look after your horse, if it's acceptable to you, mistress." She again nodded. "Zachary, bring the horse a bucket of grain and see he's watered. Be quick about it, boy."

As the squire ran to do his knight's bidding, a commotion on the platform above brought the same soldier who had gone to find Prince Konall. The soldier leaned against the railing to catch his breath, waved his hand, and caught the attention of Taliesin and Sir Rikard.

"Prince Konall asks the Raven Mistress be brought to him, Sir Rikard. He's waiting in the study with Sister Constance. Shall I tell him you're coming?"

"Mistress?"

Sir Rikard waited for her acceptance of the invitation. His manner was polite and his behavior chivalrous. Taliesin had never seen Sir Rikard's name among knights known to fight in tourneys throughout the kingdom. The knight was apparently of value, or Prince Konall would not have placed Sir Rikard in command. He extended his arm for her to take, treating her like a lady instead of a fellow warrior. She doubted most of the soldiers and knights had seen a female warrior, for they watched as she placed her hand upon Sir Rikard's arm. Zachary returned with a bucket of oats and stood beside Thalagar. The red scales vanished from the horse as he nosed the oats, and the squire toweled off the layer of sweat before he commenced to brush him down.

"I said he was a good lad," Sir Rikard said, guiding Taliesin toward the stairs. "So is Prince Konall. Of all the princes, he has the kindest heart, which I suppose is why his father sent him here, out of harm's way. It's the same for Sister Constance...the king's sister, for she is not a prisoner, mistress, but a guest. The king thought it wiser to bring her here, the one place he thought safe, though it's proven to be quite the contrary."

"Do you know Sir Roland Brisbane of the Knights of the White Stag?" she asked. "Sir Roland is a...a dear friend of mine."

"Roland? Yes, I know him well. We jousted against each other many times. He guards King Frederick, along with his order. The king is well-protected. I'm surprised to hear you say his name. I wasn't aware Sir Roland was friends with the Raven Clan. If he is your friend, then I will consider you as one as well. We could use your help, as I'm sure Prince Konall will agree once he meets you."

"Thank you for the compliment," she replied.

A door stood open, and gold light flowed from the interior. Sir Rikard placed his hand upon hers, stepped inside, and drew Taliesin into the prison warden's study. Lined with bookshelves and carpeted, it was a comfortable room given the austere exterior of the castle. Two knights in gold armor wearing the royal crest sat at a long table with a grizzled-looking man in a black tunic, gray-peppered hair, and hard eyes. This had to be the warden, thought Taliesin. A slender young man with short black hair, dressed in a dark red doublet with a thin silver crown on his head — presumably Prince Konall — sat close to the fireplace. Beside him, in a large chair, was an older woman with a regal face and auburn hair pinned in a bun wearing a fur-trimmed cloak with diamonds hanging from her ears. The prince stood, looking from Sir Rikard to Taliesin, slightly nervous and unsure how to respond.

"Your Grace, allow me to introduce Taliesin of the Raven Clan. Mistress, I have the honor to present you to Prince Konall and his aunt, Princess Calista. If it pleases you, Prince Konall, I suggest the rest of us excuse ourselves. Prince Sertorius has a battering ram and five catapults, so we should prepare for a night assault. He's here and has brought the entire Garridan army with him."

"Yes, yes," Prince Konall said. "Do that, Sir Rikard, and see my brother knows I have no intention of speaking to him. As far as I'm concerned, he is a traitor, and I do not talk to traitors. Warden Stuart, would you and the Royal Knights please go with Sir Rikard and see our defenses are in place?"

Sir Rikard turned and left with the warden and knights, closing the door. The fire crackled and popped, and for a moment no one spoke. Her mother turned in her chair to scrutinize her, no emotion on her face, while Konall acted like an awkward boy.

"I met you before, Your Grace," Taliesin said, offering a smile. "When I was a child, I used to play in the royal garden with your younger brother. My father, John Mandrake, was the royal swordsmith." She noted the lady's eyes moistened at the mention of her father's name and sat straighter. "Must we really pretend we don't know one another? I'm Rosamond Mandrake, and you are my mother, Princess Calista. The sisters of Talbot Abbey thought you needed rescue, so here I am. Perhaps I can be of service and help you both leave the castle."

"I knew at once we were related. You are quite lovely, cousin," Prince Konall said. He gave a friendly smile and hurried to his aunt to offer his hand. He helped her from her chair and returned with her to Taliesin.

"You are Rosamond? My little Rose?" the princess asked in disbelief. She clung to Konall. "It can't be. I was told she died years ago along with my husband. No, it can't be her, dear nephew. I see nothing of John or me in her face."

"Mother, are you...are you not glad to see me? I thought you died during childbirth. When I heard otherwise, it was like a dream come true. I had to come and find you. Please say you remember me. I want so much for you to love me."

"Rosamond," Calista said, her voice cracking. "It is her, Konall. I know it."

"Yes, Aunt Calista," the prince replied. "It is your little Rose, and my cousin grown into a beautiful woman. What a fine reunion this is. Please. Let us make the most of it while we can. Let us rejoice and be happy, for this is a special moment. Daughter and mother are once more reunited!"

With a sob, Princess Calista threw her arms around Taliesin, catching her by surprise. The woman hugged her so tight she could barely breathe. Feeling shy, Taliesin embraced her mother, unable to suppress her emotions, and tears poured from her eyes as she recalled all the years she'd dreamed about meeting her, never knowing who she was, nor even able to imagine her face. Calista lifted her head and kissed Taliesin's cheek a dozen times before she held her back to gaze into her eyes. Love and tenderness appeared in her mother's eyes.

The moment exceeded anything Taliesin ever dreamed possible. Stunned and unable to find her voice, Taliesin let her mother guide her to a chair and sat heavily. Calista slid into a chair beside her while a gracious Konall poured wine into three goblets and handed them out before sitting across from them. Plain of the face and not at all a handsome man, Konall's infectious smile made it impossible not to like him.

"I dare say, Aunt Calista, I don't think I've been this happy, not in years. Seeing you both together like this, anyone could see you are mother and daughter. You have the same nose and chin." Konall lifted his glass. "To family. Though our time may be short together, let's always think of each other like we are now. Sertorius will soon spoil everything like he always does."

Taliesin tapped his goblet and then her mother's, so excited and delirious with happiness it was difficult to swallow the wine, for a lump had formed in her throat. She listened to the crackle of the fire and the howl of the wind at the closed shutters, staring intently from her mother to her cousin. They looked more like family with their brown hair and brown eyes, and a certain familiarity existed between them, which made it clear she had made a strong impression on Konall when he was a boy.

"My father was wrong to send you both from the court," Konall said. "When Sir Roland told me the Raven Mistress was really my cousin, I knew we had to meet. I don't approve of what Almaric or Sertorius are doing. Not at all. Father has always doted on those two, ignoring me and barely tolerating Dinadan. Father didn't bat an eye when he learned Almaric sold Galinn to the Skardans, and not once did he try to buy him back or even send a message. Imagine if Galinn was here with us. He was very nice, Rosamond. You would have liked him too. I suppose he is dead now."

"Konall has spoken about you the entire way from Talbot Abbey," her mother said. "The famous Taliesin of the Raven Clan is my little girl. It's hard to even imagine that you have grown into such a strong woman."

The prince laughed. "I told her all about your adventure in the Salayan Desert and how you found *Ringerike* in the Cave of the Snake God. Sir Roland is my friend, and he told me what happened, only I wish you hadn't left him behind. He said you were quite close. In fact, he seemed very sad when he mentioned your parting in the desert. I thought it surely had to do with Master Xander and the Eagle legionnaires. They never should have gone after you. I don't like Xander or his father. If I were king, I'd get rid of the other two clans and re-build Black Castle for you, dear cousin. Now that I have seen you both together, I know it was fate that brought us here at this time."

"Konall, really," Calista said, "you are talking far too much. You act exactly as you did when you were a boy. Men tend to grow up after they marry, and your father should have let you marry years ago. Give us a moment to become acquainted, Konall. I've been away from court for so many years, I know little enough about your brothers and their affairs, let alone the king's, so let us focus our attention on Rosamond and give her an opportunity to speak."

Taliesin was surprised Konall was thirty years of age, for he looked younger than she did, and a privileged life had kept the wrinkles from his face. He was the fourth son, and she noted he wore a ring with an emblem of a yellow rutting stag on a field of black, the same as the tunics worn by many of the knights. He finished his wine, set it aside, and bounced to his feet.

"Have you eaten, cousin? Are you hungry? I shall have the servants bring you dinner and then you must tell us all about your adventures."

"Very well, cousin," Taliesin said, though she felt they should be on the battlements. She watched the prince hurry to the door, shouting to the servants. When she turned back to her mother, she caught a strange look in her eyes. "Are you disappointed in me, Mother? Am I less than what you hoped for in a daughter?"

"John kept a journal with the names of every magical weapon in it. He was quite the artist," Calista said. "In the book, he had a portrait of King Korax. You look like the Raven

King, not my dear, sweet John. I had hoped you might have John's eyes. Oh, well. It was not meant to be. Let us talk about something else, for I am sure you have many questions, Rosamond. May I call you that? Or do you prefer 'Taliesin.' Yes, I can see you do. It's quite all right. I understand perfectly."

"Please tell me what happened. I want to understand."

"You must not think too harshly of my brother, my dear. I fell in love and married your father knowing Frederick would never approve, but I didn't care, nor did John, for we were very young. The few years we had together were wonderful and enough to keep me warm every night since we parted. After the wizard took you from me, I never heard about you again. I'm sure Frederick had spies surrounding the abbey and intercepted all messages from John. Is the wizard with you?"

"No," Taliesin said, feeling reluctant to say more. She didn't want to talk about Zarnoc or reveal that her clan was now at Penkill Castle. Both swords were quiet, too quiet, for neither had offered an opinion about her mother. The moment she thought about *Ringerike* and *Calaburn*, they urged her to join the soldiers; they were not at all interested in the family reunion. When she told them to be silent, they obeyed.

"And you came here, alone, to find me," her mother said. "I always wished John would find me and take me away. I used to dream about running away with him to the Isles of Valen. Dreams have a way of keeping hope alive when wishes fail to produce results."

Taliesin offered a thin smile. "I mean to take you to Padama," she said. "I know the king sent you and Konall here to keep you both safe. It really wasn't well thought out. There are many other places where you would be better protected, including the camp of the Ghajar or my own camp."

"We are fine here," Calista said, smiling.

"Konall is very kind and not at all what I expected," Taliesin replied. "He is grossly outnumbered, though, and while I want to stay and talk with you, I feel I should help defend the castle. Not only am I the Raven heir, but I am also a

Sha'tar, and *Ringerike* rightfully belongs to me, and it is a powerful weapon. I also have *Calaburn* with me, Mother."

"Both swords?" Calista took a sip of wine, her eyes rolling upwards before she stared directly at Taliesin and said in a firm voice, "Then you will help my brother defeat that rebellious brat Almaric. If Sertorius knows you will defend my brother, then he will join us. Yes, I should think that settles any dispute between Sertorius and Konall. All you need do is reassure both boys you will help their father, and we can all go to Padama together. Go do that now, won't you?"

Taliesin tensed. "I'm willing to help Konall, and I do like him, but it sounds like you have already planned this out," she said. "You were expecting me, weren't you? You do know King Frederick...." She fell silent, unsure why she'd felt justified to bring her mother more pain by bringing up the murder of John Mandrake. "Well, the king doesn't like me, and he doesn't like magic, but since I'm here, I'll be glad to act as a mediator between Sertorius and Konall."

"What is it, darling?" Calista asked. "Something presses on you. Tell me what you were going to say about Frederick. I am your mother, and there is nothing you cannot confide in me. I long to know everything about you, child. Konall said Sir Roland went to Raven's Nest months ago on behalf of my brother and found you, which surely is Frederick's way of atoning for his cruel treatment of us both."

"It was cruel, wasn't it? Very cruel."

Taliesin drank every drop of her wine when her mother stared hard at her, searching for what she didn't want to tell her. Both were relieved when Konall reappeared with a servant carrying a tray covered with a cloth, the aroma of roast beef and fresh bread tickled her nose as it was set before them. Taliesin's hands were dirty, but she cared not, and removing the cloth, she grabbed a loaf and set her teeth into the thick crust. Her mother and cousin watched her uncivilized behavior with tolerance.

"I interrupted your conversation, and I apologize. Father has long since feared the return of magic and only recently, due to Lord Arundel's influence, has done away with Magnus's unjust law against it," Konall said, launching without tact right into a delicate discussion. "Thousands of witches and warlords have been executed in the past, or at least people suspected of using magic. Lord Arundel says magic must be used to defeat Almaric and the barbarian horde coming to Tantalon. I suppose I should employ your services, cousin. The truth is, we don't have enough soldiers. I brought two hundred with me, and Sertorius has thousands. Father couldn't spare any more, and he thought Sir Rikard and Warden Stuart could take care of us. He was wrong."

"You're quite impetuous, Konall," Calista said. "I made it quite clear I wanted to spend time with my daughter, and you want to rush her outside to wage war upon your brother. I suggest you invite Sertorius here to talk. *Taliesin* has agreed to help your father, and if Sertorius knows this, he'll join you both, you'll see. I remember Sertorius quite fondly. He was only three when I was forced to leave. I remember he had such beautiful eyes. Over the years, I have held my tongue and not written to your father, Konall. It was a mistake on my part, I readily admit. Being silent and keeping secrets among family is no way to garner trust or love or their support."

"Sertorius already killed one messenger, Aunt Calista. Our flag of truce was ignored," Konall said. "I can't expect either of you to understand the rules of chivalry handed down from a knight to his squire or the military rules of engagement each commander and his officers are to adhere to under Caladonia Law, but Sertorius has broken every rule. He has since he was a boy, cheating at board games, stealing ribbons from girls, and hoarding items that didn't belong to him."

"Konall, I may only be your aunt, separated these last twenty-odd years, but I can assure you, I'm well aware Sertorius was always naughty. I will pray he sees the light of Stroud. It is the only thing I can offer that will help, for Stroud...."

"...always listens?" Konall threw his hands into the air. "Each night I dream about the Gods of Mt. Helos, about how they manipulate us mortals into doing what they want and turn us against one another. The last thing I want is Stroud's intervention. Riders from the Eagle's First Legion, under Sir Cerasus, reported seeing Ragnal in the Tannenberg Forest. Surely you can appreciate the danger this places us all in. When the gods walk among mortals, it can only mean destruction and death will soon follow. Already there are numerous signs the Age of the Wolf is upon us, Aunt Calista. If you really believe Stroud will help, if all your years in the abbey have led you to this conclusion, then, by all means, say your prayers, but leave me out of them. I want to defeat Sertorius on my own terms. My own way!"

Taliesin washed a slice of roast beef down with another glass of wine. She wanted to eat more and needed to rest, but there wasn't time for such niceties. She wiped her hands on the cloth covering the table, suppressed a belch behind a raised hand, and pushed back her chair to stand. Her mother remained seated as Taliesin walked toward Konall, seeing in him a boy frightened by the thought he might die at the hands of the gods in a battle against Sertorius. He was a gentle soul and the complete opposite of Sertorius, yet he was right.

"It's war, Konall, and people do horrible things when they are afraid," Calista said. "I will pray for you, for Taliesin, and even for Sertorius." She bowed her head, hands pressed together, and whispered prayers.

"Ragnal is interested in what happens here," Taliesin said. "This is just another one of his games to cause my bloodshed and death, for *Varguld* is upon us, cousin. He's shown himself to me twice, and I defeated him in battle the last we met. I cut him. He bleeds just like you or me. The gods are powerful, yes, but they are not indestructible. If you have dreamed about the gods, then you know Ragnal, Mira, and Navenna each want to use us for their own purposes. I know how it sounds, but Mira has been influencing my ability to use magic when the moon is high, and Navenna wants me to restore my clan to its former glory. Picking one over the other has always caused me heartache, Konall. When I went to the abbey to find my mother, I saw another face of Stroud, one that is loving and protective. If we are going to stop Ragnal from turning brother against brother, and son against father, we need the All Father's help. I have to believe he doesn't approve of what his children are doing and will at the least offer his protection."

"You've...you've actually talked to the gods?" Konall asked, shocked.

"They're an ancient race, not unlike the Lorians and Hellirin," Taliesin replied. "I've met many people during my travels, Konall, and have been to the Magic Realms. The fairies and *darklings* do not want to share their magic. They don't need to because it's been here all along, right in Eagle's Cliff, until I went there last night and...." She paused. "Well, you don't need to worry about their magic guild."

Konall pointed at *Calaburn*. "Hey, I know that sword! I've seen it in tapestries, held in the hand of Prince Tarquin and burning with fire," he said. "That sword belongs to the Royal House of Draconus. Yet, you also carry the legendary Raven Sword. How can you have two swords, opposed to one another and each possessing powerful magic, and control them? Is this the influence of Mira? Or is this because you are a *Sha'tar*?"

"I'm far more than that, Konall. And by no means am I in control."

"Then what good are you, if you can't help me against Sertorius?"

"I didn't say I couldn't help you, but it is complicated," Taliesin said. "The Garridan army will follow whoever takes command. Sertorius must either agree to stand down, or we should capture him and take his army."

"My brother will not listen to you," the prince said. He kneaded his delicate hands in frustration as beads of sweat dotted his forehead. "He came here to kill me, Taliesin. To kill your mother and to kill you. The only reason he's backing Almaric is that he too wants the throne. If Sertorius can whittle down his enemies by playing both sides against each other, that's exactly what he'll do. I've heard the gossip. People say I joined Almaric and I hate my father. It's not true. Not at all. I love my father, Taliesin, and will do whatever it takes to help him."

"Then let me bring Sertorius here, and you can talk to him."

Stepping away from her cousin, Taliesin went with instinct and used the saltshaker to draw a circle on the floor. She removed a raven feather and the remains of a small stalk of dried lavender, items Sertorius had touched, from her pouch and placed them in the circle. She knew no spell to conjure Sertorius, nor was the moon shining. As her mother quietly prayed to Stroud and Konall looked upon her with such hope in his eyes, Taliesin knew she needed a miracle. She pictured Sertorius in her mind, clapped her hands three times, and spoke in a loud, clear voice, "Come to me, Sertorius." She felt *Ringerike* vibrate, and even *Calaburn* jiggled in its scabbard. "Appear before me in this circle. Come now."

Konall gasped, and in his haste to move away from a glimmer of light, he fell over a chair and collapsed to the floor. Calista raised her head, though she continued to pray, eyes wide as Konall's as the light started to condense and take shape until Sertorius stood in the circle, looking formidable in his sparkling, bright silver armor, staring at Taliesin. His dark blue eyes glistened with anger, and his hair was matted with sweat. He reached for his sword, wasting not a moment on pleasantries. When he tried to pull it free, his hand jerked away from the hilt as if scorched.

"Witch," Sertorius hissed. "You have no right summoning me here." His eyes widened to see the swords strapped to her hip and back. "Nor do you have the right to possess *Calaburn*—that sword belongs to me. Give it to me and send me back to my troops."

"Hello, snake," Taliesin said with a smile.

* * * * *

Chapter Twenty-Seven

"You did it. You brought Sertorius here. I can't believe it," Konall said with enthusiasm. He quickly stood and pushed the chair aside. "How does it feel to be caught in a trap, brother? I bet you didn't expect Taliesin would side with me against you. Now you're my prisoner!"

"Shut up, you ridiculous buffoon," Sertorius said in his deep, melodious voice. "By allowing a witch to summon me, you have defied our laws of banning magic. I have every right to kill you where you stand and your red-haired witch."

Sertorius moved his foot and tested the circle. When he discovered he could not cross the line of salt, he again reached for his sword. It refused to budge, and magical lights sparking at the opening of the scabbard revealed its identity to Taliesin. He'd somehow found Rivalen's prized longsword *Retaliator*, which had been shown on the Deceiver's Map as buried in the Salayan Desert. Neither Taliesin nor *Ringerike* had sensed magic users in the Garridan camp, and as she concentrated on *Retaliator*, she saw an image of Djaran nomads locating it at the bottom of a dried oasis, still clutched in the skeleton hand of its former owner. Sertorius had no magic users working for him. It was mere luck he'd found a magical sword, but it was powerless against *Ringerike* and could only sputter and thump in its scabbard.

"You have no other choice but surrender," Taliesin said, wanting to laugh at Sertorius' surprised expression. "The accommodations at Dreskull Castle are a bit damp. I'm sure we can find a cell that opens to the sea, cousin. I know how much you enjoy allowing your prisoners to stand in seawater all day."

427

428 | SUSANNE L. LAMBDIN

"Wait! What? Did you call me 'cousin?' What do you mean?" Sertorius glanced at Konall. "What does she mean? I want an explanation."

Konall shrugged. "Just what she said, Sertorius. This is Rosamond Mandrake."

"Yes, I know that. But who was her mother?"

"I am. She's my daughter, Sertorius," Calista replied. "Surely you knew why I left Padama. Her father was John Mandrake, my husband and her father. Rosamond Mandrake is your cousin. Now, do you see why you mustn't storm this castle? Both Konall and my daughter want to help Frederick. You must help him as well. Stop this nonsense and see reason, dear boy."

"So, this is why you didn't want to marry me," Sertorius said, laughing. "Oh, didn't she tell you, Konall, we were betrothed as children? No? Well, it was a childish dream, after all. And here I thought her rejection was because of Sir Roland Brisbane. He is her lover, you fool." He laughed harder. "If only you could see your face. I do apologize Aunt Calista, and I'd come kiss your cheek; alas, I am stuck inside this circle of salt. While it keeps me from greeting you, I do hope it keeps Rosamond from getting inside, for no doubt she has told you her secret. Rosamond does like keeping secrets."

"Shut up," Taliesin said, fearing he was about to announce she was *Wolfen*.

Konall stared at Taliesin, his brows furrowed, trying to think of something to say. She imagined her mother was equally horrified, for Calista said nothing else. Sertorius crossed his arms over his breastplate.

"My men have orders to attack this castle at break of dawn, and they will bombard this stack of bricks until it falls. When they breach the walls, and it will happen whether I am a prisoner or not. You, my pretty witch, will be bound with silver chains and a lead ball and thrown into the sea. Konall will either bend a knee or die, and as for your mother, my aunt, I will stick her head on a pike and exhibit it at the walls of Tantalon Castle for all to see."

A gasp came from Calista. Konall ran over to his aunt and put an arm around her, offering what little comfort he could. He was afraid of his younger brother who was taller, stronger, and more handsome, and had the mind of a brilliant tactician.

"Pity you can't have either sword, Sertorius," Taliesin said. She reached for *Ringerike's* hilt and saw in her mind's eye the Garridan troops as they prepared to launch stones at the castle and brought the battering ram forward, protected by soldiers using their shields as cover. "Konall, go tell Sir Rikard the enemy is about to attack. Your brother is a liar. There are Garridan warships headed this way. Two ships are already here, anchored offshore, and men are bringing scaling ladders to come at us from behind."

"You can see all that?" Konall kissed Calista on top of the head and stepped away from her. He clapped his hands in delight. "Checkmate, brother of mine. Not only is she a *Sha'tar*, but Taliesin can read your bloodthirsty thoughts. I am going to take command of the Garridan troops. Without you, they won't attack, and you know it. I intend to take your army to father and win his approval, once and for all."

"Idiot," Sertorius muttered as his brother hurried out of the room. "Why have you sided with Konall, when you know he is unfit to lead even a child to the toilet? The soldiers and sailors from Garridan will only respect a strong leader, and that is me, cousin. Oh, they may listen to Sir Rikard. However, they'll laugh the moment Konall shows his face. All you have done is delay my plans. I am by no means vanquished."

"I am ashamed of you, Sertorius."

Princess Calista, a solemn look on her face, rose from her chair and came to stand beside Taliesin, as the prince leaned over to pick up the raven feather and slid it across the invisible barrier. His boots covered the remains of the lavender blossoms. Someone had apparently been talking to him about magic spells, or he'd found a book, for he was trying to use her own magic against her. The feather went up in flames, and he gave a quick shake of his burned fingers.

430 | SUSANNE L. LAMBDIN

Sertorius smiled at the crash of stones slamming into the sides of the castle and the shouts of frightened soldiers and prisoners. "What did I tell you? No Garridan soldier would dare surrender to Konall," he said with disgust. "My army will tear this castle down around your ears, Taliesin. Better to side with me now, than be taken prisoner. Give me *Calaburn* and all will be forgiven. I'll set aside my wife and marry you instead. Isn't that what you want? Isn't that what you want, Aunt Calista? Tell your little girl to give me what I want, and I'll be more than happy to offer my protection, love, and forgiveness."

"I don't owe you an apology," Taliesin snarled. "You owe me one!"

"There's your bark. Oh, I do love it when you're riled up."

"Taliesin, don't listen to him," her mother said. "I insist you remove this magical circle and allow Sertorius to talk to us in a civilized manner. And you're wrong about Frederick, for he did do away with the law against magic, nephew. I want you to make amends with Taliesin and then Konall. Please, Sertorius. Do it for the love of your own mother, for you know very well Aislynn would not have approved of this."

Sertorius winced and lowered his gaze. "Taliesin, kindly tell that woman not to mention my mother again," he said. "I do not like being the villain."

"I think she heard you...snake."

His dark blue lifted to hers. "Taliesin, why do you insist on being my enemy when I only want to love you? What can you do against twenty thousand men? Hmm? You are no more a commander than my stupid brother. Tell me, Aunt Calista, did you enjoy your years at the abbey? Surely Taliesin told you the sad news. It was your brother who had your husband murdered by the Assassins' Guild of Bavol. I can see on your face this news surprises you. Sadly, it is true. When good King Frederick heard rumors Rosamond Mandrake might still be alive, he sent Sir Roland Brisbane to Raven's Nest to investigate. Roland was to bring her back to Padama, but the damn fool fell in love with this red-haired temptress and ran away with her. The king, meanwhile, felt Master Osprey and the Raven Clan deserved to be punished for hiding the girl, so he ordered the Wolf Clan to destroy the Ravens. Lord Arundel and the Eagle Clan, being deceptive and cunning, did nothing to help. In fact, they have gone out of their way to help the Wolf Clan get rid of these nasty scavengers, which does seem suspicious, and makes one wonder if Lykus and Arundel have a secret pact."

"You lie," Calista cried out. "John was killed by thieves who were after the five swords he made for you and your brothers. Frederick sent word to tell me what happened. He said the thieves were caught and executed. It's all in the letter he wrote to me, a letter I have kept all these years." She reached into the front of her dress and removed a frayed, worn piece of parchment. As she hurriedly opened it, she tore an edge and caught her breath, trying not to sob. "It's right here. He…he told me what happened, and I grieved, I grieved terribly for the loss of John."

"Yet, not for your daughter," Sertorius added. "Interesting."

"You have no idea what true love is, nephew," she wailed. "If you loved my daughter as much as I loved her father, you would never lift a hand to hurt her! You would cherish every moment with her and do whatever it takes to make her happy!"

"I did love her, madam," Sertorius said. "I just love power more. Now put the letter away. Didn't you find it curious the king told you by messenger the two people you loved the most were murdered? Your brother didn't visit you at Talbot Abbey for the simple reason he didn't want to lie to your face. So, you lived the life of the nun, cut off from the world, while your big brother took measures to destroy any chance of happiness you might have had. I think that reason enough to hate the old boy, don't you, Aunt Calista? Don't you want him to die? Don't you think it's time he visited the family vault in Tantalon Castle, permanently?"

Calista dropped to the floor, sobbing hysterically. Whatever strength she'd had as a young woman no longer existed. "It's not true! Frederick knew I loved John more than anything," she cried. "What you are saying cannot be what happened, or Stroud would have shown me the truth. I have prayed and prayed for guidance, and with Stroud's guidance I was able to forgive my brother for separating us."

"Not another word, Sertorius. You will drive her mad with grief," Taliesin snarled. "How did you ever get to be this cruel?"

He laughed. "Don't tell me you're still upset that I stole your ribbon so long ago? If you really gave a damn about your mother, you would have told her the truth the moment you saw her instead of pretending to be so…so noble."

Another boulder slammed into the castle walls, shaking the floors and rafters in the study. A goblet on the table fell over, and the glass windows cracked as another stone crashed into the tower, causing Calista to cling to Taliesin's arm. The dragon armor and the winged helmet immediately appeared, and *Ringerike* slapped her back.

"The king is a murderer, Aunt Calista," Sertorius continued. "He only brought you here to lock you away, and he sent Konall to do the job because he didn't need him at court. Konall is a bumbling idiot and serves no purpose. Taliesin wants to kill the king as much as I do. She hides the truth from you because she wants to keep peace in the family. Peace is something this kingdom will not have until I sit upon his throne, dear aunt."

"Taliesin?" Calista turned to her. "Is this true? Did Frederick order John's death? Is this what you were going to tell me?"

"I really can't say, Mother," Taliesin said.

Sertorius laughed. "Forgive me, Aunt Calista, for being the bearer of such dreadful tidings. The truth hurts, and that is why people lie."

Smoke drifted into the study. Taliesin heard thousands of arrows hitting the castle walls and the panic of men fighting on the battlements. Her mother's pain was difficult to watch, as a myriad of emotions appeared and vanished on her face. She finally collapsed in a chair, holding the letter against her chest, sobbing. Soldiers ran past the opened door, headed toward a nearby tower.

"Damn you, Sertorius. Stop hurting the people I love," Taliesin shouted, wanting to reach through the magical circle and strangle him. "I have to stop this battle. When I subdue his army, Mother, we'll all go to the king and let him explain what happened that night. Until I return, please stay strong for me. Please don't let Sertorius turn your heart and fill it with hate and bitterness. It's what he does."

"So, it's hate now, is it?" Sertorius puckered his lips. "Sweetheart, I never thought I'd hear the truth, and finally I have, and you hate me. First, it was love...."

"You really must shut up, cousin!"

Turning, Taliesin slid past the guards entering the study, dashed along the platform, down the stairs, and entered the courtyard. Boulders sailed overhead and slammed into a group of soldiers and the walls of the keep where a fire burned, lapping at the windows while workers used buckets of water to douse the flames. Zachary stood beside Thalagar under the eaves of the stable, trembling each time a rock came over the wall. She patted his shoulder and climbed into the saddle.

"Zachary, go to the study and take care of my mother. Prince Sertorius is with her, and I don't want him spreading his vile lies and upsetting her further. Pray with her," Taliesin said. "Pray I am able to stop the Garridans before they get inside."

Thalagar flew into the sky under a hailstorm of fire arrows, rising high above their arc and the smoke from the fire as they headed toward the Garridans. She glanced at the clouds in the sky as water pelted her face. Rain fell on the castle, dousing the flames, while the battering ram slammed into the gate, splintering wood each time it struck. It needed to be destroyed before she took out the catapults.

A blaze of blue light surrounded her and the winged horse as she drew *Ringerike* from its scabbard, attracting the aim of enemy archers who fired upon her as she flew over the causeway. The arrows hit the blue orb around her and bounced off harmlessly. She imagined the waves lapping at the rocks beneath the platform rising to cover the men holding the battering ram and heard their cries of alarm as she watched a monstrous wave close around them and clear them from the causeway.

Taliesin reached for *Calaburn* as she flew over the soldiers, and with the weight of a sword in each hand, steadied herself in the saddle. The Draconus sword burst into flame, and a fireball shot from its tip when she pointed it at the nearest catapult. Fire engulfed the catapult and reached the nearest men, setting them alight like torches. She fired a ball of red flame at each siege engine, creating five massive fires that hungrily licked at the closest soldiers. The Garridan soldiers scrambled to move aside as the fire spread to the supply wagons and tents. Bows in the archers' hands turned into torches, and human flesh melted inside plate mail. As cries of agony filled the night, Taliesin sensed the God of War watching under the camouflage of night, taking pleasure in the high death toll.

Calaburn wanted to kill them all, to protect both Draconian princes and the princess inside the castle and to serve her. But *Ringerike* cautioned Taliesin not to help Ragnal's quest for total destruction and begged her to send for rain.

"Yes, rain," Taliesin said, as if already able to taste it on her lips. "Rain, rain! Please, Mira, Navenna, or Broa, whoever is listening, please, let it rain!" But no rain came, and the vicious flames roared like beasts, snatching knights off horses and overwhelming entire platoons. Frantic to end the madness, she lifted both swords into the air and screamed, "Stroud! Help me!"

Lightning streaked through the smoky sky, and bolts slammed into the ground, routing the Garridans, who mounted what few horses remained and tried to escape as a loud clap of thunder released a deluge. Huge waves slammed into the cliffs and shoreline as thunder rumbled like a deep voice in the sky. A strong breeze from the sea lifted Thalagar higher and threatened to topple both horse and rider from the sky. *Calaburn's* fire went out, and she managed to slide the sword into its scabbard as the blue orb produced by *Ringerike* dwindled. With both hands, she grabbed the hilt of the Raven Sword, every muscle straining as she fought against the scabbard, and she slammed it home as the wind thrust her forward. She clung to Thalagar's neck, terrified, as the horse frantically battled the wind.

"Land! Land! Anywhere!"

Concentrating solely on her horse, Taliesin imagined Thalagar landing lightly upon the ground as a blast of wind scooped them into the sky and tumbled them through the air, away from Dreskull Castle and out to sea. If this was Stroud helping her, the All-Father was doing everything imaginable to make it impossible to reach the ground safely. Stroud was the worst sort of god, she thought, and no sane person would pray to him, yet she had, and she'd left her mother doing that very thing.

"*You will die if you do not submit,*" the voice of Ragnal said, his laughter crackling along with the lightning strikes that slammed into the castle. "*Stroud seeks to destroy you! I alone offer safety, but you must pray to me! Remove the necklace or die!*"

A shrill whinny of pain from Thalagar brought her gaze toward his left wing which hung at an odd angle, broken by the strong wind. He was no longer able to fly, and his legs kicked, helpless to prevent their descent as they fell toward the waves. Taliesin knew their armor would drag them to the bottom of the ocean. Her magic was useless against a superior power, and her mind gave in to terror as they approached the crest of a wave.

"No," she shouted. "I *wish* none of this had happened!"

"*Done,*" a deeper voice bellowed from the sky.

The wind vanished along with the storm, and the moon shone bright overhead. Thalagar suddenly spread his wings wide, the bones no longer broken, able to fly over the strangely calm water toward the lights of Dreskull Castle. As he flew over the wall, Taliesin gazed in horror at the destruction within, for every Maldavia soldier laid dead, as well as the prison guards. The entire front side of the castle was gone, destroyed by the catapults that had never burned, and the Garridan army marched across the causeway. Sir Rikard lay in a crumpled heap beside his squire, Zachary, his eyes open and mouth twisted in a silent scream. The prisoners, now armed, moved through the royal troops and slit the throats of the survivors, killing everyone. Warden Stuart hung from a window in a noose, and what few knights remained loyal to the king were lined up and beheaded by an executioner with a long-handled ax.

"I never should have made that wish, Thalagar! What have I done?"

With an angry snort, Thalagar dipped lower and swerved to avoid a shower of arrows. He buckled and tossed Taliesin off his back, flying off while she fell to the ground and landed on a pile of fresh corpses. As she scrambled off the bodies, soaked in the blood from dozens of butchered soldiers, she reached the edge and stopped at a pair of boots worn by a tall figure in silver armor. She lifted her head and stared at Prince Sertorius, his magical sword in one hand, and the head of Konall in the other. He tossed the head beside her as guards grabbed her arms and yanked her onto her feet.

"Thank you for your help, sweetheart," Sertorius said, laughing coldly. "One second I was your prisoner, and now you are mine. Perhaps I do like magic." He snapped his fingers at a knight. "Remove her sword belt and harness, and quickly, Sir Morgrave. Bring me *Calaburn* and place that cursed Raven Sword in a crate and seal it shut. Almaric can decide whether he wants it or not. Sir Duroc, remove that sapphire ring from her hand. The Raven Mistress doesn't need it. Find some silver chains. We can't take any chances with this…this *Wolfen*."

Rough hands held her arms while Sir Morgrave cut through her belts and two other Knights of Chaos took possession of her swords. Sir Duroc, an older man with gray hair and beard, grabbed her right hand and pulled off the sapphire ring. Duroc handed the ring to Sertorius, who slid it onto his own hand and held it up for a closer look.

"Ah, the ring of Tarquin Draconus," Sertorius said. "It fits me much better than you, cousin. While you were casting spells, your mother has seen the light. Praise Stroud! I think she hates the king more than either of us." He glanced at the iron nail that hung around her neck, reached out to touch it, and lowered his hand. "I won't take this silly token from you. What do I want with an iron nail? I have everything I want, Taliesin. As for you, while your mother will be taken to Padama in style, I intend to let you keep Konall company for the duration of the trip. Sir Barstow, toss the pair into a gut wagon, and don't forget the head." He lifted Konall's head by the hair and handed it over to another knight. "Don't lose that, Sir Gallus."

"Now you belong to us," Sir Barstow snarled.

He had a large belly, a red beard, and silver chains over his shoulder. As he approached Taliesin, he dropped the chains and pushed back his visor, allowing her to see his face. She remembered the ugly brute from a prior encounter at an Aldagar inn. Sir Barstow watched as two guards placed cuffs on her wrists and chained her arms behind her back, not knowing the Broa necklace kept her from turning *Wolfen* and rendered silver powerless to harm her.

"That should hold her," Sir Barstow said, chuckling.

"As soon as we leave, Barstow, burn this castle to the ground. One of you, bring my lovely aunt to the courtyard and ready her horse," Sertorius said. He walked forward, placed his hand under Taliesin's chin, and lifted her head. "I don't know what you did to change events, cousin. Somehow, you allowed me to be victorious this night, and for that I thank you. We'll burn a few bodies in sacrifice to Ragnal, for it's very obvious he protects me. Pity you didn't join me when you had the chance."

"Is that regret?" Taliesin asked.

Sertorius lifted an eyebrow. "I regret nothing, *cousin.*"

"Get out of my way," a sharp female voice ordered.

Princess Calista, dressed in a traveling cloak, stepped through the bodies of armed men, and her gentle face twisted with a hatred that filled her eyes as she gazed upon Taliesin. Sertorius, a smile on his face, joined Calista, placed his arm around her shoulders, and gave further insult by kissing her cheek.

"I told you she was dangerous, dear aunt," Sertorius said. "She brought about Konall's death and the deaths of his men, trying to protect the very king she hates, though all she had to do was tell you the truth about John Mandrake. I will see you safely returned to the royal court and provide you with a lifestyle you so richly deserve. Have you anything to say to your daughter?"

"This is no child of mine," Calista snarled. "Take her away — the sight of her offends me!"

"Mother? How can you? I tried my best!"

"Obviously, it was not good enough," spat the princess. She turned away with Sertorius, her hand grasped tightly in his as they walked toward their horses. "I always favored you over your brothers, my dear, sweet boy. One should never put any worth into what a Raven says. They are nothing but thieves and murderers who rob from the dead to fill their pockets with gold. I shall see their clan is wiped from the face of the world and see Frederick suffer before he dies."

"I leave the prisoner in your capable hands, Sir Barstow."

"Yes, sir. I'll see to her comfort."

"No food or water. Remember."

"No charity will be offered, Your Grace."

Dumped into the back of a wagon with the bodies of dead Garridan soldiers, Taliesin found Sir Rikard and Zachary already waiting for her. Konall's body was tossed beside her, with his severed head facing her, his eyes open, as if accusing her. Sir Barstow climbed onto his horse and rode beside the wagon as it rolled out of the castle and along the causeway, jostling her among the dead. Taliesin gazed at the sky, wondering how she'd come so low when victory had been so close. As she wept for Konall and his men, hating herself and Stroud for letting them down, a sliver of the moon slid from behind the clouds. She'd tried to serve Navenna, then Mira, and lastly Stroud. In the end, it didn't matter, for the gods were capricious and cruel.

"Oh, Zarnoc," Taliesin cried, in a broken voice. "What have I done?"

As the wagon headed away from Dreskull Castle, Taliesin wondered if anyone would notice or care if she died and joined them. At least then, she would no longer be alone.

# # # # #

About the Author

Susanne L. Lambdin is the author of the *Dead Hearts* series of novels. A *Trekkie* at heart, she received a 'based in part' screen credit for writing a portion *of Star Trek: The Next Generation: Season 4, Episode 76*, titled '*Family.*' She is passionate about all things science fiction, horror, and high fantasy. Susanne is an expert on the subject of zombies and is affectionately known by many of her fans as 'The Zombie Lady.' She lives in Kansas with her family and two dogs.

To contact Susanne and to learn more about her current and upcoming projects, visit www.SusanneLambdin.com.

The following is an
Excerpt from Book Three of the Realm of Magic:

Queen of Magic

Susanne L. Lambdin

Winter, 2017

eBook and Paperback

Excerpt from "Queen of Magic:"

"Kill the bitch!"

Every *Wolfen* in the vicinity answered his master's command. Lumbering forms on hind legs with monstrous heads swarmed the blue orb. *Wolfen* pressed their heads inward into the orb, which stretched outwards like a bubble. Taliesin reacted and stabbed each pointed-eared head through the jaws or lopped off their muzzles as she stabbed and hacked her way to Lykus. Her sword arm never wavered—Ringerike cut down the furry bodies and left a butcher shop in her wake. When at last she faced Chief Lykus, Taliesin was eager to kill him. He dropped the knight's body he had ripped apart to feed on and glared at her.

"This battle was over before it was fought," Lykus snarled with his mouth full. He paused to swallow a large section of raw flesh, and his yellow eyes narrowed. "Almaric will be king, and I will be his chancellor. The Wolf Clan will feed on the flesh of Ravens and Eagles. But you are mine, Raven Mistress. I will eat and digest you, leaving your remains along the road enroute to Penkill Castle."

"You talk too much, old man!"

Ringerike lifted her arm and sped toward Lykus's chest. His eyes opened in surprise as a crackle of blue flames slid along the length of the blade, and the tip slid between his ribs. A throaty snarl burst from his jaws. Lykus swept one clawed hand toward her head. On his finger gleamed a ring, and it possessed an ancient, dark magic. His hand passed through the blue orb and smacked against the side of her helmet. Small scales fell from her hood, and it vanished, but when she stepped on the plates, they reattached to her armor at her feet, and just as easily, returned to her head as a new helmet with wings.

"Die, girl," the chief snarled.

* * * * *

Also by Susanne L. Lambdin

A Dead Hearts Novel Series:

Morbid Hearts
Forsaken Hearts
Vengeful Hearts
Defiant Hearts
Immortal Hearts

Dead Hearts: Bloodlines

Exordium
Medius
Ultimum

The Realm of Magic Trilogy

Seeker of Magic
Mistress of Magic
Queen of Magic

* * * * *

Made in the USA
Monee, IL
09 January 2021